Bilge Rat - Pirate Adventurer

Black Tarantula
(Book Two of a Series)

Kevin Charles Smith

1S

Journey Publications, LLC

© 2015, Kevin Charles Smith
This book is a work of fiction. All rights reserved and protected
under International and Pan American Copyright Conventions.
Published in the United States by Journey Publications, LLC

Library of Congress Cataloging-in-Publication Data
Smith, Kevin Charles
Bilge Rat – Pirate Adventurer / Book Two, Black Tarantula
A novel by Kevin Charles Smith
LCCN: 2015933477
ISBN-10: 0-9798171-7-X
ISBN-13: 978-0-9798171-7-5

Printed in the United States of America

Journey Publications, LLC
POBox 2442, Warminster, PA 18974

www.piratetale.info

Film/TV/Subsidiary Rights: Mark B Miller Management. (markbmiller@aol.com)

Dedicated to the eldest and the youngest members of the Smith clan. To my mother, Dolores, for the precious gift of life and the continual love and outstanding support she has showered on me throughout my entire life. To my newest grandson, Van, may your infectious smile follow your travels for the remainder of your life.

CONTENTS

ACKNOWLEDGEMENTS

A most grateful and heartfelt thanks and appreciation to everyone who assisted in allowing my dream to reach fruition. Special recognition to my wife and invaluable contributor, Patricia, for unswerving support and encouragement along with the numerous hours spent typing and her contributive critique. To my talented naturalist daughter, Kari, I very much value her knowledgeable direction and counsel on herbal and natural healing advice and direction. To my historically rooted daughter, Shannon, I also very much value her guidance that enabled me to maintain time accurate and appropriate information and context. To my son-in-laws, Ryan and Clay, my deepest appreciation for their enthusiasm, encouragement and honest appraisals. To my number one fan, Sue Deetjen, I treasure her devoted support and continual reinforcement. To all of my brothers, sisters, relatives, friends and associates, I am blessed by your optimistic reassurances that kept me motivated and moving forward throughout the entire process. To my departed father, Charles, I am forever grateful for his guidance and inspiration which is dearly missed. To my loving mother, Dolores, I treasure her for her ability to instill confidence and motivation in her outstanding loving manner.

In addition, I have great need to express my appreciation and deepest thanks to the talented team of professionals who enabled my scribblings to transform into a credible work. For outstanding graphic and artistic work, my grateful appreciation to my Creative Director, Rocio Amovadar and my unsurpassed illustrator, Mike Saputo. To my friend and long-time associate, George Brigandi, I am thankful for his wise counsel and his agency's full support. A tremendous thanks to my outstanding editor, Ali Bothwell Mancini, for her wise, concise and constructive suggestions, recommendations and consultations that enabled this work to evolve in a concise and proper manner.

ACKNOWLEDGEMENTS

To my hard-working digital team, Neil Harner and Melissa Cherepanya and the entire Inverse Paradox team, I am thankful for all of their outstanding efforts. Finally, My gratitude and utmost respect and indebtedness for my agent, publisher and very close friend, Mark B. Miller, whose undying faith and belief in my work enabled it to reach actualization.

Kindest and most grateful regards and thanks to you all!
Kevin

AUTHOR'S NOTE

Without a historical guide to shed full light on pirate exploits, Bilge Rat…
Pirate Adventurer is a fictional account of the true to life times of these
merry reprobates. Chock full of whimsy and quirkiness, this trilogy
is a rollicking tale of adventure and romance set in an age long-past
but hardly forgotten. This saga is intended to capture the essence of the
period…a hard and brutal epoch where life expectancy was woefully
short and men and women were born to stations in life that rarely
altered. Spiked with exciting sailor tales and stories, this action-packed
trilogy attempts to relate a clearer understanding of those popular sea
vagabonds in an entertaining and captivating way.

Book Two: Black Tarantula

"Grommet Billy's Lament"
(Traditional Sailor's Song-Author Unknown)

Boys and lads drawn to a hard life at sea
Death, famine and loss paving their way
Fortune and fame...A dream for them all
A sailor's fate is hard work and misery
Young men grow old while chasing history
    Grommet Billy...Grommet Billy...Man the sheets
    Grommet Billy...Grommet Billy...Ain't life sweet!
Most ships are gone for years on end
Time for young men to grow some hair
Forget your Mom...Forget your Dad
Forget your duties and taste the whip
Grow up and grow old...Enjoy the trip!
    Grommet Billy...Grommet Billy...Man the sheets
    Grommet Billy...Grommet Billy...Ain't life sweet!
Food's so dreadful, we're served in the dark
Maggots and weevils are constant mates
Scurvy and pox haunt all of our days
Forget the Doc...He'll bleed you for sure
Past practice and schooling demand this cure!
    Grommet Billy...Grommet Billy...Man the sheets
    Grommet Billy...Grommet Billy...Ain't life sweet!
Sea monsters and demons will lead to your doom
Boys mature to old men...Weathered and seasoned
Storms called hurricanes will cross your path
Cry for you Mom...Cry for your Dad
Complaining too loud will keelhaul a lad!
    Grommet Billy...Grommet Billy...Man the sheets
    Grommet Billy...Grommet Billy...Ain't life sweet!

PROLOGUE

Welcome back aboard...landlubbers! My dire predicament has certainly not altered one bit during recent reminiscing on my past life's choices. The chunks of floating debris that surrounded me are ever so slowly disappearing one-by-one below the crashing waves. There are serious engulfing flames on each of the still floating fragments of wreckage. Some have even laid claim to my minuscule sanctuary. These fires are certainly not assisting my plight. As for my fellow wreckmates, the circling sea jackals have eliminated a vast majority of these hell-bound degenerates. With their brutal demise, the sea surrounding me has gone deathly quiet.

While my tale is far from concluded, I am certain that my floating wooden asylum will provide ample time to continue reminiscing. As previously disclosed, my early childhood was fraught with continual hardship and danger. Having successfully survived these harsh times, I can honestly vouch that I was blissfully unaware of the cruel and brutal realities that I routinely faced. In fact, I can faithfully attest that I subsisted in a seemingly contented state: albeit fraught with constant battles with sadistic bullies such as Scarf Rockingham and Mr. Bass.

Reminiscing on my past, it has been extremely difficult not to smile outright remembering jubilant times spent with my long-lost brother and aged uncle. These retrospectives remain vivid and wholly comforting until I happen to muse upon their horrific fates. Of paramount, Toby's disappearance and my inability to locate him has proven to be a continual nagging and haunting phantom that pays uninvited visits on an acutely regular schedule. These sudden negative reflections close the curtain on my heartwarming and stirring mental flashbacks invariably jolting me back to grim reality.

In making a detailed examination of the choices I had made thus far in my life, I can attest that I have chosen quite wisely. While self-preservation forced me to end the lives of several miscreants who threatened my very existence, by no means do I consider myself a murderer. Rather, I have simply taken strong measures to protect and safeguard my livelihood even though these choices led to the destruction of several of my nefarious foes. Correspondingly, my quick thinking and ingenuity had served to save both myself and my closest friends on a number of occasions. While I have been hailed a hero and savior, I fully realize that in reality I strictly acted out of extreme necessity in each of these instances. Consequently, I judge myself a survivor not a hero, but obviously my companions perceive these matters in a wholly different light.

Since my story is far from finished, I have decided to continue my circumspect review in the short time that I have remaining on this earth. At this point, I return to my recuperative interval on Jamaica following my victory over the odious Sir Jonathan and the grievous demise of my mentor and closest friend, Handy.

Chapter 1: Rest and Recuperation

My recovery from my duel with Sir Jonathan persisted for a very long time, actually more than a full month. As I journeyed in and out of a dream-like fog, I never realized that the wound delivered by Powder Monkey's late owner was as serious as it had proved to be. Gertrude continued her continual ministrations so that I was dosed with every herb and medication known to mankind. While I certainly was in no condition to complain, it proved to be a slow and painful voyage to full recovery. Powder Monkey and I developed an even closer bond during this extended recuperation period. As we spent many long days alone, I discovered yet another rather startling talent that my new ward had kept secret. You see, Powder Monkey could actually talk! While the majority of the sounds and tones of his words were indeed strange to my ears, I nevertheless had no real difficulty understanding each and every word he vocalized.

After uncovering this ability fraught with unnatural enunciation, I made a solemn promise to continue to keep his secret masked, which earned me a huge smile of relief. In my mind, this shrouded talent coupled with his uncanny ability to read an individual's lips more than made up for his loss of hearing. As we spent more and more time together, we became very adept at communicating rapidly. Between his lip-reading, his somewhat slurred and mangled speech and our very unique sign language, we evolved into conversing with each other in a remarkably swift and efficient manner. I explained to Powder Monkey that his abilities were quite astonishing, and I was sure that the future would prove these skills to be extremely valuable.

Another frequent visitor during my convalescence was our very concerned Captain. He visited almost every morning to ensure that I continued my recovery and to engage in our daily game of chess. During one of his early visits, he had informed me of his vital need to fill the vacant position of First Mate. Despite Captain Adams' knowledgeable assistance, there seemed to be no likely candidate on the entire island to fill this position. The Captain confessed that he had given the matter much thought and believed he had arrived at a very proper solution. Confused to the extreme, I quizzed him as to who he had decided upon to fill this vital post. Smiling broadly, he informed me that he was now looking directly at that individual. Still confused for a moment, I finally realized the startling message in his words. Marking my understanding, he continued by informing me that I knew as much about the everyday operation of the *Amafata* as he did. He confided that the crew not only liked me but trusted my judgment without question. He further divulged that my superior navigational abilities made me a sea artist in every sense of the title. Moreover, he confessed that my past quick thinking and ingenuity had saved his ship, his precious cargo and most importantly his life. He finished on a solemn note by informing me that our late mutual friend, Handy trusted in my abilities implicitly. For all of these reasons, the Captain was offering me the position of First Mate of the *Amafata*. Shocked and yet extremely pleased by this prospect, I begged the Captain for just a little time to think over his fabulous offer. Smiling once again, he responded that he had anticipated just such a response and would certainly allow me all the time I required. Winking as he moved a chess piece into a rather precarious position, he returned his full concentration to our ongoing match. For my part, concentrating on the match was almost impossible given the tremendous opportunity that I had just been offered.

Later that day, I received two much unexpected visitors. Long Tall Willie and Angry George. They had jointly decided to pay their respects to their recovering comrade. After filling me in on all the recent island scuttlebutt, I confided in them about the offer our Captain had recently proposed. They listened patiently as I described the Captain's logic and reasoning on his offer of promotion. When finished, I questioned both of my friends on their true feelings. Grinning from ear to ear, they both laughed and patted me on the back. They announced that I was perfectly suited to the role the Captain was offering. With their strong endorsement, I made my decision at that moment to accept the Captain's offer and planned to advise him on the very next visit.

Chapter 2: The Trial of Mr. Bass

A portion of the scuttlebutt reported by Long Tall Willie and Angry George concerned an almost forgotten Catstalker Gene. Frustrated and feeling lost and despondent over the incarceration of his mentor, Catstalker Gene reverted to his old tricks of torturing, mutilating and desecrating helpless animals. When the local cat and dog population proved inadequate to sate his sadistic tendencies, the lad decided to move onto larger and more challenging prey. Sneaking into Fat Dog's chimpanzee enclosure one night, the mentally diseased juvenile selected one of the weaker and more defenseless baby chimps to exercise his perverted mania. In plain sight of the entire chimpanzee troop, the knave tortured and brutally slaughtered this poor defenseless creature. Knowing the immature monster as I did, I was certain that he laughed in utter delight to the hoots, screeches and screams of the entire chimp pack as he went about this filthy work.

Having had a delightful time with his new victim, Catstalker Gene decided to repeat the experience the very next night. Once again, the vicious brute snuck into the barn that housed the apes. He had made a decision to repeat his depredations on yet another younger and more defenseless member of the troop. Having identified the victim the previous evening, he stealthily approached the cage where he had noticed the young ape. What he was not aware of was the fact that Fat Dog had taken the time to rearrange the cages in the simian compound following the unfortunate and suspicious death of the baby chimpanzee the previous night. As Catstalker Gene opened the cage holding what he believed to be the younger twin of his recent victim, he was greeted instead by a huge surprise. The cage he had unlocked no longer housed the defenseless infant but rather a fully grown male chimpanzee.

As he unbolted the cage, the fully matured male inside recognized his human liberator as the very devil who had grievously tortured and murdered one of its kind. The enraged beast literally tore the poor tar apart. Afterwards, all that remained of Catstalker Gene was a blood-soaked and mutilated torso. The poor unfortunate's arms and legs had been literally torn off and scattered in every corner of the enclosure. His noggin had also been savagely torn from its moorings and was nowhere to be found. The bloody torso appeared as if it had been trampled by a herd of stampeding oxen. Besides the massive pool of blood, the mutilated body had been flattened to unrecognizable proportions. The shredded clothing that remained clinging to the murdered victim resembled sailor's slops, but without a head or any kind of recognizable marks on the corpse's trunk, the identity of the victim remained a total mystery. Eventually, the head of Catstalker Gene was recovered inside one of the chimp cages. Once identity was established, inquiries were made of the Captain and crew to attempt to determine the details surrounding the exact cause of death. Based on answers received, the authorities had no other choice but to rule the death purely an accident. They surmised that the unlucky youth had in all probability too much to drink and stumbled accidentally into the ape enclosure. Since one of the cages appeared to have been opened, the authorities ruled that the boy had made a series of inebriated mistakes that eventually cost him his life. Given his rabid addiction to bully, torture and annihilate all manner of weaker creatures, I felt absolutely no pity or remorse whatsoever for his tragic demise. The perverse lad was nothing short of an apprenticing monster and I concluded that his horrific end was more than justified

The trial of the hated First Mate, Mr. Bass opened during the weeks I was recovering. My weakened condition did not allow me the opportunity to witness the trial in person, so I dispatched Powder Monkey to act as my eyes and ears and to report back on each day's outcome. Since Sergeant O'Toole was very popular with the troops stationed at the fort, there was an abundance of fellow soldiers prepared to testify to his good nature. The first several days of the trial were spent hearing from these soldiers extolling the virtues of their former comrade and commander. Further, his loyalists trivialized his murder of Handy as a misguided attempt by their comrade to defend himself after his mortal wounding by Mr. Bass' dagger. Specifically, several witnesses proclaimed that their fellow compatriot retaliated entirely out of self-defense after being mortally struck by the defendant's blade, and as a direct result it altered his aim to a great and tragic degree.

Additional witnesses next took the stand and testified to Mr. Bass's barbaric actions at Fat Dog's Pub on the day the First Mate went berserk while watching the ape fights. Other local citizens further swore to the crude and ugly behavior of Mr. Bass while he was on liberty. When it came time to produce witnesses on behalf of Mr. Bass, there were simply none to be found. Catstalker Gene was scheduled to testify, but the unfortunate death of this key witness left the trial defenders without viable options.

The court magistrate was absolutely convinced of several facts prior to handing down a verdict. Sergeant O'Toole's character was deemed in good standing, given the numerous positive testimonies by witnesses during the trial. Mr. Bass's character was judged to be less than scrupulous, given the negative testimonies by important island residents. Finally, the murder weapon was clearly identified as belonging to the defendant. The case was extremely one-sided, but the military magistrate decided to allow Mr. Bass a chance to speak on his own behalf. The First Mate used this opportunity rather unwisely. Once on the stand, he proceeded to lambaste the court, its proceedings, the Governor, the residents of the island and finally his former crewmates. His accusatory tirade served no real purpose other than convincing everyone in the courtroom of his criminality. The magistrate ruled him guilty of the dastardly crime of murder and sentenced him to be hung from the gallows as rightful punishment. His hanging date was set for the very next morning and the court was dismissed.

As it happened, my enemy did not hang the next day. You see, as he was being escorted to the awaiting gallows, he somehow managed to overtake his guards and escape. In the process, he killed two soldiers and critically injured two more. A warrant was summarily issued for his immediate arrest under multiple murder charges. A citywide search was conducted for the murderer, but no trace of the feared criminal was found. My fervent hope was that this madman was gone completely from my life!

A number of days later, the Captain visited to match wits in our daily game of chess. He was pleasantly surprised to find me up and about, since Gertrude had finally declared me cured. After fully assessing my condition, the Captain informed me that it was now time to prepare for our continuation to Barbados. The hurricane season was near at end and sailing preparations had begun aboard our ship; my presence as First Mate was sorely missed. I promised the Captain that I would report for duty the following morning which pleased him tremendously. Saddened at first by my departure news, the sisters eventually understood my calling and assisted in my preparations to return to the ship. Before I actually vacated the house, the sisters announced that they intended to host a celebration in my honor prior to our departure. Invitations were prepared and couriered to all of the leading families on the island so I quickly realized that my presence would be mandatory. Since the party was scheduled for later in the week, I bid my heartfelt thanks for the sisters' ministrations during my convalescence and returned to my ship.

The joyous reception I received from the entire crew immediately lifted my spirits. As I took stock of the situation, I could see that my crewmates were furiously involved with sailing preparations. As I stepped aboard, they all stopped their work and rushed to my side. Hearty backslaps and well wishing was the next order of business. These continued for much longer than I certainly wished, and the spontaneous show of emotion was finally ended by the Captain, who ordered all hands back to work. As I made my way slowly below decks, I had an intensely grief-stricken feeling as soon as I entered the galley. This familiar location as well as the entire ship seemed rather empty without the presence of my old friend, Handy. I knew in my heart that it would be a long while before these sad and melancholy feelings would lessen and eventually dissipate!

Since I was now the First Mate, I moved all of my belongings into the cabin once occupied by Mr. Bass. Given my previous adjustment to the limited space aboard, this cabin seemed quite large and cavernous. Once settled, I checked in with the Captain to receive my orders. The Captain announced that sailing preparations were proceeding smoothly. He then commanded me to take an inventory of the ship's food and water supply to ensure that we were fully stocked. With a crisp salute, I was on my way to the hold to complete my assigned task. As I reached my destination, I realized that I was not alone. Powder Monkey and Long Tall Willie were busy at work sorting barrels as I entered. They both ceased their work to acknowledge my presence with broad grins. It seemed to me that the two had formed a tight bond in my absence, which I found totally reassuring. Completing my assignment expediently, I returned topside to assist in the many other chores necessary to prepare us for our upcoming voyage.

After a few more days of exhausting labor, the *Amafata* was fully readied for departure. As it happened, it was also the night that the sisters had chosen for my bon voyage gala. Cleaning myself up, including donning a new set of clothes more befitting my new rank, I collected the Captain and we made our way to the Adams' mansion. When we arrived, the party had already begun, and we were treated to food and drink of the most exceptional quantity and quality. As I made my rounds, Hortence asked for a moment of my time. Leading me to a secluded alcove, Hortence confessed to me that she had decided to perform a singing exhibition in my honor. As the time neared, she had become more and more nervous about performing in front of her neighbors and friends. As she was notifying me of her fears, three island society ladies wandered by our location so rapt in their own conversation that they did not take notice of our presence. Their conversation centered on the exact topic Hortence had just brought to my attention. As we listened, we clearly heard them snip that everyone was simply aghast that Hortence had the unmitigated gall to actually attempt to perform for her assembled guests. As we both listened to these cruel women and their snide remarks, I could easily sense Hortence's hurt and anger rising with each malicious word uttered by these society snipes.

When these ladies had finally drifted away, Hortence whimpered that was exactly the type of negative reception she feared she would receive. She announced that she simply would not perform under ugly conditions such as scorn and ridicule. Realizing the depth of her suffering, I questioned if she might be persuaded to perform if she had a willing partner at her side. Giving me a skeptical glare, she inquired who I had in mind. I answered that I would be honored to share the stage with her. Brightening, she quizzed if I was being totally serious. Informing her that I was deadly serious, she hugged and thanked me, notifying me that she was now extremely motivated to prove her dissenting ridiculers wrong.

At last, it was time for the promised exhibition. Hortence was extremely nervous and none of my calming words held any comfort or ease for her. When she was introduced, she was shaking like a snagged anchor line, so I stood up and made my way over to her side. Addressing the snickering audience, I calmly announced that I would be performing alongside my hostess. With introductions made, I signaled to the band members to start the first number and Hortence and I began to sing. Well, I can truthfully say that it did not take very long for the jeering and snickering guests to suddenly realize their huge mistake. Accompanied by my booming tenor voice, Hortence's voice was sweet and clear. After finishing our first number, the audience was totally enthralled and remained so for the entirety of our performance. As we finished with a haunting and very moving love ballad, our grateful audience cheered, clapped and shouted for more. By the long and rousing applause that followed our final number, I knew that Hortence would never again need to fear performing for absolutely anybody on the island!

Later that evening, I spied Captain Adams speaking in hushed tones to a very rapt group of gentlemen including my Captain. Making my way towards them, Captain Adams happened to glance up and spot my progress across the room. Nodding to me to join them, Captain Adams informed us that he had just received terrible news concerning our last port-of-call, Saint Domingue. At the sound of his voice and the mere mention of Rue's homeland, my heart started to beat faster and faster. The villain of his story was none other than Angry George's unscrupulous blackguard, the Black Tarantula. It seemed that this fiend had altered his normal piratical practices. Due to his notorious and fearsome reputation, most merchant ships had deviated from their normal trade routes in an attempt to avoid any confrontation whatsoever with this vicious madman. Frustrated to the extreme, the demonic lunatic switched his attack tactics from ships at sea to coastal cities with established wealth-laden coffers. To this end, he boldly sailed into the harbor of Cap-Francis, ordering his blood-maddened crew to attack, defile and destroy the city. Confronting and overcoming the minuscule military force on the island, the Black Tarantula proceeded to sack and pillage the unfortunate town. Realizing that even more could be gained from the wealthy rulers of the island, he took several of the island's leaders hostage demanding exorbitant sums for their release and safe return. Having no real choice, the islanders accumulated and delivered the vast fortune he demanded. Once satisfied that his outrageous demands had been met, he returned the hostages to the town. However, these hostages were delivered in pieces. Each hostage had been murdered and violated in unspeakable terms. Horrified by his actions along with his broken promises, the town's populace were stunned into inactivity, requesting assistance from neighboring islands to protect them from further aggression.

Sympathetic to their calamitous plight, Captain Adams intended to mount a retaliatory force to ensure their neighbor's immediate safety. Calling for volunteers, Captain Adams hoped to launch this disciplinary excursion as soon as possible. My first reaction was to immediately volunteer my services, but I quickly realized that my duty to the *Amafata* preceded my burning desire to enlist. Noting my look of perplexed frustration, my Captain came to my side and requested a brief moment alone with me. As we made our way outside, my leader informed me that he knew what I had been thinking. I responded that my true love resided on Saint Domingue. Nodding in his wise manner, the Captain notified me in his most serious tone that he, as well as the entire *Amafata* crew, was depending on me to perform the role that I had previously accepted. He was very sympathetic to my desire to return to Saint Domingue, but was exceedingly firm in his resolve to have me continue the voyage to Barbados. However, as a conciliatory gesture, he promised that once our business was concluded on Barbados that he would allow me the opportunity to return to Saint Domingue to rendezvous with Rue.

The first question out of my mouth was just how long he estimated it would be before I could return. Taking a moment to ponder my question, he announced that he expected that it would be at least a month or more before he could fulfill his promise. Noting that this time period was indeed formidable, he attempted to console me by telling me that Captain Adams' force would arrive on Saint Domingue in just a few weeks time and would restore law and order. Further, the Captain felt reasonably assured that once Captain Adams' troops arrived that the Black Tarantula would flee the vicinity in search of weaker prey. At that moment, Captain Adams made his way outside and joined our conversation. The Captain apprised him of my dilemma. Captain Adams sided immediately with my Captain and promised me that he would personally search out Rue as soon as he arrived on Saint Domingue to ensure her safety and wellbeing. Feeling totally helpless yet quite duty-bound, I thanked Captain Adams for his very kind assistance. I then reluctantly informed my commander that I would not desert my newly assigned post. Clapping me firmly on my back, he informed me that I had made the right decision. Given this latest horrific news of the scoundrel's depredations, the party came to a very abrupt halt. Upon making my departure, I thanked each of the Adams sisters for their care and assistance with my injuries and recuperation as well as the delightful party. Promising to visit them in the very near future, I took my leave along with the Captain to the tears and sad farewells of the entire Adams' household!

The Captain and I trudged silently back to our ship. All along the way, I hoped and prayed with all of my heart that I had made the right choice this time!

Chapter 3: Proving My Worth

Leaving Jamaica proved to be an acutely sorrowful experience indeed. It certainly was not that I was disappointed to be back on the brilliant blue carpet with its frothy white capped waves. Rather, I had found a temporary home on this island with very special people who cared for me deeply. During my life's short duration, these new found feelings and experiences were a very rare occurrence.

While these conflicting emotions raged through my addled brain, I also sensed that I had changed significantly from a purely emotional standpoint. I perceived that my overall view of the world had shifted. I realized that I was much less focused on past feelings and attitudes that had driven the majority of my life's decisions. In many ways, my former emotions and thinking suddenly seemed quite secondary, almost juvenile in nature. In taking the time to carefully reflect on the entire situation, I realized that I had somehow matured during my recent escapades on Jamaica. Maturity, I realized, was a curious new development that seemed to have a life of its own. You see, I had made no conscious effort to achieve this more mature state; it had simply occurred!

With Gertrude's herbal inventory and Hortence's theatrical gifts safely stowed in my new cabin, I took a moment to inspect the slim gold band that Willamina had bestowed upon me. Realizing that I did not want to endure the pain necessary to transform this good luck piece into an earring, I pondered an alternative method of sporting Zarina the Gypsy's wedding ring, so that its good luck was not wasted. Realizing that the ring itself was far too small to wear on any one of my fingers, I found an alternative home for my prize on my second toe of my right foot. It was both a perfect fit as well as a sort of hiding place for my treasure. Elated with my solution, I hastened topside to begin my critical role as First Mate of the *Amafata*.

As the hours turned into days, I began the process of becoming accustomed to my new role. My new responsibilities were broken up into two distinct categories, performing the ship's navigational functions and maintaining the operational management of the vessel. As for the first, the Captain had relinquished the role of ship's navigation into my capable hands. Since our final destination had been predetermined, it was now incumbent on me to deliver us there in both a safe and expedient manner. Given this critical task, I spent a number of hours each day carefully documenting our seagoing path, while plotting and calculating our optimal future course. Once done, I would dutifully meet with the Captain to update him on our progress, as well as laying out my recommendations. While the Captain really never challenged my calculations or navigational decisions, I felt a certain degree of comfort in sharing these recommendations with him. Additionally, these daily visits also allowed us to match wits in our daily game of chess. These matches were no longer one-sided affairs, as I began to best my master more often than not. After one tightly fought chess skirmish, the Captain turned to face me with his well-known smile and announced that it was good to have me back to my old self!

My second responsibility was overseeing the smooth operation of the vessel. While I approached this duty with a firm hand, I nevertheless performed this function in a much gentler manner than my predecessor. That is not to say that I allowed any type of lazy, inept or careless action on the part of the crew. Rather, I never went out of my way to find fault or to impose unreasonable or unjustified punishment for their mistakes. Consequently, I sensed a sort of natural acceptance of my new role by the entire crew. They dutifully performed the orders I gave, but seemed to be watching and waiting before passing final judgment of my handling of the authority that I had been granted. Thinking hard about their somewhat standoffish behavior, I came to the conclusion that the entire crew was waiting to see how I would handle myself in troubled waters. They knew with certainty that a good ship's officer could only be judged under difficult and life-threatening conditions.

Well, it did not take very long before their opportunity to judge came to pass. About a week into our voyage, the *Amafata* traveled directly into some very dirty weather. Near sundown that day, we ventured directly into the path of a very powerful storm. In a matter of minutes, the voyage had gone from an effortlessly serene cruise to a fight for our very lives. As wind and rain pelted our vessel unmercifully, I called all hands on deck. Barking out a series of orders, I sent the crew scrambling to complete the directives I deemed necessary for survival. For the next several hours, we fought a valiant battle against this powerful weather system that seemed intent on our total obliteration.

At one point in our struggles, the Captain wisely suggested that our sails needed to be trimmed to eliminate the risk of catastrophic damage. However, to do so meant sending men aloft to complete this task in a certainly less than safe environment. Thinking his suggestion through for just a brief moment, I realized that he was absolutely correct in his seasoned counsel. I also understood that sending any sailor aloft under the miserable conditions facing us was nothing less than a death sentence.

Taking a moment to reflect on the problem, I came to a swift and decisive solution. Summoning Angry George and Creeping Jeremy to my side, I explained the dire mission I needed them to undertake to ensure survival of the ship and crew. I spelled out exactly what I required them to accomplish, which basically amounted to scaling the riggings and trim the sails to alleviate the pressure the storm was placing on them, before they eventually gave way or were torn asunder leaving us utterly helpless. As I passed my orders to them, I could read the looks of dread and fright on each of their faces. They seemed to be silently questioning me as to why I had selected them to perform this highly dangerous act. Noting their dire expressions, I notified each that I believed that they were the most accomplished members of the crew at navigating the tops of the ship. Further, I informed them that I had an idea that would somewhat mitigate the extreme danger that they were each about to face.

Shouting an order to Long Tall Willie, I demanded two stout ropes be brought up from below. At the same time, I shouted for another crewmember to go below and return with two hammocks, which I required to affect my plan. As these items were retrieved, I confided my intentions to my two dreadfully terrified friends. Upon hearing my words, each relaxed somewhat understanding exactly what I had in mind. Manipulating the rope hammocks, I carefully made several quick alterations to them. When I finished my work, I was left with an unrecognizable tangle of ropes that nevertheless would serve as a very effective set of human harnesses, which I had each sailor don. I then attached each of the delivered ropes directly to these harnesses. The other end of these cables was securely affixed to the mainmast in order to provide a secure lifeline between each sailor and the ship. In addition, I looped and tied a number of discarded hammock strands around each of their arms and legs. With all now in readiness, I gave each sailor my final instructions including utilizing these hastily applied hammock strands on their arms and legs. I explained that employing these short ropes from time-to-time would provide secure lifelines at various intervals in the event either of them accidentally came free of the riggings. Should this misfortune occur, they might dangle a short way, but would remain securely attached so that they would be able to regain precious handholds on the lines. Each nodded their understanding and began their perilous assent to achieve the vital chore that lay before them.

About halfway to their intended target, Angry George was viciously blown off the lines he had been clinging to by a violent gust of wind. Screaming in utter panic, his fall was halted very quickly by my improvised climbing rig. Twisting and flailing in sheer desperation, he managed to expeditiously regain his hold and continued his upward journey. Not much later, Creeping Jeremy suffered the same fate with much the same result to the cheering encouragement of the entire crew beneath him. As intended, both sailors reached their objective and performed the necessary maneuvers to trim the sails before tentatively inching their way back down to the maindeck. Upon reaching the deck's safety, their crewmates came cheering and screaming to their sides congratulating them on successfully completing this extremely dangerous mission. Waiting just a few moments, I made my way over to the riotous party and expressed my sincerest gratitude on behalf of the entire ship for the bravery and courage they displayed in following my extremely hazardous orders. Looking directly into my eyes with renewed respect and admiration, they simultaneously thanked me for my fast thinking. The seas and winds eventually calmed and we continued our voyage, but as far as my crewmates were concerned I had passed the test thrust upon me. I had displayed superior fast thinking as well as keeping a calm and cool head in very troubled waters.

After the excitement caused by the recent tempest, I felt tired and weary down to my very core. Having set the next watch, I returned to my bunk and collapsed into a deep sleep, oblivious to anything or anyone. Upon waking the next morning, I was shocked to discover that the wooden cross given to me on Saint Domingue had mysteriously disappeared. I knew that I had clasped it briefly the previous evening to ensure that it was not lost in our fight for survival in the raging tempest. Aware that the talisman had somehow become dislodged during my sleep, I tore apart my bunk in a fruitless search for my good luck charm. Unsuccessful, I scoured every inch of my small cabin for my stringed wooden amulet. This search proved also unsuccessful and real concern began to bloom in my heart. After another rummaging of both my bed and quarters, I came to the very obvious conclusion that my wooden cross had been taken from my possession sometime during the night.

Exasperated and confused, I called Powder Monkey to my cabin to explain the devastating loss. He asked if I suspected anyone of the crime. Shaking my head in a negative fashion, I answered that I actually had no idea who would have performed such an underhanded deed. Because I was totally in the dark, I asked him to keep a sharp eye on our crewmates to determine if any of them began to act in a suspicious manner. Believing that none of my closest friends would ever have perpetuated such a dastardly act, I commanded Powder Monkey to be especially vigilant of the new recruits that had just joined our company. Understanding my meaning, Powder Monkey informed me that he would not rest until my lucky token was returned. He was then off in a flash to begin his assignment. Partly assuaged, since I knew my cross had to be somewhere aboard the *Amafata*, I also made a silent promise to myself that I would keep a sharp eye out for any suspicious activity or behavior on the part of anyone aboard!

Upon leaving Jamaica, we had been forced to add several new sailors to our small crew. Unlike my days spent as a galley slave where I would get to know each new arrival in great detail, my new position as First Mate did not allow such luxury. For the most part, these new crewmembers were nothing more than strange faces and names. However, the disappearance of my wooden talisman caused me to pay particular attention to these new men in the hopes that I might discover if any had a hand in the nefarious theft.

There was one odious newcomer that caught my attention immediately. His name was Walter Gibbons, but was quickly renamed Pigsty by his mates for very obvious reasons. You see, Pigsty was a slovenly obese and lazy animal, who smell worse than any open cesspool. This detestable tar was both inventively sneaky and conniving in all manner of conduct. Pigsty was a master at the art of *skedaddling,* translated in seaman's terms as a shirker of duties by continually inventing excuses to avoid his fair share of work. He was nothing more than a complete nuisance, instigating issues and trouble throughout the ship. To make matters worse, Pigsty signaled out Powder Monkey as a scapegoat for the majority of his troublemaking, since my friend was unable to speak or properly defend himself. I was thoroughly aware of his nasty antics and constantly alerted to the many predicaments that this obnoxious creature created. Powder Monkey had also been closely observing this disgusting swine, convinced that Pigsty had been acting in a very strange and unusual manner since the night that my cross had disappeared.

When we had an opportunity to confer in private on the matter, Powder Monkey signed that he was convinced that Pigsty was the culprit responsible for my lucky charm's mysterious disappearance. Powder Monkey informed me that he had already secretly searched the scum's few personal belongings with negative results. However, he remained staunch in his belief that Pigsty had purloined the cross and then had hidden it someplace safe aboard our ship. Because of his strong suspicions, Powder Monkey had taken to clandestinely following the stinking maggot around the ship to uncover the suspected filcher's secret repository. For the time being, all we could do was watch and wait!

My new position meant that I ate meals with the Captain and the Doc. While the food was for the most part no better than the rest of the crew enjoyed, the company was exceedingly different. While my new messmates and I spent many an evening discussing various intriguing philosophical topics, I sorely missed the camaraderie of my old friends and the wild sea tales that were part and parcel of any evening's meal. Further, I genuinely longed to hear the daily scuttlebutt of the crew. The good news was that my friend, Powder Monkey, supplied this vital information on each of his visits. Powder Monkey's reports provided me the latest intelligence on our crewmate's discussions, fears, and gossip. While the majority of this knowledge was of very little value, I understood with certainty that one day my silent companion would furnish pivotal information!

Chapter 4: Jesuit's Bark

The very next day, Pigsty made an appearance at Doc's surgery looking extremely under-the-weather. He complained of multiple symptoms including a headache, drippy nose, constant cough, stomach aches and bombarding chest pains. Doc seemed to have a suspicion concerning the cause of Pigsty's affliction, but told me he wanted to observe the rascal for a while before issuing a prognostication. As Pigsty continued to whine and complain, the Doc and I got him comfortable. Waving a hurried farewell, I quickly made my way to the Captain's cabin to provide my daily report. For a short time, I completely forgot about Pigsty and his supposed illness.

That night while we were enjoying our dinner, the Doc confessed his suspicions on Pigsty's illness to the Captain and I. The Doc believed that Pigsty suffered from the dreaded disease called typhus fever. While this disease was not as deathly lethal as other infectious plagues, it was nevertheless a proven killer. This news was extremely worrisome to the Captain, and he instructed both of us to keep him totally informed of any new developments concerning Pigsty's infirmity. Given the new recruit's delirious state, I was later allowed the unimpeded opportunity to thoroughly search the stinking scoundrel's person and possessions for my missing wooden cross. To my utter dismay, I discovered that my amulet was not on him nor among any of his filthy belongings. Relating this failure to Powder Monkey, I signed that I now agreed with my friend's belief that the thief had stashed my talisman in a safe hiding place somewhere aboard our ship. Powder Monkey nodded and signed that he would find this secret cache no matter how long it took.

The next morning I made a visit to Doc's surgery to inspect the condition of our patient and discovered that the situation had taken a turn for the worse. Pigsty was in far more pain than the previous day, evidenced by his high fever, chills, muscle aches and constant vomiting. Doc informed me that he was now fully convinced that the suffering fool was truly a victim of typhus fever. Because he was unwilling to leave his patient's side, Doc requested that I inform the Captain of this recent development. Further, he pressed me to persuade the Captain to initiate standard precautionary measures which included the fumigation of the ship and the exchange of our current water supply with that of fresh water. I immediately reported this beastly news to the Captain, along with Doc's recommended actions. While the Captain was highly agitated by my report, he ordered me to begin the fumigation process with haste. Hustling below, I enlisted the assistance of Powder Monkey and Long Tall Willie to prepare the fumigation pots.

These devices consisted of utilizing a few of the larger galley pots that would house a lethal combination of sulfur, pitch and brimstone. Setting this mixture on fire produced an odious smelling cloud of black smoke believed necessary to combat the noxious vapors that had invaded our ship. For me, it seemed to be more like creating one bad stench to overpower yet another! Because of the extreme danger our medical emergency represented, both Powder Monkey and I momentarily forgot about our mission to locate my missing cross. But I did begin to wonder if Pigsty's illness had anything to do with its disappearance, since it sure seemed like our vessel's fortune had taken a disastrous turn for the worse since the amulet had been pirated.

As our fumigation work was carried out, I was advised by Angry George that two more of our crew had reported to the Doc complaining of symptoms similar to those of Pigsty. This news convinced me that we had a full-fledged medical emergency on our hands. As I supervised the fumigation process, I thought back to the herbal remedies for tropical fevers that Gertrude had taught me. I recalled that her answer for tropical fluxes was an herb called quina, which was distilled from the bark of an indigenous mountain dwelling tree. This bark was also known as Jesuit's bark, in honor of the Spanish missionaries who had discovered its curative powers from local natives. Furthermore, she had provided me with a significant quantity of Jesuit's bark, as part and parcel of her parting gift of herbal cornucopia.

Racing to my cabin, I uncovered the bark and grabbed a fistful of this innocuous looking substance. Instructing Long Tall Willie to immediately begin boiling fresh water, I immersed a portion of the strange looking bark into the steaming water, and after a short duration had produced a very bitter tasting tea. Instructing both Long Tall Willie and Powder Monkey to drink a tankard of this newly brewed tea twice a day, I rushed the remainder of my new medicine to the Doc's surgery for the treatment of his patients. By the time I arrived, there were four additional sailors exhibiting the same symptoms. The Doc, looking quite confused at my liquid delivery, asked me exactly what I was planning to do with this strange looking tea. I explained my actions, citing Gertrude's knowledge and experience with this novel type of herbal cure. While he appeared a bit skeptical of my solution, he was certainly willing to give it a try since the typhus fever epidemic was quickly escalating out of his control.

Dosing the seven suffering sailors with the mixture, I instructed Doc that the regimen had to be repeated twice a day if we hoped to beat the dreaded disease. In addition, I ordered Doc to partake in the tea curative to prevent his contraction of the disease. Reporting this latest development to the Captain, he thanked me for the quick thinking and ordered me to forsake my normal duties so that I could assist Doc in treating the typhus-stricken patients. Worried about shirking my prime responsibilities, the Captain informed me, that given the extent of the emergency we faced, he would assume these responsibilities. The Captain also notified me that he would initiate a search for a suitable location to obtain fresh water that the Doc had insisted upon. Nodding my agreement, I returned to the hell that was waiting for me below!

The fumigation process was finally completed to the appeasement of my choking and teary-eyed companions. The crew, by this time, was fully aware of the scuttlebutt regarding the dangerous pestilence that was now roaming free on the *Amafata*. To a man, they were all very fearful and apprehensive that this horrid disease would be paying each of them a visit in the near future. As I made my way back to the Doc's surgery, I was stunned to discover that the situation had taken another turn for the worse. The patients had grown sicker, with Pigsty the very worst of the bunch. In my absence, he had developed a mass of angry red rashes all over his chest, back, arms and legs. The Doc informed me that these marks were the telltale signs of typhus fever. In addition, the sick count had risen to include eleven men, so that we needed to also utilize my cabin to house the growing number of patients. Taking some time away from ministering to the sick, I rushed to the Captain to apprise him of the severity of the situation. The Captain, accepting my news with grim determination, informed me that he believed he had found the answer to our fresh water needs on a nearby small uninhabited isle off of the French possession of Martinique.

Returning to the Doc's surgery, I alerted him of the news that the Captain had just delivered. Somewhat relieved, he told me that he doubted whether fresh water would make any real difference at this point. His patients had all developed high fevers, and many were quite delirious calling for their mothers or loved ones to countermand their suffering. Up to this point, Powder Monkey, Long Tall Willie, Doc or I had shown no signs of the disease, so I still maintained hope that the quina tea would provide the cure for which we were all silently praying. The noxious aroma in both my cabin and the Doc's surgery was so overpowering that Doc and I were forced to don neckerchiefs covering both our noses and mouths to endure the odoriferous hell. The Captain made a surprise visit to inquire about his sick crewmen and to inform us that the targeted tropical isle had been sighted, so that the fresh water issue would be solved in a matter of hours. Doc, muttering in Italian, voiced his real concern for his dying patients. These words needed no translation as the Captain had already perceived the dire nature of the situation all around him. He merely nodded to me and quietly slipped out of the room.

Once we reached our destination, I made my way to the Captain's side to volunteer for shore patrol. The Captain, realizing my strong desire to assist, turned down my request. He informed me that my work with the sick was much more crucial than any help I might provide the shore party. Continuing, he ordered me to maintain my post onboard as ship's commander, as he intended to lead the shore patrol himself. Saluting my assent, I made my way back to the sick patients.

Chapter 5: Adventure on Pig Island

The Captain and six healthy crewmates set off near midday to scout for a source of fresh water to replenish our stores. Included in this party were both Long Tall Willie and Angry George. The Doc and I had our hands full with our suffering charges, which now totaled an even dozen. Continuing to administer the quina tea to our typhus stricken comrades, both Doc and I kept a very close watch to determine if the curative herb was having any effect at all. From these scrutinies, it appeared that this medicine seemed to have little effect on those sailors who had reached the high fever and rash stage of the illness. In fact, Pigsty actually became our first ship causality, expiring not long after the Captain's departure. Since the brute never recovered consciousness, I was unable to pose any queries about the theft of my wooden talisman.

In traditional nautical manner, I had the distinct displeasure of preparing Pigsty for burial. Locating a suitable sailcloth shroud, I proceeded in the morbid task of wrapping his stinking dead corpse and sewing this moldering package shut with the traditional thirteen stitches. The last stitch was through the miscreant's nose that I had learned was meant to substantiate that the interred was truly deceased. The awful odor emanating from Pigsty's corpse was truly horrendous. Our current anchorage placed us in rather shallow waters, which meant that we would need to store this gruesome package for later burial at sea. Toting the despicable load down into the hold, I made some hasty rearrangements and nestled the putrid bundle amidst the trade cargo already stored there. I judged that this appalling aromatic bouquet would soon be lost in the overall noxious atmosphere associated with this particular location.

As I completed this grisly task, I rejoined the Doc in his surgery attending to his remaining patients. As I had already judged, the Doc informed me that the quina tea seemed to be having a positive effect on those sailors who had not yet reached the critical stage of the dreaded illness. While there was very little improvement in their condition, each had yet to progress into the far deadlier stage that had already claimed the life of poor Pigsty. In addition, the Doc was quick to point out that he, Long Tall Willie, Powder Monkey and I had yet to display any signs of typhus fever. He accredited the quina tea as the only rationale for our continued health. Hopeful that our remedy would eventually produce positive results, he ordered the herbal dosing to continue on schedule. Since Powder Monkey had little to do other than constantly brewing more medicinal tea, I asked him to spend some time in the hold in search of my wooden cross.

By the next day, I began to become apprehensive given no sign of the scouting party's return. During that night, I was called to manufacture two more burial shrouds for the unfortunate sailors who had passed into the high fever and blistering rash stage of the malady. Finished with this disagreeable chore, I joined the Doc and expressed my growing concern for the safety of the Captain's shore party. The Doc soothed my worries, insisting that only one day had passed since their departure, predicting that we would surely spot some sign of them prior to nightfall. He reminded me that fresh water could prove to be an elusive commodity on any isle. Somewhat comforted by his words, I announced that should we receive no word from the patrol by the next day, I would be forced to take action to discover their status. The good news was that our typhus patients seemed to be slowly recovering from their affliction. While they were far from being considered cured, none had as yet not progressed into the serious and lethal phase of the illness. At the same time, Powder Monkey made a brief appearance to inform me that he had not uncovered the hiding place of my wooden amulet. Signing that he still had several areas yet to search, he confessed that he still believed that we would find the hiding spot before the Captain returned from his foray.

By midday of the following day, no sign had been spotted of the Captain's scouting party. Both Doc and I were now very concerned for their safety. In discussing the matter, we agreed that it was now time to take action. Knowing that the Doc was critically needed onboard, I decided that Powder Monkey and I would make a trek to the isle to attempt to discover the reason for the patrol's delay. Our objective would be strictly one of reconnoitering. Calling Powder Monkey up from the hold, I outlined the task that lay before us. With our plan agreed, Powder Monkey and I bid farewell to the Doc and headed towards the island's sandy beach where we had last seen our companions.

Upon reaching our objective, we found it to be entirely deserted, with no visible evidence other than the shore party's beached and deserted longboat. Since there was nothing to be gained by remaining there, Powder Monkey and I cautiously made our way into the isle's interior following the tracks made by our missing mates. Not traveling far, we discovered the ruins of what appeared to be a small church. This structure looked like it had been abandoned for quite some time. All that remained of the sacred edifice was a collapsed wooden cross and the crumbling mud and stone walls, each suffering immense weather damage over a considerable period of time. The inside of the building was a mass of rubble including what appeared to be human remains.

From the abused and neglected condition of this structure, it appeared that this ruin was a mission or church of some sort that had been attacked and devastated by some unknown force. Taking stock of the situation, I came to the conclusion that the island might not be as deserted as originally conjectured. Given this realization, I signed to Powder Monkey that we needed to proceed with extreme caution to avoid any trouble we might encounter on our search. As we cautiously continued inland, we discovered yet another strange revelation. The interior of the island was marked with numerous primitive fetishes taking the unusual form of swine skulls that were affixed to hand carved poles. These skeletal pig heads seemed to be everywhere, silently marking our progress, while warning us of danger lurking ahead. In taking the time to examine a few of these pig posts, I could not determine if they were placed deliberately as a warning sign to trespassers or were simply hunting trophies. However, what they did clearly tell me was that we were not alone on this island!

As we continued to push our way inland, I suddenly heard drums beating out a faint rhythm in the far distance. To insure that we were not detected, we slowed our pace considerably and kept under the cover of vegetation to the greatest degree possible. As the drums seemed to become louder and louder, we understood that their source was very near.

Reaching the edge of a clearing, we were finally rewarded in our exploration efforts. Before us stood an entire primitive village, complete with vine, twig and branch hovels that housed what appeared to be a barbaric tribe. In the very center of the village was a huge roaring bonfire surrounded by painted warriors involved in some sort of ceremonial dance. Accompanied by the ever-present drumbeat, the warriors were circling the blazing conflagration in calculated and precise movements. The group was led by a wizened and ancient figure that was cloaked in all manner of swine skins. His noggin was adorned with a massive skeletal pig head much like those we had passed on our march here. All at once, the headman shouted something unintelligible. A number of village women rose from their sitting positions upon hearing the command. Moving in mass to the other side of the camp, these women stood directly in front of a hastily constructed enclosure. Straining my vision to uncover the enclosure's function, I was eventually rewarded as I spied movement within the strange structure.

All at once, I understood its purpose very clearly. It was a prison of sorts! Inside, I could barely make out our missing crewmembers hunched and huddled together in the very center of the framework of branches and vines. From our position, I could see only five figures inside the enclosure, but to my great relief our Captain was amongst the captives along with Long Tall Willie and Angry George. At further sharp barks from the swine adorned chieftain, the women entered the enclosure and dragged out one of its occupants. I recognized the wretch as Tommy Boyle, as he struggled uselessly trussed up on the ground. His terrified screams and wails went unnoticed by the congregation's faithful. Given a shouted order from their leader, who I had christened Pighead, I returned my vision in his direction. Pighead was slowly advancing to a stone table of some sort that also housed more pig fetishes. As I concentrated on the stone table, I suddenly realized that it was some sort of religious affair. Straining my vision further, I was able to distinguish a multitude of round yellowish-white objects on the top of this heathen abomination. With a sudden jolt of recognition, I realized that these round white object were human skulls!

Pighead seemed to be conducting some sort of prayer ceremony in front of the ghastly altar, bowing in deference to either the skulls or the pig fetishes scattered on it. After a brief moment, he rose from his position of prayer and shouted a stern command to the women now kneeling all around Tommy Boyle. Acknowledging this command with a unified grunt, the women each unsheathed a primitive knife and proceeded to slice and slash the tortured and screaming tar. My first thought was that they intended to stab Tommy to death. As I continued watching, I discovered that their attack on Tommy was executed with far less than mortal intent. Rather, it sure seemed as if they were executing deep incisions on every portion of his body.

Confused by their vicious yet nonlethal actions, Powder Monkey and I continued to watch the tragedy unfold. Finally completing their curious efforts, the women all grunted some intelligible words towards Pighead, who seemed to nod his approval at a job well done. Immediately, the crazed chief called out a command to his silently standing warriors, who made their way over to Tommy and lifted him over their heads as they returned to their places in front of the roaring fire. At that exact instant, the drums resumed and the bloodthirsty savages broke into a stomping dance as they circled the fire holding a terrified and moaning Tommy Boyle high over their heads. I was now convinced that they meant to heave Tommy directly into the roaring flames. The dancing continued on for some time as Tommy's blood dripped freely down onto his captors, showering them with his precious life's fluid. At another loud command from their superior, the men made an abrupt turn and carried Tommy to the other side of the village, where I noticed yet another stouter enclosure.

Peering intently at this new location, I spied movement from several dark shapes that were imprisoned within. With mounting horror gripping my entire being, I realized that the enclosure was filled with enormous feral pigs. As the warriors toting Tommy reached the wild pig cage, they stopped for just a short moment before tossing the bleeding and helpless sailor directly into the center of the pen. The feral pigs, smelling a potential meal, descended on poor Tommy and began their ravenous feeding. The savages, elated at the frenzied actions of their pets, began their stomping dance once more. Above the roar of the natives and the pounding of the drum, Powder Monkey and I could hear the terrified squeals and shrill screams from Tommy as the pack of hungry monsters were literally devouring him alive.

Totally shocked and disgusted by this inhuman scene of madness and depravity, I signaled Powder Monkey to start making our retreat from the village. In taking a last moment to assess the situation, I was certain that there was very little the two of us could accomplish by confronting the superior force of savage warriors. I understood that we required a plan and we needed to implement it very soon or the Captain and our remaining crewmembers would suffer the same horrific fate as poor Tommy Boyle. As we retreated through the dense vegetation back towards the deserted beach and our anchored ship, we were both tortured by poor Tommy's continued dying screams and wails that thankfully became fainter and fainter the further we moved away from the village.

Once we distanced ourselves from the heathen village, both Powder Monkey and I broke into a fast trot. Without a word between us, we realized that the rescue of our Captain and mates rested entirely on our shoulders. We certainly could not depend on the Doc or his sick charges to assist our efforts in any way. As we passed one of the heathen pig totems, a very strange thought entered my mind. Stopping for a brief moment to think this new idea through, I realized for the first time that there just might be a way for us to affect a rescue. To accomplish the plan I had in mind, I knew that I needed to prepare several items. As we both resumed our hurried march to the beach, I communicated the gist of my plan to Powder Monkey. Wide-eyed and totally terrified, Powder Monkey nodded that he understood the plan that I had just imparted. As we ran side-by-side, I signed that I needed a dramatic diversion that would frighten the savages into flight. This ruse would need to totally scare the religion out of these pig worshipping heathens!

Glancing over to Powder Monkey, I asked him if he could provide some sort of explosions to scatter the villagers in utmost terror. Thinking over my request, Powder Monkey suddenly lit up and informed me that he had an idea that would provide the type of diversion I required. At once, Powder Monkey separated from my side and raced over to a grove of palm trees. Once there, he began to inspect various coconuts that had fallen around the trees. Working his way meticulously through the fallen fruit, he began separating the coconuts he deemed worthy and began placing them into the longboat. Noting my quizzical look, he signed that he now had the proper vessels to provide the dramatic explosions which I had requested. Shrugging my confusion aside, I hopped into our boat and we quickly rowed out to the anchored *Amafata*.

Upon reaching our ship, I sent Powder Monkey off to prepare his explosive surprises, while I ran to the Doc's surgery to inform him of our ghastly discoveries on Pig Island. The Doc was shocked and astounded by my report and questioned me on what plan I had in mind to save our captured Captain and mates. I briefly laid out my outrageous scheme noticing that the Doc continued to stare at me as if I had completely lost my mind. Reminding the Doc that we were severely undermanned to execute any type of frontal assault, I finished relating the startling diversion I had in mind. Once done, the Doc could do nothing more than shake his head in complete bewilderment and wish me the best of luck in this insanely dangerous venture. Additionally, he informed me that his patients were recovering quite nicely due to my quina tea. Since my last visit, there had been no further deaths due to the illness, and the sick sailors under his care were definitely showing signs of marked improvement. He congratulated me on my resourcefulness, and sent me off to prepare for the grand deception with his very best wishes for success.

I made my way to the galley to check on my accomplice, Powder Monkey. Once there, I found him busy in concentrated work on the coconuts he had so meticulously selected. He was totally absorbed in the process of drilling holes into the top of each nut with one of Chip's augers. Once he completed each hole, he drained that coconut of its milk and asked for my assistance in carefully reaming out the majority of the wet fruit from its core. Confused totally by this frenzied work, I asked him to explain his scheme to me.

Stopping briefly, he informed me that he was turning the harmless coconuts into grenados. Still stymied by his words, he continued by explaining that a grenado was an age-old Spanish military tactic that if executed properly would provide the explosions that I had requested. Taking one of the coconuts into his hands, he demonstrated the process of making a grenado. Pouring a mixture of gunpowder and small shot into the hole bored in the coconut, he finished the device by plunging a small piece of a slow match into this hole at the top and then sealing it in place with pliable candle wax. Once finished, he held the coconut with the slow match stem in front of my eyes explaining that the slow match acted as a primer for the weapon. Once the slow match was lit, all he had to do was lob the coconut at a desired target. When the fire from the slow match reached the gunpowder, it would cause a tremendous explosion that would propel the shot in every direction destroying anything and everything in its path.

Suitably impressed with the device now resting in my hands, I asked him if he thought that this miniature explosive would actually work. Giving me a huge wink and a lopsided grin, he informed me that he surely hoped it would work because both of our lives depended on its performance. Nodding, I notified him that we had very little daylight left to enable us to return to the accursed village. Once there, the plan was to utilize the cover of darkness to carry out our daring ruse. He informed me that he required only a little more time to finish his arsenal, since most of the preparation work had already been completed. Assisting him in the final stages of manufacture, we eventually had our grenados ready. Bagging the lethal coconuts in two sacks, we carried them back to the longboat and made our return to Pig Island.

As we rowed ashore, I explained the full details the grand hoax we were about to perpetuate. To ensure success, I instructed Powder Monkey that he needed to separate when we reached the village of swine-worshipping savages. My grand design called for allowing us a chance to get close enough to our intended targets to unleash the devastating grenados. I further confided that his signal for commencing action was the moment I detonated my first grenado. Upon this signal, Powder Monkey was instructed to throw his first grenado at an agreed upon target. From that point on, he was ordered to toss his lethal armament as quickly as he could manage at the other targets we had both deemed appropriate.

Laughing at the sheer audacity of our plan, I informed him that should our hoax fail that we would surely be joining our friends for a dinner date with some very hungry swine. Understanding my sinister message, he nodded and related that he had great trust that his brainstorm would prove successful. I absentmindedly reached towards my chest to take hold of my trusty good luck piece, only to find it missing due to an unknown crew member's thieving ways.

We landed on the deserted beach and made our way inland just before the sun set. Arriving back at the village, I was gratified to observe that no further swine sacrifices had occurred in our absence. As we waited for complete darkness, I signaled the spot where I needed Powder Monkey to position himself. As soon as he disappeared, I began to ready my grenados for the performance that was about to start. As I made these preparations, I noticed that the drums had suddenly resumed their dreaded beat and the warriors had begun to assemble in front of the roaring fire to initiate their ceremonial dance. I was fully aware that this drumbeat signaled another victim would be chosen shortly to appease the ravenous hunger of their avaricious pets.

As I continued to watch, Pighead repeated all of the drama from our previous visit. At his initial command, the village women moved to the captive's prison and dragged their next victim out to prepare him for unholy sacrifice. The victim chosen happened to be our very own Captain. As the women bent over the Captain to tenderize him for the voracious swine, I utilized my *special voice* to project the haunting screech of a pig in mortal pain and distress. This sound came easily as I had previous familiarity in Londontown listening to swine in the throes of being slaughtered.

I was gratified that my ruse was having its intended effect by the stunned looks of surprise and terror on the faces of each and every tribe member. As I approached the village center, I continued to issue my vile swine screeches at full volume. I then quickly lit my first grenado and lobbed it into the center of the village. Before it detonated I lit and tossed the second grenado towards the nearest edge of the village. When both exploded, the deafening din and flying shot sent the villagers in haphazard flight in opposite directions from our positions.

Powder Monkey observing my first strikes released his initial grenado. In a matter of seconds, the entire pigpen was alighted with the thunderous detonation of his well-aimed explosive. The result was truly wondrous as the deadly shot spread its path of destruction, completely obliterating the entire swine herd huddled inside the enclosure. Continuing our attack, we lobbed grenado after grenado into the village. They began to explode virtually everywhere. I watched in awe as one of these sinister bombs detonated directly in the center of the ceremonial fire spewing fiery shards throughout the village igniting homes and humans alike. All in all, it was like observing a biblical Armageddon!

Well, the savages needed no further encouragement as they furiously scattered in all directions to avoid being slaughtered. As they made their frenzied escape, Powder Monkey came to my side signing that he intended to heave his remaining grenados in the villager's wake to discourage any brave or curious soul from returning. Nodding my assent, Powder Monkey lit the remaining four fuses and heaved his deadly devices in the fleeing tribe's wake. As he executed this final assault, I ran over to our captive crewmates to free them from their bindings. As I reached them and opened the enclosure holding them prisoner, I was greeted by their looks of absolute terror and fear after experiencing the devastating explosions we had unleashed. Shouting that we had little to waste, I severed the vines that had kept them prisoners. Instructing all on the planned escape route, I hurried to the Captain's side to also free him. Relieved at finding him dazed but virtually uninjured, I severed his bindings and got him to his feet. Once finished, Powder Monkey and I led the Captain and our dazed crewmates back to the deserted beach. Once there, we all piled into the two waiting longboats and made our way hastily to our beloved ship.

As we rowed out to the *Amafata*, the Captain thanked both of us for saving both his life and those of our crewmates. Now fully recovered from the shock of the ordeal, Long Tall Willie laughed loud and hard as he remembered the terrified faces of the savages. He conjectured, in a fit of laughter, that the villagers were in all probability still in full flight! Given his humor, the tension and strain felt by all of us seemed to dissolve as we all began joking and laughing with each other.

As we climbed aboard, the Doc raced to the Captain's side in obvious relief that our rescue mission was a success. He then joyfully reported to the Captain and I that the typhus fever patients were near full recovery due to the quina tea treatments. The Captain ordered the anchor weighed to distance us from the odious Pig Island and its vicious swine worshipping heathens. Wrapping his arm around my shoulders, he thanked me in the most sincere manner for the incredibly brave and resourceful rescue that I had just engineered. Flattered by his sincerity and embarrassed by his emotional overture, I informed him that all was really made possible by Powder Monkey's quick thinking regarding the deadly grenados. Nodding in total agreement, he turned and gave Powder Monkey a congratulatory slap on the back for a job well done. As we sailed away from this insidious pagan lair, we all felt an enormous sense of relief that we were back aboard our beloved *Amafata*.

Chapter 6: Taken by the Devil's Spawn

It was now quite apparent that our ship was critically short of manpower. The typhus scourge coupled with our unfortunate losses on Pig Island meant that everyone aboard was forced to add additional duties to their daily routines. The positive news was that the typhus epidemic seemed to have abated with no further outbreaks of the dreaded illness. We still had three typhus victims ready for sea burial stored in the hold, and plans called for their funerals the following morning. Powder Monkey had renewed his search for my wooden crucifix, which as yet had yielded no positive results. About midnight, Powder Monkey made an unexpected visit to my cabin. Coated from head to toe in filth, he entered the room sporting a rather blank expression. Noting this vacant gaze, I questioned the status of his search for my precious talisman. In response, he slowly shook his head in a negative fashion.

Noting the highly determined look on his face, I broke out in a wide encouraging smile. Powder Monkey signed that he had covered almost the entire hold. He informed me, that when he had visited the Doc's surgery, he had spied an inordinate amount of tar on Pigsty's hands and clothing. With this vital information in mind, Powder Monkey had begun an extensive search of containers that held tar or pitch. Smiling wistfully, he confessed that he was very near completing the investigation of the pitch barrels in the hold. Marveling at his incredible observational abilities, I proclaimed that I felt certain that he would uncover my treasure in no time at all. Grinning widely now, I thanked Powder Monkey for his keen dedication and tireless effort to uncover my amulet's hiding place.

As plans were made the following morning for the burial of our three typhus victims, the topman called down that a ship had been spied off of our larboard side. Racing there to gain a glimpse of this vessel, I was momentarily joined by the Captain holding his trusty telescope. Once he had ample time to observe our newest neighbor, he lowered his telescope and in a very quiet tone informed me that this ship sported no colors whatsoever! Since there was no way to ascertain their true identity presently, the Captain ordered me to stand watch with his telescope to see if I could determine the vessel's intentions.

For the remainder of the day, I kept up this tiresome vigil but there was very little to actually discern. The mysterious ship seemed to be shadowing our course and speed, while never really closing the gap between us. Reporting these meager observations to the Captain, we both hoped that our new neighbor would be gone from sight the following morning. However, our fervent wish was not granted, and we sadly discovered at dawn that our shadow had remained with us during the night. Given this ominous state of affairs, the crew began to panic fearing the absolute worst outcome imaginable--pirates!

The Captain immediately requested a private conference in his cabin. Once we reached his berth, the Captain asked for my opinion on the course of action that we should undertake given our situation. Truthfully, my recommendation was basically a choice between attempting flight or standing and fighting should our shadow prove hostile. Silently, I thought of a third unacceptable course of action, which called for surrendering the *Amafata* should our pursuers turned out to be pirates. Theorizing, I voiced the obvious fact that we were severely undermanned with many of our crew still recovering from the typhus epidemic. Due to this, our chances of withstanding an attack of any magnitude would be quite remote. I then stated that I felt our best course was attempting to make a run for safety under the cover of darkness, which unfortunately was still a long way off. To succeed in this endeavor, we would need to extinguish all of our lights while altering our course dramatically in the hopes of confusing and eventually losing our shadow by means of outright deception. Taking a moment to contemplate my words, the Captain finally nodded and told me that he agreed with my recommendation. As I made my leave, he advised me to pray that our trailing friends allowed us the opportunity to execute our agreed strategy.

As I made my way back to the maindeck, I could see immediately that the situation had changed dramatically. Our potential foe was now closing the gap between our vessels so that our escape plan was entirely negated. Given this new situation, I recommended that the crew be readied for armed conflict; including loading and priming our two recently purchased cannons. The Captain slowly nodded his approval, and I sang out the order for all hands to prepare for battle. This command caused a flurry of activity as our men scrambled for their weapons. Going below, I found my cannon team also in furious activity loading and priming the two guns. I ordered the team to hold until I gave them the order to commence firing. With that, I returned to the Captain's side to sadly discover that our shadow was now closing even faster. Since my brief absence, the ship had raised a black flag adorned with a white skull indicating their true nature--pirates!

The pirate ship was alive with activity as filthy heathens were now prancing, dancing, screaming and waving their weapons threateningly while in a highly spirited mood. This activity was accompanied by a savage war tune being played by their ship's makeshift band. They were now close enough for us to hear their barbaric cursing and swearing across the open water. As they continued their fast approach, they swung in-line with us preparing to fire their guns. From my meager knowledge of piratical practices, I knew for certain that these devils did not want to actually sink our ship. This drastic act could potentially deprive the scum of a valuable prize. Rather, I conjectured that they were attempting to terrorize us into a quick surrender to avoid any sort of skirmish. As they came into cannon range, they did fire several rounds, but all of these were well in front of our position. I raced below to direct our response to their invitation to acquiesce to their surrender demands. As I reached my cannon team, I gave curt instructions to make our two shots count dearly. Our objective was to incapacitate the pirate ship's sails and riggings. My thoughts were that if we could extract enough damage to this marauding vessel, we still might have a chance to make a run for freedom.

As the sea wolves neared, terrifying all with their continued maddened antics, I ordered my team to fire both guns. Using chainshot, which I had previously ordered, our guns caused substantial damage to their mainsail as well as considerable minor damage to their riggings and tackle. You see, chainshot is a wicked little device that was made up of two smaller lead balls that were actually iron chained together. When fired, this shot would spread out in flight and wreak havoc on any target's sails, masts and riggings. As my team began to reload both guns, I observed our enemy's damaged mainsail collapse upon their deck sending filthy scoundrels scurrying for cover in all directions. Our Captain realizing the opportunity presented him, ordered the crew to prepare to flee from our vicious adversaries. Our precise cannon work had hampered the pirate's maneuverability and speed to a significant degree, hopefully enough to allow our attempted escape from their clutches! At the same time, I noticed that our defensive actions had made the pirates madder than a nest of angry hornets, as they raised their screams and curses to an even higher level. Utilizing their muskets now, the pirates began to fire randomly at our topside crew, who were attempting to make preparations for our hasty departure.

Given all the damage we had inflicted, the demons refused to quit. Realizing their crippled condition, they immediately launched two small boats full of deadly musketeers. Meanwhile, the musket barrage from their maindeck continued to harass our crew from going about our own flight preparations. Making my way topside to personally assess the situation, I observed several of our crew severely injured or dead as a result of the deadly musket barrage. Realizing that our slim chance to escape had been thwarted, I raced back to my cannon team now prepared to make a last-ditch effort out of the dire situation facing us. Ordering my team to prepare for the battle of their lives, I commanded them to send a load of grapeshot at the lead longboat filled with gun-toting savages. For you landlubbers, grapeshot is made up of small lead balls that are affixed together that separated and flared out upon firing to form a lethal killing barrage. Our first shot came very close, forcing the rabble to fall on their faces in the belly of the boat as our deadly shot sailed directly over them. As they climbed back to their feet and resumed their insane shouting, we readied the second cannon for action. Issuing the order to fire, I was gratified to see that this time our shot was true as we turned the small boat into splinters, sending all who were not initially torn apart directly into the sea.

Watching the flailing arms of the doomed demons seeking rescue gave me a brief moment of satisfaction. However, this sensation was very short lived, as I noticed the second small boat steadily making its advance. This longboat was also crammed with musket-toting sharpshooters, probably the best shots our friends had to offer. As they neared, they began a deadly fusillade that raked our topdeck cutting down even more hands, who were still under the Captain's orders to prepare the ship for retreat. I heard several cries from above that our Captain had been wounded. Racing to the topdeck, I found wounded or dead littering our ship almost everywhere I gazed. Rushing over to our fallen Captain's side, I discovered that his injuries were indeed quite serious. He had taken a deadly musketball in his stomach, which I knew would certainly result in a slow and agonizing death. As I made him comfortable, he ordered me to continue our desperate fight since we had already angered our attackers beyond any hope for a peaceful surrender.

Nodding my assent, I hurried back to my cannon team to deliver the dire news. Quickly filling them in on our woeful plight, I ordered them to reload their guns with more grapeshot. As I watched the revenge maddened villains in the remaining longboat heading our way, I commanded both cannons to be fired in unison. The result was truly devastating as these small rounded projectiles literally ripped the approaching boat and its diabolical occupants to minuscule shreds, showering the surrounding sea with bloody chunks of human flesh.

Having dispatched both of our imminent dangers, I glanced over to the pirate ship to judge our next move. I could see that a furious effort was being applied to repair the damage that we had caused with our initial barrage. Witnessing the utter destruction of their friends and comrades in the two longboats had sent every pirate onboard into a bloodletting frenzy, as they made these hasty repairs in order to once again take an active attack role. Realizing that we were still attempting to flee, the pirate Captain ordered his cannons filled with both chainshot and grapeshot. Once completed, these villains unleashed their own deadly barrage which caused horrific damage to our sails, riggings, yards and masts. This damage and destruction was catastrophic, preventing us any chance of even modest navigation. I realized that our only course now was to stand and fight to the death. As I stood numb with shock, the Captain called me over to his side. He explained that both the ship and her crew were in my hands now. In a very calm voice, he advised me that when we were overrun by the filthy pirate scum to take whatever actions necessary to grant survival to any living crew member. Smiling weakly, he announced that it would be far wiser to play pirate than risk total annihilation at the hands of these vile brigands.

As he finished these orders, I looked up to see that the pirates had completed their hasty repairs and were now swooping down on us to extract their sweet revenge. As they neared our position, a wave of grappling hooks were unleashed that found purchase at various points along our deck. Concurrently, a continuous barrage of musket fire kept us from taking any preventative or retaliatory action. Additionally, since they had already felt the sting of our cannons, the pirates approached us from our stern, neutralizing our cannons as our last line of defense.

In mere seconds, the pirate rabble boarded our dear ship, and sporadic hand-to-hand combat was underway. However, there were far too many pirates and too few of us. Before very long, we were completely overtaken and at the full mercy of these crazed savages. As we were roughly herded together, the pirate Captain slowly made his way onboard to conduct an inspection of his captives. The furious pirate Captain stomped his way over to us, demanding to address the senior officer of our ship. I stepped forward to face him as his howling devils poked and prodded my crewmates with their cutlasses and dirks. Taking stock of the situation, I realized that there were only about a dozen of my crewmates still alive. Included in my count were Powder Monkey, Doc, Chips, Long Tall Willie, Creeping Jeremy, Angry George, Charlie Crowfeet, Muttering Moses Hart, Fighting John English and just a few more.

The first question out of their leader's mouth was how someone so young could possibly be Captain of our vessel. I responded that I was not the Captain, as I pointed to our leader lying in a lake of his own blood. Having received my answer, the pirate Captain swaggered over to our Captain and gazed down demanding to be told where all of our booty was hidden. Our Captain, weak and nearly unconscious, whispered that all money had been spent on Saint Domingue and Jamaica to replace fire damaged trade-goods. The pirate chieftain, incensed beyond reason by this response, proceeded to shove a drawn dagger directly into the belly wound of our leader in an effort to persuade him to immediately divulge all secrets. Screaming in utter agony, our Captain lapsed into unconsciousness. Wasting no time, the pirate Captain grabbed a nearby bucket of seawater and doused the dying man in an effort to revive him for further interrogation. As our Captain came around, the pirate Captain informed him that he personally planned to murder each remaining crewmember one-by-one until the truth was revealed.

Our Captain in a halting and gasping whisper told his captor that he had been deadly honest in his reply to the question put to him. Noting that further questioning would prove useless, the pirate Captain ordered Fighting John English to be brought forward and to kneel before him. Placing his cutlass on the back of the terrified man's neck, the pirate repeated his original question on the whereabouts of the ship's hidden loot. Once again he received the same weak response from our Captain. Infuriated, the beast delivered a savage downward stroke ending Fighting John's life, as he nearly severed his head completely off. At that point, our Captain realized that all was certainly lost and confessed to the heartless brute that what little coin existed was hidden in a Bible in his quarters. The pirate Captain motioned one of his insane companions to go below and deliver the promised word directly into his waiting hands.

In just a short time, the Bible was handed over to the heartless monster for inspection. Opening the Good Book, the pirate Captain discovered a pouch full of coins neatly hidden in a compartment that had been hewed out of the Bible's interior. Elated with this discovery, the pirate Captain became philosophical as he instructed us that their sole objective was virtually the same as any merchant, banker, politician or clergyman on land, to get rich. Further, he proudly proclaimed that the only difference between themselves and their landlubbing brethren was that they went about their business in an honest and forthright manner versus the sneaking and conniving methods employed by the latter. Further, he elucidated that thieving landlubbers were protected by laws while pirates operated without any assistance and invariably paid for their labors at the end of a stout rope. While he enacted this drama for our sole benefit, his crew, thirsty for revenge, began calling for our blood. Quieting his rabble with a savage wave of his cutlass, he patiently explained to them that our cannon expertise had left him with a very severe deficiency in manpower. Given our proven ability to fight, he loudly expounded that he intended to replace his losses with only those he judged suitable to filling the vacancies.

After this proclamation, the pirate Captain called over to his ship and invited his Quartermaster to join the party. I can tell you that we were all very much astonished to view Lion Babar, the Turk from Saint Domingue, make his way onto our ship. The same could be said of our old drinking companion, who shook his head in smiling amazement once he recognized all of us. Snapping out of his bemusement, he informed his Captain, named Rambling Dirk Shivvers that we were all old acquaintances, friends and damned good sailors. He then enumerated the extent of their severe manpower shortage. Due to this, Lion recommended that we all serve as the immediate replacements grievously required to continue their piratical voyage. The pirate crew certainly did not agree with Lion's proposal, calling loudly for our blood once again! As he quieted his mangy crew, Captain Shivvers shouted that taking revenge and killing us would simply make matters worse for all of them. Replacements were sorely required and Captain Shivvers bellowed that he intended to lead the investigation as to which of our number would be found worthy of that honor. Grumblings of discontent followed his proclamation, but were quickly silenced by the menacing stares of both Captain Shivvers and his hulking Quartermaster.

Chapter 7: Pirate Captain Shivvers

Captain Shivvers subsequently announced that we were very fortunate for the privilege and honor to serve on his ship, the *Midnight Crow*. Since I had been identified as the senior officer, I became the first to be questioned. Captain Shivvers began with the obvious, inquiring if I knew of any additional booty aboard our ship. Answering honestly, I confessed that we had experienced an accidental fire while at sea which had destroyed about a third of our total trade-goods. Our Captain, who was now being propped up by Angry George and Charlie Crowfeet, could only nod his agreement as he passed in-and-out of consciousness. Continuing, I related that any reserve the ship may have carried had been utilized to replenish this lost cargo. I informed my rapt inquisitor that I had not even been privy to the contents of the Bible safe. Finally, I acknowledged that our only onboard valuables were our trade-goods currently stored in the hold.

Then as a test to determine my conduct as a ship's officer, Captain Shivvers asked my terrified crewmates exactly what kind of officer I happened to be. Was I harsh and cruel or fair and forgiving? To a man, my crew responded that I was a very good and capable officer, fully worthy of their trust and respect. They also informed the pirate leader that I had saved the ship and most of them from death and destruction numerous times. To my utter surprise, Lion seconded these positive responses and vouched for my generosity and courageous actions on Saint Domingue.

I could sense that Captain Shivvers was a bit disappointed by these glowing tributes, and was now in a quandary as exactly what to do with me. Seeking further guidance, he inquired about my specific duties aboard the *Amafata*. In a very clear and calm voice, I stated that I served as ship's Navigator, First Mate and assistant to the Doctor. Blinking furiously with surprise at my response, he responded that he was stunned that someone so young could be so accomplished. Shrugging innocently, I answered that I was a very quick learner and had been well-educated as a lad back in England. Still unsure of my real abilities and qualifications, he questioned me on the identity of the person responsible for commanding our cannon team. Once again in a humble voice, I replied that I was the person responsible. Hearing my answer sent his pirate rabble into a crazed frenzy once again. One particularly louse-ridden villain actually drew his pistol and took careful aim at my chest, informing me that he would now avenge his dead comrades. As promised, he pulled the trigger of his pistol and fired a shot that was intended to put an end to my life. At the same instant, our Captain with the last vestige of his strength shirked off the two assistants holding him upright and stepped directly in front of me, shielding me from the tormentor's musketball. The lead meant to end my life, hit him directly in the heart and he immediately slumped to the deck and perished.

Lion was the first to react to this unsanctioned attack. Unsheathing his enormous cutlass, he proceeded to decapitate the pistol-shooting barbarian to the complete shock of all. After delivering his punishment, he turned to Captain Shivvers and reiterated that I was a very valuable asset, and the traitorous scum who had acted without authority deserved the fate he had received. Turning then to his crewmates, Lion shouted that the scoundrel he dispatched had been masquerading as the pirate ship's doctor, and due to his total incompetence was probably responsible for more of their own deaths than any prisoner standing before them. Captain Shivvers totally understood the logic of Lion's words, and ordered our dead Captain and the decapitated pirate's torso and head to be hauled to the side of the ship and thrown overboard.

Captain Shivvers then demanded an inventory of ship's goods stored in the hold. Taking my time, I provided a succinct inventory of all of our holdings from memory. This simple and immediate response once again stunned every one of our captors into complete silence. Finding his voice once again, Captain Shivvers questioned me on our destination. I replied that we were bound for Barbados, after which we intended to return home to England. Issuing a wicked sneer, Captain Shivvers announced that a slight detour was definitely in order!

Not quite finished with my interrogation, the pirate leader asked me to identify my cannonmates. As I pointed to them, Captain Shivvers motioned them to step forward. Angry George remained behind and seemed rather reluctant to show himself because of his past grievances with Lion. As he attempted to hide, Lion recognized him and immediately made his way over to confront his old enemy. To our great surprise, Lion grabbed Angry George and wrapped his huge arms around him in a friendly embrace, informing him that their former lover, Sugar Sally, had been brutally murdered. It seemed that she had been victimized by the Black Tarantula's assault and had lost her life in the encounter. With a sincere look of dismay, Lion reported that he missed her terribly and would someday seek retribution for her untimely death. Slapping Angry George on the back, he shouted that since the reason for their dispute was no longer living that the two of them had no further quarrel.

Glancing at the remainder of our crew, Captain Shivvers inquired if any one of us could function as either cook or a carpenter. Smiling, I pointed out Powder Monkey and Long Tall Willie, as I notified the pirate leader that these two individuals were indeed our esteemed cooks. Turning once more in Chips direction, I signaled him out and announced that he was the finest carpenter to ever sail the seas. Gratified at my responses, Captain Shivvers then questioned if our doctor had survived the attack. Once again, I pointed directly at Doc, who was more than confused as to what was happening and the reason why he had been signaled out. Understanding his apparent confusion, I spoke to him in his native tongue explaining all that had transpired since our ship had been taken over by the pirates. Relieved at my explanation, the Doc stepped forward and in his native tongue acknowledged that he served as our ship's physician.

Since none of the pirates understood Italian, I loosely translated that the Doc was excellent at his profession, and had saved numerous lives throughout our journey. Once again, Captain Shivvers was both shocked and impressed that I could understand and speak the Doc's strange sounding language so effortlessly. To end his apparent confusion, I confessed to the reprehensible sea leach that I had been taught several languages as a lad. Captain Shivvers seemed to believe that I was lying to him, so he quickly turned to a fellow scoundrel and ordered him to converse with me in his native tongue. The rascal immediately began speaking to me in French, asking for clarification on which languages I was fluent. Understanding him, I answered back in French that beyond English, French and Italian, I could communicate in Spanish, German, Dutch, Latin and Portuguese. My curt answer not only impressed the

Frenchman, but also the entire scurvy crew of murderous rascals. I could also tell by his appraising expression that Captain Shivvers had finally realized my true worth.

Having made his decisions, Captain Shivvers informed us that we really had only one chance in order to continue living. To do so, he announced that we all had to go on the account and become members of his pirate band or suffer and die in utter savagery at the hands of his revenge-minded crew. My crewmates all agreed to become pirates rather than face the disagreeable alternative. Turning in my direction, Captain Shivvers informed me that he was in desperate need of my skills to serve as ship's navigator and translator. After taking a brief moment to consider his offer, I replied that I would certainly not turn pirate at any cost, choosing death rather than serving alongside his mangy lot of heathens. The pirate crewmembers applauded my choice and seemed very eager to oblige my last request. However, Captain Shivvers was undaunted by my negative response. He informed me that unless I agreed to his terms, he would murder each and every one of my friends in a slow and truly agonizing manner. I responded that this course of action would only deprive his ship of valuable and able-bodied seamen to replace his numerous losses.

Realizing that I was deadly serious in my denial to turn pirate, he attempted to negotiate a compromise between us. He divulged that if I willingly agreed to serve that this condition would only be temporary. He further promised that he would issue a written statement that I and my crewmates were forced into piratical service under pain of death should we ever be asked to explain our actions to questioning authorities. Still sensing my reluctance, Captain Shivvers pulled out his own pistol and held it to Powder Monkey's head encouraging me to make the right choice immediately. Having no real option, I agreed to go on the account, but insisted that my crewmates not be harmed in any way by him or his filthy crew. Turning now to his band of savages, he swore this oath on his very life!

Because this entire interchange had taken quite a long time to complete, I came to the obvious conclusion that pirates were painstakingly methodical in their interrogation for two very important reasons. First, we were quite isolated in the calm tropical waters surrounding us with absolutely nobody remotely close enough to harass or arrest the efforts of these insidious thieves. Secondly, their patient and thorough methods allowed them to be utterly sure that no valuable loot was overlooked.

Once Captain Shivvers had obtained my agreement, he prepared to unleash his filthy minions to strip our vessel of anything of value. Besides our trade-goods, the savages were ordered to plunder all manner of ship necessities including sails, riggings, cables, anchor, arms, food, water and medicine. Scattering in frenzy as they prepared to obey his order, the voracious ruffians virtually drooled over the prospect of stripping the *Amafata* clean, as they whooped, hollered and screamed the entire time. Captain Shivvers ordered me and my crewmates to go below and gather anything we deemed necessary to fulfill our new roles. Once done, we were then instructed to transport these items to our new home aboard the *Midnight Crow*.

Turning in Lion's direction, Captain Shivvers issued a strong command that we were not to be interfered with in any way under penalty of a brutal and painful death. Further, Captain Shivvers ordered Lion to accompany me and to assist the procurement of my possessions with special emphasis on any nautical navigational devices I deemed essential. Captain Shivvers then charged another of his filthy swine to accompany Doc and assist in the transfer of his entire medical store. He also instructed Chips to garner his carpentry tools and to transport them to his ship so that necessary repairs could begin at the earliest possible time. Finally, Long Tall Willie, Powder Monkey and Angry George were assigned the duty of managing the transfer our cannons, shot and powder to the *Midnight Crow*.

We all watched in absolute horror as the *Amafata* was literally torn asunder by the crude efforts of these despicable heathens. Lion accompanied me to my cabin and assisted my efforts to pack and transport all my required instruments, charts and maps. Included in my indicated needs were the special trunks of supplies given to me by Gertrude and Hortence. Never once questioning my motives or choices, Lion proved a valuable assistant in helping me to transfer my entire lot of possessions aboard my new home.

As the defiling of the *Amafata* continued, one very interesting occurrence came to my attention. Just before Lion and I began the tedious chore of transferring my required possessions, two extremely shaken pirates returned from their very brief visit to the hold. Running to Captain Shivvers' side, these terrified tars reported that there were three dead bodies wrapped in sailcloth in the bowels of our ship. This announcement from the two pirates, now white with fright, brought a temporary work-stoppage to the entire pirate crew. Their announcement seemed to raise a very high level of anxiety amongst these marauding savages, causing many of them to make the traditional sign-of-the-cross on their bodies to ward off evil. In a stuttering and frightened tone, Captain Shivvers demanded to be told why these dead bodies were being stored in the hold. I informed my new leader that these men had died of deadly fever and were duly scheduled for burial, which had been interrupted by his insidious attack. Making his own sign-of-the-cross, Captain Shivvers ordered Charlie Crowfeet and Muttering Moses Hayes to go below and bring the three dead wretches topside so that a proper burial could be performed.

Noting the abject fear and superstitious terror on the part of each and every pirate, I decided to tuck this information away for later when I could employ this powerful weapon to my advantage. When the *Amafata* was finally stripped of every worthwhile item, the gleeful rouges set fire to our beloved ship. As our ship began to burn uncontrollably, my crewmates and I watched with utter sadness as our dear *Amafata* slipped steaming beneath the white capped waves. Reflecting on our loss for a moment, I decided that I would especially miss the bare-breasted mermaid that had adorned our bow.

Chapter 8: On the Account

We were now settled aboard the *Midnight Crow,* at the total mercy of the murderous brutes who had captured us. The Doc and I were afforded a small cabin, to serve as both our domicile and his surgery. The ship itself was a schooner that was constructed quite differently than our dear departed vessel. While our merchantman was designed strictly for cargo transport, our new home was engineered to maximize their devilish thieving intentions. While the *Amafata* had spacious cargo space and carried a small but adequate crew, the *Midnight Crow* was tight and confined below decks. This confined space only allowed the barest amount of space necessary for accommodating its much larger crew and her prodigious stock of fearful munitions. By comparison, our new vessel carried well over triple the number of bodies and cannon firepower as the *Amafata.* Once a prize had been captured, I realized that the confiscated goods were stacked and piled in every empty and available nook and cranny throughout the ship. Since the pirated goods never stayed very long on the ship, the burden of having crammed booty everywhere never seemed to be an inconvenience or significant hindrance to my new shipmates, especially when the end result put coin in each of their pockets!

The other noticeable difference between the two ships was the significant speed and maneuverability of our new narrow hulled and shallow drafting vessel. These features played a major role to any pirate ship on the prowl for prey. Speed and maneuverability obviously enabled economical location and capture of valuable prizes. In the case of running up against trouble from an adversary with superior forces and firepower, speed and maneuverability also played a vital difference between escape and disaster. Further, a shallow draft enabled a fleeing ship to take full advantage of the numerous shallow water escape routes and hiding spots that larger and more cumbersome ships were unable to navigate or follow due to their tendency to breech or beach.

There were also a number of other less significant differences between the ships that really fell into two specific categories, overall upkeep and warfare precautions. As far as overall upkeep, there was very little to report since virtually nothing was ever really done aboard. In fact, the pirate crew seemed to take very little interest in any housekeeping tasks, choosing instead to perform just the minimal amount of upkeep or repair work to keep the *Midnight Crow* barely afloat. As I learned later, the concept of maintenance and upkeep was foreign to pirates, who would simply abandon their current ship in favor of a captured prize, if it proved more seaworthy, in order to continue their diabolical thievery.

As for warfare, this notion was taken very seriously indeed. To start, the *Midnight Crow* cast a low profile while at sea. This effect was accomplished on purpose in order to provide maximum stealth and secrecy in the pursuit of quarry, or as a defensive weapon providing maximum escape possibility and minimum detection against mightier foes. The munitions aboard were also fearsome including a total of six cannons. All in all, our new ship was fully armed, ideally fast, difficult to detect, extremely maneuverable and easy to hide in the many shallow hiding spots that dominated the Caribbean, an almost perfect pirate's warfare tool!

The pirate gang was made up of a virtual kaleidoscope of varying nationalities and races. I was surprised to discover pirate crew members hailing from darn near every corner of the world. There were definitely no race, creed or color distinctions of any sort. Black, yellow, brown or white skin tones held no special place or rank among these heathens. National or racial differences of any sort seemed rather inconsequential to this insane band of thugs, loners, sadists, criminals, deserters, derelicts and psychopaths.

As I had the distinct displeasure of observing them firsthand, I realized that they hardly made up a seasoned team of battle hardened veterans melded into a formidable nautical fighting force by their years of service together. Rather their ultimate quest at achieving maximum personal liberty coupled with a flux of continual crew changes resulted in a mismatched and unmanageable mob of ruffians, whose only loyalty was individualistic first and foremost. These scoundrels came from every possible quarter, but most were naval deserters, landlubbing paupers, indentured servants, captured victims and voluntary enlisted men to round out the list. Compared to any sailing crew I had encountered, they were nothing more than a rag-tag bunch of malicious misfits and miscreants, an extremely odd mixture of human trash!

As I silently mused about all of these things, I could not help but take notice of the small gold ring that was still seated on my toe. The intent of sporting this gift had been to encourage good luck and fortune. As I assessed my current situation, I could not help but question the type of luck this talisman had delivered.

I can truthfully say that drinking was the main pastime of my new crewmates while at sea. When we were initially captured, I came to believe that their blatant drunkenness was of a celebratory nature. As time went by, I realized that it was more a way of life rather than any sort of temporary or isolated situation. Reeling and gibbering their way around the ship at all hours of the day or night, the only thing that really surprised me about their actions was that they managed to keep from haplessly falling overboard to their deaths. Because of their love of rum, the only time that they seemed to become ornery was when the spirit level ran low. This nasty situation brought out the very worst in these degenerates and forced Captain Shivvers to expediently seek an immediate replenishment source. In listening to their insane ramblings, I also learned that this freedom to overindulge was only slightly curtailed when a potential prize was spotted. When this occurred, a short self-abstinence period was observed to ensure a successful takeover of the unwary and unfortunate vessel that had crossed their path.

Due to this copious liquor consumption, the Doc and I were continually besieged with besotted crewmembers complaining of a variety of both real and imagined woes. Broken bones, deep cuts and scrapes, bumps and bruises of all varieties were our standard fare. The other standard complaint of these tipsy demons was the insistent demand of a cure for the pox, which was a direct result of their heathen lifestyle while on land. When I was not assisting Doc, I was extremely busy with my navigational duties. At first, Captain Shivvers was very leery of my overall abilities in this regard, constantly challenging every navigational decision I made. Thankfully as time passed, he seemed to accept my innate ability to guide his ship and ceased second guessing my every calculation or decision. This did not mean that he fully trusted me by any measure, but rather found other problems to occupy his time onboard.

Yet another surprise awaited me about my new home, these rascals actually operated under a series of loosely agreed to rules! In fact, a very odd crewmember named Booby Bird Dooley took full responsibility in providing me a complete explanation for each of these dictates. Booby Bird was a small slobbering drunk, who seemed to suffer from a severe case of mental instability. Any serious discussion with this toothless miscreant was a real adventure as his trembling lips jumped from subject to subject in a disturbing and distracting manner. One minute, he would be discussing his favorite port-of-call, while the very next he would instantly diverge into the merits of sand crabs as perfect beach scavengers. One had to pay very close attention to his disjointed soliloquies to glean any useful knowledge he might impart.

Booby Bird's eyes were also a strange mismatched pair. His left eye cast a downward gaze at all times. His right eye, on the other hand, wandered aimlessly, here, there and everywhere. Quick with a smile and a laugh, I judged him to be rather harmless for the most part and a reliable source of truthful information concerning life aboard the floating asylum that I now occupied.

In a rare moment of clarity, Booby Bird launched into an explanation of the specific rules adopted aboard the *Midnight Crow*. He explained that the majority of these bylaws were standard fare on most pirate ships. As he began his discourse, he informed me that there were eleven regulations that basically controlled the crew's conduct while aboard. The first of these was that the pirate ship operated as a democratic society, with each man having a vote on any decision that needed to be made at any time. While this law seemed to explain the utter anarchy I had experienced in my brief stay aboard the *Midnight Crow*, Booby Bird was quick to notify me on the true nature of this ship's commandment. He confessed that while all aboard had a vote on matters, Captain Shivvers actually made all the decisions for everyone, using Lion as his enforcer should any of his decisions be questioned. Losing track of his explanation, Booby Bird then launched into a disjointed narrative of the high value of tobacco as an export crop.

Patiently directing him back, he revealed that the second bylaw of this nefarious company was that all prize goods were to be shared equally amongst the crew. Any person found guilty of attempting to defraud the group of any sort of valuable booty would be immediately marooned on a deserted spit of land to face his eventual doom. Again, Booby Bird confessed that this rule applied strictly to the crew only, since Captain Shivvers was known to secret gems, gold and silver taken as booty from captured prizes. To question Captain Shivvers on this unpopular habit meant an instant saltwater swim. Wandering once again, Booby Bird began a serious discourse on ravenous monsters that roamed the sea lanes in search of sumptuous human flesh. He eventually revealed the third rule which was self explanatory. This law stated that every crewmember was responsible for keeping their personal weapons ready for battle at all times.

The fourth rule he explained dealt with the treatment of the tender sex. To start, he lectured that bringing any woman onboard was strictly outlawed upon pain of castration. I understood the sound reasoning behind the regulation. A female aboard any ship usually meant disaster due to the crew's jealousies and lustful desires. Booby Bird elaborated that any woman made a prisoner during sea raids was to be treated with proper respect and dignity. The reason for the decent treatment of captured women was that this conduct became a part of the reputation of any particular pirate band. A positive reputation in this regard usually insured a quicker and easier surrender by any encountered prey. Again Booby Bird was quick to point out that even Captain Shivvers adhered to this regulation, once he had defiled and had his way with any unfortunate female prisoner.

Losing his train of thought once more, Booby Bird began rambling about the value of bilge water to cure the pox. Once again, I patiently directed this muddled soul back to the ship's bylaws. He disclosed that the fifth rule was that any person who deserted his duties during battle was to be branded a coward and subjected to death at the hands of his fellow mates. The sixth rule was also very standard aboard any vessel at sea as it outlawed any personal fights amongst the crew. Any personal disputes could only be settled onshore. Again losing Booby Bird to his mumblings about killer dolphins, I managed to return my addled compatriot back to the topic at hand.

The seventh rule also did not surprise me at all since it outlawed gambling for coin aboard ship. To maintain peace amongst this shipload of feral beasts, it made perfect sense to restrict money wagering while at sea. The eighth rule he divulged gave me pause to remember my old friend, Grommet Jemme. Simply stated, any man carrying a naked flame below decks, a candle without a holder or a pipe without a cap, would be duly punished by receiving forty lashes from the dreaded cat-o-nine-tails. Remembering the utter destruction wrought by Grommet Jemme in this regard, I had to concur that this rule was indeed necessary and mandatory. Before I had the chance to move to the next bylaw, Booby Bird began to explain how the red savages from his homeland would torture captives with lit torches on their victim's privates.

The ninth rule related to the compensation for injury or loss of any bodily part while engaged in warfare. While I found it interesting that these scum would have any sort of compassion for injured comrades, I was not really at all interested to hear more about this type of renumeration so I prodded Booby Bird to continue with his litany. The tenth law did indeed surprise me since it called for peaceful quarter to be given to any prize that offered to surrender prior to confrontation. Booby Bird laughed as he informed me that peaceful quarter usually meant a saltwater swim whether a prey put up a fight or peacefully surrendered. Once again, Booby Bird was off on a divergent tangent as he discussed the best way to recover one's health after imbibing copious quantities of rum.

The last law called for the fair and equal distribution of loot at the end of any voyage. Each member of the crew was allotted an equal share of the booty with the captain receiving two full shares and the quartermaster receiving one and a half shares. Providing an evil smirk, Booby Bird divulged that this allotment normally occurred only after Captain Shivvers had purloined more than his fair share of valuables from any prize. Further, should any crewman take affront with his actions, that individual's share was reduced to nothing and the dissenter would be quite lucky to keep his life in the bargain. In all, it seemed that our dear Captain held command by total intimidation, having Lion constantly at his side to administer all the reason and justice that any matter required. After listening to Booby Bird and his mad ramblings, all I could think of was how our pirate Captain was stealing from the pirates he commanded. He was truly a pirate among pirates! Meanwhile, Booby

Bird had lapsed into a very serious discussion on the distinct difference in taste between American and European weevil meat.

On the way to the Doc's surgery, I stopped off at the ship's galley to check on how Powder Monkey and Long Tall Willie were coping with their new captivity. Reaching the galley, I found a group of fellow seamen totally rapt in awe listening to one of their own spinning a tale of horror about the dreaded Black Tarantula. I had thought I had heard the last about this spawn of the Devil with our departure from Jamaica, but to my great surprise his black exploits seemed to be following me wherever I roamed. Total exhaustion caught up with me as I sat to listen to further tales of horror and wanton destruction on the part of this madman. Before long, I dozed off missing the salient details of his latest evil antics.

Chapter 9: Cursing Challenge

Upon awakening, I made my way to my cabin to assist Doc. I was immediately put to work and did not notice Powder Monkey's arrival. He made his way to my side and signaled that he had something important to discuss. Nodding my understanding, I signed that I would meet him in the privacy of the hold. Upon reaching our agreed destination, I found my friend in a state of extreme anxiousness. He signed that while serving in the galley, he had picked up some disastrous scuttlebutt. He communicated that a trio of pirates were determined to see to my ultimate demise.

The trio was led by a knave who went by the name of Danny Goldtooth. His compatriots were known by the names of Little Joe and Penny Short. Danny Goldtooth's brother had died in one of the attacking longboats that my cannon team had obliterated. Believing me to be no more than a common murderer as a result of this occurrence, Danny Goldtooth had convinced his two dimwitted friends that I had to be eliminated by whatever means possible. Made aware of their intended treachery, my loyal friend communicated the salient details to me.

It seemed that the trio had somehow discovered that I did not partake in liquor of any sort. Knowing this, the three dolts had planned a convoluted scheme to coerce me into a drinking bout with them. Once intoxicated, they intended to coax me above decks and send me over the side for a midnight swim. Their plot was to embarrass me into this drinking contest, knowing that my avoidance of hot spirits would put me at a huge disadvantage in any sort of imbibing affair. Once they had me sloppy-drunk, they reasoned it would be a simple task to coerce me topside for my date with death. Given the simplicity of their plan, Powder Monkey was very concerned that they might actually succeed in eliminating me on a very permanent basis. Sincerely thanking Powder Monkey for both his concern and his foresight in identifying their nefarious intentions, I assured him that I would engineer a counterplot that would foil the fools' hastily made plans.

Making my way back to my quarters, I began to devise a method of turning the tables on my detestable enemies. Once I cogitated a seemingly workable solution, I made the necessary preparations to thwart their conspiracy. Locating the needed items in Gertrude's medicinal trunk, I snatched these ingredients and proceeded to create a very special surprise of my own for my empty-headed foes.

That night, I was called to the galley by Penny Short, who explained that my medical abilities were promptly required. He recounted that a Dutch pirate had sustained a nasty splinter while attending his lookout duties. The filthy chunk of wood had produced an infection and had caused the tar to lapse into a delirious state spouting only Dutch, so that nobody could understand him. Realizing this to be nothing more than a ruse, I collected my prepared concoction and followed him to the galley. Once there, I was greeted by his two co-conspirators along with a very large group of rum-drinking buddies.

Danny Goldtooth stepped forward and confessed that the emergency to which I had been summoned was nothing more than a ruse. He continued by informing me that he and his friends had engineered my attendance to thank me for the kind medical assistance I had provided them all. As a sign of appreciation, he shoved a full bottle of rum into my free hand as his way of expressing utmost gratitude. Aware of his intent, I deftly switched the proffered bottle with the one I had doctored earlier in my cabin. Urging me to drink to our new found friendship, Danny Goldtooth clapped me on my back and guided me to a free seat amongst the inebriated pirate swine. Before hefting the bottle to my lips, I inquired if my three new friends would like to partake in a little drinking game that I had learned while on liberty on Jamaica? Sensing no harm in my suggestion, Danny Goldtooth and his two cohorts immediately agreed to participate.

Seated at a galley table with my three adversaries, I proceeded to enlighten them on the rules of the contest I had christened the *Cursing Challenge*. You see, pirates for the most part prided themselves on their nimble tongues for rough talk. This simply meant that they cursed and swore continually. Fully aware of their pride at issuing outlandish curses and highly immoral speech, I utilized this knowledge to bait my trap. As I explained to the trio seated around me, the rules to the *Cursing Challenge* were quite simple. Each contestant would be given a chance to issue a curse. Once each of us had delivered our rough talk, the spectators around us would judge which contestant had articulated the very worse cruse of the bunch. The losers would be forced to take a large swig of rum. The game continued in this manner until the entire bottle of rum was consumed.

The trio wolfishly agreed to participate since they realized that the game would be a perfect method of accomplishing their evil plan, which was to get me as drunk as a beast! What the trio had failed to realize that I was far from being considered a novice at the fine art of cursing. While I had limited time in my short life to hone this insidious art, I had the experience of time spent on London streets listening to my fellow citizens filling the air with foul language. I also had the distinct advantage of intense private tutoring under my deceased friend, Handy, who could utter oaths and curses that would even make a prison guard blush bright red. So began our game, with each of my nefarious competitors entering their first attempt. Stringing together a series of utterly lewd and blasphemous phrases, I easily prevailed in this first round to the riotous roar of the slobbering and brutish judges.

Since the three co-conspirators were judged sadly lacking in their first effort, they were all forced to take a swig of rum from the bottle I had placed on the table. But this was no ordinary bottle of rum, for I had previously doctored this bottle with copious quantities of Gertrude's wormwood herb, fully aware that its effects would wreak havoc on my unsuspecting prey. Each of the murderous trio swilled their obligatory tote of rum and the game continued.

Well I can tell you that total victory was mine from that point on until the last of my special tonic was imbibed by Danny Goldtooth and his two moronic friends. By the time the game ended, my would-be assailants were quite literally out of their minds. Having secured complete victory, I innocently invited my three new friends to the topdeck for a breath of fresh air. As we made our way to the ship's rail, I knew that I was in total control of the situation. Once there, I whispered to the uncomprehending fools that I thought I heard someone calling from the dark water that surrounded us. My adversaries, now quite fearful, strained to listen to the sounds that I had just reported hearing. I then utilized my *special voice*. Directing it as if it emanated from the surrounding sea, I imitated a drowning call for assistance, which caused each pirate to lean even further over the rail. Finally, I issued an additional plaintive cry for help distinctly utilizing each of their names as well as identifying the caller as the lost brother of Danny Goldtooth.

With all three completely addled by the effects of the wormwood rum, I watched calmly as they foolishly dove over the side of the ship in a valiant effort to save their drowning comrade. As they hit the water and began their totally ineffective attempt to swim, several of their crewmates rushed to my side to discover the reason behind their suicidal leap. Acting completely shocked and ignorant, I repeatedly shouted in a panic-stricken voice that my friends had just jumped overboard for no good reason. Shaking my head in a somber and solemn manner, I confessed that perhaps they had consumed too much rum as a result of the game we had all just enjoyed. Acting visibly shaken and very remorseful, I shouted for the helmsman to bring the ship about so that my new friends could be rescued from the inky saltwater. Knowing that the chances of actually locating them much less rescuing them was infinitesimal, I continued to play the role of the grieving compatriot as our ship began its laborious course reversal to retrieve the drunken fools. After several unfruitful hours of searching, Captain Shivvers ordered the helmsman to return to our original course, declaring the drunken trio officially lost at sea. Glancing over to Powder Monkey with false tears of sorrow and regret in my eyes, I received a conspiratorial nod for a job well done by my young accomplice.

The very next day, I was called to the quartermaster's cabin by Lion. Upon reporting, I found the hulking brute laying in bed suffering from a tremendous blinding and pounding headache. Unable to even stand, the alarmed Turk begged me to cure him of this crippling malady. Totally petrified that his head pains were a precursor of death, the fearful giant actually pleaded with me to save his life. Understanding his need for immediate relief, I raced back to my quarters to prepare a curative.

As I made this journey, I remembered something Gertrude had told me about a remedy for severe headaches. Moving to her medical supplies, I found the item she had so long ago provided detailed instructions, belladonna root! She had laboriously tutored me that this deadly substance could be utilized in rather weak concentrations to cure severe headaches. Snipping off a tiny bit of the root, I proceeded to make a very weak tea which I bottled in an empty rum jug. I raced back to Lion's side to administer a spoonful of my elixir. As Gertrude had instructed, I placed a cold damp rag over Lion's face. I then ordered him to stay in that position with the damp rag over his face until I made my return to check on his progress. Setting the filled bottle of elixir at his side, I warned him further that the contents were highly potent and extremely deadly if too much was consumed. Taking my leave, I ordered Powder Monkey to stand outside the Turk's door and allow nobody to enter until my return.

About two hours later, I made my way back to check on my patient. To my great surprise, I found Lion sitting up in his bunk seemingly cured of his crippling head pains. With a huge smile, he announced that I had just saved his life! His gushing gratitude was totally unexpected, but I nevertheless accepted his words of thanks in a calm and serious manner. Further, I informed him that I was providing him the remainder of the magical elixir I had prepared in the event that his headache should ever return to plague him. Sniffling back real tears of joy, the behemoth wrapped me in his monstrous arms and broke completely down into tearful gratitude at my miraculous cure. Swearing an oath of everlasting loyalty and friendship, he informed me that I could count on his assistance whenever and wherever it was required.

Acknowledging his solemn oath, I informed him that I was overjoyed by his speedy recovery and overwhelmed by his pledge of loyalty. Pleading with me to stay and converse, I complied by pulling up a chair at his bedside. After a few moments spent on trivial scuttlebutt, I questioned if he had any news to share on Saint Domingue. Issuing a doleful sigh, he disclosed that although his news was now dated, it was certainly not good. He then revealed that his final days on the island were filled with pain and misery due to the evil antics of the Black Tarantula. As I had previously been informed, Lion validated that this sinister scoundrel had invaded and sacked Cap-Francis.

Sailing unopposed into Cap-Francis' harbor, the Black Tarantula instigated his campaign of terror and destruction. Sending his blood-crazed crew ashore, they proceeded to torment everyone they encountered. Because of their utter viciousness, it did not take very long to completely crush all local opposition, virtually enslaving the city's entire populace. While his minions wreaked havoc, he decided to personally acquaint himself with the many pleasures the city offered, including a special visit to the Palais Le Monde. Upon arriving at this renowned den of inequity, he proceeded to torture and torment the tavern's owner, Madame La Montaine. At this point in his narrative, Lion seemed unusually agitated and unwilling to continue his story, but my gentle prodding eventually persuaded him to proceed.

Lion related that he and his friends, sequestered in the pub, were powerless to stop the madman from sating his unholy desires. My mind leapt immediately to my lover, Rue, and I questioned the Turk on how she had fared in this nasty predicament. Lion confessed that he was well aware of my feelings for the lass. To placate my troubled mind, he informed me that Rue had survived the pirate's onslaught, but was unable to furnish any further specifics since she had taken flight. The news absolutely stunned me and I begged for more details.

He continued by reporting that once the Black Tarantula had established control of the Palace, he ordered Rue to perform for him and his wicked band of parasites. Reluctant to agree to his demands, Rue finally relented when a sharp blade was placed against her mother's throat as serious inducement. In a steadfast and proud manner, Rue utilized her magical voice in an attempt to calm the murderous audience that demanded song after song from the terrified girl. Lion divulged that her wondrous voice had a very startling effect on the sinister pirate leader, as he became entranced by her wondrous voice. Upon finishing her performance, the depraved madman called her to his table and paid her generous compliments and honest gratitude for her recital. Going further, he offered her an exalted entertainment position on his vessel that would reward her with wealth beyond her wildest dreams. Responding in a definitive fashion, she informed her insidious admirer that she had no intentions of leaving the island and had absolutely no desire to sail with the immoral fiend and his despicable band of rogues.

Surprised by her outright rejection, the Black Tarantula signaled to the men restraining her mother. In an instant, a cutlass was drawn across her poor mother's throat ending her life. In a near hysterical state, Rue rushed to her mother's side, only to comprehend that the wound was mortal. Turning in rage to face the Black Tarantula, she spat out a series of horrid curses. With that, she raced out of the rumhouse before anyone could stop her. Enraged to the point of complete madness, the Black Tarantula ordered his entire crew to hunt the ungrateful songbird down and deliver her back to him. His companions dispersed in all directions to locate Rue, torturing, maiming and murdering innocent townsfolk in their determined search to find the girl. At the same time, Lion and a few of his companions took advantage of this distraction and silently slipped out the backdoor of the Palace unnoticed.

After a full fruitless day of hunting, the fiends reported their failure to their leader. Incensed far beyond reason, the Black Tarantula ordered that the Palace be boarded up detaining all present. Once completed, he commanded his minions to set fire to the pub, incinerating all those inside the structure. With a tear now rolling down his massive cheek, Lion whispered that one of the unfortunates trapped inside the burning building was his lover, Sugar Sally. Lion watched this malicious slaughter in total horror unable to save his beloved. Chocking back his emotions at this point, Lion whimpered that he still vividly recollected the hideous screams and wails of the victims as they were roasted alive in the conflagration.

Giving the giant a chance to compose himself, I questioned him gently on Rue's fate in the matter. Shaking his head sadly, he informed me that once the building burnt to the ground, he and his associates made their desperate escape and signed on as a crewmen on the *Midnight Crow*. Therefore, he had no idea of what happened to Rue once he left Saint Domingue. However, he did impart an ominous prediction that he believed that the Black Tarantula would never stop searching for his entrancing songbird.

Chapter 10: Grand Carouse

Captain Shivvers made the decision to head for the French isle of Guadeloupe, better known as Butterfly Island because of its unique shape. Making for the secluded harbor of Pointe-a'-Pitre, the nefarious bandit intended to peddle the stolen cargo from the *Amafata* for much needed funds. At the same time, he informed me that the *Midnight Crow* was acting sluggish in her movements, and it was high time to free her hull of weeds. In doing so, he informed me that the time required to complete this backbreaking chore would allow for a *Grand Carouse*, a pirate festival of sorts complete with loose women, potent spirits, delicious food, games of chance and entertainment for all. To accomplish the careening chore, we needed to locate a perfectly safe spot far enough away from Pointe-a'-Pitre so as to avoid notice or discovery, while remaining close enough to garner the required party supplies. As we entered our targeted port, we were immediately greeted by a small boatful of the island's dignitaries, who acted as our welcoming committee.

Included in this illustrious group were some of the island's elite, church dignitaries and several key trade merchants. Welcomed aboard, these authoritarians were directed immediately to the Captain's quarters. I was stunned when Captain Shivvers invited me to attend the meeting to act as ship's translator. My first impression of our newly arrived guests centered on the outright greed and avarice they each displayed. In fact, it was very difficult for me to determine who the actual pirates were in this unfolding drama. After formal introductions and pleasantries were exchanged, Captain Shivvers presented each member of the delegation with a small bag filled with coin as insurance to ensure smooth negotiations. Once accomplished, he signaled me to begin translating for the sale of our purloined booty.

Almost at once, I reasoned that Captain Shivvers was nothing more than an incompetent fool by the initial terms of sale he suggested, asking for only a quarter of the total value of our goods! Instead, I opened the affair by offering our entire cargo for three quarters of its value. After strenuous haggling back and forth, we settled at a sum worth a little more than half of the cargo's value along with two new longboats to replace those that I had destroyed. This sum was more than double the value that our shiftless Captain had been willing to accept! The dignitaries promptly delivered the agreed coin and longboats while our goods were quickly loaded without incident onto transport boats that they had provided, a very smooth operation indeed! With our deal completed, an elated Captain Shivvers informed the crew that he had successfully arranged a very lucrative deal at forty percent of the total value of the goods. Therefore, by my calculation, he was purloining a quick ten percent for himself prior to distribution to the crew. Turning this coin over to his trusty quartermaster for dispersement, he made it abundantly clear that the new recruits from the *Amafata* would receive nothing. In doing so, he announced that we had not earned the right to share in the plunder. In other words, no prey, no pay.

After this distribution was completed, we headed a few miles further up the coastline and located a peaceful shallow cove that was perfectly suited to our needs. As expected, the new recruits from the *Amafata* were assigned the harsh task of careening the ship in the hot, humid and bug infested shallows. As we began our assigned labor, I realized that this insect-laded atmosphere would slow our work prodigiously. Remembering a helpful tip from Gertrude, I mixed a salve for our protection utilizing camphor leaves from my trunk of herbal ingredients along with tallow from the ship's galley. The salve worked its magic and kept the filthy blood-sucking parasites from interrupting our labors. As we began our toil, we witnessed the remainder of the crew making preparations for the Grand Carouse.

A clearing of sorts was hacked from the dense jungle surrounding the sandy beach, and thatched huts were hastily raised to house the fun and games. A fight ring was also erected to accommodate bare-knuckle brawls. At the same time, our two newly acquired longboats were sent back to town to purchase wine, rum, beer, food and women. We were told to expect their return prior to nightfall. Deciding to lighten up our hard and tedious burden, I led my co-workers in a series of nautical work chanties to take their minds off the sweat and effort they were expending. I led these chanties in a clear melodious voice, while my mates provided the refrains as our hard effort seemed to pass quickly. These traditional sailor's songs also drew the attention of the shore-bound pirates, who halted their preparation work from time-to-time to listen to our singing. In fact, we were applauded vigorously at various points throughout the day in honest appreciation of our fine vocal efforts. Our singing also provided another surprising benefit, as many of the appreciative pirates actually joined our company and assisted in the filthy careening labor. In fact, we received so much volunteered assistance that we completed our efforts on the exposed hull long before nightfall.

As we completed our backbreaking labor for the day, both longboats arrived fresh from town with all the party necessities and the Grand Carouse began in earnest. I also spotted a trailing third boat that had accompanied our shipmates back to our location. This boat was loaded with gamblers from Pointe-a'-Pitre, who operated games-of-chance. From past experience, they were hoping to achieve quick gains in fortune from drunk, free spending victims. Upon their arrival, the celebration furiously commenced. It certainly felt like I was home in London once more, enjoying the madhouse atmosphere offered at Slugger's Emporium. Roaming from hut to hut, I witnessed obscene drinking contests, who's only aim was to render its contestants into complete insensibility. In other huts, lewd and licentious pirate and trollop orgies were in progress, with various human extremities extending randomly from sweaty gyrating piles. In yet other huts, activities were regulated to gambling consisting of dice games, card games and other inventive novelties.

One of these games caught my immediate attention and drew me in for a closer look--the cup and pea game! A London street acquaintance had taught me the finer nuances of this game, so as to allow me to take his place whenever his gin consumption got totally out of water. Fearful of losing lucrative funds during these times of impairment, my friend allowed me to take his place along with pocketing significant profits in the bargain. To succeed, my comrade was forced to teach me how to optimize this scam to the maximum. As I observed the twitching, shifty-eyed weasel now operating the game, I could see that he was an adept master of the scam. However, the problem was that he was far too greedy for his own wellbeing.

The rules of this contest were quite simple. A pea runner, the game operator, played the game straight relying on his speed, manual dexterity and ability to utilize verbal and physical distractions to skew the odds in his favor. An important aspect of this sham was to allow patrons a chance to win from time to time. You see, a happy winning bird leaving the game with extra coin in his pocket would draw two or more new unsuspecting birds into the nest. In other words, allowing a patron to win occasionally was acutely good for business. The actual scam came into play when the pea runner had a fat fish on the hook. Carefully handling this big catch, the pea runner would allow the mark to win a number of times at the start of play. From there, he would engineer building the size of the bets until the poor soul wagered all that he owned. At that critical juncture, the pea runner would execute his cheating ploy. The object of the deception was to rid the board of the elusive pea, thereby guaranteeing a win for the pea runner. In a series of deft hand motions, the pea runner would rotate the cup with the hidden pea closer and closer to the edge of the gaming board. If operated correctly, the hidden pea would slide off the edge of the board neatly onto the fraudster's lap without notice. As the victim selected any one of the cups, he was assured of being a loser. Concealing another pea in his hand prior to the start of the round, the experienced charlatan would then deftly drop this second pea behind one of the other unselected cups. In dramatic fashion, he would then reveal the correct hiding place of the pea. After achieving a big score, a savvy pea runner would make sure that the next several customers were made happy winners, thereby feathering the nest for the next fat fish.

Well, that was how I was taught to successfully operate the scam. I can sincerely report to you that the greedy scum running the game was operating in a much different fashion. Rather than allowing the wagering pirates any sort of opportunity to win from time-to-time, this miscreant constantly claimed victory and extracted coins from the pirates in a continuous and far too efficient manner.

While I found his tactics highly distasteful, I offered no assistance to the miserable losers, since they were spending stolen *Amafata* funds. I was simply content to watch the weasel fleece his ignorant flock of gamers with very little recrimination on either his or my part. That is until the greedy operator made a very costly error in judgment. It happened that Powder Monkey was also mesmerized by the proceedings and had edged closer and closer to the action in order to watch the pea disappear and reappear under unselected cups. As he carefully observed the cup hiding the pea move haphazardly around in intricate circular rotations, he was truly amazed and also fully confounded when the rascal would divulge the hiding place of the pea in a vastly different place than where the lad thought it should have been. His extreme confusion was written all over his face, and the pea runner mistakenly took this expression as one of complete and utter stupidity. Deciding to have some fun at my friend's expense, the operator called Powder Monkey forth to play the game.

The pea runner informed the gathered crowd that the game he operated was so simple that even an idiot like the one standing before him could play. With that, he proceeded to fleece Powder Monkey of the few coins he had in his possession, while carrying on a derisive banter to the pirate spectators on the unbelievable stupidity and ignorance of the imp playing the game. Stunned at his inability to correctly locate the pea and highly embarrassed by the surrounding mirth solely at his expense, Powder Monkey finally took flight with heavy tears of shame running down his dirty face. Well, I can tell you that this sight infuriated me beyond words, and I decided it was high time to take an active part in the proceedings.

Stepping up to the game board, I announced my intention to play. Placing my meager coins down, I told my fellow spectators that I felt very lucky. The pea runner eager to strip me of my money prepared the three cups allowing me a glimpse of the elusive pea. Asking for a chance to inspect the pea, I made a point of closely looking it over before returning it to its home. The shyster began his distracting banter as he rotated the three cups round and round. Executing the missing pea ruse, he confidently instructed me to make a selection. After careful deliberation, I reached down and picked up a cup revealing a pea hidden underneath. Shocked to the extreme at my victory, the cheater was grudgingly forced to pay on my bet. Agreeing to continue, I placed my entire stack of coins on the board as my wager. Well, my ruse worked successfully a second time to the absolute bafflement of my foe.

My success brought a roar of approval from the pirate horde that had grown to inordinate size due to my success. On the other hand, my competitor was stunned into total silence by having his time-tested hoax fail for a second straight time. Shoving the enormous winnings in my direction, I could see that the cheat was not going to let it occur a third time. He had carefully watched every one of my movements and had a very good idea what I was doing to reverse his fraud. Anxious about defeating me and greedy to return my winnings back into his own pocket, the despicable trickster questioned if I would like to play one more time.

As I pushed my huge pile of coins forward, the pea runner matched my wager, which amounted to everything he owned. Turning a cup over to reveal the pea's location, I reached to inspect it only to have my hand rudely slapped away by the now savvy scammer. I realized then that he had finally deduced the scam I was running. You see, I had been snatching and holding on to the pea under inspection rather than returning it to its intended home, and then I deposited it deftly under my cup of choice to gain victory. As he brushed away my hand, he advised that I had certainly studied the pea quite thoroughly the first two times so that a third inspection was totally unnecessary. Smiling innocently at his remarks, I agreed that he was probably right. Upon my consent, the swindler again began his furious maneuvering of the three cups in a blur of both sound and motion. When he had successfully eliminated the pea, he issued an evil sneer and asked me to make my choice. Pretending total confusion as to the pea's location, I asked for assistance from the huge audience surrounding me. Utilizing this distraction, I suddenly moved with blinding speed and picked up all three cups at once. As I had theorized, there was no pea under any of the cups, which startled the pirate audience as they gasped in shocked unison. Continuing, I seized the pea runner's hand that held the pea he was prepared to deposit in order to declare me a loser. Squeezing the cheater's paw, he slowly opened his clenched fingers to reveal the hidden pea.

Well, I can tell you that all hell broke loose at that moment amid accusatory shouts of cheater and thief coming from all quarters. In a weak effort to defend himself, the sinister pea runner attempted to talk his way out of his serious trouble. As he mumbled and stuttered, I pulled the weasel to his feet and pointed to the numerous peas that flew earthward in all directions while informing my mates that this rogue had been cheating them all along. Well, the cheat never really got a chance to explain anything as he was dragged to a nearby palm tree and lashed securely.

As this occurred, I extracted my original wager along with Powder Monkey's losses. Holding the remaining coin in both of my hands, I suggested that the considerable sum of money be turned over to Lion for fair redistribution to the crew. This act of generosity was answered by several rousing rounds of cheers by the pirates. The ultimate fate of the cheating pea runner was certainly not a happy one. Securely bound, he became the perfect target for the entire pirate band to practice their weaponry. After painful wounding time and again by pistol, musket and knife, his miserable life finally ended when Captain Shivvers severed his cheating head from his body. In the meantime, I tracked down my friend, Powder Monkey, and returned his coin. Vastly relieved and now smiling, he thanked me and vowed to stay well clear of all games of chance in the future.

The rough treatment of the gambler caused the remaining gamesters to hurriedly pack their belongings and return to town. None of them objected to the poor scoundrel's harsh treatment, since cheaters of any ilk fared very poorly anytime they were discovered. Wherever I roamed that night after my little adventure, I was greeted by wide smiles, kind words and friendly backslaps. I knew I had made a lasting impression on my pirate brethren, but it would take a little while longer before I realized just how profound those feeling were.

The next morning we were back in the bug-infested shallows careening the other side of the vessel. As was the case the previous day, we worked with a song on our lips. As the morning passed, we were joined by several of the pirates as they awoke from their night of debauchery. By midday, I was stunned to realize that nearly the entire crew had now turned out to assist in our hard labors. I believed that the reason for their assistance lie in the songs and camaraderie we all shared as we went about our toils. Explaining my theory to Powder Monkey as we went about our chore of dislodging the insidious barnacles from the ship's hull, he was quick to disagree with a curt shake of his head. Rather, he signed, it was due to my efforts at debunking the cheat and my show of utmost generosity the previous evening. He went on to inform me that our new shipmates felt obligated to assist after the simple kindness I had shown them all. He then laughed and signed that I would need to be careful or before I knew it I would be commanding the entire pirate band as their elected Captain!

Mirthful at his joke at my expense, I could not shake this thought from my head, no matter how farfetched it seemed. A while later, Powder Monkey returned to my side with a crazed smile racing across his face. He then held out a filthy tar-encrusted object for my inspection. Taking time to carefully inspect his gooey offering, I suddenly realized what it was. Somehow, he had found my precious wooden cross which was now covered in pitch. When I questioned him on where he had located the talisman, he signed that he had just recovered it from the bottom of one of the pitch barrels that had originally come from our ship. Continuing, he signed that the thief must have secreted the cross in the barrel, safe from discovery due to the filthy nature of its hiding place. Accepting the wooden amulet from Powder Monkey, I quickly jammed the tar-covered cross into my pocket to avoid any of our company discovering my obsession with the object. I silently vowed to never let the lucky talisman out of my sight again.

Clapping Powder Monkey on the back for his invaluable assistance in returning my wooden amulet, I genuinely offered my friend my deepest thanks and gratitude. Nodding his full understanding, he skipped off to return to the careening labor. As he pranced away with his usual lopsided grin, I was momentarily reminded of my missing brother, Toby. Haunted still by his strange disappearance so many years ago, I swore to myself to one day unravel his mysterious disappearance once-and-for-all!

By mid-afternoon, we had finished our arduous work on the ship's hull with the invaluable assistance of all of our pirate volunteers. After the long hours of toil, we all drifted off to find a shady place to rest so that we could fully enjoy the evening's upcoming activities.

Chapter 11: Fight Night

As the sun descended, we all began making our separate appearances, and the raucous party resumed in both insanity and intensity. Even the frightened gamblers of the previous evening made their reappearance, a bit wiser about attempting to cheat us in any outright manner. The strumpets had never left our company, and the evening sparked yet another round of raucous lewd behavior. Booby Bird notified me that tonight was Fight Night, when all seaborne squabbles would be settled in the ring. Captain Shivvers was responsible for any additional pairings, after all of the seaboard disputes had been arbitrated. Given that there was always a prodigious number of ship disputes, Booby answered that it was usually highly unlikely that anyone else would be raising their fists tonight. When he launched into a rambling lecture of the various dangers of vicious and bloodthirsty mermaids, I made a quick escape.

I soon encountered Powder Monkey who seemed unusually upset. Sensing his heightened agitation, I questioned him on the source of his worries. He signed that he had just spotted the Captain, who had been in whispered conversation with a few of our pirate brethren. Able to read the Captain's lips from a discreet distance, he hurried to locate me to warn me that the Captain was distinctly displeased by the entire crew's reaction to my generous behavior the previous evening. While he was unable to discover exactly what our dear Captain had in mind for me, he was certain that Captain Shivvers felt very uneasy about the sudden popularity I had gained with the crew. Fearing that I might replace him as the leader of this band of heathens and cutthroats, Powder Monkey was sure that Captain Shivvers was scheming my demise. Laughing now, I informed Powder Monkey that I had no such intention or desire to command this villainous troop of scum. Nodding vehemently, Powder Monkey warned me that our Captain was certainly not privy to my private intentions and certainly feared the very worst in this situation. As he prepared to take his leave, he signed that regardless of my feelings or intentions, I needed to keep a sharp eye out for trouble at the hands of Captain Shivvers.

Suddenly the clanging of a small but noisy bell announced that Fight Night had officially commenced. As I made my way to a spot on one side of our laughable ring that would provide a proper view of the proceedings, I was greeted by more smiles and backslaps that seemed totally genuine in nature. As I took my place, Captain Shivvers strutted into the center of the ring to formally announce the opening of Fight Night. He declared that a small disagreement had arisen while onshore between two members of our company. Continuing with a savage smile, he shouted that One Eared Pete had summarily challenged Pig Snout Jones to hand-to-hand combat over the love of a local trollop appropriately named Strumpet Janie. Each contender was vying for the sole affection of this notorious wench, regardless of her dubious occupation or evil reputation. In the matter of Strumpet Janie, it was widely rumored that the soiled dove was as common as a public privy-seat, servicing a new stranger as soon as another jumped off and in all probability in much worse condition! This lewd and licentious reputation certainly did not deter either pathetic pirate from declaring his true love and admiration for the jezebel. It was also rumored that Captain Shivvers had personally propagated the feud between these two dimwitted lovers, so he could have his way with the tramp the previous evening. Either way, the pirate fighters were committed to do battle in order to settle the account once and for all.

As I gazed across the ring at each fighter, it seemed to me that the two assailants were very evenly matched. The wagering that accompanied the fight mirrored my observations, calling for even odds. From my vantage-point, I could smell the noxious aroma that wafted off these two clueless tars. The opening bell was finally rung after copious idiotic tantrums from both fighters. As the two swarmed into each other with both arms and legs windmilling in comical fashion, I realized that neither fighter was accomplished at all in the art of self-defense. Rather, the match quickly degenerated into an animalistic struggle of grappling, kicking, head butting and most especially biting.

The two pirates continued to scuffle and tussle their way from one side of the ring to the other. With neither scoring any kind of meaningful blow, it seemed that this match would continue forever. At one point, Pig Snout got a mouthful of One Eared Pete's arm and chomped down as if it were a leg of mutton. Meanwhile, One Eared Pete pounded his opponent's head with his free arm in an attempt to free himself. Once liberated, One Eared Pete inspected his wounded arm. He quickly issued snorts of disgust, discovering one of Pig Snout's rotted teeth still implanted firmly in his forearm. Shivering with revulsion, he brushed the human fang from his arm before resuming the contest. Meanwhile, Strumpet Janie was standing in the front row alternatively rooting for both of the fighters. Her wild cries of encouragement for both combatants were comical in nature, and had us all laughing hysterically.

It was not long after that both fighters showed utter exhaustion from their strenuous pugilistic efforts. Each was reeling and staggering around the makeshift ring as their ineffectual blows caused little harm to their opponent. With no end in sight, Pig Snout decided to take matters into his own hands. Drawing a hidden dirk from his filthy plaint of hair, he managed to seize a secure hold on One Eared Pete and viciously rammed the sharp blade directly into his chest. Continuing this dastardly tactic, he furiously pummeled One Eared Pete's chest again and again.

At this point, Strumpet Janie had ended her shrieks of encouragement, and my pirate brethren had also gone deathly still. Standing to make his presence known, Captain Shivvers shouted that the match was finished, but even his announcement did not cease the mechanical hammering from Pig Snout's blade. Clearly frustrated that his order had been ignored, Captain Shivvers drew his pistol and ended Pig Snout's attack with a direct shot to his face. Both fighters were now dead and were dragged unceremoniously from the ring. Captain Shivvers, laughed heartily at the match's tragic outcome and declared that he had certainly devised a highly effective method of getting the poor tar's attention!

Before the next match began, Captain Shivvers announced that a special event would follow the two remaining grudge matches. Turning in my direction and sporting a very devious smirk, he proclaimed that I had agreed to demonstrate my own pugilistic abilities against none other than Rooster Bill. In a stunned state, I glanced over at my colossal adversary and came to the stark realization that I now had no real choice in the matter. With the match proclaimed to all, my choice was to either face the monster or be branded a coward by my crewmates. The pirate horde erupted in appreciative chaos, eagerly anticipating the now promised match. While I was not terrified, I certainly did not relish the thought of combat with Rooster Bill, since the latter was truly enormous and powerful, more like a machine than a man.

Aware of Shivvers' intent, I realized that I would need to employ every nasty and underhanded trick I had ever learned to survive the upcoming battle. My immediate thought was that if I could outlast the gargantuan, then the match would be decreed a draw, and we could both proudly walk away from the ring. Truth be known, I had developed into a rather fine specimen of a young man, but I understood that strength alone would not guarantee the outcome I desperately desired. Rather, I was sure that it would require a nimble mind and agile reflexes to avoid disaster. In order to collect my thoughts, I wandered away from the madness of the fight ring.

As I stumbled onto the beach, I ran directly into one of the more mysterious rogues of our crew, South Sea Tan! Nobody knew his real name since he spoke only in his native gibberish and responded to overt sign language exclusively. As we converged, I was suddenly airborne and I landed hard on my back both dazed and having difficulty breathing. Regaining my senses, I found Tan standing over me with a very concerned look on his face. Assisting me to my feet, he continued to sign his apologies for his rough treatment. Tan then communicated that he wished to extend his sincere thanks for returning his coin from the cheating gambler. I signed that I was happy to help and moved cautiously away so that I could continue my wanderings. Holding up his small hand to stop my progress, Tan signed that he wished to award a gift as a matter of repayment for my generosity.

Well aware of my upcoming fight, he signed that he had vital information he wished to impart. Tan signed that his secret knowledge was rather simple, attack my opponent's feet! I was quite unsure whether this little yellow devil was making a joke at my expense or was serious in the advice he had just delivered. Smirking innocently at my apparent confusion, Tan signed that Rooster Bill had been endowed with tiny and very delicate lower appendages. They were indeed his weakest point, but few ever came to realize this fact given the sheer size of this hulking colossus.

Edging his way past me, he signed that he wished me good fortune as he disappeared into the night. While his insider knowledge buoyed my hopes, I realized that I needed to pay close attention to those oversized paws my opponent called fists or I would be beaten into a senseless pulp as I attempted any attack on Rooster Bill's supposed weakness. The funny thing was that I had yet to feel any real terror at the upcoming encounter. In the past, I had observed a fair number of smaller men prevail in the ring over much larger opponents utilizing a wide variety of tactics and maneuvers. My strategy was to withstand his early barrages, so that I would have an opportunity to retaliate later in the fight. As our match neared, I secured my valuables with Powder Monkey for safekeeping. Angry George had volunteered to act as my cornerman. As I entered the ring, I was heartily greeted by the vast majority of the spectators. However, the betting line was twenty-five to one against me, but all that really meant was a chance for me to earn some extra coin. I hastily instructed Powder Monkey to wager every bit of money our old hands of the *Amafata* had in their possession on me to prevail against my highly favored opponent.

Amid a smattering of hisses and catcalls, my opponent entered the makeshift ring. It is a puzzling phenomenon to me that large things seem to get bigger and small things get tinier the closer we come to them. Well, I can faithfully report that Rooster Bill appeared more like a mountain than a mere mortal as he stood snarling and growling over me. Before the start of the match, he glanced over at Captain Shivvers and received a conspiratorial wink. With a signal from Lion, who acted as ring referee, the bell was struck and the match began. With speed that caught me off guard, Rooster Bill raced across the small ring and began his murderous assault. From the very start, I recognized that he was certainly no stranger to the ring, and he moved with incredible agility given his immense size. Noting this information, I took several evasive steps to avoid his serious and deadly blows as I continued my evaluation. My second bit of wisdom was that Rooster Bill's right hand was definitely the more serious weapon of the two. Further, I noted that he preferred to throw round-hammering strokes versus utilizing any type of short jabs or punches. This meant that I needed to keep us both close to negate his long-rounded assaults. I also favored his left side to avoid the chance of suffering one of his massive arcing blows from his powerful right hand.

Do not for a moment believe this vital knowledge came without a heavy price. In a very short time, he had delivered several wicked shots that both stunned me and provided a spectacular mental light show. Never failing to let my attention wander, I discerned that he was in excellent physical shape complete with superb stamina. In a very short time, I knew that I could not hope to outlast the brute as I had originally planned. As I continued my study, I was rewarded with another key observation. This insight was the exact information I had been hoping to gain. You see, when he was just about to lash out with one of his murderous rights, his massive stomach muscles clenched giving me a momentary warning of the upcoming strike. This information also did not come cheap since he had successfully landed one of these murderous punches that almost decapitated me. As it was, the blow sent me prone on the sandy ring's floor.

Taking my time to shake off the disastrous effects of this punch, I slowly rose to my feet prepared now to take the fight to my adversary. Rooster Bill, convinced of victory, waited patiently for my slow recovery. When I was finally able to clear the many bright lights exploding in my brain, I signaled my opponent to continue our battle. As he closed in on me, I kept a sharp eye out for his involuntary warning signal. When I noticed his telltale stomach muscle bunching, I eased further to his left and managed to duck under his sailing right paw. As I did so, I delivered my very own lethal combination, striking my opponent with a powerful right uppercut, followed by a furious left cross and finishing with a devastating looping right strike. These three blows were executed in a surprising blur of motion, and I could see that they had rocked the monster temporarily.

A bit surprised that my powerful punch combination had not leveled the beast, I prepared for his retaliatory onslaught. Again and again, I utilized the very same combination of blows in direct response to his stomach muscle signal, and I judged that my strategy was succeeding. Shaking off my latest barrage, I perceived that my opponent was a bit stunned and confused at my success. With an inhuman roar, he steadily advanced intent on ending the fight in his favor. Judging that the time was right, I unleashed my secret weapon. As he closed, I stomped down hard on his lead foot causing him instant pain and anguish as his confident smirk was replaced with one of total disbelief. As he hopped around the ring in misery, I utilized the same devastating combination of blows twice more in rapid succession. He was staggering and reeling from their thunderous effects when I lashed out and crushed his other tiny foot with my right heel. This time my huge opponent howled in mortal agony as I pressed the advantage and landed my trio of punches twice more. Dazed and groggy, Rooster Bill skittered away from me to nurse his injuries. Blood was pouring out of his broken nose and his eyes were glazed over, but I was far from finished.

Advancing steadily, I once again hammered down on both of his sensitive feet while delivering the best right uppercut I had ever thrown. As my wicked blow connected and shattered his jaw, he should have fallen face first onto the sand, but his unbelievable stamina and determination kept him erect. The savage and riotous crowd went deadly silent as I surveyed my opponent. It was clear that he refused to fall but I was not quite done. Taking careful aim, I sent a powerful straight right fist directly into his broken nose, and I could see the lights go out in his eyes. As he landed face down in the sand, it was clear to me that he was not going to rise again. The bell was struck signaling the end of the match. I faintly heard the Doc declare that Rooster Bill was indeed far beyond his need for assistance, the monster was dead. In hearing Doc's pronouncement, I felt a fleeting sense of remorse for the death of this hulking brute, but was exceedingly relieved that I had survived the murderous contest.

My victorious exploits in the ring proved extremely advantageous, as my pirate captors now viewed me in a whole new light, one of both respect and admiration! There was little sympathy for my dead opponent, as he was dragged feet-first from the ring and dumped unceremoniously into a nearby refuse pit. Lion held up my hand signaling me the victor, as the entire crew went absolutely wild calling out my name time and time again. Noting my new friend Tan gloating with pride at my decisive victory, I silently signed an appreciated thanks in his direction. Scanning the delirious throng of pirates, I noticed that only one of them seemed quite unhappy with my victory, a scowling Captain Shivvers!

As I was hustled out of the ring on the shoulders of my new supporters, Captain Shivvers continued to shake his head in sad disbelief that his nefarious plot to end my life had failed so convincingly. Since no other fights were scheduled after my battle, Fight Night was declared officially over. As we all made our way over to the food and drink that had been assembled beside a roaring bonfire, I whispered a silent thanks to Saint Agnes, Papa Legba and Willamina's Gypsy Queen Zarina for sparing my life, a truly multi-denominational entreaty indeed! As we all partook of the delicious feast prepared by Long Tall Willie, I noticed that our conniving leader was conspicuously monitoring my every action. Forgetting my adversary for a brief time, I feasted on the many delicacies that were shoved my way by my adoring fans. I knew in my heart that my struggle with our nefarious leader was hardly at an end, and that I would need to keep a sharp eye on the brigand who wished me dead!

Chapter 12: The Tale of the Black Monk

As our appetites were finally sated, a call came from my companions for a horrific tale of ghosts and goblins to make the evening complete. Since I was the hero of the hour, I was duly appointed to lead the storytelling. Thinking back to the time when these murderous villains were cowed in utter dread by the dead corpses discovered in the *Amafata's* hold, I launched into a story that I had been devising since that incident occurred. A tale that was sure to scare the senses out of these thieving animals. I was also certain that I could further capitalize upon this tale of horror as time passed. In a slow and deliberate manner, I announced that my tale concerned a horrid phantom, which had been haunting me since early childhood. This spectral apparition was known to me as the Black Monk. Gaining their full attention with this theatrical introduction, I launched directly into my story.

The imaginary account began one gloomy evening when my brother, Toby had wandered the basement area of Saint Agnes' and had managed to lose his way, a regular accomplishment for my brother! Struggling to reorient himself in the endless maze of rooms and discarded rubbish, Toby ambled, lost and confused, in a determined effort to navigate his way back to me. As he meandered, he came across a hidden alcove that was littered with a myriad of what he believed to be animal bones strewn across the floor. In a quick appraisal of these skeletons, he identified dog, cat, goat, pig and rat bones that had been scattered everywhere. To Toby, it seemed like these defiled animals had been literally ripped apart, but he was perplexed on discovering no blood trails or flesh remnants of any kind. Frightened beyond words, my brother fled the alcove terrified of encountering the demonic resident of this unholy lair of pure savagery.

As he fled from his grisly discovery, he suddenly thought that he heard distant and eerie sounds. Unable to identify the source of this unnatural clamor, he stopped moving to listen more closely. The strange noises sounded more like threatening growls or grunts, while the creature issuing them seemed to be closing in on him. Finding an empty cabinet, Toby took refuge. Scared senseless, Toby held his breath so as not to be discovered. Able to utilize a small crack in the cabinet, Toby kept a watchful eye on the area just outside his improvised sanctuary. In a short time, the ghastly sounds became extremely loud as his tormentor finally made an appearance. The problem was that the basement was steeped in darkness so Toby could barely discern any details of his adversary. Unable to readily identify the fiend, Toby realized that his hunting demon seemed much darker than the inky blackness that surrounded it, blacker than black in fact! As he continued his terrified surveillance, he perceived that the creature seemed to be dressed in some sort of hooded black robe that precluded further identification.

As the demon passed his hiding place, it suddenly stopped its skittering movements and made sniffing sounds much like a canine, as if sensing that someone was very near. At this point, Toby was so terrified that he involuntarily began to urinate, which added an extra measure of fear believing that the black goblin would now smell him for sure. The demon continued to glance back and forth but never identified where my brother was hiding. Seemingly satisfied that the area was unoccupied, the black nightmare began its scuttling movement back towards the unholy alcove that Toby had just vacated.

Waiting for the creature to disappear entirely, my brother made his escape in the exact opposite direction. In desperate flight, Toby finally located our well-marked trails and quickly worked his way back to me. As he approached, I could see that he was shaking and deathly white in color, while breathing in a ragged manner with eyes nearly bulging out of his head. When I questioned him on the reason for his strange manner and outright frightful state, he described his dreadful encounter with the mysterious and ghastly creature.

Laughing at his childish fear, I informed him that I held strong doubts about his fantastic story and asked him to supply some proof. Staunchly reluctant to return to the hellish alcove, I finally persuaded him to accompany me near the source of his terror. We searched and searched but were never able to discover the beast or its hiding place. Returning to our quarters for breakfast, we reported Toby's unusual sighting to our Uncle Archibald.

In a halting and frightened voice, Toby repeated his horrific experience including the hellish alcove and the black sniffing creature that had pursued him. Upon completing his account, Uncle Arch took on a look of extreme concern. Taking a long measured breath, our uncle unsteadily took a seat and then began to perspire and shake uncontrollably. Asking for a moment to compose himself, Uncle Arch eventually declared that Toby had just experienced the demon named the Black Monk. Continuing in a terrified voice, he divulged that Toby's experience was indeed unusual since the specter rarely made his presence known to mortals. With these words, our uncle related the specter's story.

It seemed that the Black Monk had at one time been a highly regarded clergyman, who was assigned to a monastery that long ago occupied our exact location. While extremely eccentric and brooding, this strange individual was considered brilliant by his peers and overseers. However, this unusual man did have a tragic preoccupation with the study of the occult, including witchcraft and devil worship, thereby earning him the title of the Black Monk. His superiors were concerned with his fascination in these dark arts, but could not deter him from these studies. Finally in desperation, he was strictly censured and ordered to cease all investigation and education in these forbidden subjects.

To those nearest him, he seemed to comply with these dictums and resumed all of his normal routines and duties. As time passed, the Black Monk seemed to become even more aloof and secretive in nature. Coincidently, laborers living near the monastery began to complain of domestic animal disappearances to the abbot, but a formal investigation into these matters was never conducted. However, once this formal protest had been reported, the disappearances ceased rather abruptly and things returned to normal. In a short while, matters really digressed as neighboring children began to disappear during the night. The townsfolk once again turned to the abbot for his assistance, and this time a formal investigation was conducted into this now grave situation. Each of the monks in the monastery were questioned extensively but no real answers were uncovered to explain the missing tots.

At wits end, the abbot widened his investigation to include everyone associated with the cloister. When a small and frightened stableboy was questioned, he confessed that he had been enlisted by the Black Monk to abduct the children from their sleep and deliver them to his superior. Informing the abbot that he had no real idea of what happened to the children he abducted, he broke down completely into a sobbing wail asking the head of the monastery for forgiveness for his sinful actions.

The Black Monk was summoned to the abbot's chambers, but upon questioning denied the lad's tale while claiming total innocence in the matter. However, when a thorough search was made of his living quarters, a small black box was discovered that was filled with bones of human fingers, small and delicate and certainly emanating from children! Confronted with this damning evidence, the Black Monk once again professed his innocence, claiming that the black box had been planted in his room by his enemies. Not believing him, the abbot ordered the monastery fully searched once more including the ruins of the old basement.

What was discovered in the basement truly revolted and disgusted the search party. A very strange altar was found in this evil lair, complete with an upside down cross and other demonic icons and fetishes. Additionally, the horrified monks found the butchered and partial remains of several children in the state of rapid decomposition. It appeared to the sickened searchers that the children had been slaughtered and cannibalized in the performance of some sort of satanic ritual. The Black Monk was hauled before a hastily convened church counsel, and eventually convicted of various heinous crimes including murder, satanic worship and cannibalism. He was sentenced to the harsh punishment of being burned alive at the stake. The abbot decreed that his execution take place in the same unholy temple that the monster had utilized for both his demonic rites and horrific crimes. The Black Monk was executed in this most hideous fashion, and in the process the entire filthy area was set ablaze and destroyed to eventually remain abandoned and in ruin.

Not another word was uttered about this horrible and demonic matter, and as time passed most forgot this unfortunate incident entirely. Over time, strange and disconcerting noises and sounds were reported by several of the monks stationed at the abbey. It was determined that these sounds seemed to emanate directly from the old basement. At the same time, reports arose that a number of the monks had viewed a strange black creature that seemed to appear out of nowhere and disappear accordingly. Once again, an extensive search was made of the lower levels with absolutely nothing strange or unusual detected. While these terrifying appearances continued, in time they slackened and became less and less frequent. Eventually the monastery burned to the ground one fateful night killing all of the monks in residence. The church reclaimed the property, and the Saint Agnes Basilica was erected on this old site of the monastery.

While Uncle Arch confessed to us that he had never seen or experienced this phantom, there were those who had claimed to have seen a strange scuttling figure from time to time in the basement of the basilica. I solemnly reported to my captivated audience that Uncle Arch's ghost story totally scared the religion out of my brother and I. We certainly did not sleep very well for a number of subsequent nights, but all eventually returned to normal. Being naturally inquisitive, I began my own exploration of the basement.

I continued these vain searches every now and again as opportunity presented itself. One night, as I was haphazardly roaming a particularly cluttered section of the basement, I thought I detected very strange and mysterious sounds. Hiding myself in an extremely dark and secluded recess, I took the time to listen intently to these strange noises. Not long after, I was rewarded by a series of grunting and growling emanations that seemed to be getting nearer and nearer. All at once, I spied a black hunched specter appear out of nowhere, scuttling and sniffing its way towards me.

White with fright, I remained rooted in my hiding spot, praying furiously that the fiend would not locate me. As the figure slowly and steadily approached, I realized that I needed to take quick action or I was doomed. Shaking and shivering, I began to chant the *Lord's Prayer*. The ruse seemed to work as the black specter ceased its advance, and took full measure of the words that I was issuing. With an inhuman and disgusted sigh, the monstrosity turned around and made its retreat. Easing myself out of my hiding place, I began to shadow this ghostly apparition. I followed this mysterious creature for several minutes before it seemed to disappear completely into a solid basement wall issuing a trailing wail in its wake. Try as I might, I just could not work out exactly how the ghoul had made its escape, but I was extremely grateful that it had!

Returning shakily to the church's upper level, I vowed to remain silent on my grisly discovery to avoid panicking my brother further. Later when

I was alone with Uncle Arch, I questioned if he knew of any significance attributed to the sightings of the repellent specter. He informed me that there was an old superstition that the loathsome wraith sought out special victims to terrorize and haunt until their eventual death. It was rumored that the Black Monk's eternal soul had been rejected by Satan, and was doomed to roam the earth practicing his sordid deeds for all eternity. Uncle Arch then sincerely warned me to take precautionary steps to avoid contact or communication with the phantom, so as to avoid the possibility of a lifetime of horrific visitations and hauntings.

Well, I reported to my now frightened and utterly captivated audience that being a mere lad, I believed myself immune from such a tragic fate, so I continued to stalk the black shade in the church's dark, dank underworld. I had managed to spy the fleeting black shape on a number of occasions, and my rendition of the *Lord's Prayer* always caused the satanic goblin to flee. In fact, I came quite familiar with this specter's presence, and it seemed after a while that I no longer had to perform any sort of search, he simply found me!

Continuing, I narrated that having signed on as a crewmember of the *Amafata*, I had been quite sure that I had experienced the last of the Black Monk as my ship set sail for foreign ports. I then related to my now stunned and terror stricken listeners that we had been at sea for a goodly number of weeks before this black phantom decided to make his first appearance. I explained to my mesmerized audience that my role as galley slave forced me to make numerous trips to our hellish hold in search of wood fuel for the stove. It was during one of these trips that I spied the familiar malignant spirit creeping around in this vermin infested environment. I was both shocked and stunned at discovering that the Black Monk had been able to manifest himself so far from his hellish home.

I informed my pirate audience that I followed the black phantom in the lowest level of our ship, and was not surprised when it seemed to disappear directly into the vessel's hull. From that point on, I explained that I had experienced a few more glimpses of this evil demon at no particular time or place. It seemed that one minute he would appear and in the next he would be gone! The only consistent feature of these short visitations was the demon's departing wailing howl, which never ceased to unsettle me. As I finished my tale of horror and dread, I noticed that the entire audience was now hanging on my every word.

Deciding to grace my tale with a semblance of truth, I utilized my *special voice* and issued a loud mournful wailing howl, which I directed as if coming from somewhere deep in the isle's interior. Completely terrified, my savage assemblage were now staring into the black void that surrounded us, waiting for the horrific specter to make its dreadful appearance. Once again issuing the same mournful wail, I concluded my tale by informing everyone present that for reasons unknown to me the Black Monk seemed drawn to my person. Because of this, I beseeched them all to be constantly vigilant for my hellish ghoul, since I was absolutely certain that he would make his presence known sometime in the not too distant future. Taking the opportunity one last time, I issued a parting howl that sent my audience scurrying for far safer confines.

As my comrades were in the process of full-fledged flight, Strumpet Janie reeled into the firelight in a very drunken state. Cursing and screaming obscenity after obscenity, she called for Captain Shivvers and shouted that she had something vital to impart to him. Because of the noisy and inebriated scene she was creating, many of my fleeing pirates returned to the firelight to determine the cause behind her delirious issuances. Captain Shivvers finally stood and confronted the hysterical trollop. As soon as Strumpet Janie spied her target, she launched into a series of very wicked curses aimed at our disingenous Captain for the role he had played in the murder of her two lovers.

Laughing at the sheer idiocy of her threats and accusations, Captain Shivvers strode directly up to the wench and delivered an extremely savage blow. Knocked to her knees and bleeding copiously from an apparent broken nose, Strumpet Janie hissed her final curse. Menacingly, she informed Captain Shivvers that he was certainly doomed to a tormenting and painful death for his evil actions. Continuing in a halting and now weepy voice, Strumpet Janie announced that she carried a particularly nasty disease, the pox of all poxes! Since he had taken his pleasure with her a multitude of times during our Grand Carouse, she was absolutely convinced that she had passed this hellish present on to him. Stunned into complete silence, Captain Shivvers turned homicidal and proceeded to beat the poor doxy to death right before our eyes!

Chapter 13: A Cure for the Dreaded Pox

With the *Grand Carouse now* officially at an end, we all made our way back to the *Midnight Crow* to continue our piratical practices. Although I had chosen to persevere in my association with this nefarious band of rogues, I was continually plagued by the question of whether or not I had made the right decision. As I thought back to Willamina's palm reading prophesies, I decided that I was now quite enmeshed in the radical life change that she had foretold. While I had no inclination or great desire to assist these sea brigands in their thieving efforts, I remained hopeful that time and circumstances would permit me to uncover a method to free myself and my old crewmates from their evil clutches. I was determined to keep a very sharp eye out for this opportunity. In the meantime, I found myself merely a prisoner of my forced decision and decided to make the very best of the entire ugly situation.

My crewmates seemed to adjust quite nicely to the madhouse atmosphere that surrounded us. Life aboard the *Midnight Crow* felt more like a night at any shore pub than any sort of voyage. For me, my short time aboard the *Midnight Crow* began to feel more like a prison term than any type of adventure. The only real difference I sensed between serving time in prison and laboring on this pirate ship was the fact that I had the distinct opportunity of drowning while onboard this insidious asylum! Dancing, singing, arguing, swearing and drinking was the standard fare day and night living on this den of iniquity. I realized in very short order that there was no such thing as a dry pirate ship!

Drinking was the order of business at all hours of the day and night. The copious quantities of spirits that these vagabonds consumed did provide obvious benefits such as fortification against dirty weather, as well as enabling them to endure the miserable dampness and cold permanently existing on the lower decks. However, the real reason I surmised behind their unlimited consumption was the very simple fact that they actually could drink nonstop without remorse or rebuke. And drink they certainly did, resembling quaffing machines rather than human beings. From the moment they gained consciousness each morning to their eventual inebriated collapse each evening, each rogue carried a bottle as his closest companion that never deserted his side. It was extremely difficult for me to imagine how these pirates actually planned to capture any sort of prey given their continual pitiful condition. As I made my way around this floating grogshop, I was constantly surprised and quite often amazed by the ingenuity and novelty of the many drinking games and contests that my inebriated mates continually devised.

As I wandered the ship, Booby Bird appeared at my side and announced that Captain Shivvers had requested my presence in his cabin. Our duplicitous leader seemed to be in quite an anxious and concerned frame of mind as I sat down directly across from him. He whispered that he had made a visit to the Doc's surgery to seek his wisdom on whether or not he was stricken by the deadly pox, cursed on him by Strumpet Janie. His problem centered on the fact that he could not convey his fears, his symptoms or even his name to the foreign physician. Deciding on an alternate course, he chose to enlist my help instead. Understanding his abject terror that the doxy's curse would lead to tremendous suffering and ultimately death, I decided to use this fortitudinous situation to my distinct advantage.

Blubbering now that he was far too young to die, he begged me to cure him of the insidious disease that had been cruelly gifted to him. Promising me wealth beyond my wildest imaginings, the sniveling coward also promised my freedom if I would only produce a cure for his horrible affliction. Understanding his totally deceitful nature, I knew with certainty that all of his promises would amount to nothing the moment he believed himself cured.

Knowing from his past failed machinations that our dear Captain wished me dead, I decided to play along with his desperate wishes in order to make myself indispensable and therefore safe from his death plots. I informed the shifty pirate that I would do everything in my power to affect a cure, which brought a flood of tearful thanks from my sworn enemy. Having made this totally insincere promise, I conducted a rather bizarre series of examinations on the terrified leader. Finally, after careful inspection of his toes, I informed him that I had found no indications of the disease's progress. However, I assured him that it was much too early in the dreaded disease's life for a display of definitive symptoms. I informed him that we would have to wait for sure signs of the illness before attempting any curative efforts. In a nervous and shaking voice, he questioned which exact symptoms we were awaiting that would announce the advance of the malady. Taking my time to consider his query, I confided that if he were truly infected that he would next develop severe anxiety, high fever and horrific hallucinations. Once these telltale symptoms occurred, we could initiate a treatment program.

However, I sternly warned him that there was no guarantee of a cure, and his agonizing death could eventually occur despite any of my life-saving efforts. Nodding his grave understanding, he begged me to apply all the knowledge and resources at my command to affect a miraculous cure for him. I ordered him to stay in his cabin resting comfortably until I returned. I quietly began to slip out of his cabin before I lapsed into uncontrolled mirth at his imaginary predicament. As I made my hasty departure, Captain Shivvers called my name softly from his bunk. When I turned to answer his summons, I was greeted by a look of utter dread. In a halting and terrified manner, he softly inquired if I had yet encountered the Black Monk aboard his ship. Realizing that he had just provided me with another valuable weapon, I smiled weakly and told him not yet!

Following my meeting with Captain Shivvers, I hurried back to my cabin to procure a few items from my cache of goods required to carry out my devious plan. After locating these items and stuffing them in an empty sack, I made my way to the galley and silently signaled Powder Monkey to meet me in the hold. In a flash, I swiveled and stealthy made my way to our secret rendezvous spot. As I awaited his arrival, I began work on one of the items that I had brought along in the sack. Handling the belladonna root very carefully, I shaved off a small chunk and began dicing it into a pulpy mush. As I finished this chore, Powder Monkey made his appearance. I filled him in on Captain Shivvers condition and the plan I had concocted. Once finished, he signaled his complete approval and questioned how he could assist. I signed that our first step was to find an opportunity to usher the crushed herb in my hand into the Captain's private brandy stash. My words brought a look of apprehension to my accomplice's eyes. Understanding his immediate concern, I signed that I would devise a method to enable him to accomplish this mission without discovery.

The reason for my friend's apprehension about the Captain's brandy was an oft repeated story we had both been told by various pirate crewmembers. As the story went, an incurable thief and inebriate named Bowlegged Billy had once been caught dipping into this sacred well and had paid a very high price for his thievery. Billy was known for his side-to-side amble when he was drinking and whoring on land. While most of us sailors tended to sway from side-to-side ashore because of our continual shifting search for balance on moving vessels, Billy's swagger was so much more pronounced that it earned him his pirate name. For his brutal punishment, Bowlegged Billy was lashed naked to the mast of a small fishing craft on a brutally hot and muggy tropical morning, while the *Midnight Crow* was anchored off a series of low swampy islands. To make matters worse, he had been slathered with sweet-smelling honey that was intended to draw a virtual horde of blood-sucking guests. The instructions given by the Captain to the two tallow-swabbed oarsmen were to provide Bowlegged Billy with a slow and wondrous pleasure cruise through the insect-infested isles and lagoons so as to allow the flying scavengers a chance to sample the honeyed flesh of the poor helpless prisoner. As the story went, the punished pirate was rowed in-and-out of the shallow water passages for the entire day serving as the main course for untold thousands of diners. At the day's end, the miserable wretch was rowed back to the *Midnight Crow* so that everyone aboard could witness the terrible destruction wrought by these insidious pesky blood-suckers. The crew was shocked into silence as their crewmate was dragged roughly aboard. His body was bloated and scarred from the innumerable bites and stings he had been subjected to along his torturous journey.

The unlucky drunkard was dragged to the ship's doctor for treatment. His eyes displayed the inhuman pain and suffering he had endured at the mercy of his tiny but determined tormentors. Since his tongue had swollen to over three times its normal size, Bowlegged Billy was unable to communicate. At his eventual death, most of his crewmates surmised that he had simply lost the will to endure anymore suffering. The cost of his foolish theft was first his body, then his mind and finally his life. Given this harsh and beastly lesson, the sacred brandy supply was never tampered with again. The pirate crew to a man would sooner drink from an overflowing pisstub than ever consider whetting their palates on the Captain's brandy!

I signaled Powder Monkey that our time for action had finally arrived. Further, I informed my co-conspirator that I planned to accompany Captain Shivvers to the Doc's surgery for a variety of further unnecessary tests. I then signed to Powder Monkey that this was his opportunity. With a solemn wink, he acknowledged complete understanding and disappeared to prepare his special delivery. I hastened to Shivvers' cabin and announced that I required his presence in the Doc's surgery for a few more tests. Dutifully agreeing, he rose and we both exited his lair bound for the Doc's cabin. Prior to this planned visit, I had taken Doc into my confidence, and had filled him in on my scheme to rid the ship of our contemptible leader. As part of this plan, Doc's role was to play along with my ministrative ruses, assisting in the fantasy treatments whenever the need arose. However, should our wily skipper take it upon himself to visit the Doc for a second opinion or for an alternative treatment program, a specific strategy was in place between Doc and I that would surely diffuse this situation and strongly discourage any further private consultations by our villainous commander.

As I performed further meaningless tests with Doc as a willing assistant, Shivvers suddenly questioned me on my choice of a pirate name. I responded that I had yet to give the matter much thought. Providing one of his endearing smirks, he announced that he had given the matter serious thought. Continuing, he confessed that he had questioned many of my former shipmates following our capture, and had learned volumes about my past. After listening to my fearsome campfire tale of my basement explorations for the Black Monk, he divulged that he had struck upon a perfect pirate name for me--Bilge Rat! My initial reaction to his inane announcement was a belief that he was making a joke at my expense.

As I studied his intense features for a moment more, I decided that he was actually being truthful and honest with me, traits he certainly had extreme difficulty maintaining! Understanding his serious intent, I thought about the name he had just suggested. While it certainly held no claims on vanity or glamour, the name Bilge Rat seemed to resonate somewhere deep within me. My unnatural affinity with this loathsome ship's location coupled with my first meaningful occupation as a ratter extraordinaire seemed to confirm my enemy's affirmation that his creation was perfect. Continuing, Captain Shivvers confided that this new name would inspire terror and dread in typical piratical fashion. Laughing now, I thanked Captain Shivvers for his concern regarding my future, and agreed that his name, Bilge Rat, was both unique and totally fitting. With a beaming smile, the outlaw acknowledged my compliment and considered the matter closed with finality. From that moment on I became Bilge Rat to both my friends and enemies aboard!

Having completed my bogus examination, I thanked Captain Shivvers for his patience. With a look of dread, he tentatively questioned if I had made any crucial discoveries regarding his condition. Noting his concern, I answered that it was still far too early to prognosticate, but that I would be keeping a close watch on his progress, and would provide him answers the moment I reached any definite conclusions. Nodding his grateful thanks, he slowly made his way out of the cabin to return to his sickbed. Just before exiting, he turned and in a halting whisper petitioned me for one further favor. He then pleaded with me to alert him immediately if I happened to encounter my personal specter, the Black Monk, anywhere on his ship. Solemnly promising him that I would certainly do so, he resumed his slow death-like march back to his cabin. Moments following his departure, Powder Monkey appeared and signed that he had successfully completed his dangerous mission. Signaling my sincerest thanks, the agile little imp disappeared in a blink of an eye to return to his chores in the galley.

Having nothing better to do, I followed my friend's path back to the galley to partake in a quick meal and to listen to the latest scuttlebutt from my pirate comrades. Upon entering the galley, I realized that I had arrived just in time to be entertained by a seafaring tale being spun by Jumping Jimmy, a renowned shipboard storyteller. Jimmy informed his audience that his tale centered on a deadly account of a fellow tar, who had the odious misfortune of contracting a sinister case of the pox. I realized immediately that our Captain's current illness was the source of tonight's entertainment. I was also cognizant of my pirate brethren's fear of this insidious affliction due to their continual transgressions with port trollops. Nicknamed the brothel scourge, this infirmity was as formidable as hanging, drowning or the unthinkable calamity of an empty liquor cabinet to my thieving brothers!

Jimmy began his tale by informing his rapt audience that the poor unfortunate involved in tonight's story was a former shipmate by the name of Spanish Petey. The lad had contracted his nasty curse from a young island doxy nicknamed Cross-eyed Mary. Upon spending a night of pleasure with the diseased whore, Petey was soon beset with pox symptoms in the form of filthy boils and ugly sores on his privates. Convinced that he was doomed to a horrid death, the tar revisited the source of his malady and proceeded to beat the poor lass to death with a mallet borrowed from his ship's carpenter.

Having sated his murderous inclinations, Petey began a desperate search for a cure from several trusted island sources. His fist attempt to gain salvation was visiting a barkeep at his favorite island rumhouse. This so-called authority informed the miserable pirate that he needed to wash and wrap his maleness in sour wine for a week's time to effect a cure. Following orders, Petey obtained the necessities and spent the next week in abject agony as he attempted to drown the pox from his body. At the end of the prescribed treatment period, Petey felt no significant relief. In fact, his privates were now severely aflame and much too tender to endure the slightest touch. Convinced that he was yet infected, he turned to God for a solution.

His next stop was the local church, where he conferred with a wizened man of God for deliverance. After listening to the sailor's plight, the priest expounded that Petey needed to pray the evil out of his body. To that end, the holy man taught him a myriad of holy epitaphs and provided the sick tar with a vial of precious holy water to douse his lower regions in order to expel the demonic ailment. Petey sent another week dousing and praying to no avail. His curse prevailed and the only result of his effort was a severe lightening of his personal cache of coin to the coffers of the ineffective prayer monger.

In a panic-stricken state, Petey next visited the local blacksmith, who was rumored to possess a solution for the curse. Upon conferring with the smithy, he was told that the answer to his problem was extreme heat. The charlatan described the procedure he favored which involved the singing and cleansing of the fool's privates with a white-hot iron.

Snorting an inebriated laugh, Jimmy related that Petey wasted no time and promptly fled the man's stable before this torturous application could be effected.

Seeking a more humane answer, Petey next made a visit to a renowned island medical man. Upon examining the diseased idiot, the doctor confirmed Petey's suspicions that his new patient did indeed suffer from a malicious case of the pox. The doctor then outlined his prescribed treatment of copious bleeding followed by curative applications of mercury. Desperate and anxious, Petey agreed to the regimen and placed himself in the doctor's care. After two more weeks of evil leeching and mercury ointment wraps, Petey found himself no closer to a cure. In fact during this time, he had begun to salivate a frightening thick black spittle while his few remaining teeth began to fall out one-by-one. When confronted, the doctor's only response was: "A night in the arms of Venus leads to a lifetime with Mercury". Deciding that the promised cure was far worse than the ailment, Petey abandoned any further bleeding and mercury dousing and once again resumed his frantic search for a solution.

Desperate to the point of madness, Petey made one last attempt by visiting the island's witchwoman, renown for her natural curative abilities. The ancient hag interviewed him for all of the details surrounding the contraction of the pox and then made a thorough yet highly embarrassing inspection of his privates. Upon completion, she boldly announced that only a sandbath would cure him of his mortal pestilence. Confused to the extreme, Petey demanded further explanation. Chirping out a savage hoot, the crone responded that he needed to remain calm and that his numerous queries would soon be answered.

Petey attempted to relax as the healer began a complicated process to manufacture a strange mixture from her vast assortment of odd ingredients located haphazardly around her hovel. Once done, she shoved this greenish composite into his hands and ordered him to quaff the medicine quickly while she prepared the next stage of the cure. Holding his nose, Petey drained the odious concoction and began to experience a mystifying sensation of numbness creeping all over his entire being.

Collapsed now and unable to move any portion of his body, Petey was at the total mercy of the healing hag. The woman then shouted a command and two burly assistants suddenly appeared. Wrapping their stout arms around him, they lifted him to their shoulders and exited the hut following the lead of the smiling witch. After what seemed like hours, Petey's contingent arrived at a deserted beach and he was dropped rudely on the powdered sand. The old healer issued a series of commands and her assistants went to work digging a sizable depression just above the surf-line.

Once this hole was completed, the brutes shoved Petey feet-first into the cavity. Shoveling back the excess sand tightly around him, Petey found himself buried up to his neck facing open water. Still perplexed by the nature of the hag's cure, Petey questioned the witch on the reason for his burial. The old woman leaned in close and informed the immobilized pirate that he was about to pay for his lustful sins. Continuing, she confessed that Cross-eyed Mary had been her own beloved daughter. Given his ill treatment of the girl, the crone now promised a final retribution.

Petey, hearing her declaration, realized that he was in serious trouble. Still befuddled, he nervously inquired what she planned to do to him. Surprised by his query, the old woman laughed and told him that she intended to cure him of his disease as promised. Continuing, she informed him that the rising tide would provide the means of his ultimate salvation. With an evil sneer, she said;" What the sea does not claim, the crabs certainly will!" With these words, she collected her cohorts and marched away to the shrill wails of the terrified pirate.

Well, I can tell you that we all slept very badly that night remembering the story of Spanish Petey. Fully awake the following morning, I made my way to Captain Shivvers' cabin to check on my patient. When I reached his door and knocked, I was greeted by my smiling nemesis, who informed me that he felt wondrously alive and well this fine morning. Believing the danger of the insidious pox totally passed, he confessed in a brusque manner that my doctoring services were no longer required. Realizing the futility of arguing, I nodded and turned to take my leave. Just before the door shut, I turned and delivered an ominous pronouncement to the deluded fool. In a halting and shaking voice, I revealed that I thought that I had spied my old nemesis, the Black Monk, in the wee hours of the morning sneaking around our ship. My words acted like a strong slap to his face, as his cheerful mood disintegrated right before my eyes. With frightfully shaking hands, Captain Shivvers invited me immediately back into his cabin to discuss my recent encounter.

In order to gain some instant courage, he stormed across the room and drew a sizable quantity of his precious brandy, which he quaffed in a couple of long swallows. Noting this action with internal satisfaction, I related a totally fictitious story of my encounter with the demonic clergyman the previous evening. As I spun my fanciful tale of terror, Captain Shivvers once again made a return trip to his sacred brandy hogshead and downed another tankard. Finishing my report, I arose to take my leave promising to alert him if I experienced any further sightings of the black shade. Shaking now in terror from head to toe, he grudgingly thanked me for alerting him to the evil news, and then collapsed on his bunk in an attempt to calm his raging nerves. Noting his utter distress brought a warm feeling of satisfaction to my inner core, and I turned and made a fast retreat.

Reaching the galley, I signaled to Powder Monkey to meet me in our secluded spot in the hold. Reaching the location first, I was in the process of arranging a few necessary items when my protégée made his appearance. He signed that the entire ship was whispering about my new pirate name provided by our dear Captain. Nodding, I informed him that our illustrious leader had indeed been of service in devising my fanciful moniker. Changing subjects, I related the specific details of the next stage of my scheme, and his grin evolved into a full-fledged smile. I cautioned him that my plan involved risk. However, I was confident that if executed properly it would serve to send Captain Shivvers well over the edge of sanity. With that we both went to work on the necessary preparations that would prove critical to the ruse's success.

Having nothing but time on my hands, I retired to my cabin and conducted my daily navigational duties. As I was nearly finished with some complicated calculations, I was startled by a series of loud voices engaged in a deafening argument. Stopping my work to investigate, I was not at all surprised to discover that the uproar originated from Captain Shivvers' cabin. Upon reaching his door, I came face-to-face with Lion, who bore a very troubled expression. Lion whispered that he was certain that Shivers had completely lost his mind. Requesting explanation, the giant merely shrugged and invited me to check for myself. Knocking on the Captain's door, I entered to find my patient furiously pacing the sparse space, while muttering unintelligible words. Noting my presence, he ceased his aimless wanderings and in a death-like grip clutched my shoulders. With bloodshot-maddened eyes, he announced that the Black Monk was most certainly on his vessel in search of his immortal soul. Stifling a chuckle, I innocently questioned my addled foe on what had occurred since our last meeting. Dragging me closer, he whispered that he had spied the demonic clergyman while making rounds on the lower decks. Convinced that the black phantom was patrolling for him, he had commanded Lion to stand watch at his door to keep the demon out. Playing now to his fearful concerns, I divulged that my experience with this wandering spirit had taught me that it could appear or disappear at will anywhere it desired.

Hearing this proclamation sent visible shivers throughout his entire being. The fool then begged me to disclose the best methods to elude this noxious presence. Realizing my opportunity, I answered that the majority of my sightings of the nefarious devil were made in dark and shadowed surroundings, which indicated that this fiend seemed to shun bright sunlight. I immediately recommended that he move himself to the upper deck of the *Midnight Crow* to take full advantage of the tropical sun's strong rays. Understanding my intent, he ran to his door and bellowed for Lion to return for a new set of orders. In effect, the Captain commissioned Lion to move most of his belongings to the maindeck, where he would take up residence until further notice. Lion turned in my direction for confirmation, given the total lunacy of this request. Issuing signs of total bafflement, I announced to Lion that the fresh air of the maindeck might do my patient some good. Shrugging his shoulders, Lion called for a few pirate crewmen to relocate our leader's gear topside immediately.

Relieved that defensive action was being taken, the Captain in a weak and tearful state thanked both Lion and I for our valued assistance. As we made our departure, Lion asked for my opinion on these unusual orders. I confessed that I believed that our leader was experiencing severe hallucinations as a result of the pox. In his current frightful condition, I regarded it wiser to honor his ridiculous requests in the hopes so that we might calm his inflamed imagination. Nodding his full understanding,

Lion questioned whether I thought the Captain's condition would improve or worsen over time. Feigning uncertainty, I answered that all we could do was to continue to keep an eye on him as time passed. With a look of pity and utmost concern, he strode off to complete the idiotic commands he had just been issued.

Meanwhile, I made my way to the galley to have a quick word with another co-conspirator. When I arrived, Long Tall Willie was in the process of preparing the evening's fare. As our eyes met, he ceased his work, wiped his hands clean and came over to my side. He immediately asked what I required of him. Grateful for his help, I explained the developing situation with the Captain. I then filled him in on my plan. Requesting how he could assist in the ruse, I explained that I needed to debunk my tale of the Black Monk to the crew as nothing more than a campfire ghost story. To avoid any sort of backlash from our pirate mates, I needed him to convince them that my story was pure jest and spun for their amusement only. In a serious manner, he questioned what my plans would be if the crew decided that he was lying to them, and the appearance of the Black Monk was actually deemed as my fault. I responded that I had total faith in his ability to convince our shipmates of the truth.

As the evening approached, Powder Monkey suddenly appeared at my side and signed that Long Tall Willie had convinced the crew that my ghost story was totally fictitious in nature. He signed that Long Tall Willie had managed to plant seeds of doubt concerning our illustrious leader with his very attentive audience. Questioning the Captain's motives for resurrecting this fairytale monster while we searched for viable prey was certainly highly perplexing in his judgment. Long Tall Willie had conjectured that perhaps the Captain just wished to prolong the charade a bit longer, given the preoccupation it seemed to have on his crew. Quoting the persuasive dwarf, Powder Monkey signed that his exact words were: "What is that rascal attempting to do, scare us poor pirates to death?".

After hearing my friend's news, I made my way topside to check on my delirious patient. As I approached, I was met by a seriously concerned Lion who had been keeping watch over our commander for the better part of the afternoon. Lion informed me that the Captain's sanity and demeanor had disintegrated the entire time. He further divulged that the Captain had also been copiously consuming brandy, but seemed far from being considered drunk. Deathly afraid of the approaching night and the darkness it would spawn, Captain Shivvers had ordered wood from the galley stove to be delivered topside so that a fire could be built to prevent the Black Monk from making an unwanted appearance. I confided in Lion that such a request was highly unusual and quite delusional, since fire was a mortal enemy to any wooden ship. Nodding his total assent, Lion reported that he believed that the illness was responsible for making the Captain as "crazy as a blind-drunk pirate in a whorehouse full of naked trollops". I then asked whether these insane rambling had been heard by anyone other than him. He sadly acknowledged that the Captain's rants had been heard by a number of crewmen. Thanking his for his valued assistance, I sent him below to get some food and rest, while I took on the duty of guarding Captain Shivvers from harming himself. Urging me to be extremely cautious, Lion turned and made his way below to gratefully follow my advice.

Approaching Captain Shivvers, I could see that he was indeed in very poor shape. His face carried a deathly white pallor, and his blood rimmed eyes were in constant nervous motion. His body was taught and shaking furiously like a flapping sail in the midst of a sudden strong gale. Recognizing my presence, he questioned if I had spied the cursed Black Monk. Whispering now, I confided that while I had not seen the evil spirit, I was convinced that it would not be very long before he would make his demonic presence known. Cautioning him to continue his watchful vigil, I went about a cursory examination for the sole benefit of the topside crew, which were now monitoring every movement that our raving leader made.

A few hours into my vigil, Lion made an unexpected visit to check on the Captain's condition. Noting that very little had changed since his departure, he questioned me on my thoughts on handling the matter. In my most serious and concerned voice, I informed Lion that I was at a total loss on how to further treat our leader, since I had never experienced this type of illness at any time in my past. Continuing, I informed Lion that I was very much concerned with the detrimental effects Captain Shivvers' ravings were having on the crew in general. While I was completely sure that my campfire ghost story would have no lingering negative effects on any of us, I was now very worried that my tale had served to create a very lasting impression on our vulnerable and delirious leader.

In a whispered conspiratorial tone, I confided to Lion that these insane ravings of our leader might actually attract an evil spirit to the *Midnight Crow*. After making this admission, I made the customary sign-of-the-cross to evoke protection as well as to prove to the quartermaster that I did not relish the thought of actually being haunted by any sort of evil spirit. Once done, I moved away from his side and issued a series of bloodcurdling wails and shrieks sure to attract the interest of everyone onboard. As I finished my performance, we both were startled by a loud commotion emanating from somewhere below us. As we both glanced around with shocked expressions, there was an explosion of crewmembers furiously scrambling their way up from the lower decks led by Powder Monkey. We could both see the haunted facial expressions of our crewmates as they reached our position. Lion immediately demanded an explanation from the nearest pirates for their sudden flight. Speaking in unison, the sailors reported that the Black Monk had just been heard prowling the lower decks of the ship. You see, all Powder Monkey had to do was convey his recent sighting of the black creature belowdecks to a few terrified crewmembers and the panicked tars provided further imagined certification of the fantasy eventually forcing a stampede to the topdeck to avoid confrontation with the horrid cannibalistic fiend.

Realizing that the crew was on the verge of group panic, Lion took control of the situation, ordering the formation of search parties to discover the source of the recent mysterious noise. Hiding my absolute delight, I volunteered to join one of these groups to fully investigate the recently experienced caterwauling.

At the same time, Captain Shivvers issued a low mournful wail of complete alarm and panic upon hearing the disastrous news that the demon had truly invaded our ship. Blubbering and sputtering almost complete nonsense, he ordered his loyal crew to abandon ship immediately. With this ridiculous announcement, he ran to the nearest rail and prepared to launch himself into the dark sea. Lion ordered the nearest pirates to subdue their leader before he could attempt his suicidal plunge. In all, it took seven strong crewmembers to restrain the

Captain from his maniacal efforts. Lion then ordered more pirates to go below and fetch stout ropes to bind the Captain from head-to-toe before he caused serious injury to himself. Once this order was executed, the Captain continued his furious struggles to escape, as he cursed and swore unspeakable epitaphs and threats to us all for preventing his desperate escape. Lion, realizing the adverse effects the Captain's words were having on the crew, ordered our commander to be tightly gagged and relocated back to his cabin until he regained his senses. Captain Shivvers was hauled like a flopping fish to his cabin and securely tied to his bunk for the wellbeing of the entire ship.

Chapter 14: First Prize Taken

With the Captain sequestered in his cabin trussed from head-to-foot, I was able to relax more than I had for quite some time. Returning to my cabin, I fell into my bunk and slept quite well. As morning dawned, I made my way back to the Captain's quarters to check on my patient. As I had suspected, the belladonna laced brandy was beginning to wear off, and it was evident that the Captain's vicious and dishonest temperament was swiftly resurfacing. Prior to my visit, I had concocted a series of harmless herbs that I had brought along for this very reason. As I prepared the mixture with some fresh water, our leader questioned warily what medicines I had been utilizing to relieve his frightful symptoms. Responding innocently, I retorted that my remedy included a series of natural herbs that, judging by his present condition, seemed to have a positive effect in battling his dreaded illness. Nodding in uncertain agreement, he called for Lion to join us. When the Turk appeared, the Captain invited him to share in the mixture I had manufactured. Sensing no danger, Lion quickly quaffed the proffered liquid in two huge gulps. So as to give the concoction time to work, Captain Shivvers questioned Lion on the crew, weather and current sea conditions.

After a lengthy discussion in which Lion seemed to exhibit no visible reaction to my herbal medicine, the Captain reluctantly drank down a portion of the potion. Again sensing no real change to his behavior, he gratefully quaffed the remainder of the medicine. After doing so, he questioned Lion on whether any sign of prey had been spotted. Receiving a negative to his anxious query, he ordered Lion to continue searching and to report back the moment a prospective quarry was sighted. Before releasing his quartermaster, the Captain demanded to be freed of the bonds securing him. Glancing in my direction for formal confirmation, I nodded my silent approval. With a sharp knife extracted from his belt, Lion freed our leader in a tentative and very hesitant manner, given the Captain's wild antics of the previous evening. Once freed and acting much like his old self, Lion breathed a sigh of relief, saluted and exited the cabin to fulfill his orders.

Turning in my direction, the wily rogue inquired exactly what my prognosis was on his illness. Taking a moment to ponder, I responded that I was certain of a few conclusions. Firstly, I informed our leader that I was now sure that Strumpet Janie had passed her dreaded pox on to him, given his strange symptoms and actions over the past few days. Continuing, I divulged that I was also certain that his condition would deteriorate over time. Lastly, I appraised him that our meager medical supplies aboard the *Midnight Crow* were not sufficient to affect a cure. Nodding his understanding, he asked what actions I would recommend concerning his predicament. Responding without hesitation, I answered that he required intense medical assistance and treatment that I believed only existed in large civilized centers like London or Paris. Once again thanking me for my opinions, he casually dismissed me and commanded that I return later to continue my ministrations.

As I headed back to my quarters, I heard the topman sing out that a sail had been sighted in the distance. Since I was fully against participating in piracy from the very moment I had boarded this floating madhouse, I found this news extremely depressing. Making my way to the maindeck, I discovered that the majority of my shipmates shared my curiosity, as we all crowded around attempting to gain a glimpse of our potential prey. As I glanced around, I spied Captain Shivers making his tentative way to the ship's side with his telescope clutched firmly in his hands. Taking a long look at our new neighbor, the Captain ordered Lion to continue to shadow her to determine their reaction to our presence prior to taking action. Realizing that our cat-and-mouse game might continue for some time, the crew began to disband to ready their weapons should the opportunity turn favorable.

After a period of standing watch, Lion reported to the Captain that the vessel appeared to be a merchantman flying Dutch colors. Further, he informed our leader that the ship had taken steps to flee, since it appeared that they carried little armament to defend against attack. At this news, the Captain ordered our ship into battle-mode and chaotic preparations were begun throughout the ship. Our course was duly altered, the cannons loaded and primed, the majority of the crew reported to the maindeck with weapons readied, and our band was assembled. Rum hogsheads were delivered topside to spirit up the crew, and the chase for our first prize was officially underway. As the rum was freely distributed and thirstily consumed, I could sense the wild-eyed excitement that was building all around me. The band broke into a series of lively military tunes, which for the most part left me with a confused and disoriented state. In fact, this cacophony of noise was quite distracting for all of us. Personally, it never appeared to achieve its intended purpose of eliciting pure terror amongst our prey. As we drew closer and closer, we could all see that the Dutch trader had little choice but to surrender. A broadside warning delivered by our cannons assured our victory as our grappling hooks were unleashed in a furious wave of aggression.

As predicted, the Dutch prey took no action to prevent its capture and surrendered totally without firing a single shot. Once we had gained total control, Captain Shivvers made his way topside, but I could sense that his movements were quite irregular. I concluded that our dear Captain had partaken in a wee bit of liquid courage from his trusty brandy supply. Acting strictly in the role of interested observer, I also made my way aboard the prize to watch the proceedings first-hand.

The Captain and officers of the vessel had been separated from the rest of the crew when I arrived. Our Captain was in the process of interviewing his rival as I drew near. Moving closer, I heard Captain Shivvers demand the location of all hidden loot aboard his new prize. The Dutch Captain, terrified by the savages who had invaded his ship, was having a difficult time answering the vicious queries thrown his way. Finally mustered enough strength, he responded in pitiful English that his ship carried very little cargo and no hidden booty. This answer did sit well with our Captain, now shouting and screaming at the cowed officer to reveal his secrets or perish. Under the influence of the belladonna brandy, Captain Shivvers was again resuming his past role as a crazed and deranged lunatic. Glancing over at Lion, I could see the confusion and concern on his face as the mindless interrogation continued.

Suddenly with eyes flashing absolute madness, he questioned the petrified Dutchman on where he was hiding the demonic specter called the Black Monk. Our crew was stunned into total silence, as they gazed and gawked at one another in utter bewilderment. The Dutch Captain now utterly confounded, responded that he had absolutely no idea what he was now being asked, since he carried no clergymen aboard his vessel. Angered beyond reason, our deranged Captain drew his cutlass and proceeded to deliver a vicious strike that severed the poor creature's right arm. Once accomplished, Captain Shivvers again questioned the grievously wounded officer on the location of the Black Monk. Receiving an identical response, our mad Captain ended the Dutchman's life with a savage cutlass strike that all but decapitated him. Sensing that the situation was now out of control, Lion ordered several of our men to restrain our delirious Captain before he proceeded to slaughter the entire Dutch crew. This task was accomplished by six of our members, as Captain Shivvers continued to scream that he knew that the Dutchmen was lying about the demon's presence.

Shrieking an almost inhuman wail, our Captain was dragged back aboard the *Midnight Crow*, and once again restrained in his cabin. Lion immediately assumed command. Questioning each of the remaining officers in a precise manner, Lion came to the eventual conclusion that the junior officers were intentionally not privy to their Captain's secrets. When their Captain was brutally slain, his secrets went with him to Davy Jones Locker. Aware of this painful truth, Lion barked two simple orders. The first bore the officers and any dissenting crewmembers into a lowered longboat without oars, sail or their clothes and set them adrift to face the merciless sea. The second sent his ravenous pirates to sack and plunder the trader. With wild jubilant whoops and savage yells, they were off like a pack of wild hounds on the scent of prey. They literally tore the ship asunder stopping their mindless and wanton destruction just short of sinking her. While they never located any serious plunder, they managed to procure small worthwhile items as they made their ruinous rounds. To their utter dismay, they discovered that the now deceased Dutch Captain was telling the honest truth about the cargo for none existed. They did discover some black ivory in the form of ten African slaves shackled together in the hold. Eventually freeing them from their hull-secured brackets, they dragged the sun-blinded troop onto the maindeck for inspection.

As these poor devils were escorted topside, I had the chance to appraise them. The first thing that struck me was the utter defiance displayed by the entire group. In the face of harsh piratical tyranny, they seemed totally unconcerned, as if nothing really mattered. The second was the overall size and muscular development of each and every member of this shackled band. They were certainly warriors, as their physical presence and demeanor trumpeted. The group differed to one individual, who I assumed to be their leader. The man was truly enormous with tightly corded and bulging muscles. While not quite as large as our own quartermaster, this giant was not very far off. He sported a bald scalp complete with strange looking tattoos that gave him a very war-like appearance. The other distinctive feature was his eyes, which were a vivid green color and radiated pure intelligence. It was my understanding that each of these men would eventually be given an opportunity to join our pirate rabble, but Lion wisely withheld making any decisions until more was known of the group. If they proved unsatisfactory or troublesome, the simple solution was a trip to the slave auctioneer's block at any one of the accommodating islands surrounding us.

Since the ten slaves were the only real cargo of the merchantman, the prize was judged to be inferior in terms of value. The rape of the Dutch ship took another hour before the disgruntled pirates returned to the *Midnight Crow*. The ten warriors were sequestered in our hold. Lion ordered two pirates back to the Dutch vessel in order to set her aflame. As soon as these two rouges had scampered back aboard and the grappling lines severed, we could all view the brilliant flames that were devouring our disappointing prey.

When the ship disappeared from sight, Lion appeared at my side to ask if I would kindly check on the condition of our Captain. Making my way to his quarters, I could hear his muted wails and cries. Inside, I found Booby Bird in a terrified state as he guarded over his bound and gagged charge. Relieving the now grateful pirate, I inspected our Captain more closely. Undoing the gag stuffed in his mouth, I was greeted by the same inhuman wails that had marked his hasty departure from the captured Dutchman. Realizing that it would be hours before he regained a semblance of sanity, I stuffed the gag back into place and hurried back to Lion's side to make my report. Keeping this communication terse, I informed Lion that the Captain was suffering from a relapse of his disease. From his odd behavior, I announced that I expected this recent bout of insanity to last for several more hours before our dear commander would return to us. In the meantime, I recommended that he remain bound and gagged.

Lion once again questioned if I thought I had the skill necessary to cure the poor unfortunate. Shaking my head sadly, I informed Lion that this strange malady was well beyond anything I had ever encountered. Lion agreed, inquiring what I thought we should do given the intensity and resulting madness that the disease seemed to incite. I stated that I had strongly urged the Captain to search for a cure with more competent medical professionals on land. Understanding my meaning, Lion asked that I keep this conversation strictly between us until he had a chance to think the matter over. Promising my silence, I left Lion's side. Meanwhile, my crewmates had decided to drown their massive disappointment in spirits, and I knew it would not be very long before they all would be stumbling and mumbling incoherently throughout the ship.

After a brief time, I was once again summoned to Lion's side on the quarterdeck. As I reached him, I could see that the weighty responsibilities of commanding the *Midnight Crow* was causing him much worry and consternation. He confided that he had made a decision to return to Guadeloupe to allow the Captain to disembark and seek proper medical care. I agreed with his decision, which seemed to provide the Turk instant relief. Lion then informed me that when we reached our intended destination that the crew needed to vote for a new leader. He then surprised me by informing me that he was not interested in the position, since he felt the role was far too onerous for his liking. Giving me a long appraising stare, he confessed that he believed that the crew would appoint the appropriate leader when the time was right.

Changing subjects, he inquired if I would join him in the interrogation of the ten slaves. He admitted that he required my language skills to converse with the black savages. He also conceded that he respected my thoughts and opinions and felt strongly that I could assist him in making the right decisions about the fate of these captives. Smiling, I announced that I would be pleased to provide any support he might require in this matter.

To properly interrogate the Africans, Lion had their leader unshackled and brought up alone for questioning. Sending several pirates down to the hold to execute this command, Lion and I awaited their return. The party finally emerged from below with their prisoner under gunpoint.

Upon reaching us, Lion asked the man for his name. Clearly unable to understand the question, Lion turned to me in frustration and asked if I would attempt to communicate with the man. Glancing at the man's fiery expression, I repeated the question in French. Once again, he shrugged that he did not understand the request. At that moment, he blurted out in Dutch that he hoped someone aboard spoke the language. I answered that indeed I did, which brought a smile to his face for the first time since capture. Switching to Dutch, I asked him for his name. He responded that his people called him Tiger Eyes, and that he was the son of a tribal chieftain. As he spoke, I related his answers to Lion. Lion then requested that Tiger Eyes relate his story.

Tiger Eyes informed me that he had come from a small tribe of people who were in constant conflict with their neighbors. His tribe was finally overcome by a much larger one that had been assisted by Dutch weapons of death which he called firesticks. Upon defeat, in which his entire family with the exception of a younger sister had been slaughtered, he and the surviving members of the tribe were bound and marched a very long way to a town on the Great Sea. This town was run by Dutch traders, who specialized in the buying and selling of humans. Once there, his people were put to work building a Dutch missionary hospital for the desperate needs of captured humans prior to their shipment to many locations across the Great Sea. Following the orders from his new masters, he happened to gain the notice of a young Dutch missionary, who recognized the raw intelligence in the young warrior. This good man taught him how to speak the Dutch language night after night following the finalization of his daily toil. Since the completion of the hospital took many months, the missionary had ample time to instill this new and strange sounding language on his charge. When the hospital was finally finished, Tiger Eyes and the remainder of his people were crammed into a large sailing ship and sent for a long voyage across the Great Sea.

At this point, Tiger Eyes became almost pensive, as if waging an internal struggle that prevented him from continuing his story. Sensing that he needed a moment to come to terms, I used this time to bring Lion up-to-date. Having imparted a summary, I was pleased to find that Tiger Eyes was again composed and ready to continue. He began by confiding that the voyage across the Great Sea was without a doubt the worst experience of his life.

He explained that the decks that housed them were cramped and confining. He indicated that the height of these slave decks were only as tall as the length of his arm. There was not enough space for even a small child to stand upright. Each transport was shackled to a neighbor at the wrist and ankle. His people were forced to occupy their coffin-like space lying side-by-side. What little air that reached them came from grated hatchways that also precluded escape attempts. While pisstubs were provided in various places on these confining decks, Tiger Eyes explained that the exertion and energy required to crawl over the numerous shackled pairs was deemed too burdensome by all. Therefore, they simply fouled themselves where they laid. Smiling sadly, he confessed that the stench of human waste, the odor of rotting dead corpses and the abundance of human sweat and body odors were much more than simply appalling.

Taking another moment, I related his words to Lion. Tiger Eyes continued by informing me that the only relief from the horrific conditions was the once-a-day maindeck feedings, weather permitting. To ensure no trouble occurred during this time, extra sailors were always present with loaded firesticks and cutlasses. This time also allowed the slave decks to be washed and aired. The next issue the transports faced was serious illness. Due to the inhuman living conditions and the extremely close confinement, sickness ran rampant. Since no medical treatment was provided, these insidious illnesses claimed one member of his group after another. The unfortunates who died were unshackled and dragged out to be dumped overboard to the delight of an army of hungry sharks tailing the ship.

Many individuals chose suicide over the horrendous living conditions. Tiger Eyes had observed many men and women attempt to jump overboard. These deluded souls were either stopped by their armed captors or greeted warmly and viciously by the hunting sea scavengers. Some of his people attempted to starve themselves, while others simply lost the will to live and wasted away. Overall, death was the only relief to this personal hell, and this escape route accounted for one in every four of his people which was both a staggering and sobering number!

Tiger Eyes then stated that he would never allow himself to be subservient to any man. Realizing that suicide was not the answer, he began plotting mutiny with his most trusted warriors. They understood that this course was extremely foolish, since none of them had any experience operating a ship. They decided to wait for the right time to stage their revolt. When the blackbird, slave ship to you landlubbers, was nearing the voyage's end and land had been spotted, Tiger Eyes and his mates made their move. During mealtime when the guards were lax, Tiger Eyes and his men revolted and took the ship, treating their captors to a deadly shark-infested saltwater bath.

Once in control, they began to blindly experiment with various equipment to navigate the ship. In reality, Tiger Eyes knew, that if his people failed or if the ship wrecked, that he and the remaining survivors could survive by swimming to shore. Laughing now for the first time, he confessed that they were indeed wretched sailors. Even though he had ordered a sharp watch kept on sailing activities during their daily feedings, this limited knowledge was woefully inadequate. As they attempted navigation, a dark shadow descended and they found themselves once again captured, but this time by pirates.

As this ravenous scum assembled his people on the maindeck, a sinister figure dressed in black came aboard the blackbirder to inspect his new prize. Tiger Eyes sensed the presence of pure evil reeking from the new arrival. Since the pirate leader spoke no common language, he used a series of crude signals to announce his intentions. His first order separated the men from the rest of the group. With his warriors surrounded by heathen pirates armed with firesticks and drawn cutlasses, the pirate leader signaled a child to step forward. When nobody obeyed his order, he drew his cutlass and beheaded the nearest child. Once accomplished, he again signaled for a child to step forward. This time his demand was met. At the same time, he shouted to several of his demons to tie a woman to the mainmast. He then roared another command and was rewarded with a fearsome whip which he thrust into the volunteering child's hands. He then signaled the terrified youngster to use the whip to lash the helpless woman at the mast. Once again the child disobeyed and paid dearly by losing its head.

The child's body was casually thrown over the side. Proceeding, the pirate leader signaled for yet another small victim. This time, the child was Tiger Eyes' younger sister. Watching helplessly, his sister was given the whip and signaled to whip the whimpering woman. Turning to gaze at her brother with cheeks running with tears, she obeyed the monster and lashed the woman several times. The black devil was not yet satisfied and ordered the girl to continue the punishment. Tiger Eyes' sister returned to her gruesome task, finally collapsing in hysterical tears when her assignment was completed. The suffering and bleeding woman was cut loose and heaved overboard leaving a trail of dripping blood in her wake. Well, Tiger Eyes informed me that this scenario occurred time-after-time until the last of the whipped women were thrown overboard to the sate the ceaseless appetites of the ravenous beasts.

At this point, Tiger Eyes required some time for composure. I utilized this break to relate the tale to Lion. I could see by the giant's saddened demeanor that the story affected him deeply. Fearing the truth on the perpetrator identity, Lion questioned if the warrior had yet mentioned his tormentor's name. Answering no, I turned to Tiger Eyes and asked if he knew the name of the black demon. Tiger Eyes responded that he really never learned the creature's name. All he could tell me was that the demon seemed to be named after some sort of vicious insect. Upon hearing this answer, I quickly asked if the pirate leader was wearing a mask. Tiger Eyes nodded furiously and begged to be told the villain's name. I responded that I was certain that he had encountered the pirate known as the Black Tarantula. With a grateful nod, Tiger Eyes declared that he intended to kill this black devil. Before he was returned to the hold, I unwittingly questioned him on the fate of the surviving children, not knowing the worst was yet to come. Appearing utterly devastated, Tiger Eyes whispered that all of the children were murdered in a most gruesome manner imaginable. With utter anguish and misery etched across his face, the rugged warrior whimpered that the children's agonized shrieks and high-pitched wails persisted for what seemed like an eternity. Once the pirate demon completed his unholy atrocities on the innocents, he unceremoniously dumped their desecrated and violated bodies overboard to appease the insatiable scavengers. Lion and his warriors were subsequently sold to an unscrupulous Dutch associate of the evil pirate. The new Captain intended to return the mutinous swine to the nearest Dutch authorities to collect a sizable reward. We had interrupted this journey. Thanking him for his honesty, Tiger Eyes was led back below to join his men and await his fate.

Lion and I agreed that the warriors should be granted freedom and given the chance to join our ranks. However, since neither of us was acting as commander, the decision of fate of these warriors rested in the hands of Captain Shivvers. Understanding that our skipper was clearly not up to making any type of rational or sane decision, Lion and I decided to wait for the right opportunity to discuss the matter with him. Informing Lion that I was headed down to the galley to eat, he answered that he would be most happy to join me in this endeavor as we made our way below in search of sustenance.

Chapter 15: New Recruits and Command Change

Upon entering the galley, we found it overcrowded as many of our fellows were intently listening to one of the new recruits from our Dutch prize. The rogue's name was Scuttle. He was a hunchback, who had been bragging that he was a master blacksmith as well as an exceptional cannonmaster. Quick with a smile and seemingly good natured, he divulged that he had been born a misshapen oddity and had been subjected to continual torment. He confided that turning a blind-eye to ridicule had proven to be his best defense. He stated that when he simply ignored the laughter directed his way that his tormentors generally ceased their jokes and snide remarks.

Born and raised in the English colony of Massachusetts, he had been taught the art of blacksmithing by his father. His early years were spent in relative comfort and joy until a fire destroyed their home killing his entire family. Despite his losses, he continued to toil at the family's forge to avoid reminiscing about the tragedy. Maturing, he fell in love with a young lass, who was quite ignorant of his strong feelings. Her father was a local farmer who relied on Scuttle's burgeoning blacksmithing skills to keep his farm running. As the years progressed, he watched in dismay as his beloved eventually made an awful choice for a husband, a son of a very influential banker. Scuttle confided that the love of spirits had a very terrible influence on the young husband, who began to take his anger and resentment out on his new bride whenever he was fully intoxicated. The young bride, fearing her husband and his influential friends attempted to secret this ugly situation, but her visible bruises and broken bones made this task exceedingly difficult.

Having nobody to turn to, the young woman found a sympathetic ear in Scuttle and poured out her marital problems to him. Scuttle stood silently by for the next five long years as he watched his love nearly beaten to death time and time again. Perplexed, he approached the young woman to ask if he could assist in ending her dreadful predicament. Shocked by his intentions, the woman forbade him from getting involved. Eventually, the worthless husband went too far one evening and murdered his young bride in a fit of alcoholic fury. Upon hearing the tragic news, Scuttle was despondent and blamed himself for allowing the travesty to go unreported. Given the father-in-law's exorbitant influence, the authorities ruled the girl's death purely accidental. One evening while Scuttle was enjoying a meal at a local tavern, he happened to overhear the murdering husband boasting to his cronies that he was far better off without the meddlesome bitch. Incensed beyond reason, Scuttle staggered out of the pub before his temper erupted.

At this point, Scuttle announced that he was suffering from a very dry palate and was duly rewarded with a full bottle of rum. Resuming, he explained that in order to avenge the heinous crime and at the same time keep his involvement discreet, he carefully plotted his revenge. Remembering the disastrous fire that had taken his family, he decided that this was the perfect calamity required to avenge his beloved. Following the stumbling drunk home, he confronted the villain just as he was entering his domicile. The young man was momentarily shocked by the savage accusations leveled by this pathetic specimen of a man. When surprise turned to rage, the drunkard physically attacked Scuttle for his uninvited involvement. Totally prepared, Scuttle beat the beast to death with his bare hands, carefully taking his time to deliver an inordinate amount of pain and suffering along the way. Once done, Scuttle placed the deceased blackguard in his bed and set fire to the house.

The incinerated body of the banker's son was discovered the very next day, and authorities ruled the matter an unfortunate accident. Scuttle, deep in shame and remorse, decided to seek a new life. Announcing his intentions to a few friends, he packed his meager belongings and moved to a coastal town in the English colony of Virginia, that boasted a new military fort in desperate need of a competent blacksmith. Scuttle was hired to serve as the fort's smithy soon after his arrival. Included in his responsibilities were the general maintenance and upkeep of the fort's mighty guns. During the next several years, he perfected his blacksmithing skills while becoming an unheralded expert with cannons of all types.

Taking a long swig of rum, Scuttle resumed. It seemed that one of the young fort officers formed a jealous hatred of Scuttle due to his burgeoning cannon expertise. This miscreant staged an accident that led to the detonation of the fort's powder magazine, killing more than a dozen young soldiers. As part of his nefarious plot, the jealous officer planted Scuttle's smithy tools nearby the location of the accident which caused suspicions to fall the hunchback's way. An extensive investigation ensued that eventually ruled the fort's disaster an accident. This pronouncement did Scuttle little good as he was summarily dismissed from his duties at the fort. Despondent and seeking a new start, Scuttle signed on with a merchant trading ship as a simple seaman. Adjusting to his new life at sea, disaster stuck once again in the form of pirates. His ship was attacked and destroyed by these thieves, and his only alternative was to go on the account or perish. Since that time, he had been forced to serve on a number of piratical ventures to his utter disdain.

After the conclusion of Scuttle's tale, I decided it was again time to pay our sickly Captain a visit. I found the sneaky rascal sitting up in his bed issuing a series of orders to Lion. He seemed to be gaining a semblance of his old self, which made me more than nervous to say the least. Lion hustled towards the cabin door to fulfill these new directives. As he passed, he gave me an exasperated look. Upon completing a series of tests, I announced that I believed that the pirate rogue had successfully weathered the latest bout of his malady. Nodding, he questioned my best guess on the timing for the next attack. I informed him that I had absolutely no idea, but reconfirmed that I still recommended that he required greater medical assistance than I could supply. Sneering, he informed me that he was quite aware that I had been cleverly plotting to oust him from his dear ship. Realizing that arguing the issue would be a waste, I confessed that I did not give a hoot one way or another for leadership of this ship of fools. Frustrated by his latest accusation, I announced that since he required no medical attention at the present that my job was finished.

Reaching the quarterdeck, I found Lion in a very serious mood. In a solemn voice, Lion informed me that the Captain had decided to sell the African warriors as slaves when we reached Guadeloupe. Additionally, Lion forewarned me that Captain Shivvers had also decided to get a second opinion on his condition and had wandered off to visit Doc's surgery. With a disinterested shrug, I informed Lion that our Captain had the right to consult anyone aboard concerning his health. Secondly, I told Lion that I believed the Captain's decision on the warriors was based solely on greed and certainly not logical thinking. Going further, I notified Lion that I was certain that these physically fit captives would serve our cause faithfully. Lion agreed, sadly stating that the Captain had the last and final say on the matter. Admitting to Lion that we were a long way from Guadeloupe, I bid the giant goodnight and began to make my way below. As I navigated down, I ran into a pale and shaken Captain Shivvers. Pointing his finger at me, he screamed that Doc knew absolutely nothing about medicine, as he had attempted to cover his body with bloodsucking leeches as a remedy for his poxed condition. Continuing his rage, he also howled that I was responsible for bringing the Black Monk aboard his ship. Snorting my derision, I calmly announced that the Black Monk story was nothing more than a fairytale. Going further, I pointed out that our bedevilment was his own fault since his own mindless preoccupation with this yarn had beckoned some sort of demonic phantom to haunt and badger us. Lastly, I assured him that Doc was the best medical man I had ever met and suggested that leeches might bring him some temporary relief from Strumpet Janie's pox. With a mincing smile, I wished him a peaceful night and made my way back to my cabin with his continued taunts and rants trailing my retreat.

Before attempting sleep, I decided to check on the well-being of Tiger Eyes and his men. Stopping by the galley, I signaled Powder Monkey to tote along some food to feed our hungry prisoners. Upon reaching them, I questioned Tiger Eyes on how they were coping with the damp and awful conditions of the hold. Smiling, he answered that current conditions were far better than those experienced on the blackbirder. He then confessed that he and his men were very hungry. As he made this announcement, Powder Monkey made his appearance and handed each of the men an empty bowl and then filled them with the vittles he had liberated from the galley. I located a barrel of water, which I rolled over to their side to accompany their meal.

Nodding thanks, Tiger Eyes suddenly stopped and stared intently at my wooden cross that had popped out of my shirt as I dragged the water barrel into position. In a hushed and reverent tone, he inquired how I had obtained the good luck charm. Deciding that honesty was best, I related my entire Voodou experience, including my meeting with my friend and protector, Papa Legba. As I narrated the adventure, his eyes went wider and wider with astonishment and awe. When I concluded, Tiger Eyes questioned if I had been completely truthful about this encounter. Laughing, I assured him that it would be quite an imaginative tale to create. I then responded in a serious tone that it was indeed the truth. Just like Rue, he quietly begged me to describe Papa Legba. Slowly and in full detail, I described my wizened friend along with his canine companion to my entranced listener. After providing the description, he quickly turned to his men and communicated a legion of words that had no meaning to me. After this exchange, the eyes of each of his warriors also underwent the same startling transformation as their leader. The entire group was staring at me with eerie awe-filled expressions.

Taken aback by their intense reactions, I questioned Tiger Eyes for the reason. Apologizing, he informed me that I was very special to merit such an important visit from this sacred *loa*. At that moment, I finally realized the truth of the matter. Rue had instructed me that Voodou rites had been brought over with the island's slaves from their African origins. Believing this to be the case, I questioned Tiger Eyes on Papa Legba's existence in their native religion. To my surprise, he answered my query in an almost exact replication of the one Rue had provided.

I explained to the warrior that Papa Legba had provided this wonderful talisman to keep me safe and protected. Further, I confessed that the kindly old man had instructed me to call upon his assistance in time of extreme need. Once again, Tiger Eyes translated my words to his men. When he finished, they all discussed the matter in their strange and rather harsh sounding language. Issuing a strong command that rendered them all mute; Tiger Eyes turned and informed me that their decision on the matter was both unanimous and unquestionable. At that moment, they all got down on their knees before me. Glancing over at Powder Monkey, I could see that he too was totally stunned by their strange actions. Peering down at Tiger Eyes, I questioned what he and his men were doing kneeling in the vermin-infested bilge water. Looking reverently at me, he announced that he and his men had just sworn a sacred oath to serve at my side for the remainder of their lives! He also announced that they were all willing to die carrying out any order I might give them.

Confused to the extreme, I questioned if this was some sort of jest. Shaking his head in a very serious manner, he responded that their solemn death oath was certainly not made in jest, but a lasting pledge of loyalty. I calmly articulated my humble acceptance, and ordered he and his men to rise. Smiling now, I announced my gratitude for their professed loyalty and willingness to obey my commands. I explained that the Captain wished to sell each of them back into bondage. This statement brought a look of tight concern to Tiger Eyes' face. Continuing, I articulated that I had other plans for them and that in no way would I allow them to be resold as slaves. I then requested their patience on setting matters right. With a look of utmost gratitude, he communicated my words to his men and they all expressed their mumbled thanks. Clapping Tiger Eyes on the shoulder, I announced that I had work to accomplish but would return soon to grant them freedom.

On the way back to my cabin, I filled Powder Monkey in on the gist of the conversation with the African warriors. For the most part, he was as mystified as I by the warriors' actions we had just witnessed. Stopping me, he questioned how I planned to make good on my promise to Tiger Eyes and his men. Winking, I signed that I would just have to think of an answer and continued my way to my cabin.

The next morning, I toiled on the ship's navigation and made my way to the Captain's cabin to report my course recommendations. I found our leader in the same foul mood as the previous night. He was issuing more orders to Lion as I knocked and entered his domain. Explaining the reason for my visit, I provided my recommendations in a succinct manner and quickly turned to make my departure. As I was about to open his door, he inquired if I also had any parting medical recommendations to offer, since I would no longer be involved in treating his malady. Realizing that this was my opportunity, I confessed that I had one final recommendation on his illness, avoid all alcoholic beverages until the disease passed. In my heart I knew that this advice would be summarily disregarded because of his fondness for hot spirits. I hoped that my drastic recommendation would drive him to imbibe in even greater quantities as a means to further spite me. Listening intently, he scoffed at my advice and informed me that he would sooner die than stop drinking. With a noncommittal shrug, I announced that it was his life and his decision and that my services were officially at an end.

Well, it did not take very long for my ploy to have its effect. Summoned to the quarterdeck by Lion, I was informed that despite my warnings Captain Shivvers had been drinking rather heavily again. The result was devastating as he roamed the ship in a strange and disjointed manner. In a state of manic anxiousness, he was posing strange queries to any member of the crew he happened upon on this dysfunctional journey. Convinced that the illness was driving him utterly insane, every crewmember made an attempt at avoiding the wild-eyed raving lunatic. In desperation, Lion questioned what I thought we should do. Once again shrugging indifference, I repeated my original prognosis that I believed the befuddled fool required specialized medical care. Given his unwillingness to comply, I suggested that Lion assign a crewmember to closely follow the Captain's movements to avoid any disastrous actions on the part of our highly unstable leader.

Nodding, he ordered Jumping Jimmy to shadow the Captain and keep him out of harms way. I also told the quartermaster that we needed to get some food into the Captain to provide his body the proper nutrients to combat the illness. Again agreeing, he asked me to have the galley prepare a special meal for our sick leader. Saluting, I hurried to the galley to help prepare one last meal for my devious enemy. Stopping by my cabin, I procured an additional amount of belladonna and continued on my mission of mercy. I deposited the additional deadly herb into the fish stew that had ben prepared for our dear Captain. Carefully delivering the meal to Lion, he ordered a few strong men to locate and return our leader to his cabin. The sputtering and spitting degenerate was summarily dragged back to his cabin and force fed the delicious meal that I had delivered. Taking my leave, I made my way to my cabin to await the start of fun.

About an hour later, I heard a loud commotion occurring on the topdeck. As I reached the spot, I witnessed a very strange sight. Captain Shivvers was high in the ship's riggings completely nude, shouting and screaming obscenities like a raving madman. As I gazed up, I could see that he was leading a merry chase with six of our pirate comrades in close pursuit. Moving over to Lion's side, I expressed my deepest concern that our esteemed leader seemed bent on self-destruction. Lion confessed that the situation had reached a critical stage, and that it was time to begin contemplating his replacement. Glancing up, I watched in horror as the Captain attacked the nearest rescuer and proceeded to viciously kick the individual away from him. In the process, the rescuing tar lost his grip on the ropes and plummeted down to the maindeck with a sickening crunch. As several of us rushed over to check the condition of the fallen pirate, I was saddened to the extreme to discover that the dead sailor was Charley Crowsfeet.

Infuriated, I informed Lion that the remaining pirates needed to be recalled before any more deaths or injuries occurred. I stated that I would ascend the riggings and attempt to talk our mad Captain down. Issuing a surprised look, Lion questioned my decision to enter the chase. As I began to explain, a shout rang out from above which drew both of our gazes back to the Captain. Our crazed leader was now severing several of the lines that surrounded him for unknown reasons. Informing Lion that the situation was beyond critical, I began my swift assent toward the lunatic's position. As I passed members of the rescue party, I ordered them to return to the maindeck before someone else was injured or killed. With looks of relief, they began their descent to the safety of the maindeck. Continuing on to Captain Shivvers, I realized that he was certainly beyond my help given his nonsensical gibbering, hooting and screaming. As I neared, I could hear him strangely humming to himself between his mad caterwauling. Calling his name to gain his attention, I quickly realized that he was well past recognizing anything or anybody. He was absolutely stark raving mad!

Suddenly, he sensed my presence. Smiling, he proclaimed that he would destroy me. Naming me the Black Monk, he immediately scrambled and clawed his way towards me. As he closed on my position, I used my *special voice* and issued a series of low wails and moans that halted his advance. Moving his head from side-to-side in a jerking manner, he searched for the source of the haunting sounds. Failing, he again focused on me and issued a bloodcurdling scream of both frustration and blind rage and resumed his advance. When he was nearly upon me, I issued my last desperate attempt to stop him. Utilizing my *special voice*, I sent a whispered threat of damnation in Strumpet Janie's hissing voice, making it sound like the dead doxy was directly behind him. Spinning to face his ghostly enemy, the delirious fool lost his hold on the ropes and plummeted down into the bright blue sea. I continued to watch the spot he had entered for signs of his surfacing. After several minutes, I located his body rising to the surface. From my towering view, I judged that his fate was not very promising at all. Lion ordered a boat dispatched to fetch the corpse as I descended back to the safety of the maindeck. Captain Shivvers body was quickly retrieved from the sea, but he was long past any sort of assistance. He was as lifeless as a gutted mackerel!

The departure of our nefarious leader brought a sudden pall over the entire ship. Both bodies were prepared in nautical tradition including the thirteen stitches. Lion came to my cabin and asked if I would preside over the somber ceremony, since he was totally uncomfortable with Christian religious rites. When I agreed, he thanked me several times prior to making his departure. At dawn, we all gathered on the maindeck to wish a final farewell to our comrades. Citing several Bible quotes from memory and providing a very compassionate eulogy for both sailors, we sent their bodies over the side to enter Davy Jones Locker. After the ceremony, the crew utilized the occasion to drink to insensibility, nothing really novel for these rum-soaked salts! As the crew sought their alcohol oblivion, I took the opportunity to secure Captain Shivvers brandy supply and launched the half empty hogshead off the quarterdeck and into the sea undetected.

That night, Lion approached to inform me that the *Midnight Crow* could not continue to operate without a Captain. He knew that I had resisted turning pirate from the very start, but begged me to seriously consider the opportunity of leadership for the good of all aboard. Informing the Turk that I would only consider the role of Captain under my own terms, he swiftly questioned what they entailed. Firstly, I revealed that I would only assume captaincy if the ship operated under a formal *Lettre of Marque* from the Governor of Guadeloupe. Smiling, he mentioned that obtaining such a document would not prove very difficult as long as the proper incentives were provided. My second demand was to revise the ship's bylaws under which we operated. Shrugging, he confessed that I could certainly alter these rules to suit my needs, but getting the rogues aboard to abide by them would prove much more difficult. Understanding his meaning, I informed him that I was more than capable at seeing the amendments obeyed as long as I had him at my side. With that, I divulged that I would not take command unless he agreed to serve as my First Mate. Suppressing a sprouting smile, he answered that he would be honored in that regard. Lastly, I announced that the African prisoners now shackled in the hold would be given the opportunity to join our crew. With slight concern on his face, he confessed that the slaves were our only profit for our present voyage. In a very plaintive voice, he questioned how he and his mates could afford needed liberty without adequate funds. Noting his dilemma, I promised that I would provide the necessary funds from my own pocket so that our crew could thoroughly enjoy liberty. This final act sealed the bargain and I was voted the acting Captain of the *Midnight Crow* that very afternoon to the rousing cheers and well wishes of the entire crew.

Having been granted the supreme authority over the ship and crew, I called for the African warriors to be brought up from below with their restraints removed. As Tiger Eyes and his men were ushered to my side, they squinted furiously due to the effects of the tropical sun's brightness. Finally assembled before me, I spoke to Tiger Eyes, summing up the changes that had just occurred, pointing out that I was now in command of the vessel. Under these circumstances, I gave him and his warriors the opportunity to be a vital part of our crew. Barking out the news to his followers, they all kneeled before me swearing their undivided allegiance and loyalty once again!

Chapter 16: A New Captain Emerges

It was a most difficult challenge adjusting to my new title of Captain. I realized that I was quite young to merit such a prestigious honor, and promised myself that I would perform my new duties in both an honorable and fair-minded manner. I also understood that the crew was depending on me to provide for their wellbeing and protection. I vowed that I would strive to ensure that this objective was faithfully accomplished. I moved my belongings into my new cabin after cleansing the room of Captain Shivvers meager possessions. In the process, I discovered a secret hiding place that our former leader had utilized to stash his stolen loot. His concealed cache was indeed prodigious and included all manner of coin, rare jewels and a horde of precious gold and silver bars, a veritable king's fortune! As I added my meager coin supply to this significant treasure, I knew that I could provide for my crew's liberty needs for an eternity. Finished with the moving process, I roamed the ship taking a mental inventory of all required changes and vital additions that needed to be made. As I made my way around, I was greeted warmly and given many well-wishes by my crewmates. Returning to my cabin, I summoned Scuttle the Hunchback and Powder Monkey.

In no time at all, both sailors appeared at my door. Warmly greeting them, I informed them that I had a couple of matters that I needed to discuss. I first proclaimed that I respected each of their proven prowess with formidable armament. In this regard, I gave them orders to study our current gun inventory and to report back with their recommendations for strengthening our overall firepower. They nodded their clear understanding of my directive. I then explained that once this list was finished that I would provide the necessary funds so that they could properly purchase and fit these added munitions. By the gleaming look in each of their eyes, I knew that they would both thoroughly enjoy the orders I had just given.

Finally, I came to the subject of grenados, which had been so very effective in defeating the savages on Pig Island. While I believed that these vicious devices were the future of close-encounter naval warfare, I was slightly disappointed in the results we had initially achieved. Because of the unpredictable nature of coconut housings, I informed both powder specialists that I needed them to develop a far nastier and more destructive grenado utilizing metal in place of a fruit shells. Realizing my ultimate objective, they both smiled and agreed to act as a functioning team to turn my dream into a nightmarish reality. I ordered them to begin working out the plans prior to our stop on Guadeloupe. Once anchored, I commanded them to procure the lease of the finest smithy on the island to produce these lethal devices for our use. Providing them with a sizable bag of coin, I issued a firm warning that our clandestine operation must remain secret. They both understood my intent and promised to fulfill each of the orders I had given. Saluting, they both rose to take their leave. Before exiting, I asked Scuttle to remain so that I could discover a little more about his past history.

As Scuttle sat down, I informed him that I had overheard his life's tale a few nights ago. Based on this, I divulged that I had a few questions for him. Swallowing away his anxiousness, he hesitantly questioned what I wanted to know. I answered that I understood that he had been forced on the Dutch slaver to assist in the shackling of the African mutineers. I also confessed that I had heard him relate to our crew that he had been pressed onto the Dutchman from his previous ship because of his expertise with iron implements of restraint. He simply nodded his assent to my statements. Continuing, I questioned him on the name of his former commander. With eyes twitching and with a voice that shook with trepidation, he answered that the rogue's name was the Black Tarantula. I then commanded him to regale me with his first-hand knowledge of this notorious brute. Expressing a look of torment, he responded that he had spent less than a few short months on the monster's ship, but would divulge all that he had observed during this time.

He began by declaring that the Tarantula's ship's name was the *Spider's Web*. For the most part, Scuttle's information proved to be of little value, since he had been confined to the gundeck of the *Spider's Web* to ensure the proper functioning and maintenance of the ship's cannons. However, he was able to provide a detailed inventory of the ship's armament and specific tactics the sea demon normally employed when on the attack. From his knowledge, I realized that our ship was far out-gunned by my enemy. I also learned that this insidious marauder was not opposed to firing directly upon unsuspecting prey, unconcerned with the amount of damage inflicted. This was especially true anytime a foolish captain made the mistake of attempting a defense against the fiend. Remembering one incident, Scuttle imparted that the monster blew a ship into splinters as punishment for sending a defensive barrage against his advances. Scuttle also related that the demon consistently invented new and unique methods of torture each time he was granted the opportunity. Scuttle was quick to point out that outsider's fears were nothing in comparison to the day-to-day dread experienced by each crewmember aboard the *Spider's Web*. Driven by witnessing the inhuman treatment of captured unfortunates, the crew did everything in their power to please their monstrous leader for fear of becoming the madman's next victim. During his short time aboard, he had observed no less than seven crew suicides. In a terrified voice, he explained that these poor tars were so desperate to end their living nightmare that they took their own lives in the most imaginative and horrid ways!

Scuttle was now sweating profusely recalling the absolute hell he had experienced during his two short months of servitude. Switching focus, I mentioned that I had been told by reliable witnesses that the Black Tarantula had an unbelievable obsession for a young female singer from Saint Domingue. He answered that the ship's scuttlebutt mirrored my information. I then innocently asked if the Black Tarantula had found his French songbird. Shaking his head, Scuttle confided that the hunt for this woman continued. Stopping his narrative abruptly because he recalled a pertinent detail, Scuttle informed me that a close friend of the woman's had been captured and hauled aboard to face the monster's creative questioning. At the mention of this friend, my entire body went rigid anticipating the worst. Interrupting Scuttle's dialogue, I questioned him on this individual's name. He answered that he was never privy to the poor lad's name since the entire incident was rather short in nature. When I queried him on a description, he answered that the boy was rather ordinary in appearance with the exception of his red hair and crossed eyes. At that moment, I knew that the devil had taken my old friend Grommet Jemme in his unending quest to find Rue!

Managing to get myself under control, I quizzed Scuttle on any further details he could remember about this encounter. Scuttle confessed that the treatment of this young man was of a most horrible nature. The interrogation took place in three separate phases, each becoming more brutal as the session continued. The lad was first forced to dance a bloody hornpipe jig on a bed of broken glass for failing to reveal the French songbird's location. Even given this tortuous treatment, the boy refused to divulge any information to his pirate captor. Entering into phase two, he was subjected to the loss of his ears, thumbs and most of his toes. Once this insane punishment was carried out, the damaged youth was then forced to cannibalize his own appendages as punishment for his silence. Scuttle informed me that the brave boy continued to refuse providing the Black Tarantula with answers. Incensed beyond reason, the fiend ordered the lad brought to his quarters to experience phase three of the interrogation. Scuttle and the crew were not privy to this very private affair, but were nonetheless subjected to the boy's piteous screams and cries for the next few hours. Eventually the young man's desecrated and mutilated body was hauled up to the maindeck and unceremoniously dumped overboard. Since nothing more was ever said, Scuttle was unaware if the Black Tarantula was able to elicit the information he desperately sought.

Issuing a silent prayer for the soul of my deceased friend, I dismissed Scuttle so he could begin to collaborate with Powder Monkey on their crucial assignments. I then called for South Seas Tan to join me for a few words. Tan arrived and made a low bow and signed that he was delighted that I had been appointed Captain. Thanking him for his support and loyalty, I asked this hand-to-hand combat expert to conduct a series of lessons for our untrained crewmates. Informing me that he would be most pleased to carry out my request, he hesitated and questioned if I really believed that the crew would submit willingly to such training. Winking, I revealed that I would ensure their participation through simple bribery. Requesting an explanation, I divulged that I planned to award a gold doubloon to each crewman who he deemed had mastered his lessons. Stunned by the sheer generosity of the offer, he replied in sign that he was sure that he would have a slew of willing students for his new school. I signaled to Tan that I would make the announcement on the formation of his training school and its sweet reward later that day.

My next visitor was Long Tall Willie. After exchanging pleasantries, I got right down to business. Like Tan, I commissioned the combative dwarf to utilize his abilities with blades to train his fellow crewmen. As I had explained to Tan, I was willing to reward each sailor who graduated from his school with a gold doubloon! Smiling, the merry dwarf confessed that he was sure that his special combat school would prove a grand success. I informed the diminutive warrior that I would announce the opening of his special classes later that afternoon. With a mock salute sent my way, Long Tall Willie skipped merrily out of the cabin to begin preparations.

Realizing that several more special instruction classes were also required, I decided to wait before I made any further plans. In the back of my mind, I knew that Powder Monkey and Scuttle would need to train additional crewmembers to become experts with our guns, as well as making them proficient in the handling and throwing of the deadly grenados that they had been commissioned to manufacture. Additionally, I knew that musketeer teams led by Lion, a deadly marksman himself, were required to be trained properly. Realizing that all of these important skills were not immediately pressing, I planned to commence this training at a later time so as not to completely overload my new crew. You see, I was not preparing our ship for piracy but rather for war!

Later that afternoon, I made my announcements of the formalized training classes planned for the entire crew. My news was met with some grumbling and groans, until I mentioned the enticing reward offered for their graduation from these combat classes. Upon hearing this news, the entire crew broke out in several spirited hurrahs. As I was about to return to my cabin, a topman sang out that Guadeloupe had been spotted. Calling Lion to my side, I instructed him that we would be spending two weeks or more at anchor making necessary preparations and alterations. I ordered him to split the crew in two groups. Each group would be allowed four days of liberty, while the second group labored at accomplishing these required duties. This liberty rotation would continue for the duration of the time we spent in port. I communicated the important assignments that I had given Powder Monkey, Scuttle, Tan and Long Tall Willie and asked Lion to exclude these individuals from the liberty roster. I also told Lion that I would be visiting the island's Governor to negotiate our future status, including obtaining the *Lettre of Marque* that would legitimize our upcoming voyages. Saluting his understanding, he was off in a flash to begin compliance.

As we neared our destination, I was once again stunned by the island's natural beauty. The two main landmasses of the island were called Basse-Terre and Grande-Terre. Each was significantly different in appearance as we made our approach. Basse-Terre on the western side was comprised of a series of high volcanic mountains with dark sand beaches dotting its shore. Several of the men knowledgeable with this landmass informed me that it was far less populated than its sister. Grand-Terre, it seemed, was much more accommodating to human habitation with its brilliant white sand beaches and an interior suitable for extensive agriculture.

Our final destination, Pointe-a-Pitre, was located on Grand-Terre, with a harbor well protected and sheltered from strong winds and raging storms. The coastal area surrounding the city was made up of dense mangrove swamps. The interesting thing for me about these strange trees was that they grew right out of the water! As we entered the spacious harbor, we were greeted by the sight of a number of vessels already enjoying the expansive accommodations of the port. We observed that the city was made up of two distinct parts. The lower portion existed in rather swampy surroundings, boasting large warehouses and trading facilities that dotted the shore. The upper portion was built on a limestone plateau well above its subservient lower sister. This upper portion housed the majority of the island's population in beautiful tropical splendor, residing in white houses with red tile roofs.

Once anchored, I headed towards the Governor's office to negotiate our future. As we landed on the beautiful white sand, I was greeted by the seedy and course atmosphere of the lower portion of the city. Non unlike any other bustling waterfront, the air was filled with loud noises and obnoxious odors with mud everywhere I trod. This section of the city was made up of shoddy buildings and small lanes weaving their way throughout. Fishermen, sailors, pirates, rogues, scoundrels, trollops and peddlers dominated the scene with wild dogs running amok in the chaos that ensued. Upon surveying this den of iniquity, I knew with certainty that my new crew would spend most of their liberty right here in what they would term, glorious conditions!

The upper portion of the city presented a stark contrast. Home of the tradesmen and merchants, it was noted for its gracious hospitality with an emphasis on delicious food, bracing drink, novel music and festive dance. The planters of the isle held the highest positions and lived in huge rambling manor homes close to their cultivated fields. Trade on the island consisted mainly of spices, sugar, tobacco, rum and coffee, a recent arrival. Another large and growing industry was exportation of a strange yellow soft fruit called a banana. As I roamed and made these observations, I discovered that the Creole language was spoken sporadically by black and white inhabitants alike. All in all, Pointe-a-Pitre represented a tropical paradise in all of its squalor and splendor.

I received directions to the Governor's office from a number of friendly locals and arrived at a splendid two-level white building that was both grand and imposing in design. Dressed in somber attire complete with shoes and stockings which certainly gave me much discomfort, I was made to wait an intolerably long time while my petition for an audience was carried through bureaucratic channels. As the day progressed, I was finally summoned for my appointment with Governor Louis LaCouturie. As I entered his beautifully appointed office, I was a bit surprised by the individual sitting smugly behind the large wooden desk. The first thing I noticed as I approached the man was his size. He was rather diminutive in stature as he rose to shake my hand. Hardly reaching the middle of my chest, I was tempted to inquire if he was related to our dear cook, Long Tall Willie. The second thing I detected was his unusually thin frame. It seemed like a strong gust of wind would knock the esteemed official right off his feet. As I drew even closer, I observed that his light grey eyes seemed dull and expressionless. His lips were reed-thin and he sported a rather large nose that seemed totally out of place on his small round noggin.

He was dressed in an impressive suit of black velvet that was dotted with scraps of food. As I extended my hand in greeting, I formally wished him well and announced that I was Captain Bilge in precise and fluent French. He answered that it was indeed a pleasure to make my esteemed acquaintance. Offering me a seat directly across from his desk, I moved to the intricately-carved wooden chair and sat. He opened the conversation by questioning how I had arrived at his fair island. I answered that I had recently arrived on the schooner named the *Midnight Crow.* Somewhat surprised by my response, he asked in what capacity I served on the vessel, since its captain was very well known to him. I explained that a sudden and very serious illness had taken his dear associate, and that I had taken command of the ship. Frowning now in confusion, he questioned how such a young man could assume the many responsibilities demanded of a captain. I explained that I had served in many capacities aboard my original craft including First Mate and Ship's Navigator prior to serving under Captain Shivvers as Chief Navigator and Official Translator. In prior years, I confessed that I had been highly educated as a young lad by a learned private tutor.

Nodding his acceptance of my response, he questioned me on the reason for my visit. In my most humble voice, I answered that I had made the visit to formally petition a *Lettre of Marque and Reprisal.* Somewhat stunned by my request, he questioned my need for such a document. Without hesitating, I informed him that it was my sole intent to rid the beautiful and bountiful Caribbean waters of filthy sea scavengers who called themselves pirates. Before he could make a comment, I further added that I was especially dedicated to hunting down and eliminating the worst rogue of this nefarious group, the villain who called himself the Black Tarantula. Well, these words had a great effect on the little man, whose eyes opened wide in abject terror. Making the traditional sign-of-the-cross on his person, he informed me that he had just recently been apprised of this black demon's atrocities on Saint Domingue.

In a very nervous voice, he haltingly queried why I wished to risk my very soul in the pursuit of this villainous rabble. I passionately declared that this demon had perpetuated unconscionable acts on dear friends and acquaintances on Saint Domingue. I also added that he was responsible for the murder of my future mother-in-law, Madame LaFontaine, and had attempted to kidnap my fiancé, Rue LaFontaine. Finally, I concluded by divulging that the villain was answerable for the deliberate acts of thievery, murder and property destruction against honest and good French citizens. Nodding, Governor LaCouturie agreed that the madman had committed grievous crimes against the French Empire in the course of his rampages. He confided that he had commissioned a French Man-O-War to hunt and destroy him for all of his nefarious atrocities. With a very saddened look, he informed me that this commissioned ship had in fact done battle with the pirate demon and suffered significant damages and severe causalities, including the death of her appointed captain. This ship had barely escaped capture and had limped its way back to port. In a whispered voice, he confessed that the entire affair had caused him much embarrassment with the King. Using this information, I promised the functionary reprisal for the nefarious deeds of this scoundrel and the reestablishment of his personal honor if he would be kind enough to issue me the *Lettre of Marque.*

As I watched, his lifeless grey eyes suddenly came to life as he questioned what arrangements I had in mind to secure such an honor. Feigning ignorance, I answered that I was aware of the normal arrangements necessary to secure such a document, but was willing as a gentleman to discuss the matter with him to arrive at agreeable terms. With these words, I pulled a bundle from my coat pocket and slowly opened the cloth wrap to reveal a magnificent emerald ring, whose prodigious magnitude and brilliance was utterly entrancing. Unable to keep his eyes off of this prize, I handed it over to him for his inspection. As he clutched the valuable ring in his sweaty paws, I informed him that I wished to offer the ring to him as a goodwill gesture for future dealings. In a flash, he pocketed the prize and smiled for the first time, informing me that he was sure that we could reach a gentlemen's agreement.

Governor LaCouturie, with pure greed emanating from his every pore, then informed me that the normal terms upon receipt of the document was a split of thirty percent for the King's coffers and seventy percent staying with the appointed ship. I knew these terms were a bit on the high side, but I reasoned that the accounting of the booty from any prize was highly subjective. Given this, I could easily lower his exorbitant rate by a simple inventory readjustment. However, so as to not be taken for a complete fool, I informed the Governor that I believed the normal governmental split was closer to twenty percent. Before he could react to my comment, I smoothly continued by informing the avaricious civil servant that I would increase the rate to a full one quarter of the prize, while offering an additional five percent directly to his office to cover all administrative expenses. Knowing that he stood to accrue a total of over ten percent personally, my offer plus his normal five percent from the King's share, he quickly agreed to my terms as he patted the emerald ring now residing safely in his pocket. So that he could draw up the necessary documents, he asked me to provide my full name and the name of my vessel. On a scrap of paper, I penned my name as Captain William Bilge and added my ship's name as *Rue's Revenge*. Smiling he put this information in his top drawer of his massive desk and stood to shake my hand, finalizing our bargain.

As I stood smiling and shaking the hand of this greedy little functionary, I heard a rather large commotion occurring just outside the Governor's door. At once, the door burst inward and a pompous naval officer strode purposely into the room followed by the Governor's protesting attaché. The brash officer marched straight over to the Governor's side and roughly censured him for the rude behavior of the trailing assistant. Turning a bright shade of red, Governor LaCouturie dismissed his attaché and questioned the new arrival on the reason for the unexpected visit. Totally ignored during the exchange, the French officer suddenly turned my way and rudely inquired just who I was. Biting back my obvious displeasure and total embarrassment due to the officer's tasteless behavior, I took a deep breath and told the brazen military fool that I was Captain William Bilge of the recently arrived *Rue's Revenge*. Giving me quick scrutiny, he turned to the now flustered Governor and questioned what a common pirate was doing meeting with the island's leader. Taken totally by surprise by the sheer audacity of his statement, I turned to the Governor and boldly inquired if the absence of good manners was island-wide or just practiced in the privacy of his esteemed office. Well, I can tell you that my words had a startling effect on both parties standing before me. While the Governor stuttered and stammered an apology for my treatment, the brazen officer drew his saber and advanced threateningly in my direction. Sensing the utter rage in the officer's eyes, I turned and met his gaze in a calm and detached manner. As he raised his sword to strike me, the Governor regained his composure and in a loud and commanding voice ordered the military man to halt his attack and sheathe his weapon or suffer harsh consequences.

The order stopped the malicious officer in mid-stride and he returned his weapon to its scabbard. With a snide smile, the officer faced me and in a deadly serious voice informed me that he did not care for my impertinence and would one day repay me for the personal insult. With these menacing words, he turned abruptly and headed for the door. In a calm and detached voice, I answered that I hoped to be armed for our next encounter. Red now with rage, the crazed lunatic continued his stomp out of the office, slamming the door in his wake.

As soon as the brutish officer had made his departure, I returned my gaze to the Governor, who was now assessing me with renewed interest. Professing his sincerest apology for the inexcusable behavior of the officer, he invited me to join him for dinner later that evening. He informed me that he was hosting a small celebration for a few prominent local planters and would be more than delighted if I would agree to attend. Smiling, I informed him that I would be delighted to dine with him as a celebration of our agreement. The concerned look on his face dissipated to one of total relief upon hearing my acceptance, and he gave me directions to his home. I shook his hand in a most friendly manner and turned to take my leave. At his door, I turned back and questioned him if my newest military friend would be joining us this evening. Shaking his head in a quick and decisive manner, he answered certainly not! Addressing his confused stare, I stated that I just wanted to know whether I needed to come armed or not and slid quietly out of the room.

As I began my return to the street, I stopped at the desk of the Governor's assistant, who still appeared quite shaken by the recent encounter with the arrogant officer. As he glanced up at me with remorseful eyes, he managed to voice a hushed apology for the entire incident. I quickly came to his rescue by informing him that a herd of wild horses could not have stopped the impertinent officer from breeching his intended target. Relieved by my words, he questioned if I required any assistance while I was onshore. I mentioned my need for a tailor who was accomplished and accommodating. He immediately provided a name and a location complete with directions on the Governor's official letterhead, knowing that the same would grant me an instant introduction when presented. Thanking him, I questioned him in an innocent voice for the name of the officer who had just invaded the Governor's office. In a disgusted tone, he answered that the officer's name was Captain Jean Bernard LeMerde, and that he had recently arrived from France under very curious circumstances. Observing utmost discretion, he offered no more so I bid him a grateful thanks and good day.

As I exited the building, I followed the directions provided to the tailor's shop and entered the small modest structure. I was greeted at the door by a diminutive, overly nervous man who resembled a human pincushion. Displaying my introduction and receiving its intended reaction, I told him that I required a new set of clothes for a dinner with the Governor that evening. He began to wag his head from side-to-side in a negative fashion, until I produced a number of gold coins that altered his direction to up-and–down! Taking a series of quick measurements, he scooted away in a blink of the eye shouting for me to return in three hours time. With that, he disappeared into the back of his shop and I was abandoned to find my own way out.

As expected, the Governor's mansion was the finest in the city. Beautifully appointed both inside and out, the house was managed by an army of servants who performed in flawless and skilled precision. The Governor gave me a warm greeting and then made several introductions, before whisking away to play the role of genteel host to some of the late arrivals. In total, there was about a dozen guests scattered about the open garden area. The guests all seemed to know each other quite well, as small comfortable groups formed all around me. Being a complete stranger, I wandered from group to group eavesdropping on the latest island scuttlebutt. As I was making my rounds, I noticed a handsome and intelligent looking gentleman standing alone sporting a very forlorn demeanor. Navigating my way to his side, I introduced myself and he responded that his name was Francois Rene Turbout. We orally traded personal information, and he seemed quite intrigued upon hearing my details. He recounted that he was a sugar planter on a small island southeast of our position, called Marie-Gallant. The more time I spent in his company, the closer we became acquainted and the more I found myself truly liking the man. Rene, as he preferred to be called, was highly intelligent with a very keen sense of humor. Highly educated and very accomplished, he displayed an air of confidence rather than arrogance.

The two of us kept each other company throughout the evening, and the time virtually sped by until guests all around us began to surreptitiously take their leave. Realizing that it was time to depart, I turned to Rene to inform him that I had thoroughly enjoyed his company. Shaking his hand warmly, I articulated that if he ever needed a favor all he had to do was call and I would be honored to oblige. With these innocent words, an extremely saddened expression stole over his face and he confessed that he was in need of some assistance with a very crucial matter. Nodding my head, I questioned if he would like to discuss his urgent issue in private quarters. Eyes shining with the greatest of relief, he laughed and divulged that was exactly what he needed to do. Informing me that he had a small boat in the harbor that would transport us back to his plantation house, he promised that I would be received in the greatest spirit of hospitality by he and his bride. Secretly I had always yearned for the opportunity to visit one of these great manors, and snapped at the chance he had just presented. With the matter settled, we both bid our sincerest thanks and well wishes to the Governor and left the gathering together.

Chapter 17: Rene and Lille Turbout

Rene's boat was manned by his own hirelings, and they expertly made the journey to his home in very short order. As we landed at a small dock on his private white-sand beach, it was difficult to discern any of the surroundings due to the late hour. A carriage drawn by a pair of magnificent horses whisked us to the manor house, where we were met by his beautiful bride, Lille. After assuring our comfort, she bid us both a goodnight with a saddened smile and a kiss for her husband. Promising to spend time with me in the morning, she floated out of the room and disappeared. Settling us in his impressive library with a glass of wine for him and fresh lemonade for me, he finally confided the source of his problem. His younger sister, who had been residing in France, had decided to pay her older brother a visit. On her journey to Guadeloupe, her ship had been taken by a band of pirates and she had been abducted by the rogues and spirited away to their lair.

Interrupting his narrative, I questioned how long ago this abduction had occurred. He reported that her captivity had begun a month ago, hence his growing concern for her safety and wellbeing. Continuing, he related that the prior week word had been messaged to him that his sister was safe and well tended. This note also demanded an exorbitant ransom sum for her release. While a very daunting sum, Rene had raised the amount, but awaited instructions for its delivery. Two days ago, he received a second note that increased the ransom amount significantly, but once again failed to provide any specifics on delivery. Confused and extremely agitated, Rene was highly tormented by the entire affair. I inquired if he had sought assistance through the Governor. Providing me a weak smile, he confessed that he had indeed done so, but very little had been resolved. The Governor was much more interested in appeasing his own priorities than solving a crime of abduction. He had volunteered the loan of a few retired military men to assist in the retrieval of Rene's sister, but was unable to provide any further support. It seemed that the bulk of the navy under his command was committed to the eradication of the notorious Black Tarantula. Rene had met with the recommended retirees and had found them nothing more than old broken sailors with huge appetites for any sort of hot spirits. He was now quite stymied as to how to proceed.

Assuring him that I would personally involved myself in his plight, I requested a peek at the ransom notes. Scurrying from the room, he returned carrying the requested documents. As I accepted them from his trembling fingers and began my perusal, I was instantly stunned by the bold signature at the bottom of each. I could hardly believe my eyes since the name read Captain Bass! Thinking the name to be a mere coincidence, I made a closer scrutiny of the actual writing style and choice of words and came to the stunning conclusion that the author was none other than my old enemy, Mr. Bass, First Mate of the *Amafata*. I was sure that my registered surprise was written all over my face because Rene immediately inquired what was troubling me so. Taking my time, I relayed the entire sad story concerning the insidious bully and his brutal actions aboard our lost ship.

At the end of my tale, I perceived that Rene was now even more concerned and anxious about the safe return of his beloved sister. Attempting to calm my new friend with empty reassurances, he appeared totally lost, confused and frightened. Deciding on a bolder plan, I looked him directly in the eye and informed him that I would deliver the ransom personally to the fiend. In doing so, I confessed to Rene that I would be settling two scores simultaneously. For him, I would be ensuring the safe return of his sister, whose name per the note that I had just read was Amiee. For myself, I would be settling an old score with the murdering miscreant. With an anguished look of relief, Rene snared my shoulders with his powerful grip and stared into the depths of my eyes promising that anything I required would be made available. Informing him that as soon as the next missive from Captain Bass arrived, he needed to send word and I would return and fulfill my pledge. With an inquisitive eye, he questioned exactly what I planned. Winking, I confessed that I had something extremely devious in mind but required a little more time to work out all of the details!

The next morning, we were joined by Lille for a delightful morning meal on their spacious and rambling verandah. Rene had informed Lille on my volunteered assistance in the matter of Aimee, and she too seemed quite relieved. During the meal, they both questioned me on how I had managed to become Captain at such a remarkably young age. The best method of answering their query was to provide them with a brief recounting of my time at sea, which seemed to have a captivating effect on both of them. Upon completing my tale, they both marveled at the unbelievable ingenuity and strategy that I had employed time after time. We continued to discuss various topics. I happened to mention my visit to the Governor yesterday and my incident with the brash and arrogant French officer. At the mention of his name, both of my hosts exclaimed that the man was certainly no gentleman under any circumstances whatsoever.

It seemed that Rene had approached Captain LeMerde when the news of his sister's abduction had first reached him. The Captain had laughed in his face, informing Rene that he had far greater issues to solve than the retrieval of a wayward lady. Lille had been appraised of Captain LeMerde's background by the Governor's wife. The information communicated from their homeland was that the Captain had been demoted in rank and mandated to this far outpost as punishment for a grievous act of defiance that had cost the countless lives of French sailors. Driven by insatiable ambition, Lieutenant Captain LeMerde had disregarded the direct orders of his immediate supervisor and proceeded to make a foolhardy attack on a British naval squadron in an effort to win the day. Instead, the Lieutenant Captain's squadron was decimated. The French Naval Command decided that rather than risk a scandalous court martial for his treasonous actions, he would be summarily demoted and shunted off to the West Indies to live the remainder of his life in nondescript oblivion. Arriving barely nine months ago, he had made bitter enemies with anyone coming in contact with him. His sole obsession seemed to lie in the desire to eliminate the infamous pirate leader called the Black Tarantula. By accomplishing this burning obsession, he hoped to regain his former status with the King as well as the Naval Admiralty. Whispered to be a sadist and devil by his more than rough treatment of selected island women, the word among the entire population was to avoid him at all costs. Rene summed up the rather ugly account by informing me that the man had no grace, no wisdom, no mercy and certainly no soul!

It was now time to return to *Rue's Revenge,* so I thanked my hosts for their splendid hospitality and complimented them on the stunning grace and magnificence of their lovely home. Promising that I would return shortly to complete my solemn vow, I bid them a fond farewell. The same transport returned me swiftly to my ship, and I rewarded Rene's sailors with a few coins as gratitude. Upon scaling the ship's rope ladder, I was pleased to observe that my instructions were being carried out quite efficiently. Both Long Tall Willie and Tan were conducting combat lessons in various locations on the maindeck, so I wandered over to watch the proceedings. Pleased with the progress of the two ongoing classes, I returned to my cabin to await Lion's appearance. In just a short while, the giant knocked and entered my cabin with his news. He reported that all of the ship's alterations were proceeding smoothly. Included in these was an overall change to the color of our ship, which was being transformed from black and blood-red to a nondescript sea green hue. Also underway was the strengthening of much stouter bulwarks and additional disguised gunports that I had ordered. I asked if Chips was proceeding on the figurehead I had designed for the ship and received a positive response. I then filled him in on the Governor's meeting and my new association with Rene Turbout, including my solemn promise to assist in the retrieval of his sister. Noting his confusion, I informed him that the island that Rene controlled would provide an excellent safe haven should the need arise. Nodding his understanding, I also notified him of my purchases while on Guadeloupe and to expect delivery of these items as early as the next few days. Lastly, I informed him that a local artist was working diligently on our new flag which would also be delivered soon.

As I was plotting a strategy to deal with Mr. Bass, a knock sounded on my door. Inviting the caller to enter, I was not surprised by Tiger Eyes' presence. He reminded me of the nautical lessons I had offered to conduct for he and his men. Rising, I made my way topside and began a long series of instructions on the ship and her many complicated parts and procedures, so that the warrior group could function as able-bodied seamen when we resumed our voyage. While their initial knowledge was extremely limited, they displayed a sense of eagerness and dedication to study conscientiously. I remained on the ship for the next several days caught up in my varied responsibilities and duties.

The time aboard passed rather quickly and I was surprised when the first liberty group returned to the vessel. Included in this group was Angry George, who had dragged back an old friend in hopes of my accepting him as a crewmember. He introduced his friend as No Nose Nottingham, an appropriate name I thought, given the total absence of his olfactory organ. Inviting both men to take a seat, I turned to No Nose and requested a brief history of his past before passing judgement. No Nose informed us that he was English by birth and a sailor by trade. Raised in a very large family, No Nose was sent to sea at a young age to earn his keep. He had served on a number of merchant ships in a variety of roles. During one stint, he had met Angry George and they became fast friends.

On liberty on the Spanish possession of Cuba, he had been jailed unjustly by a minor bureaucrat for theft. Tried and found guilty, he was sentenced to three years of hard labor on the Spanish mainland. He joined a crew of rough individuals fated to harvesting logwood to meet its increasing demand. Logwood was a rather small tree that tended to grow only in certain dense forested areas on the Spanish Main. This tree was known for its hard thick wood that appeared almost black in color. The wood itself was the source of a rare and valuable purple dye that fetched a very high price in European markets. The tree was not easily forested due to the many dangers that plagued the harvesters. These hardy individuals faced sickness, animal attacks and local Indian hostilities. No Nose was immediately put to work in a prison labor camp that was run by a harsh and cruel overseer. As No Nose was completing his punishment, he was bitten on the nose by a small poisonous snake. His overseer, fearful of losing yet another prisoner, utilized his own knife to lop off the unfortunate's nose, believing that doing so would stop the spread of the deadly poison injected by the venomous serpent.

No Nose spent the next several weeks lingering between life and death, attended by an incompetent physician. Somehow No Nose survived the ordeal and eventually escaped his jungle hell as a stowaway on a Spanish logwood transport. When the vessel made a brief stop on Cuba, No Nose abandoned ship and managed to find a birth on a passing Dutch trader. Before he abandoned the isle, he made an unannounced visit to his Spanish accuser and ended his life with a dagger shoved into his right eye. Subsequently, the Dutch trader he had joined was attacked by a band of French pirates, and No Nose was forced on the account until he made a successful escape on Guadeloupe. For the past year, he had been unsuccessful at obtaining nautical employment due to his grotesque appearance. He promised that he was loyal and a very hard worker, who only required an opportunity to prove his worth. Convinced by the poor tar's hard luck story along with the strong vote of confidence from Angry George, I agreed to allow No Nose to join our merry band of misfits and outcasts. Thanking me profusely, Angry George led his friend from my cabin to get him settled onboard. As they were leaving, Angry George turned and with a mischievous grin informed me that his friend also had a very interesting hobby. Looking up from the papers that were spread all across my desk, I questioned the exact nature of this unusual hobby. Smiling now, the horribly disfigured sailor told me that he bred and raised a most peculiar type of spider, tarantulas!

Chapter 18: No Nose Nottingham and Pets

Our vessel was undergoing significant changes right beneath my feet! Chips had added several new layers to the bulwarks surrounding the ship to protect our men should we face armed conflict. He had also completed our new figurehead, which Booby Bird was in the painstaking process of painting. This new addition was the image of a beautiful mermaid who resembled my beloved Rue. All of our sails had been transported to town for mending and repair with an additional set of sails ordered as valuable replacements. We had swapped all of the ship's old ropes, cables and riggings with newer and stouter substitutes. The drums that I had ordered in town were delivered and crew volunteers were being educated in their use by several of Tiger Eyes' warriors. The significant quantities of fine throwing knives, high quality cutlasses and hand-crafted muskets that I had purchased while in the city had begun to arrive and Tan and Long Tall Willie had pressed them into immediate service. Lion held target practice sessions to select three crews of marksmen, five men in each crew with two expert loaders, and would initiate further specialized classes with these individuals that very afternoon.

As these alterations progressed, I utilized the time to participate in the daylong classes being conducted by Tan and Long Tall Willie. Tiger Eyes and his men accompanied me in this crucial training, whenever they were not being drilled on navigational knowledge. As I had hoped, every crewmember was being transformed unknowingly into seasoned and very dangerous close-encounter fighting expert, while they all toiled to attain the golden doubloons that I had promised. As I joined these sessions, I knew that my own combat skills were rapidly improving. During this time, I traveled back to the Governor's office to procure the *Lettre of Marque,* which had been prepared in haste and most importantly in greed by our esteemed island despot. Wishing to avoid any further contact with the arrogant Captain LeMerde, I hastily procured the needed document and provided my thanks and well wishes to the Governor. I had a few more vital errands to accomplish, and began with another visit to my accommodating tailor. Placing my order for a variety of different outfits, the man was more than willing to undergo this labor, having already been generously rewarded for his prior efforts on my behalf. Stopping at a number of different shops along the way back to the harbor, I transacted further requirements and was finally free to return to our ship. As I passed a lively tavern on the way, my progress was halted by a loud commotion occurring inside.

The name of this pub was *La Licorne Aveugle* or *The Blind Unicorn* to us Englishmen. The sign raised high for all to notice was very unique and fanciful as it depicted a sidelong view of the head of this mythical creature in all of its spender and glory. The critter's magical horn was protruding into space, a sure attention getter to anyone passing by the pub. However, the most interesting detail about this unique signage was the black eyepatch that completely covered the beastie's eye. The end result of this curious addition transformed the glorious and fabled animal into a laughable and humorous seaman's parody!

Curious about the uproar heard inside, I peeked into the punchhouse's front window to discover the cause of the ruckus. My eye was immediately drawn to the enormous painting above the serving bar of a timeworn and battered portrait of yet another version of the legendary unicorn. The beast had been painted from the neck up and without any sort of covering over the creature's eyes. This shabby and tattered painting had certainly seen better days as it was riddled with musketball and dagger holes from previous bar frivolities. At the far end of the room, I spied that the extremely disagreeable Captain LeMerde was up to no good. Sputtering and stammering about the total lack of manners, grace and intelligence amongst the local population, he had backed a portly gentleman against the far wall at the point of his saber demanding an immediate apology. The poor obese fool could hardly voice these words given the utter fright that oozed from his entire being. While the malicious brute seemed to be enjoying his tormenting labors, I entered the pub and edged closer to the confrontation. Asking a nearby spectator about the source of the ruckus, I was informed that the gentleman in question had merely brushed against the odious officer, and was now in the process of paying the heavy price for this grave mistake. A few well aimed strikes followed by the offending bully that opened minor wounds on the terrified transgressor, who blubbered his sincerest apologies in an attempt to forgo further harm. While his earnest attempts produced no results, I decided that there was very little I could do so I decided to vacate the premises before the egotistical beast spotted my presence.

I turned to navigate my way out of the tavern, but unfortunately my rival spotted me and shouted for all to hear that a pirate of dubious renown had just entered the fine establishment. Continuing, he bellowed that my very presence sullied both the pub's fine reputation as well as all present partaking in its wondrous fare. His boisterous clamoring drew all eyes in my direction as my new audience eagerly awaited my response to the brute's injurious slights. Caught completely off-guard, I stammered a quick retort that I was a simple ship's captain and certainly not a pirate by any measure. My serious and seemingly honest reply drew a series of acquiescing nods from the now attentive patrons. Continuing, I reasoned that it was probably best that I take my leave so as to not cause any further disruption to the pub and its fine customers. With these words, I swiveled and made my way back to the entrance door. As I almost reached my destination, a well aimed dagger was flung in my direction finding a home in the portal just above my head. Extremely irritated by this unprovoked attack, I ignored the quivering projectile and turned to face my foe. With all eyes on me, I explained that I was leaving and bid the Captain a very good day. Sneering at my words, the officer informed me that I was no more than a cowardly pirate, who ran at the first sign of violence. Smiling I informed the bloody fool that I had important business to conduct and had no quarrel with him. With these words, I once again turned and attempted to open the door to escape further unpleasantness. As was the previous case, a matching dagger was launched which managed to knick my left forearm drawing a thin line of blood.

Realizing that the situation had escalated out of my control, I extracted both daggers from the door and turned to confront their owner. In a loud voice I repeated the claim that I was certainly no pirate. Continuing, I bellowed that only a pirate would keep the spoils of any raid. With these words, I flung both blades back in my aggressor's direction but intentionally well above the bullying villain. Both dirks landed with a sonorous thwack as each pierced a different eye of the unicorn portrait above the serving bar. The entire tavern congregation were stunned into an eerie silence by my bold act, and after assessing my marvelous knife-wielding feat broke into a clamorous roar of approval at LeMerde's total expense. Following up my circus-like performance, I shouted that now the unicorn was totally blind as the tavern's name demanded. This statement brought yet a greater thunderous outcry from my captivated audience who now were pointing and mocking the totally embarrassed French officer with wild abandon. Glancing back in the direction of my nemesis, I saw Captain LeMerde advancing on my position with his drawn saber raised in a most threatening fashion. As he neared, the maddened officer reared back and swung his blade at my head in a serious attempt to decapitate me. Ducking under his wild attack, I proceeded to dance neatly out of range of his flailing sword. Laughing now, I offered to buy the enraged rogue a drink to end our hostilities. My words amused the attentive patrons to such a degree that they began echoing them in a taunting fashion towards LeMerde, which only served to enrage him all the more. Spitting out a firm refusal, he advanced once more like a maddened bull totally intent on causing me serious injury to revenge the utter public humiliation I had caused him. Having no choice, I drew two of my own dirks from my waistband and calmly waited for his approaching barrage.

Parrying blow after blow, I danced and ducked away from his flashing saber repeating the claim that I was no pirate over and over. My words and these defensive actions only seemed to enrage the maniac to a bloodthirsty frenzy. Realizing the seriousness of the situation, I glanced around the room for a means of deliverance. Spying a group of four unsavory looking characters in a far corner, I immediately angled my way towards their position. Captain LeMerde followed my lead continuing to lash and slash at my retreating form to the continued taunts and laughter of all present. As I neared the group, I used my *special voice* to project a string of obscene insults in LeMerde's tone and timbre their way. Angered to the extreme by these crude and awful slurs, the scoundrels all rose to their feet to confront their source. Centering their gaze on the mad dog who they believed had voiced the injurious epitaphs, they freed their blades and went on the offensive. Attacking in unison, they descended on the unsuspecting bully and mounted their own furious assault. At this point, the pub's patrons were hysterically enjoying LeMerde's tribulations and issued further mockery and pointed ridicule at the prideful and cheeky bully.

Caught completely off-guard, LeMerde now had his hands full parrying the flashing blades of my four rabid saviors. Since I was now freed of his advances, I skirted the fray and dodged safely out of the tavern to safety. Just before exiting the donnybrook I had instigated, I glanced back over my shoulder at the French psychopath defending himself in the middle of the Blind Unicorn free-for-all. Momentarily shifting his gaze from the conflict, he returned my stare. Etched completely across his face was a look of pure menace and utmost hatred towards me for the insults and utter embarrassment he had suffered at my expense. I realized then and there that I had created a very serious enemy of this maniacal and highly prideful individual. As I made my successful escape, I could hear the savage clashing of metal and the belligerent curses continuing inside the grogshop war-zone. Later that afternoon, I was informed by a few of my returning crew that a brutal brawl had taken place in an island's pub that had resulted in the deaths of two sailors and the severe injury of a haughty military officer named LeMerde. Spectators of the battle confessed to authorities that the officer had been attacked without provocation. He was currently sequestered in the fort's infirmary nursing his multiple wounds as a direct result of the attack. They further disclosed that the entire island had been made aware of the total humiliation and mortification of this extremely loathed and reviled navy man received at the hands of a would-be pirate. His total shame and the ridicule that followed was shared and received exceedingly well by everyone on the island. Laughing heartily at this news, I promised myself to remain out of harms way by completely avoiding my newest nemesis, the French madman, for the remainder of my stay on the island!

In the next several days, numerous items that I had purchased in the city continued to arrive and were quickly stowed aboard the *Rue's Revenge*. My preparations for my scheme to rescue Rene's sister were now complete. Having the time, I continued my daily lessons with my dutiful crew. Later, as I was studying some nautical charts in my cabin, I heard a soft knock on my door. Granting access, No Nose entered with a sheepish look on his face. I had summoned the new man to understand a little more about his unusually curious hobby. Fearing censure or worse, No Nose stood before me in an extremely anxious and stressed state. Ordering him to relax, I informed him that I had some questions concerning his weird obsession. Smiling with relief, he urged me to fire away. My first query was how he had become so fascinated with spiders, especially the fearsome tarantula.

Laughing now, he responded that his love of the wee beasties had begun at a very early age. Since his parents were poor people, he was not allowed to keep pets. Instead, he turned to spiders that habituated the damp dark cellar of their house. Finding these creatures quite fascinating, he spent many of his boyhood hours in their company. When he signed on in a seaman's life, he shelved his passion since most sailors considered any spider aboard a ship bad luck. No Nose confessed that he had the chance to reacquaint himself with the creatures in the dense tropical forests where he harvested logwood. Smiling, he informed me that the area was crawling with spiders, some harmless and some quite deadly.

During this time, he became totally mesmerized by the largest spider he had ever encountered, the formidable tarantula. No Nose then launched in a litany of facts and interesting tidbits concerning this species, which I must admit surprised me greatly. To start, he confided that while the creature's appearance was quite horrifying, this breed was relatively harmless. Their bite could prove somewhat sharp and painful, but it was certainly not poisonous or life-threatening. Being the largest of its species, their gigantic bodies were covered with a sort of short fur. Besides their sheer size, the other features that led to their fearsome reputation were the two prominent fangs and their retractable claws, like that of a cat, at the end of their eight bushy legs. Hailing in a variety of colors and bright markings, they did not spin webs but hunted prey by slowly stalking their victims. Being nocturnal, their slow and deliberate movements proved an asset rather than a hindrance in their hunt for nourishment.

I was also told that they made their homes in burrows in the ground living on small insects and rodents that had the misfortune of crossing their path. Eating rarely, they lived for as many as ten to fifteen years! No Nose informed me that he currently had a dozen of the creatures in the hold, where there were enough cockroaches to keep them alive for an eternity. He reported that these varmints would naturally rear up when frightened presenting an even more fearsome appearance. No Nose disclosed that he kept his charges in small wooden cages, and had actually trained a number of them to perform actions by hand commands such as rearing up, biting, extending their claws and scurrying away. After listening to his report, I thanked No Nose for the illustrious biology lesson and commanded him to take good care of his precious pets because I believed they would play a very important role in our future efforts. Snapping a salute to my command, he left my cabin with a very perplexed expression on his face as he tried to fathom the exact role I had just intimated for his charges.

A few more days passed and the ship was almost entirely refitted. We were still receiving shipments of grenado shells from Scuttle's leased blacksmith shop on a daily basis. Work was completed on the disguised gunports, and the efforts to install our new cannons were nearly finished. I assigned six men to accompany Powder Monkey to shore to practice throwing our new grenedos for accuracy. Since the devices were armed, I ordered Powder Monkey to conduct his classes on a deserted beach not far away. With these final preparations underway, I received the summons from Rene explaining that the time had come for my promised rescue. Arriving on Marie-Galant, later that day, I was greeted by my friend who had been anxiously awaiting my arrival on his small dock. Thanking me for my prompt response, he hustled me into his waiting carriage that whisked us to his marvelous home. As we arrived, Lille met us graciously and welcomed me back. We gathered in Rene's library to study the latest ransom note from Captain Bass. The note was short and terse in nature, demanding that the requested sum of money be delivered to an isolated beach on Basse-Terre by appointed functionaries under the cover of darkness in three days time. While the exact location was not detailed, the note specified that a shoreward bonfire would signal the delivery site. Once the money had been safely handed over, Rene's sister would be deposited on that same beach the following night. The note was signed by my former supervisor.

Reading the note carefully, I dropped it onto Rene's desktop and informed the anxious couple that my plan and preparations were complete. Rene was first to speak, confessing his reluctance regarding paying the brigand prior to his sister's return, fearing the unscrupulous criminal would renege on the arrangement. Smiling, I informed him that I had no plans to deliver anything of value to the murdering swine. Shocked by my admission, I decided it was time to convey my plans in its entirety to my two new friends. After familiarizing them with the ruse I had carefully devised, they both seemed stunned by its sheer audacity.

After dining, I was escorted by both to my small transport for my return. Upon arriving back, I summoned Lion, Powder Monkey, Tan, Long Tall Willie, Tiger Eyes and No Nose to an emergency conference in my cabin. Once assembled, I informed them of the details and my plan to rectify this intolerable situation. I further explained the ruse I had concocted as well as their individual roles in the upcoming performance. Smiling and laughing when I concluded my briefing, they all promised to faithfully carry out their assignments. Informing all but Lion and No Nose that we would be returning to Marie-Galant in the morning, I ordered each to ensure that the necessary items were secured in our transport prior to our departure. Turning to No Nose, I issued a specific set of orders that I needed him to follow before I arrived back on our ship. Saluting smartly, they hustled off to carry out my detailed instructions.

The next morning, I informed Lion that I would to be away for at least a day. Further, I commanded that our ship had to be fully prepared to sail before the day was over. I then provided him with an exact location and timing for a rendezvous with us at the southern end of BasseTerre. Saluting, he promised that all would be ready and would be there as ordered. My small group assembled in the longboat with all the necessary items stowed and covered by an old sail. We quickly made our way to Rene's home to affect my scheme. We were met at the dock by Rene's men and taken directly to the manor house. When introductions were completed, I sent Scuttle and Powder Monkey back to the beach to prepare their grenados. Dispatching Tan and Long Tall Willie to handle Rene's contributions, I informed them to tell the others that we would sail the following day. The remainder of the day was spent traveling back and forth to the beach to check on last minute details. With all in readiness, we set out on our mission of mercy with the sincerest of well wishes from Rene and Lille.

Chapter 19: Rescue and Revenge

My plan called for the utilizing two separate small boats for our mission. Situated in one of Rene's small transports were I, Tan, Long Tall Willie with Rene's pilot at the rudder. I and my mates were all disguised to avoid recognition by our former shipmate. A key assumption in my plan was that Captain Bass would be present at the ransom location to receive and secure Rene's kidnapping payment. My conjecture was that our former First Mate would trust nobody from his crew with this sizable prize. Since Long Tall Willie and I were very well known to the evil sadist, I recognized early in planning that our ploy would require unquestioned disguises. Thinking hard and long about this key aspect, I decided to employ religious garb that would enable us to fully cloak our identities, while appearing seemingly weak and totally harmless to the pirates awaiting us on the undisclosed beach. My purchases from the talented tailor on Guadeloupe included three clerical vestment robes complete with hoods to provide total concealment. However, the robes I had commissioned were also quite voluminous so as to cover the arsenal of weapons each of us carried. As planned, Tan and Long Tall Willie would remain completely mute, acting strictly as unwitting assistants.

The second vessel in our grand charade was one of our own longboats. This vessel carried Powder Monkey, Scuttle and Tiger Eyes. Secured in the belly of this transport were specially designed grenados, muskets, and a slew of cutlasses and knives. While its occupants were not disguised, they represented a shadow within a shadow. You see, our boat was painted completely black and the passengers were also clothed entirely in black with black tar covering their faces and extremities. Their assignment was to shadow us and beach as close as they dared without being seen. They had orders to flank the scum on the beach and attack when the appropriate sign was issued. The plan also demanded that our group stall for some time in order to allow this second team to reach an ideal point for attack. The ruse was risky and daring and acutely time sensitive, providing me a sharp inner thrill!

The second act in this rescue drama involved No Nose, who was now arranging details in my cabin for an informational session scheduled later that evening. By my instructions, the cabin had to be cleared and a guest of honor's throne had to be fully prepared. No Nose would arrange for a marvelous reception of his trained and horrid pets eager to make the honoree's acquaintance. No Nose and I had previously rehearsed our parts, and we were both quite prepared to enact our little drama!

Time seemed to stretch very slowly as we navigated our way towards the appointed delivery site. At last, we spied the specified roaring bonfire burning on a secluded beach, and I commanded Rene's pilot to steer for the spot in a slow and deliberate manner. As we navigated our way towards the beach, we were met with a myriad of questions concerning our identities. I was gratified to recognize the voice of my old enemy Mister Bass among the inquisitive shore mob. Answering their questions in a confused and effeminate voice, I responded across the thundering surf that I was Father Jericho. Continuing, I informed the insidious welcoming committee that I was a family friend of the Rene Turbout and was acting as an intermediary for the safe return of the man's sister.

Convinced that our presence was non-threatening, the pirates ordered us to come ashore and deliver the ransom money. We were eventually dragged to the beach by the anxious pirate crew, who had waded chest-high into the surf to provide their assistance. When safely grounded, I pointed to the chest, and Tan and Long Tall Willie hefted the rock-filled container gently from the boat and carried it onto the beach. Captain Bass suddenly appeared and I noticed that he had changed very little over time other than sporting much more stylish garb. The mean-spirited bully stomped his way over to the chest in order to inspect the booty, only to find it secured by an imposing lock. Extracting his pistol, he hammered on the lock guarding the chest's secrets with no success. Turning in my direction, the impatient kidnapper demanded the key to the lock. I answered that I had been instructed to open the lock only after Rene's sister had been returned to us in safety. Furious over the delay, Captain Bass informed me that the unfortunate woman was sequestered on his ship which was anchored very near our position. He then recited that she would only be released upon deliverance of the agreed amount. I answered that I could not comply with his wishes until the girl was produced.

At my words, Captain Bass pulled a cutlass from his scabbard and stated in his typical cruel manner that if I did not open the chest immediately, he would be forced to amputate both of my arms. As he spat out these words, I noticed movement coming from behind his position indicating that my flanking team had arrived. Losing no further time, I raised my hands and shouted for the Lord's protection and assistance. This was my prearranged sign and I stood in calm composure as the villain advanced on my position. As he neared, something flew out of the dense underbrush behind him. In that moment, several more smoke grenados were lobbed into the surrounding crew of pirates. At once, the air was filled with noxious fumes and the battle officially commenced.

On cue, Tan and Long Tall Willie heaved off their robes and grabbed their weapons. Long Tall Willie was flinging blades in all directions, killing pirate after pirate in a blur of motion. Tan also attacked the stunned heathens with two whirling cutlasses that mowed down every thug in his path. The terrified fiends who chose the underbrush as an escape route ran directly into fearsome black creatures who sliced them apart with razor sharp machetes. The battle was over in seconds with the lone survivor being a mystified Captain Bass. Stunned and confused by the sudden turn of events, the vile kidnapper turned in my direction and aimed his pistol. Not giving him a chance to fire, I moved swiftly forward and delivered a vicious blow to his midsection followed by a crushing right uppercut to his jaw that totally disabled him as he crumpled to the sand. Jumping on his back, I secured his hands behind his back with a stout rope, lashed his feet together and finished my efforts with a filthy neckerchief stuffed in his mouth.

Wasting no time, we lifted the rogue into the bottom of our boat and dumped the chest of rocks directly onto his back, which evoked a painful grunt through his oral blockade. Ordering Powder Monkey, Scuttle and Tiger Eyes back to their longboat, I commanded them to make their way south to our waiting ship. Wasting no time, Tan, Long Tall Willie and I joined our odious passenger and made haste in the same direction to also rendezvous with our vessel. All that remained on the deserted beach was a slew of dead pirates, who would soon provide needed nourishment for the hungry crabs that would be drawn to the feast by the scent of rotting flesh!

As we navigated south, I turned Captain Bass on his back and removed my hood. With a look of innocence, I calmly requested the position of his ship. Glaring at me with an expression of raging hate, he struggled to sit upright but his progress was immediately halted by a sharp knife that was pointed directly at his left eye by Long Tall Willie. Begging the bully to try his best, the dwarf flicked his sharp blade further to the left and neatly removed a portion of the Captain's ear. Bleeding copiously, the villain struggled and squirmed to avoid any more punishment from Long Tall Willie's dirk. Asking him once more for the position of his ship, I yanked out his gag fully expecting the answer I received. He spat out that I was nothing more than a meddlesome murderer, and that he would never reveal the location of his awaiting craft. Smiling, he informed me that he had left specific instructions concerning the female tramp. He snidely swore that the lass would be slaughtered at dawn and then fed to the sharks. However, he wickedly added that he had granted his entire crew ill-use of the strumpet before seeing to her untimely dispatch. Stuffing the filthy rag back into his mouth, I promised that he would reveal all once I had a chance to interview him under proper conditions. Shaking his head side-to-side to emphasize his refusal, I simply smiled and informed him that I was looking forward to watching his change his mind.

We arrived at our ship a short time later and were met by the crew from the second longboat already topside. Heaving the villain over his powerful shoulders, Lion delivered him to No Nose's waiting hands. I made my way to my cabin and found my enemy completely incapacitated in a stout chair with rope bindings from head-to-toe. In surveying the evil carrion, I could see that the only portion of his anatomy capable of movement were his eyelids, which fluttered with a mixture of fear and rage. So began the second act of our desperate rescue attempt.

Introducing No Nose, whose horrid facial appearance gave Captain Bass something further to fear, I informed the good Captain that No Nose had a very peculiar hobby of raising spiders. Reaching into a wooded cage at his side, No Nose drew out a fearsome looking black beast that was adorned with brilliant orange stripes on its furry legs and back. Disclosing that my new mate trained and bred the largest spiders in existence, I nodded my approval and No Nose gently placed the monster on Captain Bass's chest, which had been prudently bared for the performance. Motioning with his hands, the hairy nightmare began a slow and tentative crawl upwards. By the furious blinking of my enemy's eyelids, I knew that our creeping abomination was having its intended effect.

I then revealed that No Nose was an expert with these horrid beasts. I further informed Captain Bass that No Nose had previously become careless with his training exercises and subsequently had suffered a grievous bite on his nose. The brave sailor had actually severed his own nose so that the lethal poison from the bite was stopped from entering his bloodstream, which would have resulted in an extremely painful and horrific death. Grinning now, I continued that I now believed that No Nose had learned a valuable lesson that fateful day.

At these words, I pulled out the gag and a bloodcurdling wail of fear erupted from Captain Bass, who begged for the removal of the monster crawling slowly up his chest. I informed the prisoner that I would comply once he divulged the information I sought. Gaining a moment of sudden courage, the evil brute spat a decided negative in my direction. Gagging him immediately, I motioned No Nose to make his next move.

Reaching into another wooden cage, he extracted the largest spider I had ever seen. It was blackish-brown behemoth that was larger than my fist. He then gently placed the tarantula on Captain Bass's forehead and motioned with his fingers to direct the slow and cautious giant to crawl down the prisoner's face. Informing the horrified scum that any tarantula seemed to love the smell and taste of honey, I slathered an ample supply of the gooey substance all over his nose. Informing my hated adversary that his face would soon look just like that of my mate's or possibly worse, I signaled No Nose to proceed with the next step. Leering directly over the prisoner, No Nose made a few more hand motions and the hideous creature crawled directly over Captain Bass's right eye, suddenly reared up exposing its two lethal looking fangs. As this occurred, the first spider had reached the scoundrel's neck and was slowly making its approach to the honeyed scent using its retractable claws to make purchase on the swine's sweating flesh. With abject terror now dominating his expression, I removed the gag once more demanding that my question be answered.

Emitting a very shrill child-like scream, he shouted that his ship was anchored north of the rendezvous point in a small hidden cove. He then confessed that the girl was being kept prisoner under guard in his cabin. Positioning a nautical map of Basse-Terre's coastline in front of his eyes, I drew my hand up the outline of the shore informing him to stop me when I had pointed to the exact spot. With one eye on the marauding creature directly over his eye and his other fixed on my traveling finger, he finally yelled stop when I had reached the proper location. Stuffing the rag rudely back into his gaping maw, I ordered No Nose to retrieve his pets. Before I vacated the cabin, I bent over the black-hearted barbarian and hissed that if he had not told me the truth that I would allow No Nose to have more fun with his odious pets. Noting the awful aroma arising from Captain Bass, I realized to my delight that the poor soul had soiled himself in a most disgusting manner!

Leaving No Nose with two wickedly sharp cutlasses to guard our prisoner, I raced topside to provide the crew with sailing orders. Because the pirates held Aimee in bondage, I communicated the exact sequence of steps that needed to be accomplished before it was safe to storm the pirate ship and send her filthy occupants to Davy Jones Locker. I explained that we needed to first make a quick stop at the deserted ransom rendezvous point to borrow some required props. When we reached the spot, I was rowed ashore sporting Captain Bass's clothes which had been liberated from the sadist in a very harsh manner. That is, only his shirt, coat and hat, for every article of clothing below his belt was left undisturbed on the filthy-fouled animal!

Tan and Long Tall Willie along with a dozen other crewmembers accompanied me to shore. Once aground, we borrowed the clothing from numerous deceased pirates as well as their longboat and headed back to our ship. Once aboard, we began our trek northward to the exact location conveniently provided by Captain Bass. As we neared the spot, I placed Lion in charge of our ship and Scuttle in charge of our batteries. Their orders were to wait for our signal before entering the hidden cove to confront our foes. My plan called for utilizing the pirate longboat with a dozen of my crew dressed in the dead pirate's slops to create an appropriate diversion. In our blackened longboat, Tan, Long Tall Willie, Powder Monkey and Tiger Eyes would utilize the diversion I would create to sneak onto the opposite side of the ship, liberate the prisoner and then give Lion the signal to attack. As we neared the hidden cove, I ordered our disguised blackened launch to remain well hidden until we began our diversionary ploy. I then added the ransom chest full of rocks in the pirate's boat, finalized my disguise and jumped aboard to initiate the fun!

We entered the cove and were very relieved to spot the pirate ship resting easy at anchor. I had selected this exact timing aware that the majority of the pirate scum would be unconscious or deeply asleep from the night's debauchery. Noting that the enemy's ship was under a skeleton watch, we continued our bold advance. When we arrived at the pirate's side, I called above, imitating perfectly Captain Bass's timbre and tone demanding immediate assistance. My calls were finally answered by one of the sleepy watchmen, who stuck his head over the rail responding to his Captain's familiar commands. I then ordered the pirate to assemble the watch to assist in the transfer of the money chest sitting in the bottom of our boat. Jumping to attention, the fool rushed off to find help to execute my terse orders.

After an agonizing wait, several more sleepy faces peered over the rail to receive further instructions. Informing them that the chest was heavy with coin, I ordered them to swing a yard over with hauling tackle attached to heave the chest aboard. As I waited, I began to become anxious for the sign that Powder Monkey would provide signaling that the prisoner had been rescued and announcing our call to battle. As the sleepy rogues continued to follow my barked commands, a large and thunderous explosion was heard above us. Saying a quiet prayer of thanks, I quickly ordered my men to sever the mooring ropes and to row us away from the side of the pirate ship with great haste.

As we were in the process of distancing ourselves, I heard several more explosions coming from the pirate craft. These loud noises woke the pirates from their nightly slumber and the rabble started to flood the topdeck to discover the source of the thunderous clamor. I then spied *Rue's Revenge* entering the cove to engage in battle. Having the huge advantage of surprise, Lion navigated our ship into a position that allowed Scuttle and his cannon teams a chance to unleash a barrage of shot that caused catastrophic damage to our enemy. Our cannons now concentrated on the pirate swine crowding the topdeck. Once again our guns boomed and a large number of pirates were swept completely off the deck by this bombarding shot.

Since this second salvo was our signal to board, I urged my crew to return to the pirate ship's side to join the fun. We reached our enemy and clambered aboard with frightful vengeance. As I watched in awe, our boarding crew tore through the villainous pirates at will. Between the furious musket fire from *Rue's Revenge* and the brutal hand-to-hand combat on the pirate ship's deck, our adversaries were being slaughtered at a most fearsome manner and rate. While enjoying the scene, I was suddenly attacked by one of the pirates who had snuck up behind me. Suffering a serious slash to my right arm, I utilized my left to fling a knife at my attacker, arresting his advance.

Prepared now to meet his charge, I ducked under his wild swing and gutted him with a savage left handed cutlass thrust. Kicking the brute over the side, I could see that the battle was practically at an end. The few remaining pirates were easily slaughtered by my advancing marauders and their deaths signaled the battle's conclusion. Reaching Long Tall Willie's side, I questioned him on the status of Rene's sister. With a wide smile, he informed me that she was safe with Powder Monkey. Asking about her condition, Long Tall Willie related that she was terrified and suffering nervous confusion, but otherwise seemed in very good health. Thanking him for a job well done, I ordered my men to scour our prize to uncover its secrets and to eliminate any pesky survivors. With a yelp, my hounds were off on their hunt. I was now bleeding quite freely so I made my way back to our dear ship to receive some medical attention from Doc.

Anything of value was stripped from Captain Bass's ship and transferred to our vessel including two stout chests of coin. Before dawn, we stacked the dead on the enemy's deck ignoring the numerous floating corpses surrounding us. We had lost two men and had sustained several severe injuries in the conflict, but our hosts had fared far worse. My wound was attended to and my arm was now in an immobilizing sling, but otherwise I was fine. I used Lion's cabin to house our rescued damsel and had visited her to assess her condition. She was in very good health but still terribly frightened. I assured that her reunion with her dear brother and sister was very close at hand, and invited her to use the remaining time to rest and compose herself. Traveling topside, I was met by Lion who informed me that the pirate's vessel had been gutted as ordered. When I questioned him on the suitability of our prize for our own use or sale, he sadly reported that the ship was in absolutely dreadful condition. Agreeing, I ordered her fired and sent to the bottom along with her scurvy crew. Once this task was accomplished, I commanded our return to Marie-Galant with all haste.

We reached our destination in the early morning hours in a jovial and celebratory mood. Our first encounter as a combat team had proven itself to be an extraordinary success. We had met and defeated our enemy in both a devastating and efficient manner. As we anchored in Rene's cove, we beheld that a welcoming party had already formed on the beach to greet our return. By the singing and dancing of our crew, I was sure that the assemblage on shore realized that we were the bearers of only good news. Escorting Rene's frightened sister to our awaiting longboat, we rowed to the small dock to deliver her to her brother and sister. The reunion was filled with joyous tears and laughter as Rene and Lille swarmed their sister with hugs and kisses. Breaking away from this celebration, Rene approached me and clasping his arm around my shoulder thanked me over and over again for the daring rescue. With an invitation to the manor house, he ordered food and drink for my crew. His decree brought a loud roar of approval from my men.

Placing Lion in charge, I returned to the mansion with the reunited siblings. Upon arriving, Lille led her sister-in-law off to be attended to, while Rene and I retreated to his library to discuss the events of the rescue. When we were comfortably seated, I related the entire adventure from start to finish, leaving out no detail. At the conclusion of my narrative, Rene informed me that he was amazed and thrilled by our exploits. In a very serious tone, he confessed that he owed me a great debt which he was sure he could never repay. With a wandering wave, he questioned what I desired as payment for the wondrous deed I had just performed. Matching his serious manner, I answered that I desired three things from him. Firstly, I asked if I could entrust my current fortune in his keeping for protection. Secondly, I confessed that I desired that we remain faithful friends. Lastly, I asked him with a huge grin for a chessboard and men so that I could enjoy friendly competitive match from time-to-time while at sea. Laughing now, he promised that each request would be happily and faithfully fulfilled.

Our discussion eventually returned to the perpetrator of the ugly kidnapping that we had foiled. Since the crime was more of a personal nature, I questioned Rene on his desires on the matter. He confessed that he would be most appreciative if I would remand the insidious kidnapper into his hands to ensure justice was served. Rene then promised to see the knave hung for his crimes. I told him that the rogue was now trussed and well guarded in my cabin. Rene then called for his plantation manager, called a busha, to attend him at once. When the man arrived, I was immediately surprised by the individual's overall size and ferocity. Staring at the behemoth, I realized that Captain Bass would receive nothing but extremely harsh treatment during his detainment on Marie-Galant.

Rene explained his plan for the proper handling of the prisoner and his charge responded that all would be prepared as quickly as possible for the safe internment of the kidnapping pirate. After all was readied, the giant would lead and armed escort to my ship and transport Captain Bass to his new domicile. Rene smiled and sent him on his way to complete this task. Suddenly feeling totally exhausted, I asked Rene's leave to check on my crew and to assist in the transfer of my old enemy. Agreeing, Rene invited me back for a feast he was preparing to celebrate his sister's return later that evening.

Arriving back on the beach, I found my crew already celebrating our victory over the pirates. As promised, Rene had provided a dazzling array of delicious cuisine along with more than generous supplies of ale and rum for my crew's pleasure. I gave my respect and thanks to everyone present for the outstanding victory that they had achieved. Once I was done lauding their victory, I made my way to our ship to check on the status of our mean-spirited prisoner. Climbing aboard, I noticed very few crewmen aboard. Lion had given the majority of the men leave to enjoy the sumptuous feast. Checking my cabin, I was gratified that No Nose had maintained his vigil over the bound and gagged miscreant. I notified No Nose that his relief was expected in the next few hours. With all in place, I found a quiet place below decks to get some much needed rest.

I awoke to the sounds of commotion aboard, and made my way topside to investigate. Rene's plantation overseer, had arrived with four armed guards and were roughly transporting a bound and helpless Captain Bass to the prison cell specially prepared for him. Glad to be free of the bullying swine, I made my way to my cabin to begin my preparations for the evening's festivities at the manor house. Since No Nose had accompanied the busha's party to shore to join his mates in drunken debauchery, I finally had the cabin to myself. Dragging the ransom chest to the topdeck, I unloaded the worthless rocks one-by-one over the side. Returning to my cabin with the emptied chest, I collected the majority of Captain Shivvers considerable fortune and placed it into the container. Securing the formidable padlock, I knew that its presence would raise no questions with my crew as they would naturally believe that I was merely returning the container to its proper owner. Stripping down and easing myself over the side and into the warm saltwater, I treated myself to a long needed bath as I scrubbed off the tons of filth I had accumulated over the past few days. Gertrude had instructed me multiple times that saltwater was a marvelous method of naturally cleansing wounds. To gain the maximum benefit, I had removed the sling and bandages covering the battle wound and soaked for a long time in the briny sea. Completing my bath, I climbed onboard and donned my suit of clothes and went to visit Doc. My friend was more than happy to inspect and re-bandage the wound. He announced that I was fortunate since the wound showed no signs of infection. He then informed me that I would still be without the use of this arm for the next three weeks.

Thanking the Doc for his efforts, I returned to my cabin to collect Rene's chest and had Lion cart it down to the awaiting transport for a short ride to shore. Once there, I ordered two drunken crewmen to load the chest on Rene's carriage while I checked on the remainder of the crew. At my appearance, my tipsy cohorts gave me several loud cheers and called for a toast. Accepting a glass of water, I raised it high and toasted their bravery and skills in battle, their overwhelming destruction of the insidious kidnappers, and most importantly their manly good looks! The last statement brought a roar of appreciation and laughter. I bid them all a good evening and departed to their loud cheers and well wishes. I returned to the manor house and requested the carriage driver transport the chest directly behind me.

Entering the home, I was escorted to the library where I found my friend awaiting my arrival. When we were alone, I provided the lock's key and informed Rene that the chest contained the fortune that I had asked him to protect. Opening the lock, Rene dug into the treasure in front of him with a mixture of awe and total surprise. After giving it a brief inspection, he glanced up at me and stammered that the chest did indeed contain a very large fortune. Smiling, he questioned the logic of merely holding such a valuable and significant sum. He then proposed an appealing alternative. He informed me that he could utilize this substantial wealth to purchase a significant portion of his island in my name to allow me one day to create a wondrous home for myself and my friends. He then articulated that the land he referred to was further south of his possessions. Winking, he confided that this property also included an excellent and well-hidden cove that would serve as a wondrous hiding place should the need ever arise. In addition, he promised to clear and build an excellent road connecting his land with the hidden cove, which he would also expertly secret. In this way, goods could be off-loaded at this hidden cove and transported to his storehouses for proper handling and to ensure a fair and concise inventory prior to our greedy Governor's knowledge or involvement. His plan made perfect sense and I readily agreed to the covert partnership he had proposed.

As our negotiations concluded, he walked me over to a magnificent chess set that sat on his library desk. As I hefted a few of the intricately carved men, he explained that the set had been manufactured years ago by native Indians on the Spanish Main for Spanish conquistadors. He informed me that the Indian craftsmen had labored long and hard with local precious materials to painstakingly create the exquisite pieces sitting before me. The board was also magnificent, as it was constructed of various tropical woods. The set had originally been purchased by his grandfather and had been passed from father to son ever since. He presented the beautiful set as my reward for saving his sister. Moved by his stunning show of generosity, I thanked him in my sincerest voice for the marvelous gift. Since the set was far too valuable to carry aboard my ship, I begged his indulgence to guard and protect the treasure for me. He promised to honor my request and to provide a less ostentatious set to accompany me on my travels. Thanking him again, I immediately challenged him to a match later that evening.

With our business concluded, we rose and made our way to the large dining hall where both women were waiting for our presence. Lille had preformed miracles with Rene's sister, Aimee. She had been scrubbed and outfitted in one of Lille's elegant dresses and the lass was stunningly beautiful. Petite with long blond tresses, she also sported a cute dimple on each of her cheeks along with sparkling green eyes. As we conversed, I found her witty, entertaining and totally mesmerizing. Providing me a kiss on both of my cheeks, she thanked me sincerely for her deliverance. She confessed to all that my act had saved her life, since she had overheard the pirates' plan to rape and kill her rather than return her regardless of the ransom payment. She then announced that she would forever remain grateful. In fact, she mentioned that she had many important friends, who might prove fortitudinous to me one day. As we sat for dinner, the women pleaded with me to recount my childhood experiences and the reasons I had chosen the sea as a way of life. Slowly and deliberately, I spun my life's story as we devoured course after course of our never-ending feast. As I concluded my tale over dessert, I could see that my story had a profound and stirring effect on them all!

After dinner, we moved to the candle-lit verandah for coffee and cigars for Rene and myself. As we were lighting our cigars, we were suddenly interrupted by the butler who delivered some very distressing news. Somehow Captain Bass had managed to escape his confinement, murdering four guards in the effort. Since he was now armed and on the loose, I asked Rene to escort the women upstairs and guard over them until assistance arrived. Turning to the butler, I scribbled a note to be delivered to Lion, commanding him to post sober and observant guards in case the murderer headed their way. Realizing that in all probability I was the target of this vicious fiend, I settled into a comfortable chair on the verandah to await his expected arrival. As I was thoroughly enjoying my cigar and coffee, Captain Bass stepped neatly from the surrounding vegetation onto the verandah. With a bloody cutlass secured in his hand, he informed me that I was about to die once and for all. In his crazed state, I knew he would be quite suggestible to my taunts and ploys, as I was quite certain that I would require every advantage available to survive the upcoming encounter. While severely limited by my untimely wound, I drew my own cutlass with my left hand and calmly awaited his charge. As I stood, I was confident that Tan's lessons had significantly improved my sword wielding skills. My simple goal in this life or death match was to delay the battle for as long as I could until help arrived, which I knew could take a very long time!

With an enraged bellow, Captain Bass suddenly attacked with the fury of a madman. For the next several minutes, I dodged and parried his advances attempting to conserve my energy. As this cat-and-mouse game progressed, I studied his every movement very closely. I observed that his mouth made a curious twitching motion before any serious lunge or strike, providing me a small amount of time to counter these attacks. I also noticed that after just a few minutes of exertion that his breathing had become ragged and labored attesting to his poor physical condition. As we circled one another warily, I innocently asked him if the horrible Blood Monkeys had ever returned. This query caused a look of dread and concern to appear on his face, as he furiously glanced around for any evidence of the simian demon's sudden appearance. As he did this, I used my *special voice* to issue an ape-like screech right behind him. At this sound, Captain Bass spun around in abject terror. Finally collecting his wits, he launched another furious assault and I easily evaded his flashing blade. For no reason, he once again ceased his attack while proceeding to turn in all directions wearing a very confused look. Switching to a menacing smirk, I realized too late that his latest movements were nothing more than a ruse. He suddenly lashed out with a vicious and totally unsuspected backhand slash. I felt his blade slice deeply across my injured arm. Peering down, I witnessed another savage gash appear on this arm which caused an amazingly large outpouring of blood. I realized at that moment that I could not hope to outlast him while awaiting help.

Captain Bass came to the same realization and began smiling at me like a total madman. At once, he attacked again and again, and I was having a difficult time evading his serious blows as I continued to slowly bleed to death. The few cuts and scratches I had scored in the conflict had no real effect of slowing him down. In that moment, I realized that I was going to die.

Then a strange thought entered my mind. I remembered a trick Tan had once taught me that could only be employed in a desperate and mortal situation. The problem was that I needed to be flat on my back to allow any chance of success instituting this ruse. Captain Bass, sensing my weakening constitution, pressed his attack to an even greater degree. At that point in our battle, my extreme dizziness signaled that my end was very near. To minimize further injury, I clung to him and whispered in his ear that I knew he was not guilty of murdering Sergeant O'Toole. In fact, I confessed that my friends had actually stolen his dagger on my orders and subsequently utilized it to kill the obnoxious military man.

Incensed beyond the point of insanity by my confession, Captain Bass furiously shoved me away from him. I tumbled very hard onto my back, and I found myself in the perfect position to execute Tan's deception. Clutching my cutlass with my left hand, I glanced up to see Captain Bass leering over me and raising his sword to end my life. Tan had taught me that an aggressor standing over a victim expected capitulation not attack. In addition, an individual in this superior position normally guarded only against a high frontal strike from their opponent. Forgoing a high strike, I concentrated on my opponent's ankles. The move I was taught was executed in three separate steps. The first called for a vicious slash to your opponent's ankles. While my aim was true, my strength was waning and I managed to slice his ankles anemically causing him to momentarily falter but not collapse.

The second step was purely defensive as I rolled over and pivoted on my shoulders to vacate the spot on the ground to avoid my opponent's expected retaliation. Rolling to a sitting position slightly behind my adversary, I executed the third and most important stroke. With all the strength I could muster, I swung my blade in a flat horizontal arc aimed directly at the back of his ankles. This spot was highly venerable and housed an important soft tendon that when severed sealed the fate of any individual. My aim was perfect and my sharp blade bit deep into Captain Bass's ankle tendons, severing them both causing him to lose balance and pitch forward face-first to the ground where he flopped around like a landed fish. With our positions reversed, I slowly and agonizingly rose to my feet to end the battle once and for all. As my enemy reached and groped for his sword that had fallen from his hand, I lashed down and severed his right hand just above the wrist. Screaming in agony and seething with demonic rage, he attempted once again to reach the cutlass with his uninjured left hand. Finding absolutely no pity in my heart, I again slashed down and separated this hand also. Bellowing like a maddened bull, the helpless brute rolled around on the ground swearing and cursing my name. Full of hatred and fury, I unleashed my blade and buried it in his throat finally ending his miserable existence forever. With that, I pitched forward and slammed to the ground.

Before long, I was rolled onto my back by Rene, who together with Lion and several armed men told me that Captain Bass was dead. On Lion's orders, Captain Bass was hauled away and dumped unceremoniously in a nearby swamp as fresh fodder for its creeping scavengers.

At that point, I slipped into an unconscious state from severe blood loss. As I hovered between life and death over the next several days, I was plagued by gruesome nightmares that seemed very real to my confused mind. I also seemed to recall beautiful angels hovering over me attempting to communicate, but I was unable to translate their mysterious language. I simply drifted off to a dark and empty place. The one nightmare that seemed to replay again and again in my mind was the angry words and face of Captain LeMerde informing me that I was nothing but a pirate and as such doomed to perform a hempen jig, which is hanging to you landlubbers!

Chapter 20: Escape from a Mad Frenchman

As I edged closer and closer to consciousness, my dreams became shorter in duration and quite jumbled. I suddenly came back to the world in all its dazzling glory. As I struggled to determine my exact location, I glanced around my surroundings and recognized my friends, the Turbouts, anxiously watching over me. My first perception was that I must have been injured far worse than I had previously thought, because I was covered from head-to-toe with bandaging. Sensing my confusion, Rene was quick to explain that he had ordered the excess swaddling hoping to disguise and shelter me from my vicious adversary, Captain LeMerde, who had arrived not long after my tussle with Captain Bass. Stunned by this news even in my completely addled state, I weakly petitioned Rene to elaborate. He explained that I had made a horrific mistake when I publicly humiliated the narcissistic naval commander, who became the butt of island-wide jokes and jibes. During his convalescence, the French peacock had the opportunity to build up a raging fervor to extract revenge for the unforgivable slights I had engineered at his expense. To that end, he had commissioned a series of spies island-wide to monitor and report each and every one of my movements while he spent his time in recuperation. As luck would have it, an island physician hired by Rene to assist in my treatment and recovery had provided the revengeful villain with enough pertinent information to allow LeMerde to conduct a surprise raid on Rene's holdings. Having done so, the scoundrel had placed myself, my ship and my crew in utmost peril. After spending what seemed like a good deal of time digesting this extremely ill news, I questioned the trio on the current state of matters. They reported that LeMerde had conducted his clandestine raid just a few days prior. The prideful officer's timing could not have been any better since my crew were still in the process of celebrating our recent victory over Captain Bass and his minions. Sweeping into Rene's harbor, LeMerde had easily captured *Rue's Revenge* and had stationed his gunship alongside my vessel with orders to blow my ship to splinters if any sort of escape attempt were undertaken. To further guard his new prize, he had posted a squad of his own sailors on my vessel to keep a close watch on my loyal crew. Additionally, to stave off any escape attempt on my part, Captain LeMerde had positioned a cadre of men around the plantation manor including two right outside of this room. To my utter dismay, Rene finally confessed the very worst of the news. In a doleful tone, he stammered that LeMerde intended to see me hanged as soon as I was healthy enough to participate in the proceeding.

Stupefied and aghast at all of this horrendous scuttlebutt, I suddenly was overcome with extreme exhaustion which matched my frightful dismay, and I dropped back into restless unconsciousness. Awakening later that day, I found that Rene and his family still at my bedside. Sensing my utter dejection and worry, my friends attempted consolation by promising to assist any escape attempt I might undertake. All the Turbout's required was clear direction. Still quite groggy, I nevertheless begged them to recount the current situation in absolute detail one again. As they repeated all of the precautions that Captain LeMerde had instituted at my expense, Rene happened to mention an upcoming celebration that had been planned in Aimee's honor. This revelry was to occur in three days time, and would be attended by a multitude of dignitaries from Guadeloupe. While Rene planned to postpone the party due to my very unfortunate predicament, I convinced him otherwise. I was sure that this festivity would provide a very convenient and much needed diversion to allow me an opportunity to escape LeMerde's clutches. All I had to do now was conceptualize a plan that would enable me to do so. As a sudden swell of utter exhaustion washed over me like a rogue wave, I thanked each of them for their assistance and concern and immediately dropped back into oblivion.

I regained consciousness later upon hearing Aimee singing a very sad song from somewhere very close. As I listened to her, I realized that her voice was sweet and clear, a real talent indeed! Looking around my surroundings, I discovered that I had actually been placed in Lille's bedroom, as I identified various articles of clothing that I had witnessed my gracious host wearing. Just then, Aimee made a sweeping entrance through a side door that must have connected her room to that of her sister-in-law's. Continuing my scan of the various articles heaped about the room, an outlandish thought crept into my mind based on a bygone incident. I had previously reasoned that devising any sort of escape plan that would not further endanger my friends, or destroy my ship and crew in the process would require deviousness and cunning. Realizing that this new burgeoning scheme was daring and dangerous, I explained my premature thinking to Aimee. I was not at all surprised to witness the shocked and horror-filled expression that initially appeared on her face. As she continued to listen, this dubious and highly perturbed expression morphed into a mirthful smile. At the end of my explanation, she agreed that my plan was certainly bold enough to succeed. Jumping up from a bedside chair, she announced that she would covertly communicate the details to Rene and Lille at once so that the four of us could begin strategizing and effecting the necessary and complex preparations.

I determined that the first and most important step was to improvise a proper disguise. I was now certain that this crucial step could only be accomplished with the knowledgeable assistance of Aimee and Lille. I insisted on remaining fully bandaged since this camouflaged condition would play later into the devious scam I was engineering. The next step was to have Rene alert the pompous French officer that I had finally regained consciousness. The third step was for Rene to pass the word to Lion to prepare *Rue's Revenge* to sail, but to do only in absolute secrecy so our French enemies were not alerted to our intentions. Yet another crucial step necessary for our plan's success was to ensure that the celebration in Aimee's honor would also serve as her farewell party, as a result of her feigned burning desire to return to the safety and comfort of her home in France. Lastly, Aimee would also need to perform a singing exhibition during this upcoming celebration planned in her honor.

That same afternoon, Captain LeMerde swaggered into my room to gloat over my grim situation. Pretending to migrate in and out of consciousness, I finally greeted my tormentor in a weak and fluttering voice and welcomed him to Marie–Galant. Sneering at my words, Captain LeMerde announced that I would pay for the island-wide embarrassment I had inflicted upon him as a result of the brawl at the *Blind Unicorn*. Continuing, he promised me a most ghastly death by hanging as soon as possible regardless of the *Lettre of Marque* issued by our incompetent Governor. Continuing his litany of threats, he also stipulated that my ship and crew would be delivered to Porte-A-Pitre, where my entire crew would summarily be tried as pirates and punished accordingly. He warned me that he had placed armed guards outside my door to arrest any escape attempt on my part. Wishing me a speedy recovery with a serpent-like hiss, he proudly promised that I would die painfully before the week had finished.

As the time drew closer for the celebration, I was gratified to learn that all preparations had been completed. Rene revealed that he had informed Captain LeMerde that Aimee planned on leaving for Guadeloupe immediately after her party. He then petitioned the conceited brute for his sister conveyance via the Frenchman's warship to Guadeloupe, so that she could board an awaiting transport for her desired and expedient return to France. Explaining that his sister was quite anxious to put the nasty kidnapping in her past, he entreated the unscrupulous officer to personally see to her transference.

However, Captain LeMerde was quick to decline this privilege, explaining that his presence was vitally required at my execution. Appearing exceedingly desperate for a solution, Rene then petitioned if *Rue's Revenge* could be utilized. Captain LeMerde's first reaction was to deny this request, but Rene finally convinced him of my crew's utmost loyalty and assured Captain LeMerde that my men would comply with any command issued them aware that I was being held as a helpless prisoner. Reluctant but eventually convinced, Captain LeMerde agreed to this plan, but informed Rene that a substantial armed escort would continue to be stationed on the pirate craft to ensure the ship and crew would remain anchored at Guadeloupe upon arrival to await prosecuting and punishment. The scheme was now rigged and all that remained was its actual execution!

On the afternoon of the celebration, guests began to arrive in their small transports. Aimee had divulged that a veritable feast had been arranged for the party with copious quantities of food and drink available for their guest's consumption. The verandah had been outfitted with torches and the household came alive as the festivities were about to begin. Rene revealed that Captain LeMerde and his thugs were also present to ensure that all proceeded smoothly. As the party got underway, Captain LeMerde paid me a quick visit to gloat over my miserable defeat once more. With a wicked smirk, he informed me that a special gallows was being erected at the dock in my esteemed honor. Continuing, he snickered with extreme pleasure that I would hang in no more than two or three day's time. Bidding me sweet dreams, he stalked out of the room. As soon as he made his haughty departure, I jumped out of bed and began my own preparations. Looking in a mirror, I could see that the last few weeks of recuperation had cost me a significant loss of weight. Smiling at my thin reflection, I was quite sure that it would immeasurably assist my upcoming escape attempt.

A while later, I heard Rene make an announcement to formally introduce his sister, the honoree of the gala occasion. He explained to the gathered crowd that Aimee would be returning to France the following day to put her dreadful abduction totally behind her. However, he proudly proclaimed that she had agreed to perform a very special singing exhibition for all present prior to her departure. I could hear the loud round of applause that announced Aimee's entrance. She then proceeded to thrill her attentive audience with the tale of her rescue by me and my brave crew. After she completed the harrowing saga, she then proclaimed that Captain LeMerde intended to hang me shortly as a pirate, which was met with a series of hisses and loud shouts for my release. Rene informed me later that Captain LeMerde had turned bright crimson with embarrassment at this supportive response for me. The crowd, swayed by Aimee's tale, were duly convinced that the detested officer's extreme actions were not appropriate and continued to clamor for my immediate release.

Sensing that he was quickly losing control, Captain LeMerde threatened serious harm to anyone who attempted to stop him from justly hanging me as an insidious pirate. Striding to Governor LaCouturie's side, he whispered all manner of personal threats should the Governor not condone the hanging. Frightened to the extreme, our cowardly Governor informed the assemblage that he had certainly not issued a *Lettre of Marque* on my behalf. Therefore, I was operating as a pirate and deserved my just reward no matter how valiantly I had acted in Aimee's rescue. Sensing that nothing more could be done in my defense, the Turbout's remained completely silent on the matter. While the crowd was certainly not appeased by the Governor's admission, they nevertheless settled down and put the nasty business aside, since there was very little any of them could actually accomplish anyways.

To lighten the mood of his guests, Rene reintroduced his sister and prompted her to begin her performance. As I continued to listen intently, I could hear Aimee begin singing a popular love ballad which hushed the crowd completely. In her beautiful voice, she continued to perform a series of touching songs, ending the exhibition with her finest effort and her personal favorite, *Versailles, the Light of the World*. Aimee's final and triumphant rendition brought the entire mansion to a complete standstill. She was mesmerizing and entrancing in her performance, which completely enthralled and enchanted her doting audience.

Once finished, Aimee demurely made her rounds, thanking her new admirers for their warm and wonderful appreciation of her performance, as well as their loyal comradeship and friendship which she promised to never forget. Feigning the slow loss of her voice due to her strenuous singing efforts, she was finally reduced to hushed whispering. She then informed the crowd in an extremely weak voice her immediate need to depart, to prepare for her trip home early the following morning. In barely a whisper, she apologized sincerely for having to leave so abruptly, but promised to return someday to revisit all of her new friends. As she made her grand exit, a huge roar of applause trailed her graceful retreat.

Moving into her room and listening intently at her door, I could hear Captain LeMerde notifying her that he planned to personally accompany her to the waiting ship for her transport to Guadeloupe. Questioning the amount of time she required to ready herself, she anemically squeaked that she only needed to change into suitable traveling clothes, since her trunks filled with her belongings were already packed and loaded on a delivery wagon. Captain LeMerde then informed her that he would follow her carriage on horseback when she was ready. Nodding approval, she slipped quietly into the room leaving Captain LeMerde outside. As she entered and closed the door, she gave me a wink and we both went to work to prepare for my escape.

Per our plan, I donned her traveling clothes, which had been previously tailored to fit me, and arranged a blonde wig on my head. To conceal my face, I had chosen a bonnet with a black veil to complete my traveling ensemble. To finalize the ruse, I bandaged Aimee's face, arms and hands, and then moving back into Lille's room used drapery cords to lash her securely to the bed I had just vacated. To give her further excuse beyond her loss of voice for not alerting the guards stationed at the door, I gagged the lass prior to entirely covering her with my former bandages. Since she would be required to be in this very uncomfortable position for possibly a number of hours, I had Powder Monkey deliver a mild herbal mixture that would relax and calm her nerves as she lay in this prone position bound to the bed.

When all was completed, I returned to Aimee's room. Utilizing my *special voice* to duplicate Aimee's, I softly called for her maid to enter the room and carry her small travel bag to the waiting transport. At the front door of the mansion, I was met by Rene and Lille, who whispered that they were both fully prepared to execute their roles to ensure they did not become suspects in my plot to foil Captain LeMerde's hempen jig party. As we parted, I whispered to my dear friends that I would return soon, and thanked them once again for their invaluable assistance. As I entered my waiting carriage, I continued the performance by waving Aimee's handkerchief to Captain LeMerde to ensure he was ready to follow. He answered that he would be along as soon as he had a final word with his men inside, but instructed the carriage driver to proceed directly to the dock. Making his way inside, he returned to Lille's room to ensure all was in order. Peeking into the room, he was satisfied to observe that his detested prisoner was still lying in bed bandaged and quite helpless.

Since we had an earlier start, my carriage arrived at the dock long before my enemy. Thanking the carriage driver in a hushed tone, I boarded the waiting longboat and was immediately rowed out to my ship. Onboard, I was immediately directed to my own cabin. As soon as I reached this destination, I was greeted warmly by Lion and Powder Monkey. Asking them both if all was in readiness, they responded with quick nods. Just a short time later, Captain LeMerde arrived, and strutted his way onto our ship to ensure all was right and proper. Glancing around in a quick inspection, he called Lion over to his side and commanded Lion to weigh anchor and deliver his recently arrived passenger directly to Guadeloupe. Once he had completed this charge, Lion was instructed to remain there awaiting LeMerde's arrival. If these specific orders were disobeyed, Captain LeMerde promised horrid and dire fates for Lion as well as the entire crew. He also informed Lion that the armed escort onboard would serve to guarantee his firm directives were obeyed implicitly. At this point, Captain LeMerde saluted his prodigious onboard guard detail and returned to his longboat to row over to his nearby gunship.

As he moved away from our ship, I made a grand appearance, still in Aimee's garb, to the roars and shouts of my entire crew. Waiving Aimee's handkerchief in a fond farewell to my enemy, I signaled Lion to proceed swiftly with our prearranged plan. In the blink of an eye, Lion ordered the severing of our anchor line to allow us to cut and run. Next, he shouted the command to fire our guns. They boomed in response sending a deadly barrage sweeping across our enemy's vessel destroying all manner of masts, cables and sails. Given that our onboard armed French escorts were momentarily stunned by our surprising cannon volley, they were quickly subdued by our superior forces. Once incapacitated, they were treated to an immediate saltwater bath. Lastly, our sails were furiously unfurled and we began a steady departure from Rene's cove.

By the time I stripped off my disguise, we were steadily gaining speed as we headed out to sea. Returning to their senses, we could see and hear a mad flurry of activity aboard the disabled French warship. Captain LeMerde, still situated in his longboat, was shouting out a string of commands to his shipboard officers to halt our escape. However, our cannons had caused enough damage aboard our foe to prevent any possibility of reprisal or giving chase. Meanwhile, Captain LeMerde was bouncing up and down in his longboat in absolute hysterics, yelling continuously for his vessel to shadow our wake. Anyone viewing his performance would judge him to be totally and unequivocally deranged!

As we made our quick departure, we gave our enemies a rousing farewell cheer. Later, Rene would fill me in on our ruse's conclusion. Captain LeMerde immediately returned to the plantation intent on hanging me that very evening. Storming up to the front door, he was met by Rene and Lille, who acted startled and dumbfounded at his dire news of the pirate band's escape. Racing upstairs, he found his prisoner still bedridden. Bursting into the room and shouting my name, he demanded to know what my crew was doing by attempting to run away. Unable to elicit an answer from the bandaged occupant, the enraged officer ran over to the bed and began to shake his prisoner, demanding an answer to his question.

It was at this point that he noticed something highly unusual. As he attempted to shake his prisoner he realized that the bedridden pirate could not be moved. Yanking the covers off, he was shocked to discover that his prisoner had been tied securely to the bed. Numbed and confused by this discovery, he then peered into his prisoner's eyes, noticing their frightened and pleading state. Totally mystified, he roughly yanked off the bandages covering the prisoner's face to discover a frightfully terrified Aimee under the wrappings. He could see that she was both immobilized as well as gagged. Untying the gag, he was rewarded with a horrible and tortured scream from Aimee, which drew the guards and the Turbouts into the room. Rene and Lille pretended to be equally shocked at the discovery of Aimee fully bandaged and secured to the bed. Finally managing to calm the lass down, Captain LeMerde questioned her on exactly what had happened. In a halting and sobbing voice, she explained that I had attacked her when she had entered her room to change into her traveling clothes. I then had dragged her into this adjoining room and tied her to the bed. In a guttural moan, Aimee cried that I then gagged her and arranged the bandages on her face, arms and hands. Where I had gone remained a total mystery. Captain LeMerde suddenly had a strange thought. In a weak voice, he croaked; "If you are here, then who is on the *Rue's Revenge* in your place?" As if answering his own question, he began muttering my name over and over again.

But that was not the end of Rene's rehash of the concluding events of that evening. As LeMerde finally collected a modicum of lucidity, he donned a malicious leer and directed a blasphemous and threatening prognostication to my three trembling co-conspirators. In an ominous voice laden with pure malice and contempt, the incensed naval officer bellowed that he was quite sure that the Turbouts had somehow been willing accomplices in my escape plot. As such, he vowed categorically through clenched teeth that they would pay the ultimate price for their insidious deceit and treachery. After issuing this prophetic declaration, he stomped his way out of the manor house leaving a trail of continued threats and insinuations in his maddened wake!

As we made our escape, I maintained a northerly direction until we were well clear of detection, and then I ordered us to reverse our course and sail south. I realized that our eventual destination and ultimate destiny lay north, but I felt we still had important work to accomplish. There was more celebration and festivity aboard over our triumphant escape, and I allowed my crew to have their fun.

Chapter 21: Piratical Decisions

The next morning I was up and about greeting my crew, most of who were still recovering from the prior evening's celebration. Since I felt the time was right to discuss our future, I made for a tiny deserted isle with a serviceable cove and anchored our ship in the safety of this isolated haven. Lion, alerted to our departure plans well in advance, had fully stocked our ship stores. In no immediate need of supplies, I called all hands on deck to discuss our future.

I began by informing them that our *Lettre of Marque* protected us from swinging from the gallows, since we could now legally operate as French privateers and not as ravenous marauding pirates. In this regard, I informed them that we could continue our seafaring efforts without the danger of "performing an unwelcome dance of death at the end of a rope". Further, I pointed out that it made little sense to chase after meager prey operating as foreign traders even with the protection of our official status. I pointed out that these ships rarely provided any sort of substantial booty anyway. On the other hand, I carefully crafted a scenario of searching out and destroying scurvy sea thieves, whose goal was the rape and pillage of all manner of vessel. These thieves routinely amassed a considerable fortune in their normal operations and their bounty was ours for the taking. Continuing, I theorized that every pirate vessel we captured was worth tenfold the value of any vulnerable merchantmen.

The crew took little time in agreeing with my sound logic on these points. I continued by mentioning that while it seemed like we would be attacking stronger and better armed adversaries, I did not believe this to be a true assessment. I reminded them that, for most part, pirates did not relish the thought of armed conflict, but rather relied on speed, surprise and bloodthirsty reputations to ensure that their prey capitulated without conflict. I further explained that the vast majority of pirates were really cowards at heart. I then reminded them that our ship and crew had been transformed into a seasoned fighting force. With our superb tactical skills, our combative fearsomeness and our weapons superiority, we could easily match our skills with any pirate on the open seas and claim victory. I then made a solemn promise that I would not needlessly put the crew or the ship in harms way, but rather keep us afloat and operating successfully which would make each of them filthy rich beyond their wildest dreams. With that said, I asked them what they all thought of my plan. With a rousing cheer, they voiced their total agreement to my new course of action.

Quieting them, I explained that we needed to vote on several crucial matters. The first of these was agreement to a ship's name, since our current name no longer seemed quite appropriate. Continuing, I confided in them that I had to quickly devise a new ship's name to secure the *Lettre of Marque*, and had utilized the name *Rue's Revenge*, in honor of my well-known sweetheart and her dire predicament she faced. I informed them if they were not comfortable with my choice, that I would be amenable to allowing them to devise a substitute. The only caveat to this statement was that we would be forced to operate as *Rue's Revenge* until I was able to formally petition the Governor to alter the *Lettre of Marque*. I then divulged that this alteration might prove very expensive, due to the sizable bribes that were necessary to persuade our corrupt Governor to alter the *Lettre of Marque*. As expected, the threat of wasting their hard earned booty to change the ship's name was totally unacceptable. Therefore, with a rousing vote of agreement, they agreed that *Rue's Revenge* was the perfect name for our vessel.

I then unfurled a red flag that I held by my side. I explained that I had taken the liberty to have this special flag manufactured on Guadeloupe. Unfolding the flag, before their curious eyes, I received the exact response that I had hoped for, stunned looks of fear and horror! While the design of the flag was quite simple in nature, it was concocted to elicit a terrifying response from anyone viewing it. While most pirate flags displayed skulls, dripping cutlasses, bleeding hearts and expiring hourglasses, my design was totally unique. On a totally blood-red field, I had imposed a savage and hideous yellowed human skull. However, this is where all similarity with other pirate flags ended. Protectively cradling this ghastly image was a huge raven-black rat, as enormous as any feral cat I had ever witnessed. In fact, the repugnant rodent seemed to almost dwarf its prized trophy. The foul rat had its jaws wide-open, with its massive sharpened teeth and fangs bared, prepared to attack and protect its horrid prize. The rat was terrifying in its own right, but the fact that it was protectively curled around the haunting human skull made the image highly disturbing indeed. Regaining their wits as I carefully rolled up our new flag, my crew unanimously screamed their approval.

I informed the crew that we now required a charter of our ship's rules on which we would operate. Smiling off to my side, Long Tall Willie shouted that he was sure that I had plenty of time lying on my back in a comfortable bed to devise some new rules for us. This statement brought a huge wave of laughter at my expense. Laughing along with them, I answered that I indeed had given the issue some careful thought. With that, I launched into the list of rules that I had previously and most carefully devised. There were ten rules in all and they read as follows:

Rue's Revenge's Rules of Shipboard Operation

1. The ship shall be commanded by her Captain. All serious decisions will be made by a vote of her crew. Once confirmed by the crew's vote, the Captain shall take command with total obedience expected by all.

2. All booty shall be shared by the entire crew. Any attempt to defraud or cheat the count shall be judged as theft and the villain punished most severely as judged by the Captain.

3. No women shall be allowed onboard during any voyage. Any women rescued or captured during a voyage shall be treated with utmost decency and fair play. Failure to uphold this law will result in harsh and swift punishment as determined by the Captain.

4. Drinking shall be allowed onboard, but drunkenness will be sternly frowned upon and will elicit nasty repercussions. All crewmembers are to remain sober before and during battle. Drunken mates are not to be tolerated during this time under penalty of death.

5. Desertion of post, cowardice in battle, or unwillingness to fight shall result in forfeiture of share and immediate dismissal from the ship no matter our position.

6. No fighting or quarreling amongst crew shall be tolerated at any time. Personal disagreements will be settled solely on land in view of all comrades. Murder aboard will result in an individual's loss of life and the joy of sharing eternity with his murdered mate.

7. The Captain shall garner three full shares; the First Mate shall receive one and a half shares. Each crewmember shall be entitled to a full share. A special bonus shall be awarded as deemed appropriate by the Captain for individual actions above and beyond duty's call. A full ten shares will be held in ship's treasury for lean times to ensure the crew sufficient funds to enjoy all liberty occasions.

8. Each member of crew shall be responsible for maintaining his weapons in battle-ready condition. No exceptions granted. Failure to do so will result in harsh consequences.

9. No unguarded flame shall be allowed at anytime due to danger of fire. Breaking this rule will result in a discomforting salt water bath.

10. Mutiny or armed aggression against the ship's authority will result in the immediate death of all mutinous traitors.

I read the rules one-by-one to the crew for their agreement. In truth, they were quite surprised that I had allowed any sort of drinking aboard ship. I explained that it would be much easier for me to persuade them all to become clergymen than to get them to cease imbibing. As such, I decided the fairest compromise was to allow drinking, but punish extreme drunkenness. With a consolidated roar of approval, my ship's laws were passed unanimously. The truth was that my men trusted me implicitly. I silently vowed to myself that I would never jeopardize this trust. Having agreed to all that needed discussing, I ordered a hogshead of rum to be delivered topside for a celebration. As the rum warmed their tummies and their spirits, I joined the shipboard band in a series of old and familiar seafaring songs like *Gulls Come A Flapping, The Girl Back Home, Grommet Billy's Lament* and their absolute favorite *Poxy Doxy*. The celebration continued late into the night, when morning arrived much too early for the suffering sailors who had overindulged the previous evening. Giving them all a chance to fully recover, I delayed all combat classes until later that afternoon.

Chapter 22: Loony Louie's Mermaid

By that afternoon, all were in a much improved condition and we resumed our voyage. The anchor was weighed and we slowly eased out of our hidden cove, taking our time to ensure that LeMerde had not somehow followed our course. Relieved to find the sea clear of all vessels, I ordered all of our sails unfurled for our continued run south. Later, the starboard watch shouted that he had spotted a small craft drifting aimlessly in the currents. Assuming it to be deserted, we altered our course to give inspection. Our topman called down that he had spotted a prone figure curled up in the belly of this small boat. As we approached, the figure came to life yelling all manner of nasty threats in our direction. He seemed manic at our intended approach as he stood waving one of the boat's oars in a very threatening manner.

When we reached hailing distance, I called out to the man questioning why he was drifting in the middle of open water in his minuscule transport. Yelling back, he explained that he had recently escaped from a savage Spanish pirate, who had promised nothing but death. Then upon spying our beautiful figurehead, he went completely silent gazing up at the marvelous carving that adorned our bow. In a sort of childish sing-song voice, he then addressed our nautical protectress. In this strange tone, he thanked our icon for delivering him to safety. I ordered a rope ladder dropped over the side and invited this strange creature aboard. He was short and squat of frame with a generous belly hanging over his roped britches. Sporting a deep sea color, he was beardless but compensated for this absence with a mass of wild grey-streaked hair that angled in every direction. There was a wild-eyed look to this stranger, signaling that he was certainly one-oar-short. His crazed appearance was accompanied by his constant drooling and slobbering, like a large dog after slurping copious amounts of water. Striding up to me, he introduced himself as Loony Louie, a name I found quite fitting. Since he was famished, I sent him along with Powder Monkey to see to his sustenance. Once this task was accomplished, I asked that he be delivered to me so that I could hear his story.

Completely sated, Loony Louie was back in front of me still slobbering and drooling. I asked him to relate exactly how he had found his way into his predicament. Nodding, he launched into his sad tale of woe. It seemed that he had operated as a pirate on a number of voyages under the command of a brutal and vicious Dutch Captain surnamed Barnes. As a member of this extremely scurvy crew, Loony Louie had managed to remain alive during countless piratical expeditions that netted his ship an unbelievable amount of treasure. As his ship was on the prowl for fresh pickings, a vicious and nasty ailment broke out onboard. The disease claimed the lives of more than half of the mates, forcing Captain Barnes to stop on a deserted atoll to locate fresh water and food. While anchored, Captain Barnes made the decision to return to their sanctuary on land, since his ailing crew was significantly depleted and quite unable to defend the ship to any significant degree. This was a very difficult decision, since they would be returning home with no spoils and liberty would be extremely meager to say the least. After procuring the necessary fresh water and a small amount of the cay's fruit, the ship resumed its voyage, but was soon attacked by a vicious and bloodthirsty band of Spanish sea devils.

Since Loony Louie's shipmates were still recovering from the ravages of their recent serious malady, the ship stood little chance of defeating these Spanish marauders In an attempt to forestall bloodshed the Spanish Captain, named Juan Hector Sanchez, made his way onto the Dutch vessel carrying a white flag and demanding a parley with Captain Barnes. Loony Louie described this Spanish Captain as nothing but a vain and deceitful peacock. The Spaniard, nicknamed Captain Happy Jack, wore elaborate formal attire including a brilliant white dress shirt with laced cuffs and collar, matching white knee-high stockings held in place by two red ribbons, black satin britches with silver buckles and complemented by a heavily brocaded red greatcoat. This fancy outfit was made complete by a pair of fine leather shoes with silver buckles and a black tricorn hat that sported a huge multi-colored feather. He wore several rings on each of his hands along with a gold crucifix on a chain hanging down to the middle of his chest. His hair was long and plaited with several red ribbons. Finally, he sported a thin mustache that ran all the way down to the bottom of his chin.

Loony Louie explained that initially the rogue was all civility and charm as he greeted his new compatriots. He brought aboard casks of rum for the crew's enjoyment and proclaimed that he insisted on a parley under the cover of a white flag, a talk under neutral non-threatening conditions. While detaining the Dutch Captain Barnes and his senior officers, the Spanish pirate crew stood by patiently while their new comrades enjoyed the proffered rum. Still operating under the white parley flag, the rogues then swept down upon the poor unsuspecting Dutch crew and obliterated them, dumping their bodies overboard. In the meantime, the Spanish sea dandy unleashed his sharp blade and attacked the unarmed Dutch officers, murdering all but the Captain Barnes. Since Loony Louie was in the hold sleeping off a bottle of rum, his life was also spared in this initial slaughter.

The total absence of booty on the Dutch ship convinced the devious Captain Happy Jack that his Dutch captives had secreted their treasure somewhere aboard. Securing Captain Barnes tightly to the mainmast, the Spanish degenerate proceed to flay off swatch after swatch of the poor unfortunate's skin, demanding the exact location of the treasure. Subjected to this bestial treatment for what seemed like a lifetime, Captain Barnes was quite incapable of convincing the diabolical Papist that the treasure he sought did not exist. While Captain Barnes could not divulge a location for a nonexistent cache, he did manage a brief respite by claiming that the treasure was hidden in empty water barrels residing the hold. Once the Spanish pirates uncovered his deception, they were enraged beyond reason and the bestial skinning resumed at an even greater pace. Under this heartless and pain-wracking inquisition, Captain Barnes finally gave up the will to live and simply expired.

Frustrated and far beyond reason, the Spanish crew then voted to murder the lone Dutchman's survivor, Loony Louie. Captain Happy Jack interceded and eventually convinced his men that the Dutch Captain provided no light on the location of the ship's treasure. As such, Loony Louie was their sole opportunity to discover the truth to its hiding place. Therefore, he persuaded his crew to forestall their bloodlust until a confession was obtained by the most brutal and devilish means available. Agreeing with this sound logic, the crew forcefully dragged Loony Louie back to their ship for a very proper Spanish interrogation.

Once aboard the Spanish vessel, the insidious Captain Happy Jack, totally familiar with extreme methods of torture, decided to employ the nefarious *strappado* to loosen Loony Louie's tongue. This particularly brutal method of inflicting extreme anguish and pain was conducted by securely fastening a victim's hands behind his back and then attaching a stout cable to them. This cable was then looped over a convenient yardarm and the poor unfortunate was hauled backwards into the air. Loony Louie confessed that the pain he experienced was explosive and extreme the moment his feet left the deck. Given the tremendous strain on his arms, Loony Louie confided that his arms separated from his shoulder joints on his third climb into the air. Each time he was lowered to the maindeck, he was commanded to reveal the treasure's true location. Unable to answer because he had no knowledge of its existence and quite delirious with pain, he realized that his captors would end the game in a permanent fashion once he divulged the precious information they sought regardless of its truthfulness. Therefore, he was forced to remain reluctantly silent and endure the agonizing ride up and down on Lucifer's lifeline time and again. The poor soul's only relief came when he passed out from extreme agony.

These relief periods were short lived because he was routinely treated to a saltwater bath that rudely returned him to consciousness so he could enjoy an agonizing ascension once again. As evening approached, the entire pirate horde tired of their game and headed below for food and drink, leaving Loony Louie in a collapsed and unconscious heap. Sometime during their absence, Loony Louie awoke and quickly assessed his situation. Unable to endure any more of the horrific *strappado* and having no beneficial answer to provide his captors, he decided to end his own life by drowning. Using only his legs, he managed to scoot over to the ship's side and drop into the sea with a slight splash. When he surfaced, he discovered that he was adjacent to the pirate's longboat that was being towed behind their ship by a stout line ready to return to the Duchman to claim their rightful prize. He painstakingly managed to untie the longboat and cling desperately to its side. Eventually, the tides and swift current carried him silently away from his enemies.

As he lost sight of the lights on his tormentor's vessel, he attempted to pull himself into the small craft. Every effort was met with failure, so he merely clung to the side of the craft for the entire night. The gracious sea gods looked favorably upon him by never allowing his enemies to discover his departure. The next day he sighted land, so he strenuously kicked his way to shore. Exhausted to the extreme, he was able to drag his longboat painstakingly up on the deserted beach. Using a crook in a small nearby tree, he was able to snap both of his arms back into place, immediately passing out from exertion and unbelievable pain on each attempt. Once he eventually awoke, he managed to cover the small craft with vines and branches to avoid detection and set about searching for food and water. During the next few days, he managed to gather some food, and filled a few empty wineskins found in the bottom of his boat with fresh water. Equipped now with food and water, he pushed the longboat back into the sea to seek rescue.

He was at sea for several weeks without encountering a single ship. Swallowing now from a bottle of proffered rum, he confessed that on one of these nights he experienced a very strange incident. Just before dark as he lay exhausted in his small floating prison, he was sure that he had heard someone talking to him. Deciding that the noise was a figment of his overwrought and exhausted condition, he chose to simply ignore it. The strange sounds continued throughout the night stopping abruptly at daybreak. With the sun's illumination, he scanned his immediate surrounding to discover the source of the noises he had heard. To his utter dismay, all he could see was water stretching endlessly in every direction. Realizing that he was slowly going insane, Loony Louie curled up in the bottom of the longboat to survive yet another long day at sea.

When darkness returned, he again heard the strange voice that seemed to sound almost feminine. Rising and peering over the boat's side, he was amazed to find himself gazing into the face of the most beautiful lass he had ever seen. Long black hair and enchanting green eyes met his stunned gaze. For the next few moments, he was awestruck and transfixed by her beauty and welcoming smile. While totally unable to understand her strange speech, he nevertheless spent the rest of the evening attempting to communicate with her. At dawn, she sadly waved goodbye as she pointed in the direction of the rising sun. Following the direction she had indicated, he had stumbled across our path and had been rescued. He was convinced his visions were real, and that this sea goddess had saved his life. He also confessed that our new figurehead bore a very eerie resemblance to his rescuing sea angel. With this tale completed, he confided that he was a damned good sailor and promised to earn his keep while aboard. I ordered him to report to Lion the following morning to receive a duty assignment.

After my interview of Loony Louie, I called Powder Monkey into my cabin and related the sad tale spun by the suffering wretch. Totally at a loss to separate fact from fiction, I commanded my friend to keep a very close eye on our newest crewman. That afternoon our combat schools opened once again for business. Both Tan's and Long Tall Willie's classes were producing dramatic results, with a few industrious crewmen already earning their gold doubloons. Once done, these graduates merely moved on to the other class and began a different training anew. Concurrently, our longboats were lowered and Lion's hard-trained musket teams took target practice at brightly painted barrels that had been tossed overboard. The objective of this practice was firing speed and accuracy while negotiating the vagaries of the open water. My brief observations of their efforts convinced me that they were also developing into an extremely effective weapon. The prevailing thought of the time was that a well trained musket squad was the equal of a cannon team when it came to inducing destruction and devastation on an enemy. As I observed their progress in both speed and accuracy, I was quite sure that their value would prove far greater than the addition of three more cannons!

To increase the murderous force of each musket team, I had made a few lethal additions. To start, I assigned two grenado men to each team's longboat. These men had been selected and trained extensively by Powder Monkey. They were capable of launching the deadly explosives in any type of engagement. As each musket team went about the task of eliminating topside enemy resistance, the grenado men could be counted on to spread further death and destruction on lower or upper decks depending on the specific need at hand. The second change I made was to commission Chips to devise miniature catapults that would fit in the small confines of each longboat to lengthen the distance that the grenados could travel. Chip's had produced a successful prototype, and was now busy recreating several more which would be installed shortly. The third alteration to these miniature death ships was extending the sides of each boat upward with thick timbers to provide additional protection for each team member. The final change was to paint each of these boats black on both inside and out to provide stealth and surprise during night attacks.

As these teams continued their training, I turned to inspect yet another class that was practicing at the stern of our ship, the drummers. I had great interest in utilizing this squad to lead us into battle, rather than the noisy chaos normally fostered by a ship's band. As I was selecting the drum participants, I was informed by Tiger Eyes that his people utilized similar drums to affect crude communication. Hearing this gave me an idea, and I had each drummer begin to practice communicating with the musket teams. Our first efforts were crude and at times confusing, but steady work and practice resulted in simple commands being communicated by drumbeats. I knew that a well coordinated communication effort would prove unbeatable in armed conflict, so I continued to push our drummers to practice long and hard at their efforts. Eventually, I knew it was time to practice all of our expertise on real targets, which would certainly be shooting back at us. All we needed now was the right prey, pirates!

At the day's end, I decided to spend dinnertime with the crew and I headed down to the galley. Upon entering, I realized that the entire room was intently listening to a sea tale about mermaids being spun by Angry George. Unlike Loony Louie's extraordinary experience with his fanciful sea nymph, Angry George's tale was far gloomier and exceedingly haunting.

Angry George explained that he had heard the story from a chum who had served on an English merchantman. Aboard this vessel was a young seaman who had a knack for bringing trouble upon himself by silly omissions of duty. His name was Donny O'Shea, but unilaterally referred to as Donny Boy. The lad was quite unremarkable in appearance, with only a single distinguishing characteristic, different colored eyes. One of the lad's eyes was a dark brown while the other was a vivid sea-blue hue. During their voyage, Donny Boy had suffered punishment for a number of empty-headed stunts. His latest transgression had rewarded the dolt with the onerous task of swabbing the ship's deck under a torturous tropical sun. As he was completing this punishment, he happened to spy a beautiful creature floating on the surface beside their vessel. This mesmerizing apparition gave him a quick smile before promptly disappearing under the waves.

That evening, he confessed his strange encounter to his crewmates. Their first reaction was to accuse him of inventing the incident in order to gain attention. Since he refused to recant his tale, his crewmates demanded a full description of his sea beauty. Donny Boy detailed that his enchantress had long silver hair and bright green eyes. He also reported that the color of her skin was a peculiar greenish-white. The crew pressed for further details, but since his encounter was so brief, he was unable to provide anything further. Given the sorry lack of detail, his crewmates dismissed his sighting believing it to be totally contrived.

Donny Boy returned to his usual duties and nothing more was said of the incident. After a month a passed, Donny Boy made a surprising announcement that his beautiful friend had made another appearance. This time his crewmates merely laughed at him and assured him that he was quite daft. To prove them wrong, Donny Boy produced a magnificent black pearl that he claimed was given to him by his sea goddess. Crowding around the boy, each mate took turns inspecting the wondrous treasure. Donny Boy informed his attentive audience that the pearl was a good luck talisman intended to ward off evil. His enchantress had implicitly instructed him to carry the charm on his person at all times as protection. However, he had also been sternly forewarned that should the charm be lost that he would suffer mightily.

Donny Boy, with the assistance of the ship's sailmaker, strung the magnificent black pearl onto an elegant rope necklace which he hung around his neck. Since the immense pearl was quite visible, an odious mate named Shankhand took an envious fancy to the precious gem. Known for his conniving and treacherous nature, Shankhand sported a wooden apparatus with a wickedly sharp embedded dagger in place of his left hand due to a previous necessary amputation. One night driven by insatiable greed, the shifty scoundrel crept his way below and located the sleeping lad's position. Utilizing his ever-handy blade, the thief neatly snipped the rope necklace and carefully removed the desired prize. Instantly, the pilferer became nothing more than a shadow, as he raced topside to inspect his purloined booty. As he admired the wondrous gem against the backdrop of a brilliant full moon, he was suddenly seized by an unknown source and yanked ferociously into the water.

Later that evening, the watch leader upon making routine rounds noticed that Shankhand was absent from his assigned post. The irritated sailor immediately organized a cursory search for the missing whelp, which yielded no results whatsoever. Alerting the First Mate of the curious situation, a call was made for all hands to conduct a thorough ship-wide probe. As the sleep-deprived tars grudgingly made their way topside, Donny Boy began issuing a series of piteous wails and moans in their wake. It seemed that the hapless lad had somehow misplaced his precious talisman and was now in the process of conducting a terror-stricken hunt for its return. Neither of the aforementioned searches proved successful as no sign of Shankhand or Donny Boy's pearl were found. Calling off further efforts, the First Mate conjectured that Shankhand had somehow fallen overboard during his watch. Simultaneously, Donny Boy came to the horrified realization that his prized charm had also simply disappeared.

Believing himself doomed by the tragic loss, Donny Boy went about his shipboard duties in a very lackluster manner. Later that afternoon, his crewmates witnessed the lad hanging over the ship's rail in seemingly deep conversation with the empty sea. This strange stunt convinced the entire ship that the young scamp had gone fully mad. At dusk, Donny Boy was still at the vessel's side spouting absolute nonsense into open water. Suddenly, the onlookers were unilaterally frozen in awe as a pair of green scaly wings tipped with sharp taloned claws stretched out of the sea and clutched the defenseless lad. Issuing a sharp surprised squeal, Donny Boy was swiftly lifted of the deck and dragged down into the briny deep. Stunned speechless by this haunting occurrence, the witnesses eventually regained their senses and shouted out that Donny Boy had fallen overboard. The Captain ordered the ship turned so that a proper search for the boy could be made. However, this effort proved fruitless as absolutely no sign of the boy was found. Donny Boy had simply disappeared under the waves!

The vessel eventually returned to its original course, but its superstitious crew remained vigilant for further disaster given the two mysterious disappearances haunting them. As time passed with no further trouble, the men reluctantly put the incidents aside and returned to their normal routines. More than a week later, a tar assigned to fish for the ship's evening meal hooked a very sizable catch. As he struggled with the monster, a number of mates were drawn as spectators to follow the angler's exploits. The sailor eventually hauled his weighty catch to the surface and all were entirely stunned by the utter abomination that had surfaced.

As the monstrosity was tugged towards the ship, the bystanders were unanimously dumbfounded as they realized that the catch was a hideously bloated human torso. As it inched closer and closer, one of the onlookers shouted that the human wreckage sported a blade at the end of its left arm. Once attention was drawn to this startling discovery, mumbling rose to a high-pitched roar as the abhorrent corpse was identified as one of their very own, Shankhand.

When the swollen carcass was directly adjacent to the ship, it was impossible for anyone to further confirm the victim's identity as the wretch's face was more than twice normal size along with being exceedingly mangled and mutilated by hungry sea denizens. However, the distorted facial expression on the cadaver conveyed absolute terror and unimaginable horror. Quick glimpses convinced all that whatever the poor rascal had witnessed in his last moments had been ghastly and hideous enough in nature to etch the grisly visage on his face permanently. As the stunned crowd made perfunctory signs-of-the-cross on their chests, another sailor hollered out that the abomination was sporting Donny Boy's pearl necklace.

As all averted eyes returned reluctantly to the horrid human wreck to confirm this newest discovery, another monstrosity suddenly arose from the deep. This frightful beast was unlike anything any had ever witnessed. Its hue was a pale whitish-green and was approximately the size of a grown man. The oddity's torso was covered with huge blue spots that stood out quite plainly against its overall light coloring. Further, it appeared human-like from the waist up while sporting a large dolphin-like tail on its lower half. Wasting no time, the hideous critter grabbed the pearl necklace around Shankhand's distended neck and proceeded to viciously yank it off producing a sickening squelch. As this new abomination rotated to return to the deep, several witnesses got a good look at its face. To a man, they identified that the critter had different but very recognizable colored eyes, one dark brown and the other deep sea-blue!

At he concluded the yarn with his usual flourish, I was aware that Angry George's sea tale was completely imaginary and fanciful in nature. However, I was also certain that our vast seas held many secrets that defied explanation. Retiring to my cabin, I could not help but wonder how genuine Loony Louie's rescue tale had actually been!

Chapter 23: Unscrupulous Brethren

We continued our journey south and I decided that Loony Louie could remain in our company. The half-baked tar went about his assigned duties in a determined manner, while spending the majority of his free time peering over the ship's rail staring for hours at the blue horizon. Since he caused no trouble in his time aboard, I told Powder Monkey to lighten his monitoring efforts.

At the same time, I insisted that combat practice continue on a daily basis. I was rather pleased with the progress we were making, and knew that it would not be long before we would encounter an opportunity to employ our skills to the fullest. I began to participate in a number of these classes as my strength began to make its slow return. Continuing to practice, I participated in close-quarter combat with both weapons as well as my bare hands. One afternoon as Tan and I were feinting and parrying blows with cutlasses, I heard the topman sing out that a sail had been spotted on our larboard side, and I returned to my cabin to retrieve my telescope.

Utilizing the scope, I could make out a ship in the far distance but hardly more. Turning the instrument over to Lion, I ordered him to keep a close watch on this recent sighting. To the helmsmen, I shouted a command to begin to shadow the vessel while we maintained observation. Lion reported at dusk that the ship was a three masted schooner flying the flag of Spain. Lion informed me that the ship seemed unconcerned with our presence as they maintained a southerly course. Given the great distance between us, he could not discern any further information, and I thanked him for his efforts and sent him down for his evening meal. Before joining him, I set the night watch to maintain vigilance on the Spanish vessel, and to inform me immediately of any change. The night passed uneventfully and the next day continued in much the same manner.

About midday, Lion appeared at my cabin door to report that our Spanish neighbors seemed to be edging closer and closer to our position. Since Loony Louie was near, I asked him to assist in the scouting efforts. Handing my telescope to him and providing a quick set of instructions on use, I asked him to take a long gaze at the Spanish schooner to determine if it was the same ship from which he made his escape. Taking his time, he studied the ship intently before announcing that it appeared to be familiar, but given the limited visibility could not be completely certain. Nodding, I asked him to continue his monitoring efforts a while longer, while I returned to my charts to study our position. Upon completing my navigational computations, I was surprised by Loony Louie who rushed into my cabin and in a halting and stuttering voice informed me that his surveillance had proved fruitful. It seemed that he had specifically recognized the Spanish dog that had attacked his ship and tortured him. There was absolutely no doubt in his mind that these were the very same vultures responsible for his inquisition. They were commanded by Captain Juan Hector Sanchez, better known as Captain Happy Jack. Given his past experience with the villain, he cautioned me to treat the lying scum with extreme malice and not to believe a single word out of his prevaricating rum-hole. Thanking him for this bit of wisdom, I asked that he remain hidden in our hold while we dealt with the situation, so that he would not be recognized by his former captors. Obeying my order, he scurried off to find a safe hiding place below.

I then called a war council of my most trusted men including Lion, Tan, Long Tall Willie, Scuttle, Powder Monkey and Tiger Eyes. Believing Captain Happy Jack to be a creature of habit, I quickly laid out my plan of attack. I was sure that the deceitful scoundrel would again call for a white flag parley to reconnoiter our ship and troop strength. To completely fool our nemesis, I ordered my team to turn our topdeck into a slovenly pigsty, have our crew act like disheveled drunkards and to maintain this ruse until attack orders were issued. As I laid out my specific scheme, my trusted comrades could not hide their laughter and mirth. While they realized that we could easily defeat our enemy in a frontal assault, they also understood that the price of such a victory would certainly result in the loss of life. My approach would reach the same conclusion, but would conserve our body count as we made engagement.

As the afternoon passed, the Spanish schooner continued its tentative approach until they were within hailing distance. As expected, they had raised the white parley flag directly below its Spanish counterpart. The Spanish Captain, dressed in ridiculous finery, appeared on the deck of his ship, and using a hailing trumpet called a warm and gracious greeting. He requested a parlay to discuss matters, and promised that the white flag he flew mitigated any danger from him or his crew. Accepting his truce pledge, I invited Captain Happy Jack aboard to parley. As my devious enemy made preparations to visit our ship, I surveyed our surroundings. My orders had been followed implicitly, and the topdeck resembled a disheveled trash heap. Garbage, empty bottles, dirty slops and an unbelievable litany of debris littered our deck. Since my cabin would be used to hold the parley, I had Powder Monkey rearrange my private domicile in much the same manner. In addition to the clutter and mess that surrounded me, my men feigned drunkenness and insubordinate laxity as they slouched around the deck in aimless confusion, a floating punchhouse by anyone's definition. Nodding my approval, I disheveled my hair and clothing and awaited the unsuspecting scoundrels now entering our web.

Captain Happy Jack and several of his officers made the short trip in their longboat and were welcomed aboard by drunken antics on the part of my entire crew. Monitoring their initial reactions, I could see that my visitors were extremely pleased by the chaotic scene that greeted them. Reaching the maindeck, I strode forward and introduced myself while welcoming them aboard our vessel. Captain Happy Jack was visibly shocked by my youthful appearance, but was again all smiles, believing that he had indeed stumbled upon very easy prey. Ordering his men to remain topside, the deceitful rogue accompanied me to my cabin.

Once he was made comfortable in my cabin and plied with a delightful Spanish wine, he introduced himself and informed me that he had been originally stationed on Tortuga. He then confessed that he had fled south to safer waters, due to the nefarious actions of the feared Black Tarantula. He went on to inform me that he was now conducting honest trade with a number of neighboring islands. At that point, he questioned me on my background and our ship's intentions. In a dutiful manner, I informed my deceitful visitor that I had recently been voted Captain after the sudden and unfortunate demise of our former leader. Because of my uncanny navigational skills, the crew had decided to make me their Captain. I further informed him that we were currently operating under French *Lettre of Marque* from the Governor of Guadeloupe, and were roving these southern waters in search of pirates. Making a feigned sign-of-the-cross, he wished me success in our perilous assignment. Turning the subject back to the Black Tarantula, I questioned him on any recent scuttlebutt on this evil sea scourge.

Taking a long swallow of his delightful wine, he launched into his narrative. He informed me that the Black Tarantula had been terrorizing the northern waters of the Caribbean, attacking and destroying any and all ships that had the utter misfortune of crossing his path. He divulged that by his actions, the Black Tarantula had transformed all pirates operating in those tropical waters into sea cannibals. With ultimate disgust, he informed me that there was no longer honor amongst the Brethren of the Coast. Because of this evil villain, pirates now were attacking and destroying each other with extreme regularity. As a result of this unfortunate situation, Captain Happy Jack had made the decision to migrate to these friendlier southern waters and conduct honest trade until this evil blight had been eliminated.

I informed my pompous guest that I had heard that an official force had been sent from Jamaica under the command of a certain Captain Adams to end this sea jackal's antics. Smiling now, Captain Happy Jack confirmed that my information was indeed accurate. He divulged that a force under Captain Adams had sailed north to confront and defeat the demon. Word he had received was that the expedition had been a total failure. Surprised and quite shocked by this ill news, I pressed Captain Happy Jack for more details. He retorted that he had been told that Captain Adams' ships had met and battled the Black Tarantula off the northern tip of Saint Domingue. Captain Adams had lost half of his ships in this initial encounter. Persistent and determined, the brave Captain Adams had continued his attack, eventually issuing grievous injury upon his foe. This destruction had forced the Black Tarantula to make a retreat northward, drawing the remnants of the valiant Jamaican fleet in his wake.

Captain Happy Jack informed me that Jamaican victory had seemed all but assured until a very strange circumstance occurred. As the battered Jamaican fleet made its final preparations to attack, a French Man-O-War entered the fray and completely turned the tide of battle. The Jamaican fleet was obliterated by the combined force of the mysterious French warship and the Black Tarantula's vessel. Captain Adams had been taken prisoner, while his men were treated to cruel and inhuman deaths.

Stunned by this malevolent news, I pressed Captain Happy Jack for further information on the mysterious French warship. Captain Happy Jack was quick to plead ignorance on further details of this mystery ship. All he had heard was that this vessel had suddenly appeared, assisted the Black Tarantula in the destruction of the Jamaicans and then neatly disappeared following the victory. While I realized that my visitor was prone to deceit and lies, it seemed to me that he was being somewhat truthful on this matter. Realizing that no additional information could be gained by pressing him further, I switched subjects and questioned him on the fate of my friend, Captain Adams. Again, the untrustworthy scoundrel pleaded total ignorance on the matter. This unexpected horrific news left me miserably disheartened, and it took me a long moment to compose myself.

All the while, Captain Happy Jack had been busy inspecting my cabin with conniving interest. Noting his evil curiosity, I decided to bait my trap with a promise of wealth and fortune. In a sincere and fearful voice, I informed my visitor that we were fortunate to be far away from this evil demon, especially in light of the significant treasure we had been charged to protect. Snapping his head in my direction, he feigned a frightened expression in a weak attempt to gain my confidence. In a hesitating and shaky voice, he questioned my last statement. Pretending that I had made a mistake by introducing the subject, I answered that it was of no real importance. However, the pure greed and hunger that shown in his eyes confirmed that he had taken my bait as offered.

In a final effort to pry further news from my unsavory guest, I innocently commented that I had heard that the Black Tarantula was obsessed with the vocal talents of a beautiful young lass from Saint Domingue. Nodding, he confided that he had heard this same scuttlebutt. Pressing him for further news on this subject, Captain Happy Jack shrugged and responded that he had no additional information to provide. He did seem a bit hesitant on this subject, and that led me to believe that he had deliberately concealing crucial information. As to the reason why the scum was withholding further news, I was at a total loss. Either way, I knew that time would soon come when the devious and conniving scoundrel would divulge any and all information in a most truthful manner, an experience that would prove to be quite novel to him. Having exhausted his sources of conversation, Captain Happy Jack suddenly shouted that he had the perfect wine to share with us for this evening's meal. With that, he jumped up and made his way topside to return to his ship. Lavishly promising to return later with a few of his men, he bid us a fond farewell and departed. As I peered around at my men on the topdeck, I was pleased to observe that they had all played the roles of drunken unsuspecting fools to perfection. I was sure that Captain Happy Jack and his mangy followers had been totally deceived by their superb performances. As he made his way back to his vessel, I was also certain our nefarious comrade eagerly anticipated an easy time with our ship along with the promise of valuable booty to swell his private coffers. If my plan succeeded, we would prove him totally wrong and end his pirating days forever!

Before our guests returned to transform our promised celebratory gathering into a slaughter and rape of our ship of booty, I had some last minute details to review with my trusted commanders. Calling the group into my cabin, I reviewed our plan once again for the evening's festivities, altering a few minor details to ensure all proceeded smoothly. Having finalized our scheme, I dismissed my comrades so that they could fully prepare every last detail in advance of our enemy's return. I was not surprised to find Loony Louie waiting at my door for a chance to speak with me. Respectfully entering my domain, he begged for a chance to gain his revenge on this immoral reprobate, who had slaughtered his friends and grievously tortured him in his lust for riches. Assuring him that he would certainly have his revenge, I asked him to remain hidden until our enemies were defeated and subdued. Fearing that his presence would alert the scavenging pirates of danger, I promised that his patience in the matter would be well rewarded.

About an hour after sunset, we were hailed from the Spanish pirate ship that Captain Happy Jack and his escort would be arriving shortly. At this news, I made my rounds of our vessel to ensure a proper welcoming committee was fully prepared. Gratified, I returned to my cabin to await the arrival of the Spanish blackguards. Not long after, commotion topside announced the return of Captain Happy Jack and his heavily armed entourage. Making my way to the maindeck, I was greeted warmly and graciously by my counterpart, who had brought several hogsheads of rum and wine to spice up the evening's festivities. Commanding that the spirits to be opened immediately, he spread his men in various strategic positions topside and shouted that the party could now officially begin. Grabbing my elbow in a forceful manner, he guided me below to share a most wondrous French wine, which he had personally selected from his spirit store. Settling down in my cabin, he opened his offering and without my indulgence called for our mutual success and wellbeing before he guzzled the wine. Quickly refilling his goblet, he began to ask me a series of penetrating questions in an attempt to learn more of the valuable treasure he was certain we carried. Meanwhile, we both heard a sudden commotion on the topdeck. As I rose to dutifully to check on my men, Captain Happy Jack pushed me back into my chair, and urged me relax and allow my men and his the chance to get acquainted.

Returning to the subject of treasure, Captain Happy Jack once again questioned the exact nature of the valuables we had been commissioned to transport. Providing him a conspiratorial wink, I reported that I was not at liberty to discuss specifics, but that the total value was incalculable due to its staggering size. Avariciously pressing for further details, I simply stated that it was far easier to show him the treasure rather than attempting to describe it to him. Eager now for a first-hand peek, Captain Happy Jack jumped to his feet begging me to lead the way. As I slowly rose to my feet, I heard several more loud noises emanating from the deck above us. Appearing concerned, I told my guest that I wanted to go topside to discover the reason for all the commotion prior to our promised treasure tour. Once again in a smooth and innocent voice, Captain Happy Jack assured me that he was sure that all was well, and the noises we had both distinctly heard were just our men carousing and having a grand time.

Shrugging, I pretended to agree and led my deceptive guest down to the hold to provide the promised glimpse of untold wealth. As we reached our destination, I held up the candlelight exposing the totally empty space. Confused by this discovery, Captain Happy Jack turned to me and drew his sword. With an evil scowl now dominating his expression, he demanded to know where the great treasure was hidden. Before I could respond, Loony Louie stepped from the shadows aiming a pair of pistols directly at the despicable foe. Totally confused, Captain Happy Jack turned in my direction demanding an explanation for this type of grievous treatment. Laughing now, I answered the detestable snake that I was led to believe that he was well acquainted with my newest crew member. Feigning total ignorance, Captain Happy Jack stepped closer and gazed long and hard at Loony Louie. Like a bolt of lightening, he suddenly made the connection and his self-assured swagger and poise dissolved completely. In a flash, he was immediately surrounded by other armed members of my crew, and realizing he had no choice, dropped his weapon and raised his hands in surrender.

Upon neutralizing Captain Happy Jack, I offered him an opportunity to witness the results of the battle that had just occurred. Securing the odious villain's hands behind his back, we made our way topside. Once there, another gruesome surprise awaited the treacherous and corrupt commander. Expecting to receive immediate assistance from the men who had accompanied him onboard, Captain Happy Jack was shocked to discover that his men had disappeared. I informed the vile pirate that every member of his boarding party had been slaughtered by my men prior to our trip to the hold. Feigning uncertainty, he seemed to be experiencing trouble believing my words. To convince him, I confessed that my crew was simply playacting as drunk and disorderly tars to bait the trap we had set for him. Pointing to several dark stains on deck, I told the sea brigand that this was all that remained of the twenty pirates who had accompanied him tonight. I then pointed towards his ship and asked him to pay close attention as the second portion of our plan was about to begin.

With no moon to light the sea, all that could be seen of Captain Happy Jack's ship were its numerous lights that sparkled on the topdeck. As we watched, it appeared as if the pirate ship had suddenly caught fire, as we witnessed tongues of flames rising from its visible deck. I issued orders to let out more anchor line in order to allow our ship to move further away from our now flaming enemy. As we continued to observe, we could see dim figures and shadows through the smoke and flames as they scampering all over the deck in an attempt to fight the conflagration. In a last act of reprisal, the pirate vessel launched a full cannon broadside at our original position. However, since we had just relocated, the cannonballs simply flopped harmlessly into the sea. Once their cannons had fired, we heard a loud chorus of musket fire coming from the direction of the pirate ship. These loud reports were immediately followed by the agonizing wails, shrieks and screams of my captive's crewmen. Muskets continued firing for quite a long time, accompanied from time to time by the distinctive sounds of granado explosions.

Suddenly, all went deathly silent on the water. Straining my eyes in the darkness, I observed our three small longboats making their return. Once alongside, Tiger Eyes climbed onboard and came to my side to provide his report. To Captain Happy Jack's total dismay, he reported that we had captured the enemy ship and that her entire crew had been exterminated. Continuing, he announced that Powder Monkey and his team were currently onboard the now empty vessel awaiting my inspection. Sputtering and stammering in disbelief, Captain Happy Jack stated that this report could not be true since he had over eighty men aboard his vessel. Looking over at him, I informed him that Tiger Eye's was incapable of lying, and that he was now the lone survivor of his nefarious ship. Resorting to his cruel and savage way, he contested this ill news vehemently.

Calling Lion to my side, I ordered him to select a replacement crew from amongst our men. Once done, I commanded he and his team to row over to our new prize and take charge. At the same time, I ordered Captain Happy Jack brought back to my cabin and secured for further questioning. The once vain and arrogant leader was now quite meek and cowed as he was led from my sight. Captain Happy Jack was heard mumbling only one thing over and over as he was led below: "We have all turned into cannibals!" Once out of sight, I informed my men that when the captured pirate ship's flames were fully extinguished and a careful search was made that our celebration could officially begin. We had successfully defeated a pirate force of over one hundred filthy swine, all seasoned tars and armed to the teeth, without a single injury or loss of life, a truly remarkable feat!

Our disguised musket and granado teams had snuck up on our unsuspecting foes, filled the air and the ship with fire and stink bombs, and then the musket teams had systematically slaughtered every pirate aboard as they made their way on to the maindeck to either get a breath of fresh air or to respond to the sudden attack on their ship. Many had died without realizing exactly what was happening. In all, it was a perfectly timed and planned engagement by my crew of battle-ready combatants. After witnessing this awe inspiring demonstration, I realized that our long hours of training had been wholly justified.

Returning to my cabin, I found my adversary lashed thoroughly to a stout chair naked from the waist up and gagged securely. There were four of us in the room, Captain Happy Jack, No Nose Nottingham, Loony Louie and me. I had allowed Loony Louie to be present strictly as an observer, and promised that his fun would come once we had a chance to interrogate our corrupt and vile prisoner. As was the case with Captain Bass, I began the proceedings by informing my prisoner about No Nose and his horrific pets, including the erroneous tale of how No Nose had been accidentally bitten and paid with the loss of his nose. Captain Happy Jack had gained a bit of his arrogance back as evidenced by his menacing looks.

Leaning in close to his persecutor's face, No Nose told his bound of the horror and the grave danger surrounding his pets. His performance was quite convincing as I could see wisps of doubt now clouding the villain's face as his haughty countenance began to melt before my eyes. No Nose finally introduced one of his pets, which caused the despicable brute's eyes to begin a mad-capped dance. No Nose placed his charge directly on Captain Happy Jack's bare chest, and the monstrous spider began his slow crawl up towards our prisoner's face. By this time, I could see that our guest was overwhelmed with terror. I continued the game realizing that the more fear we could induce, the easier his answers would come. As the black nightmare reached the neck of Captain Happy Jack, I knew that the time for truth had arrived.

Motioning No Nose to remove his beast, I leaned in close and removed the cloth gag. With an inhuman squeal, Captain Happy Jack begged to be released from the bonds. Nodding, I answered that his freedom would be gained as soon as he answered my queries with truth not lies. Shaking his head vigorously in a positive manner, he pleaded with me to ask whatever questions I had in mind. My first question centered on the story he had related on the defeat and capture of Captain Adams. In a shaking and still terrified voice, Captain Happy Jack recounted much of the same tale he had previously divulged. However, there were a few differences to this version versus the original.

In the first place, he confessed that Captain Adams had been purposely drawn into the trap set by the Black Tarantula. While his ship and crew had suffered tremendous casualties as a result of the sudden arrival of the French warship, he was unsure of the officer's actual fate. All he knew was that the Black Tarantula had retreated to his lair somewhere on the isle of Tortuga. Captain Happy Jack was also ignorant of any more details on the mysterious French savior, a very curious mystery indeed!

Moving to the next subject, I probed the boastful pirate on his knowledge of my beloved Rue. Captain Happy Jack also pleaded ignorance on the fate of the young lass. All he could add was that he had been told that the satanic rascal had issued a substantial reward for anyone who delivered the woman into his hands. To his knowledge, he believed that the reward remained unclaimed. Breathing a little easier, I questioned the audacious villain on the extent of the damage suffered by the Black Tarantula at the hands of Captain Adams. Again he confessed that he was ignorant of any real details, other than the fact that the Black Tarantula's ship had been significantly crippled in the engagement and that he had limped back to Tortuga to affect necessary repairs.

We had now reached the critical juncture of the interrogation and I signaled No Nose to once again produce one of his hideous accomplices. The sight of the hairy scourge instantly brought a high pitched scream from our captive. Aware that No Nose's pet had done its work, I demanded to know where he had secreted his ship's treasure, since our initial searching had proved fruitless. True to his nature, the deceitful rogue answered that all booty had been squandered on neighboring islands in the pursuit of strumpets, hot spirits and good times. Sure that I was being told a fanciful story, I nodded to No Nose and he placed the second beast directly on the pirate's forehead. This act caused the miserable wretch to issue an unholy banshee-like wail as he lost control of his bladder, fouling the entire surrounding area. Guessing that the knave required one last bit of encouragement, I signaled No Nose to introduce one more of his panic inducing friends to our guest. No Nose complied immediately by placing another huge and hairy specimen on Captain Happy Jack's cheek, which seemed to tip the scale in the direction of honesty and truth, something quite foreign to this licentious scamp and trickster.

Captain Happy Jack eventually wailed that his treasure was hidden in the pitch barrels in the hold of his ship. He shouted that several of these barrels had been fashioned with false bottoms to accommodate and secret his cache of booty. To ensure that the churlish fraud was being honest, I called Angry George into the cabin and gave him implicit instructions to conduct a search for these adulterated casks. While we waited for confirmation of the truth, I had No Nose retrieve his creeping friends to the great relief of our prevaricating visitor. At last, Angry George returned and signaled that our prey's treasure had been found. Turning to Captain Happy Jack, I thanked him for our productive parlay, and then dismissed No Nose and his marvelously helpful assistants.

Sensing that his suffering had reached an end, the deceitful pirate questioned what I had in mind for him. With an evil smirk, I informed him that I had one last surprise for him that I was quite sure he would truly enjoy. Turning, I signaled that it was now Loony Louie's playtime, as I made my way out of the room. Wishing both Captain Happy Jack and Loony Louie a marvelous reunion, I closed my cabin door and made my way topside. It was not long after that a series of inhuman howls and screeches came to the attention of the entire ship. This dreadful racket continued unending for what seemed like a lifetime to everyone onboard, as we were forced to endure its haunting and mournful melody. After a long hour, Loony Louie emerged from my cabin drenched in sweat, but sporting a huge satisfied grin spreading from ear to ear. Sure that the world had seen the last of Captain Happy Jack, I was quite shocked when Loony Louie reported that his charge was yet alive, although not entirely whole. Curious, I returned below to survey the human carnage caused by my revenge-minded tar.

What I discovered upon entering my domicile left me speechless with revulsion given the human devastation I witnessed. Loony Louie in his effort to gain revenge against his proud and arrogant adversary had effected some permanent alterations to his enemy's once handsome and dapper appearance. In the first place, Loony Louie had sliced off each of the scamp's fingers leaving only mangled fists devoid of their appendages. To ensure that his nemesis survived each extraction, Loony Louie had slowly charred each missing stub with the use of a white-hot dirk in order to seal these gaping wounds in a most painful but effective manner. His next step was to castrate his victim, depriving him of any future manly pleasures while relegating the swine to the role of an eternal eunuch. Again the heated dagger was utilized to stop the flow of the villain's vital life-force, so that he would survive to enjoy his new station in life. Both of these treatments were brutal and vindictive, but Loony Louie had not stopped there. As a lasting testament to Captain Happy Jack's nefarious nature, Loony Louie had carved into his forehead the word, **THIEF**!

All in all, Captain Happy Jack was now a masterpiece of diabolical delight and revulsion. He was doomed to spend the remainder of his life being shunned and sneered at by everyone he encountered, a fate far worse than death for this vain and prideful pirate! Upon gazing at Loony Louie's handiwork, I could do nothing but shudder and avert my eyes. Disgusted by the entire affair, I ordered the pirate leader stripped of his clothing and loaded into a spare longboat and cast adrift to suffer the vagaries of the sea and hot tropical sun. However, even when the villain was removed from my sight, I continued to have disturbing mental visions of the satanic alterations performed on the truly deserving pirate by a survivor of his cruel and heartless torture.

Before my crew had a chance to begin their celebrations, I called my trusted leaders into my cabin to discuss our situation. Once assembled, Lion reported that our pirate prey was in excellent condition although a bit singed on the topdeck and would provide a valued weapon for our future endeavors. In order to captain and man the vessel, I appointed Lion as its new commander and christened our new vessel *Neptune's Revenge*. To assist Lion in his new office, I assigned Scuttle, Angry George and a third of our current crew to join his command. As was the case with *Rue's Revenge*, I knew that specific alterations needed to be made to turn our new prize into a formidable warship. Since Captain Happy Jack reported that the Black Tarantula had taken shelter on Tortuga to make repairs, I was certain that we could utilize this opportunity to find a safe harbor to make these necessary alterations and attempt to enlist additional sailors to our cause.

Given that we were still sailing in the southern Caribbean, I decided to take advantage of a nearby small French possession christened St Lucia. Crewmen familiar with this island had informed me that it was relatively unknown and mostly uninhabited other than a few fishing villages that dotted the coastline. One knowledgeable tar had actually spent time on the island in a sleepy fishing town called Soufriere. After listening to his description of the island, I decided it was the perfect landing spot and charted a course in its direction.

Well, it did not take long for my crew to begin celebrating our latest triumph. Rum was delivered topside on both ships, and my men eagerly launched into drunken debauchery. While I never condoned this type of animalistic behavior at sea, I realized that my cohorts had earned the right to celebrate and revel in our one-sided victory. Aware that we provided an easy target on open water, I directed our two ships to a deserted cove off of an uncharted spit of land to allow the spirited proceedings to run its course. After a full day of revelry, we weighed anchor and proceeded to our destination.

However, there was a certain seaman aboard who took this opportunity to continue his celebration long after the rum supply had been exhausted. He sported a very appropriate name for his unsanctioned undertaking, Guzzlin' Gooch! A solitary and quiet figure by nature, he changed quite dramatically under the influence of hot spirits. When drunk, Gooch transformed into a loud and overbearing beast, causing nothing but trouble and hardship. After finally depleting his purloined stash from our liquor cabinet, he weaved and teetered his way above decks causing even greater disruption and chaos.

When this news was brought to my attention, I ordered several strong lads to subdue the miscreant. Screaming and cursing horrific threats to all, he was eventually delivered to me. Consulting Doc on a cure, the medical man recommended that a saltwater grog was necessary to end the unfortunate tar's thirst for rum. This remedy consisted of first immobilizing the victim and then forcing copious amounts of fresh saltwater down his gullet. According to Doc, this insidious cure would cause extreme dehydration. Additionally, it would alter the victim's innards so that the mere smell of strong spirits would cause immediate regurgitation of any and all stomach contents. Doc had assured me that this extreme remedy would effect alcohol abstinence on the sot's part. Desperate to regain order, I ordered Guzzlin' Gooch to undergo the cure. Dragged roughly to the Doc's surgery and tied securely to a bunk, the poor fool continued to wail and lodge threats at us all. Heading below, I entered Doc's cabin to assist in the saltwater purgative for our wayward mate.

Working with Doc, we managed to force a large volume of saltwater down the throat of the struggling and squirming tippler. As predicted, this briny concoction had a pronounced effect on our patient. Our initial offerings were literally thrown back in our faces by our patient's copious vomiting. After several move messy and nasty attempts, we were finally rewarded in our efforts when Gooch did not regurgitate our curative. Once our noxious mixture was accepted, our patient lapsed into unconsciousness. The Doc promised to continue the treatment the remainder of the day to appease the tremendous thirst of our patient. Realizing I was no longer needed, I returned to my cabin to attend to other pressing matters.

At sundown, I returned to Doc's surgery to check on the status of Gooch. I found him still securely tied to the bunk but awake, coherent and complaining of terrible thirst. He recognized my presence and threatened all manner of retribution towards me before I made a hasty retreat. The next day, Gooch was released from his restraints and joined his fellow mates in normal duties. While sullen and quiet in demeanor, he showed no adverse affects form the saltwater cure, other than remaining continually parched no matter how much fresh water he consumed. When the daily rum ration was announced, I was pleasantly shocked to discover that Guzzlin' Gooch declined his share in favor of fresh water. As we continued towards St. Lucia, it seemed that the Doc's cure had been totally successful!

Chapter 24: The Appearance of Sharkface Topper

In just a matter of days, we reached our intended destination, St Lucia. The isle was a small, lush tropical gem that was virtually unknown and rarely visited. On maps, the island had the rough shape of the tropical fruit called a mango. As we sailed south to reach the small fishing community of Soufriere, we were all amazed by the stunning beauty of the island. The majority of Saint Lucia appeared remote and deserted, making it an ideal location to replenish our food and water stores. Towards the southern end of this isle, our lookout spotted our target. It appeared as a jumbled collection of shacks and hovels that served as residences for the local fishermen. Soufriere's harbor was spacious and quite deserted as we dropped anchor. My men were very eager to spend some liberty time ashore in pursuit of their usual vices. Divvying up the duty roster on a rotating basis, I assigned specific refitting tasks to those unlucky individuals who would initially remain aboard both ships completing these necessary changes. The remainder of the crew was noisily shuttled to shore to begin exploration of the debauchery that awaited them.

Because I had designed the specific alterations to our new ship, I decided to remain onboard to supervise the work. Since *Neptune's Revenge* originally served as a pirate ship, many of the necessary alterations I deemed necessary had already been completed prior to our takeover. However, I charged Chips with the assignment of adding hidden gun ports on our new prize. I also authorized him to design and carve a new figurehead for this vessel, since the weathered trollop who now adorned her bow was in desperate need of replacement. Additionally, I appointed Lion with the responsibility of altering his new ship's colors as well as refitting, reworking and repainting its three longboats to house its very own musket and grenado teams. While the former pirate ship had been stocked with an abundance of lethal armament, including a treasure trove of powder and shot, I was well aware that it was critically short of manpower. To this end, I had assigned Long Tall Willie, Angry George and Scuttle the duty of recruiting new men to our cause. While the small island of Saint Lucia was not an ideal location to enlist these new recruits, I hoped that we could uncover a few suitable candidates during our planned stop-over.

As the work progressed on *Neptune's Revenge,* I participated in daily lessons of hand-to-hand combat and sword fighting with Tan and Long Tall Willie. The many hours I had spent in strenuous practice had transformed me into a veritable combative expert. While Tan still maintained a slight edge over me in hand-to-hand combat, I was now more his equal than his pupil. I knew that this experience would prove vital in upcoming engagements. For now, my task was strictly practice, practice and more practice!

On the third day at anchor, work aboard both of our vessels was proceeding rather smoothly, so I decided to go ashore and do some exploring of my own. We had managed to recruit a few young lads whose wanderlust would certainly not be fulfilled by their current laborious lives as fishermen. These new recruits were immediately set to work fulfilling desired ship's alterations, but I realized that many more hands were desperately needed to totally fill our ranks. With this in mind, I made my way to Soufriere's shore to accomplish some recruiting of my own. Upon landing, I was a bit surprised at the overall squalor of the town. Composed of a series of hastily erected hovels and shacks, the fishing village was rooted in abject squalor. The inhabitants of this pitiful village were a mixture of various races, a testimony to the numerous seafaring visitors over the years mixing with the indigenous population. While rooted in filth and poverty, I nevertheless found these people to be warm and friendly in nature.

My men returning from liberty had boasted about a local saloon name the *Hungry Shark.* Since they had raved so strongly in its favor, I decided to pay the pub a visit to make my own assessment. As I neared my quest, I was quite surprised by the wretchedness and destitution of the building. It appeared more like a large thatched stable than an actual pub. An old wooden sign bearing its name and the illustration of a ravenous sea jackal hung above the front of this dilapidated shack, but otherwise the outside of the saloon was nondescript to say the least. Upon entering, I found the place to be quite jumbled and disorganized, as if a hurricane had recently made a destructive sweep through its very center.

Immediately upon arrival, I was greeted warmly by a number of my crew in various stages of inebriation. Sighting Long Tall Willie and Scuttle, I made my way over to their table to join them. Upon reaching them, I was immediately introduced to our host, Sharkface Topper. After an initial appraisal, I had to agree that the man's moniker certainly mirrored his physical attributes. In the first place, the rascal had an enormously pronounced and elongated jaw. Giving me a huge smile and a warm welcome, I could not tear my eyes away from his gargantuan maw that was loaded with monstrous canines. In his current pose, he surely resembled the fearsome creature for which he had been named. The second thing I noticed about him was his exceptional size. As he stood to shake my hand, I could see that he was a giant of a man, towering well above anyone else in the room. As his big meaty paws clasped my hand in friendly greeting, I was stunned by their size. My hands seemed child-like next to his prodigious appendages. With his colossal bulk and ghastly protruding jaw and choppers, he resembled more a creature of nightmares than a formidable innkeeper. This image was somewhat tempered by the huge smile that seemed to permanently adorn his face. Welcoming me sincerely to his punchhouse, the towering behemoth signaled to a serving wench to fetch me a tankard of rum. Turning to the lass, I changed the order to fresh lemonade, which brought a derisive roar from all of the nearby patrons. Ignoring their snide smirks and whispered derogatory slights, I settled into a wobbly chair to enjoy the company of my host and fellow crewmembers.

As we waited for my order, I questioned our host on how he had become the proprietor of this grogshop. Giving me one of his never ending toothy smiles, he responded that he had won the pub as a wager in a game of cards. Detailing further, he confessed that his winnings were more of a nuisance than a blessing, given his usual penchant for action and adventure. He then related that he had taken over ownership less than a year ago, and was currently in the process of negotiating its sale. Questioning him on his motivation to sell, he beamed a smile and answered that managing a tavern was about as much fun as "playing a piano in a brothel, for both relegated an individual to a life of strict observer rather than participant!" Understanding his meaning, I quizzed him on his life's story prior to winning the thatched rumhut we were now occupying. Insisting it was a long saga, he motioned for all at the table to get comfortable before he began spinning his tale.

Before starting, my lemonade arrived along with tankards of grog for my tablemates. The behemoth then informed us that he was born on the nearby island of Barbados, the product of an English father and an islander mother. Neither of his parents were very large people, so he found it a perplexing enigma as to where he had inherited his immense size. From an early age, Sharkface had been significantly taller and larger than any boy his age. Because of this, he had been constantly tormented by a slew of blighters. Rather than respond to their continual taunts and jests with violence, he had learned that humor proved a far more useful defense. He had learned to laugh off the silly and spiteful comments on this size, which more often than not defused any further taunts coming his way. Absentmindedly, I remembered that Scuttle had adopted this very same defense. Given his prodigious strength and size, Sharkface had obtained work on the shipping docks loading and unloading the cargo of the numerous merchant ships. While the work was back-breaking and the hours brutal under the hot tropical sun, he enjoyed the overall physical challenge. His life proceeded down this smooth path until a strange set of circumstances caused everything to reverse course.

Reaching the bottom of his tankard, he shouted to a dimwitted doxy for another round for our table. Being the proprietor, his command took precedent, and in a flash we were all served fresh drinks. Continuing, he informed us that his parents also birthed a daughter, who was quite a number of years younger. His eyes shone with adoration as he mentioned his younger sibling. Laughing, he stated that thankfully she has not inherited his abnormal size, but instead had been blessed with beauty far beyond compare. However, he pointed out that no human being was ever created perfect, and such was the case with his ravishing sister. It seemed that his sister suffered from a rare case of terrible body odor. No matter the number of baths or bottles of perfume she employed to combat the affliction, she carried a very disagreeable scent wherever she trod. Sharkface seemed deeply disturbed as he described his sister's scent as "reeking like an open cesspool on a mid-summer afternoon", totally and truly disgusting! Because of her condition, the locals snickered and sneered whenever the lass made one of her few public appearances. While Sharkface could in good nature laugh along with his own tormentors, this was certainly not the case when it came to his sister. In fact, he had bloodied and broken many a tormentor's nose for daring to speak ill or making jest of his younger sibling.

Well, the situation took a turn for the worse one hot tropical evening when a group of young well-to-do's decided to have some sport with the unfortunate lass. Unbeknownst to Sharkface, his sister was kidnapped right off the street by this group of young scoundrels, who had nothing better to do with their free time. Deciding that the young lass smelled considerably worse than any pigsty, they determined that a fresh bath was called for to remedy the odious situation. Trussed and covered in a large sack, they transported the poor lass to a nearby deep-water pool that was fed by a roaring waterfall. Dumping the girl into the pool from the top of the waterfall, they hurried below to the edge of the water to fish the evil scented wench back on land. As they waited by the edge of the pool for the girl to surface, they joked and laughed amongst themselves that she would surely smell sweeter after her forced bath. After a few minutes passed and having seen no sign of their victim, the group panicked and deserted the remote spot for the safe confines of a nearby rumhouse. There they spent the rest of the day and well into the evening drinking to insensibility, as they related their story of the waterfall bath to anyone who would listen.

Being a small town, Sharkface had been told the following morning of the trick played on his sister, and he rushed to the waterfall's pool to console his mistreated sibling. Reaching the site, he found his dear sister floating face down in the water still secured by stout ropes. In a frenzied state, he dragged his sister onto land but realized that he was far too late. Judging by the huge purple bruise on her temple, Sharkface surmised that his loved one had struck her head violently on one of the hidden rocks in the pool when she had been launched off of the top of the waterfall. Shattered, he spent the remainder of the day holding his sister tight and attempting to coax her back to life. By nightfall, he realized that his sister was gone for good, and he carved out a grave by the side of the pool with his bare hands, and buried his beloved with huge tears streaking down his face. Once finished, he vowed to avenge her wrongful death.

During the night, he tracked each of the young killers down and quietly abducted each from darkened streets, outside their favorite drinking establishments and even from their own beds. By dawn, he had assembled the young rogues in a hidden tidewater grotto not very far from town. He had discovered this deserted spot one day while fishing along the coast. The grotto could only be explored at low tide, since seawater would enter and flood the cavern at tide's change. Dragging each of the securely bound and gagged miscreants into this special hiding place, he made sure that the ropes binding them all were secure and tight. Once satisfied, he wished them a very safe journey to hell and abandoned them to their deserved fate.

He returned to town completely forgetting the young men he had sentenced to death. When the lads were reported missing, Sharkface was immediately hauled before the authorities for questioning on the whereabouts of the young scamps who were known to have mistreated his sister. Feigning complete ignorance, Sharkface urged the authorities to assist him in locating both his missing sister as well as the unaccounted for youths. Well, Sharkface confessed that neither his sister nor the young men were ever found by the hastily assembled search party despite their tireless efforts. While he was never officially charged with the crime, the suspicions against him were weighty and therefore he was under constant surveillance. Deciding that his island home was a constant mournful reminder of his departed sister and tired of being constantly watched, he joined a band of sea rovers and vacated the island for good. Since that time, he had served on multiple ships in various roles, until his fortune had drastically shifted and he found himself the owner of the pub.

At the end of his life's tale, I could see that he was still deeply affected by the tragic loss of his sister. He finally issued a hushed confession that his revenge had been sweet, but in no way had it compensated for the senseless murder of his sister. Brushing away a burgeoning tear in the corner of his eye, the giant rose from our table and stumbled outside to avoid further embarrassment. Giving him a moment to collect himself, I followed him outside to thank him for his hospitality and to bid him a good evening. I found him nearby sitting quietly by himself. Approaching, I told him I wanted to thank him for the evening's hospitality. Smiling now, he answered that he had also enjoyed our companionship.

As I was about to return to the ships, I turned and appraised the giant that our ships were critically short of men. Aware that he would be cognizant of any locals or drifters who might fit our need, I explained our situation in utmost detail and requested his assistance in identifying potential tars to fill our ranks. With a broad toothy smile, he answered that there was only one man he was familiar with on this island who would totally serve our needs, Sharkface Topper! Surprised by his response, I questioned whether he was being honest or just having fun at my expense. Staring at me now in utter seriousness, he answered that he was quite tired of managing the pub. Smiling once more, he promised to sell the pub if I would allow him to join our company. I informed him that the role of First Mate had recently become available, and that the position was his if he believed his seafaring abilities and knowledge merited the rank. With a wink, he accepted my offer and promised that he would be the finest First Mate in all of the Caribbean!

Chapter 25: Combat Practice Rewards

From the onset, Sharkface Topper proved an excellent choice as my second-in-command. His sheer size instantly commanded the attention of the entire crew. Although displaying an immense physical presence, he did not rely on bullying tendencies of any sort, remaining quite fair and even-keeled in his treatment of subordinates. Additionally, his easy smile and playful temperament seemed to have a soothing effect on anyone spending time in his company. His knowledge and experience were quite evident as he issued commands in a sure and confident manner. While I missed the companionship provided by Lion, I was slowly learning to put my faith and trust in my new First Mate.

Chips had made significant progress on all of our modifications with the help of his new assistant...Guzzlin' Gooch. His new recruit had forsaken his exhaustive thirst for hot spirits, and his dedicated commitment to his duties aboard was quite evident to everyone. To both Chips and my astonishment, the reformed drunkard had volunteered to assist our accomplished carpenter in his refitting projects, and had actually excelled at this work. While Chips had much greater knowledge and experience with woodcrafting, Gooch turned out to be an even finer artist with more difficult and detailed assignments. Additionally, the now sober apprentice was a far better wood sculptor than Chips could ever hope to become. Guzzlin' Gooch had produced a spectacular figurehead of the god, Neptune, in regal and life-like splendor to adorn the bow of our newest squadron member. Further, he had created a much more efficient grenado catapult for our deadly longboats. Given its improved capabilities, I commissioned our burgeoning carpenter to produce several more for immediate installation in each of these lethal vessels as well as larger versions for both of the schooners.

Now that we were operating two ships in tandem, communication became a critical necessity. To meet this need, I focused on drum communication tutored by Tiger Eyes. These classes familiarized all of our crewmembers to the specific meanings of the various drum rhythms. While not really that difficult to teach or understand, I deemed this class critical given the number of different messages that were necessary during any heated battle. The entire crew were able to interpret the messages signaled by our drums with the sole exception of Booby Bird. This poor lad found it quite impossible to discern the subtle differences that the drum rhythms and cadences were communicating. His frustrated efforts were a continual joke aboard our vessel, so that I eventually excused him from these duties realizing that teaching him drum language was virtually impossible.

After departing Saint Lucia, we continued our direction south for two good reasons. First, I knew that we required more practice at actual naval encounters. No matter how much training my subjected my crew endured, I understood that it was no replacement for real-life battle conditions. Since many pirate crews had headed south to avoid the cruel rampages of the Black Tarantula, this was the opportune location to ply our combative skills prior to confronting the Scourge of the Caribbean. Secondly, we were still woefully short of seasoned manpower. To solve this dilemma, I was certain that we could add to our numbers from captured and defeated prey as required. With this in mind, we began our formal training.

Our efforts at naval warfare proved clumsy and ineffective at first. The crew displayed various initial issues such as translating the drummed messages under stress, functioning as coordinated attack units and properly identifying sea foe from friendly merchants. While we paid the price for these questionable efforts in the loss of several good men, we were diligently learning from our mistakes and in the process becoming a seasoned and veteran fighting force. To provide a sense of this dilemma, let me illustrate with a doleful example. During a daytime encounter with a band of Danish pirates, we experienced a problem with a grenado catapult in one of our attacking longboats. As our miniature attack vessel neared its target, drum orders called for the initiation of a grenado barrage to soften up our enemy's resolve. Individuals in this longboat loaded a lit grenado to launch at the Danish rogues, but encountered a serious miscue when the catapult jammed and the grenado was tragically locked in place. Realizing their fatal blunder, the longboat's company were forced to abandon ship prior to the grenado's detonation. In the course of this gaffe, we lost two good men. The first was too late in his attempt to abandon the stricken craft and was blown to pieces along with the valuable launch. The second was unable to swim and was pounded by the swells, slipping under the briny surface to meet his maker. In an concerted effort to rescue the floundering survivors of our destroyed tender, the Danish pirates seized the opportunity and escaped.

However, as time progressed, we became very adept at our militant craft and took prize after prize. This significant improvement led to filling our drastic need for men, weapons and powder, as well as adding greatly to our treasure coffers. As we made our southerly patrol, I continued to experiment with unique methods to defeat enemies by the employment of devious tactics other than direct assaults. For the most part, however, most of the prey we encountered resorted to retreat rather than confrontation. Nonetheless, we did clash with some very brave and foolhardy miscreant bands, who chose to stand and fight against our aggressive advances rather than turn tail and run. Aware that these unique situations endangered the lives of my crew, I constantly devised unique and insidious methods to defeat these maddened criminals before they had a chance to significantly reduce our numbers.

The following is but one example. Sailing on a brutally hot tropical sea, our lookouts spotted a potential prey in the distance. Seeking a closer look, I ordered a course change to shave the distance between us. As we neared, I discerned that our prey was flying English colors. However, due to the dress and actions of their crew, I suspected that this ship was much more than a simple trader. Observing that their crew was fully armed, I found this condition highly unusual. Additionally, I made note of the numerous piratical alterations that had been made to the craft. As we continued to shadow this impostor, I marked the arrival of dirty weather. Believing that our target would utilize the brewing storm as a means to escape, I gave orders to close the gap between us and signaled Lion to do the same. As both vessels approached, our prey astonished me by altering course and heading directly towards us. At the same time, I spied that the Union Jack had been replaced with a black flag indicating their true nature--pirates!

Realizing that our enemy was intent on attack rather than retreat, I decided that this confrontation required special handling. Since the seas that surrounded us were far too rough to effectively utilize our deadly musket boats, I quickly formulated a viable alternative. Barking out a series of commands, I brought our ship away from the wind and ordered several special barrels retrieved from the hold. Situating the barrels at various points on the maindeck, I called for my crew to strip off their shirts and fill them with the contents of each barrel. Once done, I commanded them to take refuge and await further orders. Summoning the cannon crews to stand ready, I ordered our course again altered, and aided by the strength of the gale-force winds we flew directly at our prey's midsection.

As we advanced, they fired upon us with their guns scoring minor but irritating damage. Undaunted, we bore down upon them like a bolt of lightening. At the last instant, I called for a slight course change that allowed us to pass by our enemy in extremely tight quarters. With the wind still at our backs, I commanded my shirtless crew to unleash the sizable loads stuffed in their empty tunics. Your see, the barrels I had brought topside contained a caustic mixture of lye and crushed limestone. When this powdered substance was released into the wind, it carried directly into our enemy, covering them with a fine white powder that both burned and blinded them. Having totally immobilized the villains, we swung our ship around and attacked with devastating musket and cannon fire. Since they were virtually blind, we slaughtered the vast majority of these beasts in very short order. Upon confronting a surviving officer, he questioned how I had devised such a diabolical attack strategy. Grinning at his total confusion and amazement, I responded that the tactic seemed appropriate given the way the wind was blowing!

Our southern wanderings brought us very close to the Spanish Main. As we continued to conduct warfare on the numerous pirates that infested these hunting grounds, we had the misfortune of crossing paths with a Spanish war galleon that had been patrolling the waters off the Spanish settlement of Cartagena. Utilizing a hailing trumpet, their commander identified himself as Captain Ricardo Inez Viola and called for our immediate surrender. Realizing that our adversary had significantly more men and guns, I elected to retreat rather than face their superior force. Using our drums, I signaled Lion on *Neptune's Revenge* to follow our lead, and both of our ships turned east and began our flight to safety.

The Spanish warship noted our course change and immediately

added sail to pursue. Although both of our ships were much lighter and faster than our lumbering pursuer, the Spanish Captain proved to be a seasoned and adept competitor and managed to keep us in sight as he continued his merry chase. While our dangerous shadow never closed the gap between us, he proved very resourceful and capable, having greater familiarity with the waters we now transversed. After employing several devious diversionary tactics, I believed that we had finally eluded our persistent foe only to be stunned back to reality when the crafty Spaniard's sails were spotted time and again by our topmen. Try as we might, we just could not evade the hunting hound that doggedly tracked our trail.

As we reached the Dutch ABC Islands, that is Aruba, Bonaire and Curacao, I decided to employ a different strategy to outwit our harassing foe. Since both of our vessels had shallow drafting capabilities, I decided to opt for a shallow water cove or inlet among these sparsely populated islands in which to hide in order to frustrate our pursuer into abandoning his quest. As we made our way towards Bonaire, I spotted a likely hiding place on its northern tip. Heading toward this promised sanctuary, I was relieved to discover that the entrance was much too shallow for our adversary to traverse. Narrowing further as we continued inland, this emergency channel ended in a swampy lagoon, completely masking our presence. Dropping our anchors, I ordered two crewmen to row a small dinghy back to the inlet's entrance to act as lookouts.

Once anchored, a virtual horde of tropical pests descended upon us. Voracious mosquitoes, sand flies and other blood-craving carnivores seemed to instantly materialize out of the surrounding swamp. My crews were doing a compulsory dance of avoidance, as they swatted and waved at their pesky tormentors. Realizing that this ravenous throng of pests would either eat us alive or drive us totally mad, I went below to secure some insect-deterring ingredients before matters got totally out-of-hand. Gathering these compounds, I issued instructions to Powder Monkey on appropriate quantity and mixture details. At the same time, I ordered Sharkface Topper to send a small boat ashore for one last vital substance, swamp mud! Once retrieved, I combined Powder Monkey's concoction to the slimy sludge that had been collected in numerous buckets.

Once mixed, I demonstrated the proper application as I liberally slathered it all over my exposed flesh. Once completed, I ordered my men to duplicate this effort. I also sent a generous supply of the specially mixed mud to *Neptune's Revenge* so that they could also avoid the pestering attack of the bloodthirsty monsters. While waiting his turn to apply the remedy, one bedeviled sailor decided to jump overboard and find refuge in the calm green water of the lagoon. This proved a serious mistake, as he was suddenly set upon by an assemblage of vicious and savage vipers that struck the poor soul time and again in retaliation for his unwelcome disruption of their weed-choked home. We eventually managed to drag the unfortunate back onboard but his fate was sealed. Going into a series of involuntary convulsions, he was dead in no time at all. Due to this lethal danger, swimming and bathing in this deadly pool were immediately banned; not that any sane tar would enter the mossy green water after witnessing the poor lad's destruction!

Our hot and humid purgatory proved less and less hospitable by the minute, and I was sorely tempted to flee these hellish surroundings. This option became untenable once my scouts returned with their ill news. It seemed that our Spanish tormentor, Captain Viola had anchored his war galleon at the mouth of our escape route, lying in wait for our emergence. For the life of me, I could not fathom how he had managed to guess the exact location of our hiding spot. I knew with certainty that given our sizable lead, he could not have been in position to spot us entering the waterway. Therefore, I surmised that our friend had blindly conjectured on our location. I was also certain that he would eventually raise anchor and continue his nautical hunt after a short while if he witnessed no sign of us.

Given these assumptions, I returned to my cabin with Lion to plot our course once our adversary decided to vacate his position. Lion and I realized that the holds of both our ships were crammed to capacity with valuable booty from our many successful forays against pirate adversaries. Understanding our desperate need to safely offload this booty before disaster struck, I recommended that we return to Marie-Galant and consign our cargo to Rene for proper handling. While Lion agreed, he was concerned that this course might place us in the vicinity of our hated nemesis, Captain LeMerde. Concentrating on his astute concern, I offered a compromise to my original recommendation.

Rather than sailing directly into Rene's anchorage, I suggested that we utilize the hidden cove on the opposite side of Marie-Galant that Rene had previously mentioned. With relief flooding his broad face, Lion agreed to my suggestion without a hint of hesitation. But as fate would have it, all did not proceed as smoothly as I had fervently wished!

At dusk, we were attacked by an even greater concentration of noxious flying pests. Given their sheer numbers, we were forced inside each of our vessels with any avenue of egress for these bothersome brutes blocked with old sailcloth. The problem that now beset us was the stifling heat that assailed our bodies and minds as we sweltered in our air-tight floating hellholes. The humidity was so thick and cloying that it felt like we had been immersed in a cauldron of boiling water. Sweat and stink ran off our bodies in equal measure, as we suffered every waking moment. Stripped of energy, all we could manage were silent prayers that the night would pass rapidly.

Remember when I commented that time had a way of moving slow or fast depending on the circumstance. Well, I can faithfully report that our prayers went totally unanswered in our hot and humid prisons. In fact, our wait seemed to last an eternity, as seconds turned into minutes, minutes into hours and hours into days. In effect, time virtually stood still, and I had a very troubling concern that these hellish conditions would cause serious mental strain and irreparable harm to both of my crews. When dawn finally broke, there was a mad rush to the topdeck to inhale fresh air. In doing so, we experienced a repeat of the prior day's attack by our ravenous tormentors. To this end, I was unsure which was worse, the night we had just suffered or the day we were about to torturously endure, sheer madness in either case!

Once again, I sent a scout to the mouth of the inlet to discover the status of our determined harasser. They returned to sadly report that the Spanish galleon remained anchored offshore, guarding against any escape attempt. To take the men's minds off the brutal heat, I assigned various light labors on both ships. In addition, I sent several teams inland in search of fresh food and water. To lighten the moods and minds of all, I called for rum to be delivered topside. While this ploy temporarily assuaged my men, eventually the rum supply was extinguished to the continual whining, buzzing and droning of the insect hordes that enveloped and bedeviled us.

Entering our third day in our insect infested lair, I was again disappointed and frustrated when our scout reported that our enemy had not as yet vacated their position. While our foraging teams had been highly successful in locating sufficient quantities of tropical fruits and freshwater, I knew that my tormented crew could not last much longer without going completely mad. True to my predictions, the body of an unfortunate tar was soon discovered in our hold. His badly beaten remains were uncovered by Powder Monkey on one of his daily treks for galley supplies. While I had no evidence as to the perpetrator of this heinous crime, strong suspicions fell on a recent recruit, known to have hard feelings for the now deceased sailor. Confronted by Sharkface, the offender eventually confessed to his heinous crime.

The crew convened and after hours of discussions and arguments decided that the murderer was entitled to a very grisly punishment. This agreed retribution called for the killer to accompany his victim to his final resting place, sewn together in burial sailcloth and thrown over the ship's side. Since we were far too shallow to bury the deceased, his moldering corpse had been salted and deposited in the hold to await sea burial. Knowing that this rapidly decomposing cadaver required prompt handling, I decided to utilize a deep pool in our hellish hideout to inter both his moldering body along with that of his murdering mate. As I announced this decision, a look of abject terror came over the butcher's face. Before any of us could react, the condemned criminal dove over the side, and began paddling his way to shore in an attempt to escape his ugly fate. However, as he splashed and flailed in the green murk, he was greeted by a host of sinuous forms that struck time and again.

Utilizing grappling hooks, we managed to finally snag the killer, and began to tow him back towards the ship. Along his watery path, he received bite after bite from the vicious and highly angered reptiles, whose province had again been rudely disturbed. When he was finally hauled onboard, we all bore witness to the numerous puncture wounds delivered by the irritated serpents. Jerking in agony and moaning in extreme pain, the killer expired right before our eyes. As originally decreed, both bodies were wrapped in sailcloth, weighted and dropped in the deep lagoon pool to sort out their personal differences in Davy Jones Locker.

Chapter 26: Let the Monsters of the Deep Arise

I decided that it was time to take action before any more of my crew resorted again to drastic action. Calling a conference with Lion and Sharkface, I outlined the bold plan I had been devising for the past few days. Given our hellish situation, I informed my commanders that my dangerous scheme was well worth the significant risks, if it provided us the opportunity to escape. Agreeing without question, my leaders hurried from my cabin to prepare the details of my risky venture. Succinctly stated, the plan called for the employment of a highly unusual diversion to hold the attention of our Spanish foes, while a select battle-hardened team would board the galleon and perform necessary detainment tasks.

As night descended, I was elated to discover that a thick cloud-cover blotted out the moon's illumination. Patiently waiting for the onset of the morning watch, four in the morning to you landlubbers, I gave the order to proceed with our plan. In doing so, we would rely on the use of two of our blackened longboats. The first longboat's mission was to slip around the Spanish vessel and create a significant diversion on its seaward side. Once effected, the second longboat would silently make its way to the enemy's shoreward side, and its members would gain access through any open gunport. Once the second team had successfully entered our enemy's gundeck, their mission was to spike as many cannons as possible, rendering them completely useless. Specifically, this meant that my raiders would drive iron nails into each gun's touch-hole, denying the Spaniards the ability to fire their cannons until the obstructions had been painstakingly removed. Once accomplished, this team also were tasked with depositing a good luck present for our Papist tormentors, one that would surely be highly unwelcome!

Our longboats silently made their way along the inlet and reached open water. The first boat slipped unseen by our anchored and silent watchdog. When this vessel was in position, Powder Monkey lit a lantern and placed it in the carved wooden figure that had been firmly lashed to the small vessel's bow. You see, Gooch's had devilishly carved a veritable masterpiece that resembled the terrifying image of a fearsome and bloodcurdling sea monster. Its head was enormous and fashioned to house an oil lamp to illuminate its beastly facial features. Another carved cavity in its mouth held a smoke grenado that emitted plumes of smoke and flames from the wooden creature's mouth and nostrils in a rather realistic manner. To complete the ruse, we had employed old tarred sailcloth to cover the longboat completely, and, in doing so, fein a surfacing monstrously humongous beast. To further add to the creature's frighting outline, we employed the use of an oar jutting upwards like a tentpole underneath the black sailcloth. The fire-breathing and smoking leviathan was then rowed in a parallel course to our foes so that it would be quite visible to any of the Spanish watchmen topside. This daring ruse proved a total success as it drew the full attention of the enemy's spotters. The Spanish crewmen were completely mesmerized by the appearance of this fabled sea demon and stood transfixed upon the topdeck as it glided slowly by their ship issuing smoke and flames from its enormous mouth and snout. To a man, they were both silently stunned and completely terrified.

As this marvelous diversion occurred, Tiger Eyes and crew in the second longboat rowed over to the anchored ship on its opposite side and used a grappling hook to gain access through an open gunport. Once aboard, his team spread out and began spiking cannon after cannon. Completing this nefarious action, they escaped utilizing the open gunport, while dumping three sacks filled with the vicious swamp vipers that we had earlier captured from our hellish prison. Released, these lethal serpents slithered to various hiding places all across the gundeck. From their hiding positions, these vicious vipers were now poised to strike at any slight movement or provocation. Between these deadly deterrents and the spiked guns, the entire deck had been rendered totally useless to our Spanish friends. With their tasks completed, both longboats headed north to await our imminent arrival.

As dawn broke, both of our ships emerged from hiding and headed directly at our anchored enemy to wreak our own form of revenge. Upon sighting our emergence, a warning cry was sounded on the Spanish warship, and men ran hurriedly to their assigned combat positions. Both of our ships with musket teams poised and positioned on our topdeck commenced firing. These teams slaughtered any Spaniard caught out in the open. At the same time, we utilized our newly installed catapults to launch a barrage of deadly grenados that caused further death and destruction. While we could not witness the effects of our gundeck sabotage, we were quite aware of its intended effect as the Spanish guns remained silent on our approach. When our ships were in position, the order was given and our cannons opened fire raking the Spaniard's masts and sails. Striking with devastating accuracy, we swept these targets into rags and splinters. To complete our sweet revenge, both of our ships passed the crippled Spanish warship one last time, firing our guns directly into their hull creating huge gaping wounds that doomed the vessel. From these ragged openings, we witnessed numerous serpentine forms abandoning the stricken ship. We also were well aware that Captain Viola and crew would be forced to abandon their ship and flee to shore and be subjected to the attacks and ravaging of the voracious and pesky insects that had plagued our very existence on this accursed spit of land!

Having completed our devastation, we bid a rousing and raucous farewell to our enemies and headed north to rendezvous with our two longboats. Once secured, we continued on towards Marie-Galant. I looked forward to reuniting with Rene and Lille, and to hear firsthand about Captain LeMerde's discovery of the fraud I had perpetrated to effect my escape. As planned, this stopover would also allow us to unload our prodigious booty from our escapades in these pirate-filled waters. I knew that I could count on Rene to represent us in a truly fair and honest manner in reconciling the value of our cargo with our corrupt Governor. The next several days passed without incident as we navigated northward. Since several of my crew still hungered for their promised gold doubloon, combat classes were again opened and training continued unabated. Musket team target practice also resumed utilizing coconuts tossed randomly into the sea as targets. As this all occurred, our drum teams kept a steady flow of commands echoing back and forth between our ships honing their skill to an even finer degree.

Finally reaching our destination, we scouted the coast Rene had identified and eventually discovered the hidden cove. Once located, we entered and anchored in relative isolation and peace. I sent Powder Monkey and Scuttle in our swiftest dinghy to rendezvous with their blacksmith shop on Guadeloupe to produce more precious grenados for both of our vessels. I then had Lion send a scout party ashore to locate the best route to reach Rene's plantation by land. In a short while, they returned grinning from ear-to-ear, explaining that a newly constructed road had been found that led directly to our objective. True to his word, Rene had constructed the thoroughfare he had long ago promised. Since I was eager to reunite with my friends, I ordered both Lion and Sharkface supervise the unloading of the cargo, promising to send back some sturdy wagons to haul our booty to Rene's warehouse. Once both ships were freed of this burden, I commanded both leaders to work with Chips to careen and repair the hulls of both schooners.

As I traveled the well-built and secreted lane, I fingered the gifts I had selected for my upcoming reunion. For each of my dear friends, I had chosen a rare and beautiful piece of jewelry liberated in our privateering efforts. For Rene I had selected an exquisite emerald ring, and for his wife and sister stunning necklaces of priceless rubies and pearls. I knew that my friends would be overwhelmed by my grand gestures, but felt a great debt owed for their invaluable escape assistance.

As I reached their manor, my anticipated joyous reunion was dashed as I discovered my friend in a very desperate state. Rene's appearance was much more than upsetting. He seemed quite distraught and highly distracted, as if plagued by a horde of insidious demons tormenting his very soul. Physically I could see that he was significantly emaciated, drawn and extremely pale. When I questioned him on the whereabouts of his wife, he answered that she was bedridden and much too weak to make an appearance. Realizing that something was drastically wrong, I begged by friend to supply immediate answers for his horrid condition. Ushering me to his comfortable study, he related what had transpired following my escape.

Rene informed me that all had gone according to plan until the villainous Captain LeMerde returned to the mansion. Rene described the reprobate's mood as completely irrational sparked by his ferocious anger and utter frustration. Crazed to the point of total insanity, he immediately blamed the Turbouts for assisting in my flight from justice. Although all three of my friends claimed absolute innocence in the affair, Captain LeMerde would not listen to a single word and singled out Aimee as the prime culprit in facilitating my illegal exodus. Insanely intent on seeing me hanged, Captain LeMerde abducted Aimee under the guise of arresting her for abetting a known criminal. Crying out in anguish, Rene informed me that LeMerde had taken Aimee and had simply sailed away with his poor unfortunate sister. Convinced that she was the perfect bait to induce me into attempting a rescue mission, Captain LeMerde informed Rene that his destination was Jamaica. Issuing an insidious threat, he promised Rene and Lille that he would hang Aimee as a pirate's accomplice if I did not surrender myself to him for proper legal punishment. Since the villain's departure, Rene had been agonizing over his love for his sister as well as his concern for my safety. Looking directly into his eyes, I informed him that it was both my responsibility and my duty to see that Aimee was returned unharmed. I confessed that it was my direct involvement that had brought this evil down on his family endangering each and every one of them.

Chapter 27: The Governor Throws a Party

Rene questioned how I intended to honor the pledge I had just uttered, and I responded that I required assistance from our perfidious Governor before initiating my quest. Confused by my answer, I explained that our unscrupulous Governor had the power to provide a document that would lawfully sanction the mission. Still quite confounded, Rene nevertheless divulged that he and Lille had been invited to a celebration at the Governor's mansion the following evening. It seemed that the Governor was celebrating his birthday with a grand party, and had invited a host of influential people to this gala event. Continuing, Rene explained that Lille was too distraught to make the journey, and that I could attend the festivities in her stead. Rene further confessed that his feeble attempts to petition the isle's leader for assistance regarding Aimee had failed miserably, since the Governor lived in utmost fear of Captain LeMerde. Laughing now, I informed Rene that the greedy bureaucrat would certainly be quite interested in the proceeds from the prizes we captured during our latest voyage. I explained that we would utilize these positive financial tidings as bait to enable us to garner the great man's undivided attention.

I then realized that I did not have the proper attire to appear at the Governor's celebration. Rene volunteered use of his wardrobe, since the two of us were actually quite similar in size and physique. Retiring to Rene's bedroom, I was presented with a bevy of dignified and exquisite options. I finally settled on a dove grey long-coat of the finest wool, black trousers, a leather lambskin vest and black boots and hose. I also opted for a brilliant white shirt with wide puffy sleeves, the current rage for any serious swordsman. To complete my attire, I selected from my own belongings a fabulous gold watch and fob along with a massive blood-red ruby ring. I knew that our good Governor was excessively avaricious and the smoky brilliance of this exquisite gem would surely attract his attention. Rene's valet made all of the necessary alterations to my clothing choices, so that by the next evening we were both off to pay our sincerest respects to the island's esteemed leader.

Arriving well in advance of the start of festivities, Rene and I were hurriedly ushered into the Governor's study for private words. We were both greeted in an abrupt manner by the Governor, before he resumed his manic pacing. He appeared to us both as being uncontrollably panicked. Clearly remembering me, he greedily transfixed on the ruby ring I wore on my hand. Meanwhile, Rene opened the discussion by providing a short summary of the booty that my voyage had produced, and the Governor seemed somewhat enthused and excited concerning these conquests and their resulting spoils. At that moment, his faithful office attaché entered and whispered some words into his leader's ear. Completing this seemingly disagreeable task, the assistant hastily excused himself and practically ran from the room. Glancing back to the Governor, I could see that the recent tidings were indeed quite wretched, as I watched the poor fool's face fill with panic and consternation. At that point, the Governor began stammering and babbling like a drunken sot, a total blithering idiot. Like a man issued his death warrant, the Governor extended his sincerest apologies to Rene and I, and informed us that a dire emergency had arisen that desperately required his attention as he practically ran from the room. Perplexed to the extreme by our host's bizarre behavior, Rene and I stared at each other in stunned silence.

Deciding to better understand the nature of the calamity, I exited the room in search of the message bearer. Finding the faithful assistant in the massive kitchen issuing furious orders to the staff, I asked the man for a moment of his time. Pulling him off to a narrow cubbyhole, I questioned him on his supervisor's erratic behavior. Shrugging innocently, the attaché' informed me that the famed island performer and tonight's entertainment, Luc-A-Luc had contracted a sudden malady that precluded his presence for the evening's festivities. As consummate host, the Governor had panicked aware that his birthday party was doomed to failure without proper entertainment, a fate in his mind worse than death!

After thanking the helpful assistant for this scuttlebutt, I began plotting a scheme to take full advantage of this unfortunate turn of events. Searching for the elusive Governor, I discovered him in his library shouting at several cowed servants to locate a last-minute substitute to replace the villainous Luc-A-Luc. Continuing his tirade, he informed the befuddled group, that if they were not successful, he would face social ruin and substantial embarrassment, and subsequently they would perform a painful dance under the ministrations of the dreaded cat-o-nine-tails. Approaching the manic politician, I informed him that I had the ideal solution to his problem. Continuing, I announced that I could fill the role of tonight's entertainment. My statement caused the flustered and preoccupied politician to actually laugh in my face, as he named me both a total fool and complete imbecile. As he roughly pushed me out of his way and continued his path out of the room, I issued an impromptu rousing rendition of *Blind Bess* that completely arrested his retreat. Turning back, he issued his famous snide smile, still rather shocked at the demonstrated quality of my voice. Nodding slowly and mechanically, he announced that maybe I was not completely mad after all. With a sly grin, he questioned what recompense was at stake should he decide to allow me to perform, a shrewd gamesman at all times!

Responding that my price was quite modest, I informed him that it simply amounted to a proposition I wanted him to consider. Unaware of my meaning, he motioned me to continue. I proposed that should my entertainment endeavor prove to be an overwhelming success with his guests, that he would provide Rene and I an hour of his valuable time to discuss a new business venture. As I recited these words, I actively fingered the enormous ruby ring on my hand letting the best light in the room reflect through the marvelous gem creating an illusion of fire. Realizing he had few alternatives and greedy for possession of my priceless ring, the Governor agreed to my proposition, but questioned who would act as judge of my proposed talents. I answered that his guests would surely provide this measurement, for if they were not buzzing with happiness and extreme satisfaction over my stupendous performance, then I had failed in my task and Rene and I would pester him no further. Satisfied with the arrangement, we shook hands over the matter, and he immediately retired to prepare himself for his guests' arrivals. As soon as the Governor departed, Rene gave me a long questioning look. Lightly tugging on his immaculate sleeve, I winked and whispered that he needed to have faith, as I promised our mission would result in a rousing success!

The guests arrived in droves at the appointed time, and food and drink were supplied by the finely dressed servants who circled the crowd like a pack of highly attentive curs. I had a lengthy meeting with the orchestra members to ensure that they would provide the proper accompaniment, as well as gaining their agreement on my intended performance agenda. I also provided several coins to each to guarantee their finest efforts this evening. After acknowledging his gracious guests and formally toasting his own birthday, the Governor called for everyone's attention and announced my agreement to perform this special evening. As he did so, he confessed that I was a last minute replacement for the indisposed Luc-A-Luc, and requested the audience's benevolent patience and understanding in this matter.

With less than rousing introduction, I stepped up onto the small makeshift stage and introduced myself and my fellow musicians. Describing the performance they were about to receive, I confessed that as my performance progressed I would require their invaluable assistance. Smiling politely, they collectively stared up at me with questioning gazes. Without delay, I launched into an island ballad that I had heard on my last visit. Choosing a rich and strong baritone delivery, I stopped time, as the entire room became instantly transfixed and totally at my command. Continuing with a dozen more delightful and charming French love songs and ballads, the audience quieted into an adoring reverie as my voice magically enthralled each and every one of them.

Well into my performance, I once again called for their complete attention, and explained that I had planned something radically different for them. Explaining the need for strenuous labor on any sailing ship, I informed my rapt listeners that we employed special work songs called chanties to ease the labor and burden prompted by these necessary but harsh tasks. I then inquired if they would like to hear an example of a sea chanty, which was met with a tremendous roar of approval. Informing them that I required their assistance to demonstrate the song, I provided specific instructions on performing a tune called *Mermaids Ashore*. Per my direction, I explained that I would lead the individual verses followed by all of them harmonizing the chorus, which I promptly tutored them on. I then petitioned my audience to imagine that they were in the midst of performing difficult and harsh menial labor. I promised that as our song progressed, they would soon forget these imagined hardships and burdens as they immersed themselves in performing the enchanting chanty.

With that I began, and the whole house was soon thumping and bouncing to the lively tune. The entire audience enthusiastically voiced their role in the nautical ditty, and soon all was forgotten as they engaged consummately in the fun. Even the serving men and women participated, as the whole house answered the verses I delivered. Since this chanty was such a huge success, we moved on to another selection as soon as the first finished. In no time at all, we had spent well over two hours with this entertaining and fanciful diversion. It seemed that I had invented a new kind of upper-crust parlor game. At last, my voice became weary and worn from my strenuous efforts. I thanked the audience for their grateful assistance and wonderful harmonizing. They responded with a long and hearty round of applause and clamorous shouts of appreciation. As I rejoined Rene, I was personally thanked and backslapped by nearly anyone I passed which pleased me greatly. With the evening nearing an end, Rene and I hunted down our host to inquire if he would honor our bargain and grace us with an audience as soon as his guests departed. Smiling, he answered that an audience was the least he could provide, given the immense success I had made of the evening. He informed us that my entertainment had been both unique and outstanding, and that his celebration would be remembered and treasured for many long years to come.

As the evening eventually concluded and the guests sent home bubbling, smiling and ecstatic, Rene and I were alerted by the Governor's signal to follow him to his private study. Once comfortable, he opened the discussion by inquiring how my latest voyage had fared, having paid absolutely no attention to our previous account. I responded that our voyage had been quite successful, and as he would soon be appraised, quite profitable. I informed him that I had deposited all the valuables from my excursion with Rene, as I trusted him implicitly with handling the matter of settlement. Nodding agreement , the Governor warily questioned what other matters we wished to discuss.

At once, Rene launched into his dilemma regarding the abduction of his sister by the nefarious Captain LeMerde. I could see the Governor becoming more and more anxious as Rene provided the sordid details. Both Rene and I had already come to the agreed conclusion that news of this atrocious abduction had obviously reached the island leader's ears long before our visit. As expected, the shifty executive feigned total ignorance on the matter. With an ingenious apology for his total unfamiliarity regarding this horrid situation, he bade Rene to continue his account of the abduction while continuing his innocent act of pretending that it was totally new knowledge. As Rene finished, the Governor appeared stricken and lost as he contemplated extricating himself from this undesirable dilemma. Eventually formulating a cowardly course of action, he questioned what we expected of him because of the unsanctioned actions of this wayward officer. Convinced that LeMerde had lost his mind and was quite dangerous to anyone who crossed his path, the Governor apologized for the rogue's ill-treatment and manners, but made it clear that his authority only encompassed the Isle of Guadeloupe and not the entire Caribbean. In other words, the scoundrel's actions away from his island were of little and no concern to him.

Aware of the Governor's personal fear of this renegade, I launched into my own proposition. Given that the Governor's province over LeMerde was limited, I reasoned that Captain LeMerde was guilty of kidnapping while operating within the Governor's realm. Because of this serious trespass, I proposed that he issue a legal arrest warrant for the capture and return of both LeMerde and his prisoner, Aimee Turbout. Before the Governor could raise a craven objection, I further propositioned that this warrant be issued in absolute secrecy to avoid any future unpleasantness should my efforts prove unsuccessful in any way. I then vowed to keep our agreement and subsequent arrest warrant in absolute secrecy. For this consideration and cooperation, I nominated Rene to represent me as official negotiator to ensure that the crown's share of our reported treasure was truly maximized. Finally, I removed the exquisite ruby ring from my finger and offered it to the Governor as a show of good faith. Beaming now, the Governor snatched the ring from my hand, and in an official tone proclaimed that my plan was both sound and agreeable. He promised to have the necessary official arrest papers drawn-up and ready for delivery in three days.

As we exited the Governor's mansion, Rene forcefully halted my withdrawal and expressed his extreme concern in regard to my involvement in his sister's second rescue attempt. In a solemn and serious tone, he confessed that I had already risked my life once to save Aimee from Captain Bass. He insisted that it was certainly not my duty to attempt this feat a second time, especially since LeMerde was a far superior adversary. Gratified by my friend's concern, I stated that I was entirely culpable for his family being persecuted by this mad Frenchman. Given that they had risked their lives in an effort to assist my escape, I professed that his sister's rescue had become expressly personal and an awful wrong that I needed to right. Sporting a wide grin, he wrapped his arms around my shoulders and proclaimed profuse thanks for my invaluable assistance as well as my esteemed friendship!

We returned to Rene's plantation and informed Lille on the results of Governor's meeting. Receiving yet another round of grateful thanks, I made my departure to return to my ship.

Arriving with a slew of Rene's freight wagons and workmen, I instructed Lion and Sharkface to begin transferring our spoils onto the transports. When the work was underway, I called a war council in my cabin that included Lion, Sharkface Topper, Tan, Long Tall Willie and Powder Monkey. Explaining the developments since our escape, I noted that all were quite indignant upon learning of the nefarious and outrageous antics of Captain LeMerde. To a man, they voiced a need to once again rescue Aimee, and subsequently arrest and return the deranged French officer for trial and punishment. Smiling, I informed them that the Governor was currently drawing up the legal papers that would enable us to accomplish this exact task. However, I cautioned that we needed to maintain strict silence on the matter and to keep all plans to ourselves until the matter was completely resolved.

Turning to Powder Monkey, I questioned the amount of time required to complete the restocking of grenados. He signed that Scuttle's work was already underway and that the required armament would be completed in less than a week. Nodding approval, I turned to Lion and Sharkface and instructed them to make a list of any supplies they required. This list would be provided to Rene for handling with the cost to be deducted from the ship's share of the prodigious treasure we were placing in his hands. As the men returned to their duties, I wandered the ship lost in thought. I fleetingly noticed that our careening efforts and cargo unloading were proceeding efficiently. In fact, the tedious chore of unloading our substantial booty continued nonstop, as we filled Rene's wagons time and time again, truly a king's treasure indeed!

As I continued my wandering, I could not help but concentrate on the choices I had made to involve Rene and his family in my escape plan. My decision had put Rene's family in harms way. For the first time in quite awhile, I regretted the poor choice I had made in this matter and vowed to set matters right!

Chapter 28: Rescue Mission

Well, our good Governor finally completed and delivered the arrest papers for Captain LeMerde. In the meantime, Rene had successfully brokered our spoils of war and the funds were distributed to the crew. I elected to have Rene hold my share for the day when I could fully utilize them to create a wondrous life with my beloved Rue. Eager to hunt down the French reprobate and rescue Aimee, I informed the crew that they would have ample opportunity to spend their loot in the comfort of the numerous and accommodating Jamaican pleasure houses. Receiving a rousing approval, I ordered our anchor weighed and our journey initiated.

We reached Jamaica without any sort of incident. Once docked, Powder Monkey and I in disguised garb and a false whiskers and beard joined the first shore party and made our way to the Adams' residence. On the way we paid a brief visit with Fat Dog to arrange for a place for Powder Monkey to sleep during our time ashore. Since Powder Monkey's assignment was to roam, reconnoiter and report on any unusual activities, he required a berth where he could operate in a nondescript fashion. Remembering Fat Dog's apehouse, I judged that it would suit our needs perfectly. After a brief negotiation with Fat Dog, including the transfer of a very valuable gem-encrusted bracelet, the arrangement was finalized and Powder Monkey was given a key to the building. Fat Dog insisted that nobody intentionally visited the chimp's residence, so Powder Monkey was safe from notice while utilizing this novel hideout.

Once these negotiations were completed, I questioned Fat Dog concerning any news he might have on the insidious Captain LeMerde. Providing a look of utter disdain and contempt, he informed me that the madman had actually been an unwelcome guest not very long ago at the pub. Additionally, word had reached Fat Dog's ears from various sources that LeMerde had taken a female prisoner and was holding her in relative safety aboard his craft until I made my appearance. However, to ensure no rescue attempt was made before that time, the maniac had devised a cunning scheme to continually change his vessel's location until my arrival was confirmed. While it was believed that he was close, nobody knew for certain his exact whereabouts. Still quite apprehensive and distraught over this glum scuttlebutt, Fat Dog was quick to disclose that he was certain that the lass was in no immanent danger. As he put it, it was my blood that the Frenchman craved not the maiden's. Fat Dog avowed that he was confident that the lunatic's bait would not be jeopardized for any reason whatsoever. He further attempted to relieve my building anxiety by disclosing that one of LeMerde's officers in a state of total inebriation had innocently let slip that the lass was living the life of luxury while aboard and faced no impending peril. Gratified by this heartening news, I thanked my friend and petitioned him to keep a close ear to the ground for any further scuttlebutt on this loathsome situation. Giving me a wink of understanding, he scurried off to attend to an altercation that had just broken out across the room.

Once I arrived at the Adams', I was greeted in a frantic manner by all three sisters, who were quite pleased by my return. As the clamor of my arrival subsided, I was able to question them on the fate of their nephew. As soon as I opened my inquiry, Willamina jumped up and rushed from the room, like a frightened crab scuttling away from danger. She made her reappearance reverently carrying a small velvet container. Setting this box on the table in front of me, she indicated that I should open it. Reaching down, I pried the lid carefully off of the box and jumped back in confusion and horror as I recognized its grizzly contents as a human finger with a signet ring attached.

Gertrude met my disgusted gaze, and informed me that the finger was her nephew's, since the ring was easily identified as an Adams' family heirloom. Shaking off my stammered queries, Gertrude recanted the entire affair for my benefit. After his hurried departure with the small assembled fleet, Captain Adams had proceeded directly to Saint Domingue. On this voyage, a storm suddenly arose and battered half of his vessels to uselessness. As the fleet was engaged with transferring men and stores from the tempest-damaged ships, they were suddenly attacked by the Black Tarantula. Despite the ensuing chaos, Captain Adams had shown remarkable courage and fast thinking as he managed to fend off the black-hearted villain's offensive. Scoring several direct cannon strikes, Captain Adams had actually turned the tide of battle in his favor. The Black Tarantula, realizing that the battle was lost, turned his ship and attempted to flee. Captain Adams ordered his remaining three seaworthy vessels to give pursuit in an effort to end the atrocious reign of the dreaded pirate. As his ships gained ground on the villain, a late entry into the conflict suddenly made an appearance. This vessel was a French warship armed to the teeth with deadly cannons and musketeers. The newcomer proceeded to wreak destruction and havoc on my friend's remaining ships. Buoyed by this timely assistance, the Black Tarantula swooped down and destroyed Captain Adams' remaining ships one by one. Only one known survivor was plucked from the Caribbean waters, Captain Adams! Gertrude explained that she and her sisters had been informed of these developments by a passing Dutch trader, who had witnessed the entire affair from a safe distance away.

Gertrude continued by informing me that after many torturous weeks, the velvet box in my hand was secretly delivered to their front door. Included in this unpleasant package was a ransom note demanding an obscene amount for the safe return of their precious nephew. Since the arrival of this horrific package, the sisters had been in the process of amassing the fortune demanded for the release of their loved one. Gertrude proclaimed that neither she nor her sisters really believed that any amount of money would guarantee their nephew's safe return. Hence, they viewed my sudden arrival as a sign of promise and hope to end their living hell. Suddenly, all three sisters crowded around me tearfully begging me to rescue their dear nephew. With a wave of my hand, I silenced their pleas, and assured them that I would certainly assist them in their desperate time of need. With visible sighs of relief, all three sisters converged on me with tearful expressions of gratitude.

Once the emotion of the moment passed, I questioned them further on the ransom note. Rather than answer my numerous queries, Willamina raced from the room and returned with the actual note. In perusing the missive, there was no additional information to be gleaned, other than the ransom's delivery location and explicit timing. The note called for the transference of the demanded fortune within a month's time to the isle of Tortuga, where Captain Adams was imprisoned. As the note specified, Captain Adams would be released only after the ransom had been paid. Further, it warned that the Captain would perish in a most horrid manner should the explicit demands not be met or if any sort of rescue attempt was mounted. With the explicit deadline indicated in the dispatch, I knew that time was certainly of the essence if we hoped to ever see Captain Adams alive again.

Continuing our interrupted reunion, I filled the sisters in on my exploits since leaving their fair island. I informed them that I was now a Captain of two successful privateers, anchored safely in the harbor. Further, I enlightened them on the reason behind my sudden appearance. I explained that I was performing a desperate quest to locate and obliterate a nasty scoundrel, who had caused close friends nothing but heartache and misery. However, I assured them that before I could accomplish this task, there was the more pressing need to rescue their nephew before the dreaded deadline expired. Agreeing with visible relief, the four of us began to scheme and plot a host of solutions. As more and more bizarre options entered the conversation, an idea suddenly materialized in my mind. Thinking over this shrewd notion, I believed that it just might succeed as an unconscious smile stole over my face. Noting my expression, the Adams sisters ceased talking and simply stared at me, waiting for me to reveal my inner thoughts. Taking my time, I walked them through the scheme that I felt confident would solve our needs. When finished, the sisters also grew quite excited and optimistic, as they questioned how they might assist.

My first priority was to restock my medicinal stores which had nearly been depleted during recent adventures. Gertrude arose and guided me to her workroom that was located outside in a well-hidden buried root cellar at the back of the house. This structure had been carefully designed and built by Gertrude to provide a secret site for mixing, brewing and creating her life-giving ointments, tinctures and lotions. At her instruction, I carried along a small water tight chest, which would be used to store my required pharmacopoeia. To start, Gertrude quickly located and provided several large belladonna roots. In addition, she added a generous quantity of almost every valuable ingredient in her possession. Before she finished, she produced several jars filled to the brink with strange black, kidney shaped beans that were quite wrinkled and relatively scant in size.

With a voice that bespoke extreme reverence, my aged friend confessed that these tiny seeds were exceedingly lethal and formidable. She explained that these were the seeds of the Thorn Apple plant. Continuing in a hushed and apprehensive voice, Gertrude informed me that these innocent looking seeds represented one of the most virulent poisons on earth!

The plant that produced these seeds went by a variety of names including Moonflower, Devil's Trumpet and Satan's Cucumber. Ingested in minute quantities, these highly potent seeds could produce a number of horrific results, including complete insensibility, pain wracked paralysis, blurred vision, blindness, violent combative behavior, extreme agitation, uncontrollable giddiness, delirium and horrific hallucinations. However, when larger amounts of this devastating substance was employed, a painful and horrific death routinely ensued. There was no known cure for Thorn Apple poisoning, and the victim was ensured ghastly and grisly suffering which invariably ended in certain death. Further, she claimed that these seeds did not lose their necrotic potency by either boiling, cooking or drying over an extended period of time. They were surely the Devil's own design and needed to be handled and utilized with utmost care. With a wink, she confided that a victim of this bane would be hopelessly unable to register reality from fantasy before expiring in a most gruesome manner. Thinking back on my scheme, I was quite certain that the bite of the Devil's Trumpet would prove essential in Captain Adams' rescue.

Once Gertrude completed her detailed account on the preparation and use of the Devil's Trumpet seeds, I carefully included them in my valuable chest and followed her back to the house. My plot also required several unique costumes and props. Providing an extensive list, Hortence was off like a hound pursuing a fleeing fox to collect my requirements. As we awaited her return, I casually enquired about recent island scuttlebutt. In unison, the sisters informed me that since their nephew's abduction, a new commander of the fort had been named, Lieutenant Henry Hicks. Almost sneering his name, I came to the realization that there was little love lost for this new military leader. Gertrude announced that the good lieutenant was a first class coward, and therefore had not been a favored cohort of their nephew. He was nicknamed Toeless by his men, a result of a disastrous run-in with a slender reef predator, called a barracuda. This savage fish had been caught by Toeless on a recreational fishing jaunt. Putting up a colossal struggle, the nautical devil continued to flip and flop in the bottom of Toeless's boat even after being landed. Because of the fish's speed and pure savagery, Toeless Hicks had not been able to evade his captor as the demon began chomping away on the dolt's lower digits. Eventually the situation was brought under control, but not before the fool in question had lost the majority of his toes!

Gertrude confessed that while Toeless Hicks was a consummate craven, he had earned the reputation as a renowned swordsman, having murdered ten challengers in extremely one-sided duels. He had also been a very close friend of the late Sir Jonathan Brisbane. Rumors abounded that the two were actually lovers, which placed me in a very precarious position, since I was the one who ended this miserable bully's life. The sisters cautioned me on the blind hatred that Toeless Hicks held for me for this very reason. Further, they earnestly cautioned me to remain incognito during my stay on Jamaica to avoid certain unpleasantness from this nefarious officer.

There was further essential information on my newest enemy. I was told that he was protected by a pack of four vicious canines who were constantly at his side. These dangerous and powerful beasts were said to have been purchased at auction at a very exorbitant price by Toeless's former consort, Sir Jonathan, to insure his proper protection and safety. These brutal mutts were controlled by four massive handlers, who also acted as bodyguards should the dogs fail their responsibility in any way. These human ogres were immense, vile and totally ruthless. Both the vicious canines and their handlers were always present at each of Toeless' duels to ensure a happy ending to each of these bloody affairs. Rumors were whispered that Toeless had given orders to his hulking henchmen to release the homicidal hounds upon any challenger should a duel not go his way. This in effect, meant that any affair of honor with the new fort commander was an unquestioned death sentence. In fact, many challengers had made the decision that it was far less agonizing to eat Toeless' blade than be eaten by his ruthless protectors.

I then questioned the sisters on my other quarry, Captain LeMerde and received intensely sour expressions. They informed me that my enemy had indeed arrived. In fact, it was well known that the French peacock had since met several times with the new fort commander. Since these conferences were held in strictest secrecy, the sisters had no idea what was discussed or their outcome. However, they were all convinced that whatever was agreed to during these clandestine meetings would certainly not bode well for me.

Hortense then related the details behind a dastardly incident instigated by Captain LeMerde. It seemed that my enemy had attended one of Fat Dog's famous animal contests. During the insidious *Gator Gobble Game*, the arrogant Frenchman had shot and killed the star of the show before the beast could feed on any of the unfortunate baby animals. Claiming to be a winner, since the despicable villain had chosen zero as his wager in this bloody affair, he had nearly incited a riot amongst the spectating crowd due to his cheating ways. To regain peace and tranquility, Fat Dog had been forced by Toeless to pay the arrogant trickster off as well as the onus of procuring a hurried replacement for his now deceased star.

My three friends had heard no news on my beloved Rue. However, they were privy to yet another tale of cruelty and barbarity by the nefarious Black Tarantula. It seems that the scurvy swine had attacked and overrun a small Spanish coastal town on the Spanish Main. The capture and subjugation of the village was swift and brutal. The Black Tarantula ordered that all of the city leaders be rounded up and held prisoner in a local house of worship, pending an exorbitant ransom fee demanded of the town's citizens. As a measure of good faith, the Black Tarantula had promised the townsfolk that he would feed and nurture his captives while the ransom monies were being amassed.

Bolstered by this assurance, the citizens dispersed and began to uncover their hidden wealth to appease the madman's demands. Meanwhile, the confined villagers were tied securely to chairs within the church. They were then served a sumptuous meal that was laced with ground glass particles. Invited to partake in this delicious fare, the captives were given the choice of voluntarily consuming the meal or submitting to extreme measures to elicit cooperation. The demon pirate's crew proceeded to sever random digits from any member of the party who refused to eat. They only had to employ this harsh action but a few times before the lethal fare was totally devoured. When finished, the Black Tarantula ordered his men to sew the prisoner's lips shut to prevent any disgorging of their sumptuous but deadly sustenance. Pulling up a seat in the middle of the suffering assemblage, the Black Tarantula delighted in the agonized struggles and muffled moans of the unfortunates, whose insides were being torn apart by the sharp and deadly glass particles. The beast thrilled to the villagers' horrendous plight before each eventually expired. In the meantime, his insidious crew collected the entire ransom amount from the manipulated townsfolk. Once satisfied, his evil carrion proceeded to rape and defile any woman in the village from the age of five to eighty before abandoning their foray and returning to their ship.

Having completed their horror story, Willamina took the opportunity to inquire if I still sported the Gypsy Queen's ring on my person. Removing my boot, I smiled and pointed to the lower digit that proudly displayed her small gift. Grinning now, Willamina questioned whether I had reached the life changing moment that she had long ago foretold. I answered that I was not as yet certain, but believed that it could have already occurred based upon my new occupation as privateer.

As I continued to silently muse her last query, Hortense entered the room toting a small chest in her arms. When I opened the proffered chest, I was gratified to discover a veritable treasure trove of costumes, wigs and other stage accoutrements necessary to enact my plan. There was even a remarkable amount of makeup that would certainly turn any serious stage performer green with envy. Thanking Hortense for her generous assistance, I then sat down to a wondrous feast prepared in my honor.

A while later Powder Monkey made his appearance. Prior to sending him back out on a scouting mission, I commanded him to secret both Gertrude's and Willamina's trunks in his simian domicile where they would remain safe until our imminent departure. I then commanded him to return secretly to the sisters' mansion the following night to report all of his findings. Informing him of the new fort commander's nefarious reputation, I commanded him to keep a sharp watch for the villain, since I was certain he would attempt to delay our departure by any means possible. Elaborating, I informed Powder Monkey that Toeless thoroughly enjoyed his new position and would use every resource at his command to ensure that Captain Adams was not rescued. I hastily penned a note to both Lion and Sharkface that provided implicit instructions on my grand rescue scheme. I then asked Powder Monkey to see that they were delivered to both ships in the swiftest manner possible. Powder Monkey understood all, and gave me a brief salute before disappearing.

Chapter 29: Duel with the Devil

That evening, Powder Monkey returned with some depressing but not wholly unexpected news. It seemed that Toeless Hicks had been made aware of my presence in port, and had subsequently ordered my arrest for piracy. The villain had trained the fort's guns on our two ships and had promised to blow them to splinters should they attempt flight. While I was certain that this jealous fop would hang me if given the opportunity, I decided to remain undercover with the Adams sisters until I had deduced an escape plan. Powder Monkey also reported on his new roommates, who he found amusing and quite intelligent. He informed me that apes were peaceful and gentle most of the time. However, they did become extremely agitated and aggressive under two distinct stimuli, canine barking and most importantly by the starter's bell utilized by Fat Dog's to initiate chimp fights.

With my friend's exit, I conferred with the sisters to plot a ruse to escape Toeless Hicks. The first step was to assign an unobtrusive spy to follow each and every movement the popinjay made and report these back to us. The sisters immediately volunteered the same two behemoths that had proved invaluable assistants on my last visit. Once they arrived and were briefed, the two brothers gave me a mock salute and disappeared. My second chore was to identify a potential ally in the military ranks, who could replace the cowardly Hicks should the opportunity arise. In unison, the sisters blurted out that same name, Dale Houndtooth. This splendid candidate had been Captain Adams' finest officer, but had been subsequently demoted to sergeant by the new fort commander. Houndtooth was loyal, courageous and quite anxious for Captain Adams' safe return. The sisters were sure that this acquaintance would jump at the chance to regain his old title, and even happier to displace Toeless Hicks as the new fort commander. To enlist his assistance, all three sisters readied themselves for an evening out and issued orders to their staff to prepare their carriage. In a flash of capes and bonnets, they were out the door and away to meet with Sergeant Houndtooth.

A few hours later, the sisters returned full of smiles and radiating confidence. They informed me that their meeting had been successful and that Sergeant Houndtooth had promised his fullest confidence and assistance in the matter at hand. As they were completing their report, one of the brothers returned to inform me that Toeless was on the prowl for entertainment that evening. He was currently presiding over a table at Fat Dogs in all likelihood hoping to identify me among the many seagoing patrons. The bad news was that he was accompanied by his four savage beasts and their handlers.

With my detailed preparations in place, I made my way unobserved to Fat Dog's Pub to confront my enemy. Peering through a side window, I found my target comfortably ensconced at a large table in the middle of the room. I covered my face with a traveling cloak and entered the pub unnoticed. Making my way to his table, I could see that my adversary was mildly intoxicated and paying scant attention to his surroundings. Still disguised, I ambled up to him and purposely jostled his table so that drinks were spilled in every direction. Humbly whispering my regrets, Toeless jumped up from the table and shoved me savagely to the floor. I continued to express my apologies over the incident, but the mean spirited brute would have none of it. Sending several well aimed kicks my way, he promised to unleash his four monsters to viciously tear me asunder. Quite the performer, I pleaded with the man for my life addressing him by his unsavory nickname of Toeless. Well this purposeful slip of the tongue was all that was necessary to incite the evil despot to action. Pulling out his saber, he proceeded to poke and prod me as he eagerly challenged me to a gentlemen's duel to settle the matter in front of the entire roomful of witnesses.

Rising to my feet, I accepted his challenge. Since I was the challenged party, it was my right to choose weapons as well as the location and time for this deadly affair. Still remaining in disguise, I reluctantly chose swords as our weapons to the absolute delight of my tormentor. Going further, I informed Toeless that I preferred the matter settled quickly, and therefore chose that evening as the timing for our duel. Agreeing to this choice with a wolfish grin, Toeless inquired if I had a location in mind to stage our personal battle. Pretending to give the matter some thought, I finally answered that I chose the apehouse out back of the pub as our intended battleground. Confounded by my strange choice, he nevertheless nodded his agreement. Toeless then asked if I had any more conditions to our upcoming engagement.

Taking my time, I responded that I wished no audience for our fight. I also insisted that the only participants present for our duel would be each of us and our seconds. This news brought the jealous and overbearing officer to silence as he pondered my latest condition. With a savage grin, Toeless informed me that his four bristling beasts would serve as his seconds, accompanied by each of their handlers. Nodding a very reluctant agreement, I turned to Fat Dog and requested that he serve as my lone second. Fat Dog hesitantly agreed and the participants all proceeded out the back door towards the ape enclosure. On the way, I happened to glance over at Powder Monkey who was caught up in the crowd following us to our most unusual dueling destination. He gave me a silent signal that all had been prepared per my instructions. With everything arranged, I issued a brief sigh of relief and followed the human procession to the alehouse doors.

Once there, Toeless ordered several of his men to stand guard outside to prevent any unwelcome visitors. Once they took their places, Fat Dog, I, Toeless and his dogs with handlers entered the shed and prepared for our personal war. Finally removing my cloak, I turned and confronted my opponent face-to-face. Upon recognizing me, Toeless issued an audible gasp of surprise. Once he recovered his composure and swagger, he promised me a very painful death either at his hands or at the massive maws of his killer beasts. At his words, his four canines began to growl and snap in my direction. True to Powder Monkey's intel, this action brought an immediate response from the apes, who had been peacefully observing our arrival from the safety of their cages. Riled by the savage growls of the now slobbering beasts, the apes began hooting and screeching amongst themselves. Paying absolutely no attention to the chimps, Toeless approached me with his sword drawn and issued an evil sneer. He then hissed that my end was close at hand. Smiling, I answered that I was not afraid to die and our duel officially commenced.

As each of us warily moved into attack positions, I noticed a large empty cage to my right that had previously been prepared by Powder Monkey per my implicit instruction. Concurrently, Toeless issued his first attack which proved far clumsier than I had anticipated. Assessing that this initial advance had been purposely made to draw me in and lower my guard, I remained apart continuing to monitor his movements. Having determined that his first ruse was unsuccessful, Toeless snidely grinned and went back on the attack. His movements were sure and practiced as our blades met time and time again. In several lightening-quick thrusts, he was able to draw blood on my sword hand through a series of minor cuts and lacerations. Keeping my poise, I continued to circle my determined opponent. His strenuous attacks had left him breathing rather raggedly as he continued to whisper promises of my imminent demise and destruction. Judging the time right, I went on the attack with a series of blindingly quick thrusts that eventually found their mark. As I executed these, I could see my opponent's demeanor change from confident to frightened. Not slowing my advance, I attacked with additional savagery that forced my opponent to backpedal to safety. Undaunted, I pushed my attack to a higher level and bore down on the heartless officer with murder written across my face. In the virtually no time at all, my vicious assault had produced a number of grievous wounds to my opponent.

Toeless was now struggling to remain calm, but an expression of panic and uncertainty now ruled his guise. During this transition, his vicious curs continued straining at their leashes to assist their beloved master. Meanwhile, Fat Dog's apes were literally going insane as they screeched, screamed and hooted their utter displeasure at the boisterous canine snarls and growls. In a perfectly executed maneuver, I evaded my opponent's weak thrust and delivered a lethal strike that skewered the vengeful coward's chest. Stumbling back with a look of utter disbelief and sheer hatred, he commanded his handlers to release their charges so that they could rip me apart. Anticipating this response, I reeled back and grabbed Fat Dog by the arm pulling him with me toward the empty ape cage. At I did so, the burly handlers unclasped their charges and set them free to follow our retreat. Lying on the ground, in a serious pool of blood, Toeless Hicks began to snicker evilly sensing my upcoming demise.

Reaching the open cage, I flung the tavern owner in and hastily followed, swinging the gate closed as the four monstrous canine bodies struck the door slamming it shut. Not wasting a moment, I utilized my *special voice* and issued repeated rings of Fat Dog's clamorous ringside bell. Well, I can honestly report that this new sound drove the agitated apes into extreme and utter madness. Slamming at their cages with unnatural ferocity and issuing barbaric hoots and screeches, they soon discovered that the doors to each of their cages had been left virtually unsecured by Powder Monkey per our plan. You see, I had my ward use ordinary twine to temporarily secure each of the ape cage doors in place. While our clashing cutlasses and the growling of Toeless's beasts agitated the creatures greatly, it was nothing compared to the savagery and vehemence that my imitation of Fat Dog's fight bell elicited. Slamming into and hammering unmercifully upon the meagerly secured doors resulted in the shearing of the rope restraints and afforded the apes freedom to join our battle. Racing out of their now opened enclosures, they advanced as a coordinated troop on both the vicious canines and their handlers. The battle was very short lived as the apes fell upon these tormentors and literally tore them to shreds. To add to their frenzy, I continued to utilize my *special voice* to issue ring after ring of Fat Dog's fight bell, which incensed the poor creatures far beyond madness. As I watched in stunned awe, the chimpanzees ripped fur, arms, legs, heads and paws from my enemies. In just a short time, the apes completed their destruction. All that remained of my intended attackers were bloody chunks of meat scattered everywhere. Once their devastating work had been completed, the apes began to calm down and eventually believe it or not returned to their cages. Other than quiet sobs and wails from Toeless Hicks, all was now deathly silent!

Exiting the safety of our cage, I approached the mortally wounded officer to end the disagreeable affair. Seeing me approach, Toeless issued a sneering curse in my direction wishing me an everlasting place at Lucifer's side. Laughing, I answered that he would have the first opportunity to garner this exalted position as I drove my sharp blade directly into his sneering craw snuffing out the last of his miserable life. Accompanying the truly shaken pub owner, we made our way to the shed's door and exited the carnal slaughterhouse to the cheers and friendly greetings of the bystanders outside.

Immediately, another officer strode up and took full command of the situation. Once he determined Toeless' fate, he proclaimed that he was now the highest ranking English officer on the isle. He then issued a series of furious orders sending his men scattering in every direction to fulfill these directives. Reaching out a friendly hand, he introduced himself as Sergeant Dale Houndstooth. He declared the duel a fair fight and condoned my actions as those of self-defense. Whispering, he wished me luck in my future rescue mission, and turned and ordered a military detail to collect and bury the dead inside the ape house. As I stumbled away from the slaughterhouse, I looked back to judge how Fat Dog was coping. I could see that he was still in a state of complete shock over the consummate brutality and destruction he had just witnessed. Unable to answer all of the questions now being asked of him by curious onlookers, he merely kept swinging his head from side-to-side repeating one question over and over again, "Who in blazes rang my fight bell?"

With order restored and proper authority now in command of the fort, we made our final preparations to leave Jamaica. On the day we planned to sail, the sisters were escorted to the dock by Commander Dale Houndstooth to express their well wishes. They appeared hopeful that we could affect a successful rescue and wished us godspeed in the effort. With a savage grin, Commander Houndstooth informed me that his men were still collecting human and canine body parts from the apehouse!

Chapter 30: Return to Saint Domingue

Eventually, I received news that Le Merde had been sighted on Jamaica and additional reports of Aimee's presence as his protected captive had been relatively favorable given the odious situation overall. Since I believed that she would be relatively safe in my enemy's hands for a short while longer, I made the difficult decision to turn my full attention to the rescue of Captain Adams. Actually, the deliverance of his finger, the signet ring and the ransom note demanding no more than a month's delivery period convinced me that action was required sooner rather than later. Rather than making a direct approach on the Black Tarantula's stronghold on Tortuga, I decided it prudent to conduct further reconnoissance. To gain optimal information, I opted to stop at Cap-Francise on Saint Domingue, a location in close proximity to the monster's lair. The next week proceeded without further incident, and I found myself back on Rue's homeland. While I was extremely interested in news of my beloved, I realized that the main reason for the visit was to glean as much information from the locals on the fate of Captain Adams, his captors as well as their defenses. Entering the spacious harbor, fond memories of Handy, Rue and Grommet Jemme brought on quite a melancholy mood. I was sadly reminded once more that I truly missed each for their companionship, affection and friendship. As we made our way to shore in our tender, I easily visualized that the city had changed much since my last visit. Devastation and utter destruction now replaced my mental images of this once wondrous setting.

The Black Tarantula had literally shaken the city to its very core, transforming beauty and splendor to ruin and squalor. As I randomly made inquiries about Rue and Jemme, I was treated to very surprising and chilly receptions. It seemed that the citizens lived in mortal fear of the evil rampaging pirate and chose to ignore my questions with closed-mouthed caution and distrusting intimidated stares. In any event, I received no pertinent answers to my queries and I decided to visit Shantytown in the vain hope of unearthing some news.

What I discovered when I reached Shantytown was even more

depressing. This section of the city was in much worse shape with burned and destroyed buildings, shacks and hovels scattered haphazardly across its entire landscape. *The Palace*, home to us all during our previous stay, had been entirely obliterated. Just then, Powder Monkey and Scuttle appeared and made their way to my side. They reported that they had received the same cold treatment from every citizen they had approached. Dejected and quite dismayed, I asked them to continue their search in the unlikely event that they might discover some new scuttlebutt on either Rue, Grommet Jemme or the Black Tatantula. Feeling absolutely lost and despondent, I made my way to the familiar old cemetery, that I had visited frequently on my prior stop, to sit and think the matter through.

Perched alone in my usual spot in the deserted graveyard, I buried my head in my hands in desperate thought. As I was examining possibilities, I heard what sounded like a whine right beside me. Glancing up, I was shocked to to discover my old friend, Ding-Dong staring directly at me. Blinking in surprise, I shouted his name and the beast leapt up and showering me with sloppy wet kisses, while pleasurably whining his own excitement and joy. Finally settling the deliriously elated hound down, I questioned the mutt if his master was nearby. As I continued my caring ministrations, I heard a familiar voice behind me calling my name. Turning, I discovered Papa Legba in his usual garb smiling widely at me. Hopping to my feet and shaking his hand gratefully, I offered him a seat beside me. When we were both comfortable, I filled Papa Legba in on my adventures since last we had met. Once done, he complimented me on both my quick thinking and my ability to persevere under unfriendly and brutal conditions. In a serious tone, he questioned why I had failed to call for his assistance during my times of desperation. I responded that I honestly believed his help would only be made available in my very darkest and direst periods of need. Chuckling, he retorted that he would make himself available anytime I was in true need of his assistance. Smiling now along with him, I sincerely thanked him for his most welcomed friendship as well as his continued offer of assistance.

After a careful inspection, he questioned if I still carried the special talisman he had bestowed upon me. Reaching under my shirt, I extracted the wooden cross that elicited a heightened grin of pure delight from my benefactor. Taking the cross in his gnarled old claws, he announced that

I should continue to keep it close because it would certainly prove handy one day! Quite confused by this statement, I immediately probed him for more details. Waving his hand to calm my concerns, he answered that the future would reveal itself when the time was right.

As I formed my next line of inquiry, he jangled the cross and it magically came part in his rough weather-beaten hands. Shocked to the extreme, I leaned in to take a closer look. The upper section of the talisman was almost the same except for the fact that a black dirk had now replaced the entire lower half. Continuing my inspection, I deemed that the cross's bottom portion had merely served as a sheave for this wicked little blade. Sensing my wonderment, Papa Legba informed me that the exposed dagger had been specially forged from the metal of a fallen star. He explained that this black blade was sharper and stronger than any other metal in the world!

Nodding but not quite totally understanding, I questioned how he had managed to separate the two pieces. Holding both pieces before me, he slipped the bottom sheath back over the ebony blade and I heard an audible click as it returned to its original home. Continuing, he instructed that all I needed to do to unleash the blade was to push up the bottom of the cross and twist it to the right while giving it a slight tug. Curious now, I grasped the talisman and followed his instructions. Instantly, the cross separated like magic revealing the unusual inky-black blade hidden inside. Slipping the bottom cover back in place, I once again offered my sincerest thanks for his remarkable and wonderful gift.

Secreting the cross, I informed him of my inability to discover any information on Rue, Jemme or the notorious pirate responsible for their disappearance. At my words, a pain-laden expression appeared on his face. In a very soft voice, he informed me that my friend, Jemme had met his end at the hands of the aforementioned monster. As for Rue, he was elated to inform me that she was yet alive, but no longer residing on Saint Domingue. To escape the madman, who had brutally slain her mother, she had stowed away on a Spanish merchantman. When I questioned him on her current whereabouts, he sadly shook his head and confessed that he was unsure where she had gone. All he could divulge was that she was alive, safe and continuing to evade the Black Tarantula's frantic efforts to locate her. Professing his sincerest apology for not being able to answer my question in any more detail, Papa Legba looked deep into my eyes and promised that our destinies would once again see us reunited. Smiling at his encouraging prognostication, Papa Legba then dampened my spirit by informing me that he was certain that Rue would eventually require my assistance because her pursuer would never cease his determined search for her. Thanking him once again, I asked if he was aware of the current location of the Black Tarantula. Once again, he expressed his dismay at not being able to answer this query. He simply stated that all would be revealed to me at the proper time. Ding-Dong suddenly erupted in a series of menacing barks which drew my attention away from my friend. When I momentarily glanced back, Papa Legba had disappeared along with his barking familiar.

Returning to the original site of *The Palace*, I happened to spot Powder Monkey and Scuttle headed in my direction with a stranger in tow. They introduced their friend as Droopy Eyed Dick, a sailor who was currently out of work. His name was quite appropriate because the tar facing me appeared to be asleep on his feet. However, since this curious individual had been stranded on Saint Domingue for the past year, my mates had found that he was a superb source of vital information on what exactly had occurred. More importantly, he was actually willing to reveal this scuttlebutt to us.

Realizing that this might be our only avenue to glean necessary intelligence, I invited him to join us for liquid libation at a surviving rumhouse nearby. Having settled ourselves in this filthy hellhole, I proceeded to ply Droopy Eyed Dick with a number of questions. My first question concerned my beloved Rue. Upon hearing her name, the sleepy-eyed seaman began to blink in an extremely rapid fashion. Leaning closer in a confidential manner, he whispered that this poor creature was the source of much of the destruction and ruin of this once beautiful paradise. Continuing after a bracing snootful of rum, Droopy Eyed Dick related that Rue had somehow caught the attention of the insidious pirate commander. It was widely rumored that this black-hearted villain had decided to make the girl his own private property. Upon deducing his nefarious plan, Rue had taken flight with the assistance of a few close friends. Her sudden escape had brought out the very worst in the sea demon, who had systematically captured and tortured virtually everyone in town to uncover her whereabouts. When this proved utterly useless, the Black Tarantula decided that the entire island required severe punishment, so he unleashed his hellish minions to wreak total havoc and ruin.

The citizens were herded into groups and made to endure the most heinous tortures that these devils could concoct. The captured citizens were made to eat live coals, act as live targets in musket shooting practice, burned alive, dismembered and made to suffer a rash of other truly horrible indignities in an attempt to discern the location of the missing *French Songbird*. The sad truth was that none of these poor unfortunates had any idea where the girl had gone. To ease their hellish treatment, many manufactured stories about her escape and her current hiding location that sent the pirate hoard off on a series of wild-goose chases that resulted in failure after failure.

Due to mounting frustration, the level of torture and wonton destruction on Saint Domingue continued to escalate, but in the end the pirates were no closer to discovering Rue's whereabouts. At this point in his narrative, Droopy Eyed Dick informed us that the evil Black Tarantula had eventually uncovered a co-conspirator in the girl's disappearance. A lad by the name of Jemme had been captured and personally tortured, tormented and murdered by the nefarious rogue. Sadly smirking, Droopy Eyed Dick cackled that it was rumored that the brave lad had divulged nothing of real value in the midst of the barbarous treatment he received. As Droopy Eyed Dick put it, Jemme went gratefully to *Davy Jones Locker* protecting the secrets of his lady friend.

Well, I can tell you that my blood began to boil upon once again hearing of this shameless treatment of my friend and trusted cohort. Realizing that I would need to temporarily quell my burning desire for revenge, I turned our conversation in a different direction. In a calm and determined voice, I questioned our informational source on the fate of Captain Adams' expedition. Relieved to speak of other matters, Droopy Eyed Dick took another draw from his rum before responding. Sadly the tale he recounted was nearly identical to the information I had previously ascertained. However, he did have some new intelligence on the location of Captain Adams' confinement.

Downing half of his tankard, the informative yet terrified sailor confessed in a dour and stifled voice that the poor English Captain's life was all but forfeit. After his capture, he divulged that rumors declared that Captain Adams had been transported to the nearby isle of Tortuga, which served as the black scoundrel's lair. Intrigued by this news, I encouraged our source to relate all that he knew of this nearby sanctuary. Taking a deep breath, he whispered that the Black Tarantula's hideaway was actually an impregnable fortress protected by both a multitude of ferocious men and formidable armament. He explained that this location resembled a well-built and well-defended fort rather than just a safe haven to anchor the demon's vessel. The stronghold had been carefully constructed above a spacious harbor to preclude anyone from attempting to overrun it. With a lethal battery of frightful cannons facing seaward, this fortress was nearly impossible to breech from the sea without seriously endangering one's vessel and crew. This citadel had also been ringed by a series of stout battlements that allowed its defenders to easily stave off any attack from its land's side. In summary, it was imposing, secure, protected and totally immune from any sort of enemy attack!

While his latest news did not provide us any measure of solace, Droopy Eyed Dick had not finished delivering his bad tidings. It seemed that this impregnable fortress was governed by one of the Black Tarantula's most capable officers, Hurricane Jeffers. This evil hearted knave had a nefarious and renowned reputation almost equal to that of his master. Hurricane had been born a slave on Saint Domingue, performing the back breaking labor of loading and unloading the many merchant ships that arrived continuously in this bustling port. As a boy, Hurricane had been forced to watch his father and mother executed for promoting and participating in an island's slave rebellion. His vital dock duties along with his forced absence from his family had certainly spared his life. When he witnessed the tragic fate of his family members, it was universally reported that the young man had shown absolutely no emotion publicly. Later, he escaped from his slave shack by the shore and made his way to the island's mountainous interior where he rendezvoused with a number of fellow escapees and began a new life amongst them.

Although free from slave shackles, he still carried the flaming torch of vindictiveness toward his trespassers. One dark night, the brooding monster led a small group of escapees to the plantation where his parents had been brutally punished and slain. Attacking the plantation in a surprise raid, he proceeded to round up both the plantation owner's family and hired overseers along with the majority of black slaves who toiled relentlessly to ensure the farm's profits continued to flow. Driven by a vindictive lust, he utilized slave's chains to secure and bind the white overseers, including every member of the owner's family down to an infant boy. Marching these terrified and helpless individuals to a nearby lagoon with the newly freed plantation's slaves as an appreciative audience, he proceeded to personally toss each of his petrified prisoners into the water to enjoy a late night swim. It was widely rumored that he danced and sang as his victims flopped and struggled before eventually slowly sinking under the moss-green water. Rumors further told of his extreme delight in listening to the wails and screams of terror and pain emanating from the bound and chained unfortunates as they awaited their turn to die. As a result of his cruel and heartless actions against this well-liked and upstanding plantation family, he was charged with the heinous crime of murder and an outstanding warrant was issued for his immediate arrest, dead or alive! Realizing that he had unwittingly upset a hornet's nest by his savage acts, Hurricane Jeffers decided to take his leave of Saint Domingue forever. He joined a nasty group of Spanish rogues on Tortuga where he was well schooled in the fine art of piracy.

At this point in his narrative, Droopy Eyed Dick required yet another courage-inducing libation, and once his tankard was refilled he continued his woeful tale. Hurricane Jeffers took his piratical instructions seriously and before long had developed a nasty reputation for utter ruthlessness, brutality, barbarity and savagery. His evil reputation continued to grow as he performed nefarious acts time and time again. It was reputed that he had absolutely no feelings whatsoever and was born without a conscience of any sort. The fact that he was a giant of a man with huge rippling muscles adorning his massive frame did not hurt his savage reputation to any degree. To elicit maximum fear, this unfeeling animal had shaved his head and proceeded to decorate his dome with a skull and crossbones tattoo. Unsmiling and totally uncaring, this behemoth rambled through life inflicting as much pain and suffering upon innocents as opportunity allowed.

Not quite finished, Droopy Eyed Dick further reported that Hurricane Jeffers nasty and offensive reputation reached the ears of the Black Tarantula. Delighted by these reports, the Black Tarantula invited Hurricane Jeffers to sail with him, eventually promoting him to First Mate. Under the Black Tarantula's rule, Hurricane Jeffers was allowed to fulfill his barbarous fantasies to the very fullest, encouraged continually by his demonic master. While this homicidal maniac trusted nobody, he obeyed the Black Tarantula's orders implicitly. Further while not being born brilliant by any measure, he was quite shrewd and possessed an animal-like ability to identify danger and react to it long before it became any sort of issue. He was a monster at any manner of combat, defeating and destroying anyone who crossed his path. Once the Black Tarantula had completed his impregnable fortress, he chose Hurricane Jeffers to be its lord and master during his numerous absences. The perverse hellion had not taken this assignment lightly, and was fully prepared to defend his master's hideout with his last dying breath.

Droopy Eyed Dick did reveal that there was one glaring weakness to this savage ogre's personality. It seemed that he was very superstitious and deathly afraid of being haunted by the ghosts of the unfortunates he had sent to early graves. Consequently, he sported a silver crucifix as a spirit deterrent and would never consider taking it off. Concluding his terrifying and woeful account, Droopy Eyed Dick questioned if there was anything more he could tell us about Saint Domingue or Tortuga. Since we had certainly heard more than enough, we bought our new friend one more tankard of rum, thanked him profusely for his knowledge and made our way back to our ship to begin our preparations for rescue. On the way to our ship, I could see that my compatriots were visibly shaken by the news we had just received. In my heart I was fully aware that our upcoming adventure would be extremely difficult, hazardous and most likely impossible! Consequently, I was certain that I would need to devise an incredibly creative plan to prevail in the face of such impossible odds.

Chapter 31: Sailing Towards Hopeless Confrontation

As the situation now stood, I and my crew faced the most ponderous and life-threatening challenge of our lives. While attempting to rescue my dear friend Captain Adams, we would be confronted with matching wits with the most notorious pirate of our time and his legion of maniacal followers led by a ruthless and unfeeling barbarian. On top of this daunting challenge, we would need to attack and defeat these devils in their impregnable fortress under the watchful eyes of their formidable armament. In all, it was a fool's errant doomed from the start to fail. Yet given all of the significant odds against our success in this rescue mission, I, with my crew's firm approval, had committed all of our lives and our very souls to the completion of this impossible task. While we all might have been as batty as the most severely delirious lunatic in any asylum on earth, we were united in purpose and staunch in our commitment to give this vital rescue attempt our finest and most stalwart attempt. Furthermore, should we accomplish this hopeless quest, I was still absolutely committed to liberating Aimee from the clutches of the insidious Captain LeMerde. Both missions were quite futile in nature but nonetheless decidedly crucial and utterly vital.

As you can easily judge, my journey is far from finished. There still remains the almost impossible task confronting me complete with a veritable hoist of ruthless and vicious villains intent on my everlasting destruction. There is also my unwavering and resolute desire to locate and reunite with my true love, Rue, no matter the degree of abject difficulty or consummate danger involved.

For the time being, I must collect my thoughts so that I can complete my reminiscing. At the same time, I am required to make continuing efforts to avoid the savage beasts prowling the sea around my precarious position to avoid a hideous death by ingestion. After all, I am currently not ensconced in a comfortable leather armchair in a posh London men's club. Although, I can honestly report that the gentlemen who roam these exclusive environs have much in common with the man-eating sharks that are patrolling the waters around me!

To be continued in Book Three... The Pirate Demon

CHARACTERS AND NAMES

Book Two: Black Tarantula

London, England

William Echo Eden (Captain William Bilge and Bilge Rat)- Orphan, galley slave and narrator

Toby Eden-Echo's younger brother

Arch Deacon Williamson Archibald (Old ghost and Uncle Arch)- Echo's elderly uncle

Scarf Rockingham- Vicious bully

Slugger O'Toole- Owner and operator of Slugger's Sports Emporium

Amafata - English Merchantman

Jedediah Potts (Handy)- Galley master and Echo's friend and mentor

Creeping Jeremy- Storyteller and shipmate

Captain Samuel Conway-Amafata's Captain

Mr Bass- Malevolent first mate

Jemme Buttons (Grommet Jemme and Zombie Jemme) - Suspected Jonah, dullard and Echo's friend

Muttering Moses Hart- Shipmate and fife player

Fighting John English- Shipmate and fiddle player

Geovanni Perilli (Doc)- Shipboard physician

Moses Hayes (Chips)- Shipboard carpenter

Saint Domingue

Cap-Francis- St Domingue's major city

Monique La Montaine- Palais Le Monde's owner and operator

Rue La Montaine- Monique's daughter, barmaid and Echo's lover

Babar Kismet (Lion)- Turkish Pirate

Black Tarantula- Pirate Scourge of the Caribbean

Angry George- Pirate storyteller

Papa Legba- Voodou Loa

Ding-Ding- Island mistreated mutt and Papa Legba's familiar

Adams Sisters:

    Gertrude- Naturalist and Healer

    Wilamina- Palm Reader

    Hortence- Aspiring stage actress

Sugar Sally - Trollop and lover of Lion Babar

Gene Fabrege (Catstalker Gene) - Miscreant and torturer of small animals

Long Tall Willie- Dwarf seaman and knife expert
Charlie Crowsfeet- Seaman and shipmate of Long Tall Willie
Walter Gibbons (Pigsty)- Obese, lazy skedaddler
Droopy Eyed Dick - Sailor who provides basic information on the
Black Tarantula's fortress

Jamaica

Kingston- Island's main city
Fat Dog's Pub- Renown Island pub
Fat Dog- Pub's Owner and operator of renown pub
Gypsy Queen Zarina- Famous and powerful gypsy leader
Bountiful Betty- Fat Dog's fighting chimp
Sorrowful Suzy- Fat Dog's fighting chimp
Sir Jonathan William Brisbane III- Island plantation owner, bully and master duelist
Powder Monkey- Sir Jonathan's Slave and cannon expert
Captain Ronald Shuster Adams- Nephew of Adams sisters and commander
of Jamaica's Fort Charles
Sergeant O'Toole- Cannon training instructor at Fort Charles
Lieutenant Henry Hicks (Toeless)- Fort Charles Commander following
Captain Adams
Sergeant Dale Houndstooth- Captain Adams' second-in-command but
demoted in rank by Toeless Hicks

Pig Island- Small uninhabited cay off of French Isle, Martinque

Tommy Boyle- Crewman on Amafata and murder victim on island
Pighead- Heathen tribe's chieftain

Midnight Crow - Pirate Ship

Rambling Dirk Shivvers- Pirate Captain
Booby Bird Doole - Addled pirate crewman
Danny Goldtooth
Little Joe
Penny Short- Pirate conspirators involved in Cursing Challenge
Black Monk- Ghost story of cleric who was convicted of demonic worship
One Eared Pete
Pig Snout Jones- Pirate Fight Night combatants
Strumpet Janie - Trollop in love with One Eared Pete and Pig Snout Jones
Rooster Bill- Monstrous sized pirate and Fight Night combatant
JumpingJimmy- Pirate storyteller aboard Midnight Crow
Bowlegged Billy- Tortured victim in swamp ride tale
Spanish Petey- Pox victim in pirate tale
Crosseyed Mary- Poxed wench in pirate tale

Tiger Eyes- African slave and son of tribal chieftain
Scuttle the Hunchback- Rescued castaway and accomplished blacksmith
South Seas Tan- Pirate mate and hand-to-hand fighting expert

Guadeloupe- French Possession

Pointe-A-Pitre- Major city on French Isle of Guadeloupe
Governor Louis LaCouturie- Greedy Governor of Guadeloupe
Captain Jean Bernard LeMerde- Dishonored French naval officer in charge
 of Guadeloupe's marine defenses
Francois Rene Turbout- Plantation owner on nearby Isle, Marie-Gallant
 and Echo's friend
Lille Turbout- Rene's wife
Aimee Turbout- Rene's sister
Luc-a-Luc- Renown Island performer

Rue's Revenge - Privateer Vessel

No Nose Nottingham- Angry George's Friend
Father Jericho- Ruse created to free Aimee from kidnappers
Loony Louie- Pirate Castaway and Mermaid sighter
Captain Barnes- Dutch Captain of Loony Louie's vessel
Captain Juan Hector Sanchez (Captain Happy Jack)- Pirate charlatan and
 parley misuser
Donny O'Shea (Donny Boy)- Blue/ Brown eyed victim in Mermaid tale
Shankhand- Mermaid story's thief
Guzzlin' Gooch- Extreme drunkard
Neptune's Revenge- Captain Happy Jack's renamed pirate vessel

St Lucia

Soufriere- fishing village on St Lucia
Sharkface Topper- Owner and operator of island's pub
Hungry Shark- Sharkface Topper's pub

BC Islands - Aruba, Bonaire and Curacao

Captain Ricardo Inez Viola - Spanish Captain of Man-O-War patrolling
 southern Caribbean

Tortuga

Hurricane Jeffers - Evil hearted knave and soundrel who is the Black
 Tarantula's First Mate

Glossary of Pirate Terms

BRETHREN OF THE COAST

This is a self-proclaimed title invented by Caribbean pirates and privateers who made a loose pact to outlaw plundering one another. This pact was governed by a variable code of conduct that laid out command authority, individual rights, democratic-like decision making and the equitable sharing of booty. For the most part, this alliance brought together various nationalities in a common cause to harass and defeat Spanish dominion in the New World.

CANNON ORDINANCE

As with the case that there were a multitude of cannon shapes and sizes during the Golden Age of Piracy, the same was true concerning the ordinance available for their use. Each had a specific function.

Bar shot..... A close relative to chain shot except a solid bar replaced the afore mentioned chain. Like its cousin, it wrought havoc and destruction on ship riggings, spars, masts and sails.

Bundle shot..... Another relative of grape-shot, this device featured packs of short metal bars bundled together with rope. Upon firing, the rope loosened and its wave of murderous destruction swept down on enemy sailors.

Canister shot..... A relative of grape shot in which a metal canister was utilized to hold all manner of destructive material such as small metal balls or scrap like nails, spikes and rocks. Like its relative, the canister disintegrated in flight sending a wave of destruction toward the enemy's sailors.

Chain shot..... This was two small iron or lead balls that were chained together. Upon firing, they whirled their way to their target causing considerable and significant damage to a ships riggings, masts and sails thereby reducing maneuverability.

Grape shot..... This was small iron or lead balls that were contained usually in a canvas sack or affixed together. When fired at a target they spread out in flight and became a wave of destruction much like modern shotgun pellets. They caused little damage to vessels but could prove devastating to its crew.

Heated shot..... This was simply round shot that was heated white hot to incinerate targets when struck.

Round shot..... This was the traditional round cannonball fashioned usually out of cast iron. Sometimes the round shot was hollow, which provided the ball greater distance. This shot was hull piercing and could send a ship to the bottom if placed correctly.

Spider shot..... Yet another relative to bar and chain shot where two spiked projectiles replaced the spheres again providing distance and added destruction.

Split shot..... Another close relative to both chain and bar shot where split balls were utilized in place of whole spheres increasing distance.

Star shot..... A unique twist on bar and chain shot, this was made up of multiple lengths of metal chain or rods with spheres on each end connected in the center. When fired, this shot spread on its approach to form a star pattern that could devastate and dismantle ship's rigging, masts and sails.

CAREENING
Process of exposing a ship's hull for maintenance and repair below the water line. These repairs included dry rot repair, hull rupture patching due to cannon shot, shoal or reef damage and the removal of clinging hitchhikers (barnacles, seaweed and burrowing Teredo worms). This laborious and time consuming chore was necessary every six months in the warm Caribbean waters to ensure a ship's maneuverability and speed maximization.

The process was undertaken in multiple steps. The first was to expose the hull so that work could be conducted. Since the Caribbean has very little tide variation, this meant beaching a ship and hauling it over on one side exposing the hull for repairs. Once done, the next step involved laborious sanding and scraping the exposed hull free of all hitchhikers The third step was to repair all damaged areas of the hull by adding new planing where necessary or caulking the less damaged portions with oakum (separated twine mixed with tar) that was jammed into cracks, seams, crevices and holes. The forth step was to tar over the entire hull for future protection. Once the process was completed the entire operation was repeated on the other side of the ship's hull.

DAVY JONES LOCKER
This name referred to a fictional barren wasteland at the bottom of the sea as a final resting place for drowned mariners. Although the origin of this nomenclature is unknown, Davy Jones was viewed by tars as an evil spirit, possibly Satan himself, lurking at sea waiting to personally escort a dead seamen to his kingdom below the waves. It was also believed that this evil shade or devil would be seen by unfortunates just prior to disaster befalling them. Davy Jones has been described as an evil imp with horns, saucer-shaped huge bulging eyes, numerous rows of sharpened teeth and a tail.

FUMIGATION POTS
These devices were utilized to rid a vessel of evil and malignant vapors during times of sickness and contagion. These evil vapors were called miasmas and deemed responsible for the further spread of sickness and disease. A small container was filled with a variety of ingredients to effect this cleansing effort. In addition to brimstone (sulphur), other burning constituents included tarred rope, tobacco, arsenic, gun powder, steamed vinegar, mercury and tar oil. In all actuality, a crew utilizing the fumigation pots were replacing one noxious odor for another.

GENERAL SHIP LOCATIONS
Stern..... back of the ship

Bow..... front of the ship

Bilge..... lowest inner hull of the ship

Larboard..... left side of the ship facing forward

Starboard..... right side of the ship facing forward

HERBAL ARMAMENT
Belladonna (Deadly Nightshade).....
This deadly poison has been utilized for centuries as medicine and a cosmetic beyond its lethal intent. The name means "Beautiful Woman" and was used in ancient times by women as eyedrops that dilated their pupils and gave them a seductive appearance. While Belladonna is one of the most toxic plants on the planet, it was utilized by early physicians as an anesthetic for surgeries and as a painkiller for common ailments such as toothaches, headaches and ulcers. The plant is known under a series of names such as Banewort, Death Cherry, Devil's Herb, Beautiful Death and Deadly Nightshade.

The plant contains tropane alkaloids which cause bizarre delirium and severe hallucinations in weaker concentrations. While the entire plant is highly toxic, the roots are generally the most potent.

Quina (Jesuit's Bark)..... This marvelous and miraculous natural curative received its name after being discovered by Jesuit missionaries in Peru between 1620 and 1630. The Andean Indians revealed the healing properties of the "fever tree" bark to the Jesuits as a specific remedy for the dreaded tropical disease, malaria. This Peruvian bark of the Cinchona Tree is native to the Andes forests of South America. The main active ingredient of this wondrous bark is quinine.

History also reports that the wife of a Spanish Viceroy to Peru (the Countess of Chinchon) returned to Europe having been cured of malaria by the tea made from the bark. She brought huge quantities of this special bark home to Spain to introduce her

Thorn Apple (Datura)..... This innocent looking plant has a long history of causing hallucinogenic delirium and painful death. The entire plant is quite dangerous but its seeds are the most potent portion. Containing tropane alkaloids, this deadly substance causes its victims utter delirium (the inability to differentiate reality from fantasy), bizarre and violent behavior, pronounced amnesia and eventual death. Over time, this dreaded killer has been called multiple names including Jimson Weed, Devil's Snare, Devil's Trumpet, Moon Flower, Mad Apple and Hell's Bells.

Over its long history, this plant has been employed by physicians and healers as a strong analgesic for painful surgeries, toothaches, sore throats, and pounding headaches. It has also been reportedly utilized for religious and ceremonial visionary purposes. Overused, however, it can cause incoherent and inane actions and motions by victims (i.e. picking at the air for imaginary floating objects). Further, it is known to lead to agonizing convulsions, permanent psychosis, coma and eventual death. During this process, the victim experiences complete loss of motor and communication functions and the unpredictable hallucinations can last for hours or days.

Wormwood..... An age old herb that has both psychoactive and medicinal purposes. The active ingredient in wormwood is thujone, which its effects are extremely heightened by the addition of alcohol. The herb has been used over the centuries as a medicine to aid digestion since its extremely bitter taste activates the gall bladder.

Large doses coupled with alcohol can cause headaches dizziness, tremors, convulsions, loss of intellect, vertigo, giddiness, sleeplessness, foaming at the mouth, permanent mental deterioration, seizures, delirium and severe hallucinations.

LETTRE OF MARQUE AND REPRISAL

Document authorizing an individual and crew a lawful commission to attack and capture enemy vessels, as a reparation for previous injuries or war crimes. Such captured ships were to be returned to the issuing government's hands for disposition and disposal. This document gave the individual and crew amnesty from piracy laws as long as plunder came from enemy vessels. Essentially, the document ordained the holder a privateer, a self-employed soldier paid only from captured spoils.

ON THE ACCOUNT

A more gentrified description for turning pirate. Usually initiates were officially deemed part of a pirate crew after signing the ship's articles.

PIRATE WEAPONS

During the golden age of piracy standardization of weapons had yet to occur. For the most part, pirate weapons were creatively hand-crafted and more often not one-of-a-kind makeshift designs. The most important attribute for any piratical weapon was its trustworthiness and effectiveness in battle situation since an individual's life swung in the balance.

Therefore, a vast majority of pirate weapons were fashioned from everyday sailor's tools and implements. Additionally, psychological weapons were routinely utilized to cow prey into easy surrender to avoid loss of life as well as potentially damaging or destroying plunder. The following is an extensive yet not exclusive list and description of pirate weaponry.

Belaying Pin..... These implements were necessary tools found on any sailing ship. They serviced a number of vital jobs on any sea voyage. The ax consisted of a two to three foot handle topped with an iron sharpened hatchet on one side and a blunt hammer on the other. During engagement, it could serve a number of necessary functions such as a human cleaver, a boarding hook releaser, a cannon or shot chisel remover, a destroyer of shipboard encumbrances such as doors and hatches and a necessary clean up tool to remove downed riggings, masts and sails.

Blunderbuss..... This weapon was basically a shotgun with the firepower of a small cannon. The design was typified by a flared/fanned out barrel end that dispensed lead pellets over a broad area. A user normally braced the gun on his hips or side to handle the considerable recoil. It was basically a close range equalizer capable of sweeping a deck clean of opponents.

Boarding Ax..... These implements were necessary tools found on any sailing ship. They serviced a number of vital jobs on any sea voyage. The ax consisted of a two to three foot handle topped with an iron sharpened hatchet on one side and a blunt hammer on the other. During engagement, it could serve a number of necessary functions such as a human cleaver, a boarding hook releaser, a cannon or shot chisel remover, a destroyer of shipboard encumbrances such as doors and hatches and a necessary clean up tool to remove downed riggings, masts and sails.

Boarding Pikes..... They were long wood spears with a metal end fashioned in numerous aggressive and dangerous designs. They could be used to stave off boarders or thrown at opponents. They were a highly effective defense against cutlasses and dirks where room allowed.

Buckler..... A name for a rather small shield that ranged from eight to fifteen inches in diameter. Usually gripped in one hand while the other hand wielded a sword of some kind. Because of their diminutive size they provided little defense against musket or pistol balls. However, they were extremely lightweight and easy to effectively wield in either an offensive or defensive situation. Their best advantage was achieved in close quarter clashes.

Caltrop..... These insidious devices were also known as Crows Feet. They were designed as life-sized "jacks" with four sharpened points. These iron burrs were designed to always land with a sinister sharp point sticking straight up in the air. Scattered on the deck of ships, they provided a dreaded defensive weapon against aggressive barefooted invaders. These weapons inflicted crippling injuries, chaotic confusion and resistance to invading adversaries. Gripped in a defender's hands, these lethal devices could also inflict major damage in close quarter struggles.

Cannons..... These serious guns ranged from six pounds to thirty-two pounds (referring to ability to fire that sized cannonball). Cannons came in an unbelievable variety of sizes and designs based on their manufacturing origins. While the materials utilized in their manufacturer varied, iron slowly became the material of choice due to its ease of use and its economical production cost. Cannons were extremely heavy and difficult to handle aboard ships but provided prodigious firepower to overcome adversaries.

Dagger (Dirk)..... This was a small multipurpose knife absolutely necessary for routine seafaring chores. The usual design featured a straight blade with a protective hilt to protect user's hand from sliding down onto the sharpened blade. This design also avoided very deep penetrations which could cause the blade to become stuck and render it useless in battle. The dagger's design called for thrusting rather than slashing.

There was certainly no uniformity of design when it came to these weapons. While the names were virtually interchangeable, in some instances dirks were viewed as smaller knives with good balance and perfect for throwing rather than stabbing.

Cutlass..... These short thick sabers were manufactured with either a straight or slightly curved blade which was honed to a wickedly keen cutting edge capable of slicing through bone. Their hilts were either cupped or had rounded guards to protect the user's hand. These designs also made this sword easier to grip and harder to dislodge in battle.

Cutlasses were designed to be short enough to be effective in confined spaces and close quarter conflicts. Boarding aggression was not like a gentleman's duel, but rather a crazed rush to eliminate any and all opposition. Given this purpose, cutlasses became prized weapons for their ability to hack and slash rivals. They also required virtually no training or practice to utilize with crippling effect.

Grappling Hook..... These were 3 to 4 metal hooked devices that are equally spaced with a rope attached to an eye on the opposite end. Designed to catch on any victim's outcroppings they carried enough weight to cover ample distance with accuracy. In a closely contested man-on-man struggle they could also be wielded by aggressors to inflict serious damage.

Grenado..... This device was a round cast-iron ball about the size of a grapefruit or coconut. In fact, earliest designs were fashioned from hollowed out coconuts, empty glass bottles or clay containers. The device was hollow with an access hole to allow gun powder and grapeshot or shrapnel to be inserted followed by a fuse.

Incendiaries..... These were homemade buckets, barrels or bottles crammed with furious and malevolent burning materials that were thrown onto vessels to inflict awful and quite painful injuries, panic and utmost confusion. Contents and design of these devices varied widely depending on the materials available to its manufacturer.

A subset of this weapon is the stinkpot. These devices were small clay/glass pots or bottles that were packed with chemicals (brimstone) or evil smelling materials

(rotting fish, crustaceans and human waste) that were ignited and thrown at an enemy. Their use provided battle chaos and panic to an opposing force.

Lime..... Seamen toted this powder in their pockets and when tossed into their enemies face caused blindness and disorientation.

Marlin Spike..... This everyday shipboard tool was normally fashioned from wood or metal in an ice pick-like design. They were normally six inches to eighteen inches long. Used for various routine ship tasks, they were quite tough, unyielding and durable making them quite suitable for inflicting blunt trauma injuries as well as stab wounds in close quarter combat.

Musket..... This longer-ranged gun was utilized primarily for sniping rather than close quarter fighting. It was capable of crippling an opponent's crew without the danger of inflicting serious damage on the prize. After firing, it also suffered from a long reloading process and because of its overall length could prove unwieldily in close quarters.

Pistol..... This firearm was designed to be small in size and light in weight. Pistols were capable of only a single shot before a time-consuming reloading exercise which was thirty seconds at best. Since this delay was both lengthy and impractical, multiple pistols were usually carried into battle along with a trusty cutlass and dirk. Pistols could also supply a lethal boarding volley as well as being utilized as a club once fired.

Psychological Weapons..... Being natural cravens at heart in more cases than not, pirates relied heavily on psychological weapons to cower prey into submission without a fight. In the first place, a blood-thirsty and ruthless reputation went a long way into frightening prey to surrender upon confrontation. Additionally, the red or black flag promising death to all was successful in gaining peaceful capitulation. Other psychological methods included skylarking (prancing, cavorting, screaming and shouting prior to battle) coupled with a ship's band playing loud and militaristic tunes also served the purpose of cowing an enemy into submission. Finally, the strategic employment of a cannon warning shot was substantial inducement to force a non-bloody takeover.

Rope Clubs..... Simply lengths of rope that were stiffened by saltwater or tar used to inflict blunt trauma injury in close quarter conflict.

Swivel Deck Guns..... These were essentially small cannons that rested on a swivel stand or fork allowing a very wide arc of movement. Their primary use was short range anti-personal sweepers. They generally fired deadly grapeshot and proved quite effective in repelling boarders or sweeping the deck of an enemy. Because of their design, they were extremely portable and highly versatile.

PISSTUB

These were urine buckets or tubs situating in out-of-the-way corners below decks to serve as quick and temporary repositories of liquid human waste as well as chewing tobacco spittle. They also served as a handy supply of liquid to extinguish ship fires. Due to inordinate and an uneducated fear of venereal disease, sailors who contracted

the "the pox" were prohibited from utilizing these repositories.

SCURVY

Dreaded seafaring disease caused by the deficiency of vitamin C in a sailor's diet. This naval scourge debilitated its victims before killing them. The sickness was initially characterized by extreme exhaustion and lethargy coupled with pronounced soreness and stiffness of joints, especially in the lower extremities. Worsening symptoms include swollen and bleeding gums with loosened teeth, small reddish-blue spots on thighs and legs, bleeding from mucous membranes, jaundice and high fever prior to expiration. As a result of this powerful calamity, British soldiers were forced to drink lime juice while aboard to combat the disease earning them the nickname "limeys".

SLOWMATCH

A slow smoldering burning cord or twine infused with saltpeter (potassium nitrate) used to ignite firearms or cannons. The secret to its success was its ability to burn slowly and evenly. In many cases, both ends were lit simultaneously as a precaution against a lit end extinguishing upon ignition.

STRAPPADO

A medieval torture technique where victims hands were tied behind their backs with a rope secured to their bound wrists. The securing rope is passed over an upper support and the victim is hauled backwards into the air, which earned this painful treatment the name "Reverse Hanging". The full weight of the victim is supported by the extended and rotated shoulder sockets usually resulting in shoulder dislocation. To add to this brutal treatment, the torturer could abruptly raise and lower the victim with agonizing jerking motions. Additionally, weights were sometimes added to the victim's feet for added effect and pain.

SWABBING THE DECK

This tedious and laborious task was mandated for numerous reasons. In the first place, it reduced the deck's slickness due to foreign substances (mold, mildew, bird droppings, etc) lessening the chance for crewmen being swept overboard in nasty weather. Second, since there was no sealant between deck planks, this tedious effort kept planks moist and tight, lessening excess water seepage to the lower decks. Third, it kept the deck planking from warping and causing additional traction issues. Fourth, it kept splinters to a minimum, which avoided possible serious infections that could result in loss of limbs or even death. Last, this energy and time consuming chore keep an idle crew busy and occupied during long and tedious voyages.

The process was relegated to three separate steps. The first was to sprinkle the deck with sand and moisten it with seawater. The second step involved using a holystone (soft, porous and brittle sandstone about the size of a prayer book or bible) on ones knees to scrub the gritty mixture into the deck planks. The third step was to mop the dirt and grit away using a swab (mop made by tying several pieces of rope threads or cloth strands to a stick).

VOODOU LOA/PAPA LEGBA

Voodou is an ancient religion brought over from Africa in the New World's slave trade. A central belief of this religion is that nothing happens by chance including accidents or coincidences and that everything serves a purpose. This purpose is determined by a multitude of spirits called Loa. They serve as intermediaries between God and man and guide an individual through the physical journey of life. These Loa are not saints or angels but distinct beings with their own likes and dislikes. They also have distinct sacred rhythms, songs, dances and ritual symbols to honor and address each of them. They are called upon by a Voodou Priest (Hougan) or Priestess (Mambo) to make earthly appearances to guide their faithful flock. One very important Loa is Papa Legba.

Papa Legba is the spirit or lord of the spiritual crossroads, the gatekeeper in effect. He is the first and last spirit invoked in any ceremony because he has the power to open or close the doorway between humans and other Loa. He is the gatekeeper between the world of spirits and that of flesh. No Voodou ceremony can take place without his permission. He is known to be a master communicator (can actually spear all human languages) and quite benevolent in his actions. His sacred symbol is the sun and the cross and his sacred day is Tuesday. He is known to have polite and caring nature and is much loved by all believers. His favorite foods are grilled vegetables and meat and his favorite drink is spiced peppered rum (Clairin). He also has the ability to ride (take possession) of humans and control their actions and speech.

Papa Legba is believed to take a particular form when he makes his appearance. He is said to appear as a crooked (sporting a crutch or cane) lovable old man in a broad brimmed straw hat with a small tobacco pipe in his mouth and a straw bag with bits of food at his side. His body is covered with sores and usually has a familiar (mangy dog or rooster) at his side. His favorite colors are green, rose, red and yellow.

WATCHES/SHIP BELLS

WATCH	START	END
First	8PM	Midnight
Middle	Midnight	4AM
Morning	4AM	8AM
Forenoon	8AM	Noon
Afternoon	Noon	4PM
First Dog	4PM	6PM
Second Dog	6PM	8PM

Each watch was measured with a vessel's hourglass with bells being struck for each half hour increment. Therefore, the bell count during each watch started with one and ended with eight accounting for four hours of elapsed time.

Eight bells signified the end of each watch. Dog watches enabled the two separate watch crews different watches each day. This was also the time for the crew's main meal.

Rapid short rings of the bell were utilized during times of low visibility (i.e fog).

Rapid long rings of the bell signaled a general ship's alarm or emergency.

Special bell ringings were utilized for announcing the Captain boarding or special visitors.